*MARCUS*

also by Laurene Chinn

THE UNANOINTED (1959)
VOICE OF THE LORD (1961)
BELIEVE MY LOVE (1962)

# Marcus

## a novel of the youngest apostle

### LAURENE CHINN

William Morrow & Company
New York

*for Paul Reynolds*

# AUTHOR'S NOTE

The advent of gods among men has surely stirred more creative minds than has any other theme. In the twenty centuries of the Christian era no other subject has inspired so many creative works as have the events which launched the Christian church.

The first man to write the Christian story in a form which has survived and is still read was the apostle Mark. If his narrative lacks the literary excellence of later gospels, it was, with a lost document called the "Q," the primary source used by Matthew and Luke in their fuller and more scholarly works.

Mark's first appearance in the records or in tradition was as the only witness to Jesus' agony in Gethsemane. Almost his final appearance was as companion to Peter and to Paul in Rome during the terror under Nero when those two, the greatest of all apostles, were martyred. Mark survived to write his gospel and to launch in Alexandria his first independent ministry. The fact that this ministry began after the year 64 leads one to believe that the young man whom Mark modestly does not name, who fled from Gethsemane in terror in the year 30, leaving his coat in a soldier's grasp, must have been very young indeed, surely the youngest of the group of apostles found in the first Christian fellowship in Jerusalem.

The nascent period in the Christian church is bracketed by two crucifixions. A witness to the Gethsemane agony and to Peter's crucifixion thirty-four years later, Mark was deeply involved throughout this period. A bitter internal conflict existed among the earliest Christians. Native Judean Jews sought to make of Christianity a new sect within Judaism, strictly subject to the Mosaic code. Hellenists, the Greek-speaking Jews of the Diaspora, baptized Gentile converts without demanding that they first become Jews. Mark had the closest possible ties with both Hebrews and Hellenists, and witnessed the tragic but inevitable resolution of this conflict.

Most early apostles were adherents either of Peter or of Paul. Mark was close to both. He was with Peter upon the occasion of the first recorded miracle of apostolic healing and shared with Peter the ensuing imprisonment and trial before the Sanhedrin. He traveled with Peter also on various subsequent journeys.

Mark accompanied Paul and Barnabas upon the Cyprus leg of Paul's first missionary journey. He abandoned them when they sailed from Cyprus to Paphos enroute to the Asian provinces beyond the Taurus Mountains. For this desertion Paul never quite forgave him. When Barnabas suggested that they bring Mark along on the second missionary journey Paul refused. There was a "sharp contention" between them. Barnabas had long been Paul's good friend, but he was also the brother of Mark's mother. He never again traveled with Paul.

Peter called Mark "my son." But Paul's three epistolary references to Mark are aloof, and "useful" is the warmest term he employs.

Finally, Mark's Jerusalem home, with its spacious upper room, was the meeting place of the first ecclesia, and the scene of many stirring and vital encounters.

Thus we find in Mark a very young apostle, a Levite with an excellent education and some medical knowledge, heir to property both in Jerusalem and on Cyprus, no great literary light but a young man with a mind of his own and the closest possible involvement in the emerging Christian movement. I found in him also another author to add to the list of men who wrote the Bible who have absorbed my deep concern in previous Bible novels. In Mark's teacher, Agabus, I found a credible author for the lost "Q" document, which had so great an influence on later writers.

The many things we do not know about Mark are vital to the novelist, allowing latitude for creating a story which blends with the things we know. Some liberties have been taken with locales and time schedules. Chief of these was the transposition of Mark's Jerusalem home from the city's southeast quarter to the Mount of Olives. So many dramatic purposes were served by this transposition that I find it hard to believe the house was ever anywhere else. Half a dozen time schedules have been worked out by scholars for the events of this period. I therefore felt no compunction in choosing a time schedule which suited the dramatic requirements of this narrative.

In the Book of Acts and the epistles Mark is variously referred to as John Mark, John, Mark, and Marcus. I have used "Mark" when Jews are speaking, and "Marcus" in the speech of Romans or Greeks.

The ending I used for Mark's gospel is, according to modern translators and Britannica, Mark's ending. Later writers added conclusions of their own, but Mark closed with the eighth verse of the last chapter.

Laurene Chambers Chinn
Borger, Texas, and Morristown, New Jersey
1962–1965

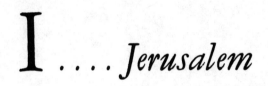

# I . . . . *Jerusalem*

# CHAPTER *I*

My mother was widowed before I was weaned. My father's property was near Jerusalem, while my mother's family for four generations had produced and sold copper wares in Salamis on the island of Cyprus. My mother early became convinced that I was a puny child, unfit for the rigors of winter in our mountain capital. She began sending me to winter in Cyprus, lest harm befall me and my father's seed be cut off from the earth.

I made the journey each year in the company of my teacher Agabus, who was Greek and a slave. Even after my maternal grandparents died of the fever I returned each winter to Salamis. My mother's younger brother Joseph was called Barnabas, which means son of prophecy. The name tells enough, surely, of his natural gifts to explain why my mother entrusted me to his care.

Agabus was a notable scholar even among Greeks. He was a small man with a large head bobbing upon a thin neck and a hitch in his walk, caused by the withering of his left leg. The pink, pouty lips curved in an elfin smile which reminded one of the limestone votaries to be seen amongst tangled vines and scuttling lizards in ancient cemeteries on Cyprus. His bony face was framed by a short beard and the curled fringe which covered his vast forehead. My reach toward maturity began when I ceased to be mortified by his odd appearance, and found justice in his complaint, "I am a slave, and halt, and I waste the years teaching a youth who cares nothing for learning."

We loved one another, then and ever after. I grew up cushioned by the love of Agabus and Barnabas, of my mother, and our two housekeepers—Phoebe in Salamis and Damaris in Jerusalem. I grew up unaware of the extent of my great good fortune.

Whenever we took ship for those annual journeys, Agabus would limp up and down the dirty little deck, skirting the heaped dunnage, muttering from his vast memory store—poetry of Homer, discourses of Plato, speeches from the dramas of Euripides. Sailors followed him as if he were a traveling entertainer.

"Know thyself!" he would shout, fixing some brawny Egyptian with a fierce glare. "There wisdom begins. Know thyself."

If Agabus could not take pride in my mind, he found a Greek pleasure in the development of my body. From the time I learned to walk he made me run. When I grew stale in the confinement of the verminous ships, he made me leap overboard and swim. I grew up tall and strong, proud as any Greek of my bronzed body.

You watch the seasons when you travel by ship. To reach Cyprus in autumn you must embark while summer winds still blow off the land. You must return after the winter gales end but before the spring winds turn contrary. If you guess wrong about the changing seasons you run into trouble. I usually reached Jerusalem before Passover, but I was never there for the autumn festival, nor ever for the Day of Atonement, that holiest of Jewish holy days.

By the time I went to Cyprus for my fourteenth winter I was beginning to resent my mother's coddling. Anyone could see I was healthy. But she had a new anxiety in the dissensions between the native Jews of Palestine and the Jews of the Diaspora, called Hellenists because they spoke Greek. Rioting and rebellion arose often in the hills around Jerusalem. The emotional climate on Cyprus was quieter.

A Hellenist herself by birth and a Hebrew by marriage, Mother valued both elements of our people. Hellenists appreciated the culture of the Greek world and the stability of Roman rule. There had been no great wars in living memory. Many Jews had received Roman citizenship in return for commercial contributions to the growth of key cities in the provinces. Children inherited this citizenship with its privileges. My mother's father had been a citizen. Barnabas therefore inherited the right to wear the toga. Hellenists traveled to Jerusalem for the great feasts on excellent Roman roads, protected from robbers by the legions. In Jerusalem Hellenists were at home in the synagogues, though in the Temple they were milked by money changers and those who sold animals for sacrifice. Nevertheless, the Hebrews were the backbone of our people. My mother so arranged my life that I grew up both Hellenist and Hebrew.

The spring when Agabus and I went up to Jerusalem for that most terrible Passover in all the centuries, the weather turned contrary. Veering winds forced our ship off course. While sailors cursed and sweated, Agabus limped about the pitching ship, muttering about Achilles, child of lovely-haired Thetis, who sulked beside the ships nursing heartsore anger whilst the other Greeks, armed with sharp bronze, engaged the Trojans on the plain before their city gate.

Whenever Agabus spoke of the bronze weapons of those long-dead Greeks (contemporaries of Moses, perhaps?) I wondered how much of their bronze had come from the copper mines of Cyprus. Legend said that our own Salamis was founded by Greeks returning victorious after the burning of Troy.

We came to land near the sandy beach of Joppa, and had to beat our way north against off-shore drafts to make port within the protecting arms of the Roman-built Caesarean harbor. I was restless for a long run over Judean hills and homesick for the sight of my mother. I fretted that I might not arrive in time to share the Passover lamb and bitter herbs with her. The sight of palm trees rising above the green hills, and in the near distance the stately marble temples and palaces of the handsome Roman city had never been more welcome.

As soon as the ship tied up at the wharf I was overside and running, past the warehouses, past the double-arched aqueduct which brought water down from the springs of Mount Carmel to Caesarea, and on to the forum. There I hired two donkeys, one for Agabus and the other to carry the luggage he would bring ashore. I wanted no donkey for myself, for I meant to walk the seventy miles to Jerusalem, following the Roman road that ran south along the ancient caravan route to Joppa, then shifted east amongst the crowding, lovely hills. I would reach Jerusalem a day ahead of Agabus, traveling light and fast on impatient feet while Agabus took the slow journey with a company of merchants.

The joy I feel when the crest of Jerusalem breaks upon the view, her massive gray walls crowning her high hills, her towers rising, and finest sight of all, the gleaming marble of the lovely Temple—this is prelude to the special joy I feel when, having crossed to the Mount of Olives, I see the rising shape of our stone house amidst our olive orchards. I ran the last uphill mile from Damascus Gate, and tumbled in at the narrow door beside our camel gate, expecting to find the house bursting with Passover guests. After all my fretting I had reached home two days before the feast.

The court was rich with the homely smells of baking bread and roasting lamb, but only Damaris was there. She knelt at some household chore, surrounded by vegetables. I shouted, "Mother! I'm home!" And Damaris turned a joyous face, chins quivering with welcome, one eyebrow frosted with flour.

"Marcus, lad! You're taller than ever, and so brown!"

I never came from Cyprus that Damaris did not weep over me, swallowing whatever was in her mouth, for she could not cook without nibbling, and reaching her busy, tireless hands for me to bend and be kissed.

I kissed both her plump, moist cheeks. "Where's Mother?" Again raising my voice I called, "Mother! Where are you? I've come!"

Damaris brushed the back of one floury hand across her cheek. "The Lady Miriam is at the house of Simon the Leper." She twinkled at my gaping disbelief.

"Simon?" For years I had skirted the house of our neighbor, whose orchard adjoined ours at the top of the mount and extended down the eastern slope toward the shoulder where lay the village of Bethany.

For years I had eyed the forbidding wall of Simon's house, filled with dread and awe for the hopeless loneliness of the good man immured within. Simon's wealth had saved him from exile to the valley of lepers. His wife had shared his lonely fate until her death a year or two ago. Servants and sons had fled when first the leprous spots appeared. Now Simon dwelt alone in that big house.

One neighbor had shown Simon kindness through the years. The farmer Lazarus brought him food from the market in a basket and remained beyond the wall while Simon drew it up with a rope, relating the gossip of Bethany and the news of the great world, and reporting the condition of Simon's orchards, for Lazarus kept an eye on the steward who had charge of them.

If Mother was at Simon's house it could mean one thing only. "Alas, poor man," I murmured. "May he sleep in peace."

"He is not dead, lad. He is cleansed! He took gifts to the Temple and the priests declared him clean. Today his court is filled with guests."

"Damaris, stop! I've outgrown your tales." Annoyed that she persisted in regarding me as a child, I rushed to my room on the roof, pausing as I passed the cistern to pick up a bottle of water. When I had changed clothes I would go in search of my mother.

Damaris called after me, "Simon was cleansed by the Galilean healer who last spring brought Lazarus from the tomb."

I grunted. That Lazarus had walked forth nobody could deny. But men were sometimes hustled prematurely into the tomb—how can such mistakes be avoided? One heard tales of a family vault being opened to discover the skeleton of the last man buried there lying against the great stone of the door, the bones of the hands broken from beating upon it, the burial wrappings scattered in frenzied swirls. I could accept the raising of Lazarus, though it was a mystery how the rabbi of Galilee had known to command that the tomb be opened. He had stood at the great stone, weeping. Perhaps he heard some sound from within. Yet Lazarus had come out with his burial wrappings intact and the napkin still over his face. The raising of Lazarus was a marvel, but this of Simon was impossible!

"Long ago Simon wasted much gold on physicians who pronounced him beyond cure," I shouted as I sloshed water over myself. I pulled on a new tunic from the pile Mother had provided against my return. I shouted, "Simon's hands are maimed by the disease. His face, they say, is a horror."

"I have seen his face, Marcus. It is not so bad, though the beard is gone. His face is as bare and bald as a Roman's."

"You saw him?" I came to the parapet, pulling my coat about me. It was a new scarlet coat, very handsome—the sort Mother loved to have waiting to surprise me when I came each spring from Salamis. I stared down at Damaris, torn between cynicism and credulity.

"I went with your mother to Bethany three days ago. She had heard that the healer of Galilee had returned with more than three score followers. The house of Lazarus will not hold even a score of guests, and the lady Miriam wanted to invite some of the women to the hospitality of this house, and offer the orchard for such men as had no better place to spread their beds at night. While we were in the road we met the healer himself, with Lazarus, and many people following. We turned to follow with the others. When we reached Simon's house the gate stood open, and Simon knelt, his face bowed over those dreadful hands.

"The people shrank back with cries of horror. But the rabbi went to Simon and touched him, saying, 'Do you believe that God can heal you?' Ah, Marcus lad, I suppose it was the first time in many years that a man had touched Simon. And Simon raised his face and cried, 'Have mercy, Lord, for I know you can cleanse me if you will.' "

"He called the rabbi Lord?"

"All the followers call the rabbi Lord."

I ran from the house. Every Passover brought to Jerusalem some new savior of the Jews. I felt a sort of shivery excitement that this year's Messiah dwelt in Bethany, that my mother had invited some of his followers to share our hospitality, along with the relatives and friends who thronged to us for the feasts from the provinces and the Diaspora. I did not want to hear the climax of this affair from Damaris. If Mother and our guests were at Simon's house today I would hear the details of that so-called healing or whatever it was from each of them in turn.

I ran up through the orchard and out onto the Bethany road. I had only half believed Damaris, but I had to credit the testimony of my eyes. The gate of Simon's court stood wide. People thronged there, craning for a sight of what went on inside. Tall as I was, I could not see much for the press and excitement of these people. Someone was speaking, but I heard only bits and pieces because of the scuffling in the gate.

I clearly saw one man of the company which sat at Simon's table. I had seen him a year ago—a follower of the rabbi, named Peter, with the heavy shoulders of a fisherman, a volatile man with ruddy flesh and a reddish cast to the brown of his thick beard.

Forever stamped in my memory is the image of Simon's maimed hand holding a bit of broken bread from which sop dripped—a hand with one whole finger and a stub of a thumb. Pink, wholesome flesh grew over the stump. The hand emerged into my field of vision, offering the broken bread. The thick beard split in a friendly smile as the fisherman opened his mouth and received the bread. That hand had dipped the bread into the common dish.

There could be no clearer evidence. Those men at Simon's table were Jews, subject to a rigid code of hygiene and cleanliness. They had dipped into the dish with Simon. He had surely been certified clean, before such a thing could come to pass. I moved away and leaned against the wall, my head spinning. I could no longer doubt that my mother was among the women who were serving this meal.

Removed from the crowding noises of the villagers I heard more distinctly the speaker's voice. "If you believe in me you will do the works I do, and greater works also."

But no man could do a greater work than this healer had done for Simon!

The voice continued. I caught fragments only, for my brain was reeling. Too much had overwhelmed me too quickly. Afterward I knew that once only did I hear Jesus of Nazareth address his friends—once only, and I should have listened to every word. But I did not. No wonder Agabus complained of me.

"Love one another as I have loved you . . . You are my witnesses. I would say more but you could not bear it . . . I am the vine, you are the branches. You cannot bear fruit unless you abide in me . . . Ask anything you will and it will be done for you."

At the time it seemed a dreamy sort of nonsense, disjointed, unreal.

"Banish your fears . . . A little while and you will see me no more. Again a little while and you will see me. Set your troubled hearts at rest."

Long afterward I could look back on those fragments of admonition and comfort and understand their meaning. But that was long afterward.

An odor exceeding sweet floated over the wall. A clamor arose. "Rebuke her, Lord! What waste! Spikenard—she is pouring the costly nard like water!"

One voice rose above the others. "Such costly stuff should be sold for money to be given to the poor."

The rabbi quieted the clamor. "Rebuke her not. Wherever you tell of my words and my works, tell how Miriam today anointed me for my burial."

Who in Bethany except my mother would have spikenard to pour upon this healer's head? Yet the folly and waste bewildered me, for Mother was a widow whose management of my inheritance had been commended in many quarters. What could have induced Mother to such ostentation?

I tried to push my way through to her, for surely a widow's son should stand with her when her neighbors cry out against her. But while I struggled with the crowd a way opened and she emerged. She was weeping. Her face was closely wrapped in her mantle. Never before had I seen her lose her composure in the company of our neighbors. Indeed, I could remember only two or three occasions when I had known her to weep even in private. She walked out into the road, immersed in grief, and I ran and took her arm.

"Mother!"

She stumbled. For a moment she rested against me. My mother was a small, slight woman, and to my eyes she was very beautiful. Her forehead was low, marked by a widow's peak. Her eyes were wide and dark, animated, responsive, and very kind. Her nose was straight, strong without being dominant. Her mouth was generous. She held a half-empty jar of fine alabaster from which rose the heavy scent of nard. This prodigal pouring must have seemed callous indeed to people for whom it would have bought a winter's supply of grain.

Mother said softly, "Mark, terrible things will happen before the Passover has ended. I wish you had not come so soon." Then, "Oh Mark, welcome home. But I wish you had not come so soon." And finally, "I do hope Barnabas came with you."

"Barnabas set out two weeks before me. But he planned to travel by way of Antioch on some business matter. I don't know when he will arrive."

"I wish he were here." Mother spoke in a lost and helpless tone which seemed strange indeed, coming from her. She clung to my arm as we walked up the hill toward our own orchard. "They will kill the Lord Jesus. Annas is his enemy, and Jesus' following has grown so great Annas can no longer ignore him."

What could I say? That not even Annas himself, chief ruler of the Jews, would dare destroy a man who had healed a leper? That a healer with such powers would not let himself be taken? But my mother was not given to hysteria, nor was I in the habit of treating her opinions lightly. Moreover, I had heard the healer say, "She has anointed me for burial." To tell the truth, I was more concerned with Mother's distress than with the possible fate of a Galilean who had contrived to make Annas his enemy.

We entered the shelter of our orchard. Mother said, "He is the greatest prophet since Jeremiah, the greatest since Moses, perhaps. Some say he is Elijah returned to us. And Annas will get him killed."

"How can Annas do that?" The Jews were not permitted to pass the death sentence except for blasphemy. Nor was it easy to persuade the Romans to condemn a man unless he was guilty of thieving, rioting, or treason. Not even Annas, surely, could bring such charges against this healer.

"Mark, I do not know how Annas will contrive it, but Nicodemus says he will. Nicodemus said I must warn Jesus to leave at once and return to Galilee."

Nicodemus was one of the youngest of the seventy rulers who comprised our Sanhedrin. He was a lawyer, a Pharisee, a man of great wealth, and the most persistent of Mother's suitors. If Nicodemus said Annas meant to get this healer killed, it seemed likely he would.

Mother continued hopelessly, "I could not manage to speak with the Lord Jesus privately. Since he teaches in parables I performed a visible parable. He understood, Mark. Yet before

I poured the spikenard he knew. All day long he has been comforting his followers against evils to come."

I protested, "This is no ordinary wonder-worker. Surely a man with the power to heal Simon can elude Annas."

Mother did not reply.

I exclaimed, "Why should Annas hate him? Annas ought to bring such a healer to the Temple and heap honors upon him."

"Jesus goes daily to the Temple. He has called our rulers sepulchers, painted white and glittering on the outside, but within full of dead men's bones. He faced Annas in Solomon's cloister and called him hypocrite."

"That was a reckless thing to do!"

Annas was president of our Sanhedrin. His sons took turns serving as high priest. Caiaphas, his son-in-law, currently held the office. But whichever son bore the title, Annas ruled. The Galilean had been rash to make Annas his enemy.

Mother said, "He called the bankers thieves. He whipped them from their booths. He overturned their tables and scattered their money and freed the sacrificial doves."

I resisted the impulse to laugh at this picture of confusion in that sanctum of privilege over which Annas ruled. For Hebrews the avarice of the Temple bankers presented no great problem. But Hellenists were forbidden to buy sacrificial animals with the coin of their native cities, or even drop such coins into the treasure chest as offerings to the Lord God. They were at the mercy of the money changers, and Annas appointed the latter. In my lifetime nothing had ever been done to relieve the burden avarice heaped on pious pilgrims from the Diaspora.

Mother said, "Mark, you will not go to the Temple while the danger continues. If they arrest Jesus there may be rioting. Many people follow him for his mighty works and some follow to hear his teaching. While he remains, there is danger. Promise you will not step off our property until the situation clears."

"You forbid me to go to the Temple?" Usually Mother could not rest until I had carried gifts to the Temple after a winter on Cyprus.

"You are growing up, Mark. I do not forbid, but I ask you to promise."

"You mean, until the rabbi goes back to Galilee?"

Mother's lovely, dark eyes were bleak. "Until it is all settled and the danger is past."

I gave her my promise. How could I refuse?

# CHAPTER 2

I early learned not to expect companionship from my mother during Passover week. This year a score of followers of the Nazarene were added to the usual guests from the provinces and Diaspora. Among these were Mary of Magdala and Salome, a kinswoman of Jesus and mother of two of his disciples, James and John. Three disciples were lodged in the house of Lazarus together with the rabbi himself. Of the seventy who had followed him from Galilee some were in Simon's house and in other houses of Bethany. The overflow bedded down amongst the olive trees in our orchard and Simon's.

On our roof was a large pavilion, made to catch the mountain breeze. Here three score guests could be fed at one sitting. My bedroom adjoined this pavilion, a summer bedroom since I spent the winters in Cyprus. That first night I lay awake, pondering Simon's cleansing and the mystery of the hatred our rulers had for Simon's healer. My pondering was punctuated by snores and grunts and other night noises from those who had spread their beds in our upper room.

Presently I heard voices over by the parapet: the high, reedy voice of Salome, the rich, low tones of the plump and handsome Magdalene, and my mother's quiet, direct speech.

"Don't fret about our Lord's safety." Salome gave her silvery little laugh. "You've seen his mighty works this week, but we have witnessed them for years. He healed the sick and fed the hungry. He once stilled a storm on Lake Galilee. Wherever he goes many follow him, while a few who overrate their own importance plot to be rid of him. When they try to arrest him, he mingles with the crowd and is gone. He has promised us a kingdom, my dear Miriam, more than once. When the time comes he will call down twelve legions of angels. Trust him. Don't worry about what certain pompous hypocrites—"

Mother exclaimed, "I wish you would not call our rulers hypocrites. They do their best. They are only human, but the preservation of the law is their whole life and purpose."

Mary of Magdala said, "They are careless about righteousness. They keep the letter of the law but not the spirit. The Lord Jesus cannot establish a kingdom of heaven on earth through compromise with hypocrisy."

"These men are sincere. Don't call them hypocrites!"

"The Lord Jesus called them hypocrites."

Salome sounded her laugh. "Jesus is a Jew. He loves the Temple and the law. He will work things out with our rulers, since all share the same loyalties and purposes. Several rulers have come by night to be taught by Jesus. If he were less courageous and outspoken they would not seek him out."

Nicodemus was one ruler who had come to Jesus by night to question him. That had happened two or three years ago, on a previous Passover visit Jesus and his followers had made to Bethany.

The Magdalene said, "The rabbi Gamaliel sends students to follow Jesus and listen. In the school of Hillel the students debate our Lord's teachings."

"Annas is his enemy. Jesus has powerful friends, but Annas—"

The Magdalene said comfortably, "When you have known Jesus longer you will understand that Annas can have no power over him."

Mother exclaimed, "You seem to think he will return to Galilee with you after the Passover. Are you deaf? He speaks daily of dying. Over and over he has bidden you farewell."

Salome said, "How little you understand him, Miriam. He is depressed by the hypocrisy of the ruling clique in Jerusalem. For a week or so he has spoken in this pessimistic vein, but for three years he has promised us a kingdom."

The Magdalene said, "He speaks in parables. He will explain the meaning of these farewells as he always explains his parables sooner or later. Trust him, Miriam. Believe in him."

Salome's silvery little laugh came again. "You should have heard him when I asked for high positions for my two boys in his kingdom. Yet they are his cousins and have been with him from the first. I have never understood why he considered my request unreasonable and pushing."

The Magdalene said comfortably, "James and John will be rulers, never fear. A mother cannot be blamed for wanting the best for her sons."

They were still talking when I fell asleep. When I woke the sun was in my face and the house seemed deserted. Before I had finished dressing another guest arrived, my kinsman Seth of Damascus. Technically Seth was Hellenist, since he was one of the Diaspora and spoke both Greek and Aramaic. Yet at heart he was as conservative about the Temple and the law as any Judean Hebrew. A heavy man and elderly, Seth never spoke to me without reminding me that he was the only living brother of my father's father. In spite of infirmities, he made one pilgrimage a year to Jerusalem. I would have been content had he chosen a festival when I was absent.

Others came and went, relatives who commented on how I

had grown since the last Passover. I was taller than Barnabas, as tall as I was likely to become. I wondered in boredom whether they would offer the same greeting when another Passover rolled around.

Another Passover. Would the rabbi of Nazareth be in Bethany next spring? Or would some new Messiah have the people in an uproar?

During the sunset meal I loitered in the court to be near Mother, though she was too preoccupied with her guests to notice me. Someone said that the Lord Jesus and the twelve apostles had gone into Jerusalem to partake together of a pre-Passover meal. I heard Salome suggest that they were planning the grand coup, that tomorrow the promised kingdom would begin on earth.

I longed to believe that Salome was right and my mother, for once, wrong. I knew Mother was counting the hours till tomorrow's sunset, when the Passover meal would be served. If Jesus survived until then all would be well. No violence would occur on the Passover Sabbath, and when the first day dawned he would go away with his followers down the Jericho road to the Jordan, and thence along the ancient, sand-packed roadway to Galilee.

That night I lay restless, staring up at the brilliant Paschal moon. I had kept my promise. While stirring forces were at work all over Bethany and Jerusalem I had stayed at home. Seth had plodded stiffly away, leading our Passover lamb to the Temple to be sacrificed for tomorrow's feast. I could not sleep, yet if I moved about this roof I would stumble over guests who had rolled their beds out anywhere and everywhere, within the house and upon it. All about me I could hear their restless breathing, their muted mutterings. I longed to escape their presence, which I found oppressive.

Voices came from the orchard. Had the rabbi and the twelve returned from their supper? Were they bedding in our orchard lest they awaken their hosts in various households? I could go into the orchard, at least, without breaking my promise to Mother, for that was our property, and she had demanded only that I remain within the bounds of our own household and farmlands.

I had never seen the rabbi. Curiosity increased my restlessness. Girding the old blue coat in which I slept, I crossed to the parapet. A gigantic grapevine climbed the wall of the house. From the parapet it had cast itself across to the spreading branches of a fig tree, and so descended to earth again. The barren old vine was of great thickness. I climbed down it and sped off across the clearing toward the shadows of the olive trees.

God knows I am not given to premonitions. Yet I was filled with a sense of impending crisis. Perhaps Salome was right. Perhaps tonight, in our orchard, the rabbi and his followers were planning the long-awaited deliverance of the Jews from their oppressors—a deliverance which tomorrow's dawn might bring. If this rabbi was truly Messiah, perhaps tomorrow the kingdom of heaven on earth would begin, with Jerusalem for headquarters and all the honorable posts going to men now dwelling as guests in Bethany! Would Jesus rule an empire, as David had? Would Rome be overthrown, and the Jews dominate the vast empire which spread over the three continents bordering on the Great Sea? The rabbi was surely no Caesar! Yet with legions of angels to command, and mystical powers such as stunned the mind, who could set bounds on what might come to pass?

My heart pounded as I crossed into the orchard which some ancestor had named Gethsemane, meaning a place of oil, the nourishing, blessed oil which richly pours from the olive press throughout the autumn harvest season. The leaves shimmered, now silver, now dark, in the brilliant moonlight.

In a moment I was within the shadows of the twisted, ancient trees.

Amongst the broken shadows I stumbled, banging my head against the knot where a branch dipped low, then twisted upward. The thing against which I had stumbled turned, groaning. A shaft of moonlight sifting between trees revealed the face of Matthias, one of the twelve.

I crawled from figure to figure, recognizing others of the twelve. These men were not founding a kingdom tomorrow! My disappointment brought back words spoken by Jesus, "A little while and you will see me no more." I moved slowly, ashamed to have been such a credulous fool, yet seeking amongst these sleepers the face which might be that of the rabbi. I found Andrew, but not his brother Peter, nor either of the sons of Salome. Nor did I see a face I could accept as that of the rabbi and healer.

I approached the top of the hill. In the clearing where the oil press stood rose an ancient, mossy stone. Legend said it had been a Canaanite altar long ago, when the land was filled with high places where carnal revels of the fertility cult occurred on nights of the full moon. These were the high places against which our prophets had railed, the high places which had tempted our people to their downfall until defeat and captivity taught them to obey the command, "You shall have no gods but God." As I approached the clearing I heard a muted, human sound. A moan? A sob? I moved quickly amongst the eerie shadows—for surely no other trees in all the earth take on such strangely weird and writhing shapes as do our olive trees. The moon-made shadows formed a setting for human agony.

From the clearing a voice came, desolate, lonely. "Peter, John, could you not watch with me?"

I froze into the hollow of a thick trunk which age had

emptied of all save its outer shell. And the voice said tenderly,
"Sleep on, my friends. You will need your rest before the night
is gone."

Great events were pending after all! Tonight would see
their beginning. Yet surely these events were not the triumphs
Salome so confidently expected. The rabbi crossed the moonlit
clearing and knelt beside the ancient stone. Whatever uses a
less enlightened people had made of that timeless stone, the
rabbi had cleansed it, as if no man had ever knelt before it till
now. His arms were crossed upon it, and the broken murmur
was resumed. I longed to go and kneel beside the lonely man.
I yearned to say, "Let me share your vigil." Still I huddled
within the hollow embrace of the old olive tree, feeling myself
an intruder in this orchard which had belonged to my father's
fathers.

I heard the murmur, "I pray for these men, the men you
have given me, my comrades in my ministry. Deliver them
from evil, when I am no longer with them, to guide and
comfort them."

His arms were extended across the stone. His face was raised
in the moonlight. It could have been the face of my cousin
Barnabas—a little older but the same type of young, vigorous,
intelligent Jew, perhaps more spiritual, but I could not be
sure, for it held such sorrow. After all that the years have
taught me I marvel that this is all I saw that night when I
looked for the first and only time upon the face of Jesus of
Nazareth. I had expected a Moses, a Jeremiah. Yet Pontius
Pilate was to look upon him next day and pronounce him
harmless. Our Jewish rulers had looked upon him and called
him schemer and imposter.

A shuddering sob was wrenched from him. "Let this cup
pass from me." The head dropped upon the outstretched
arms. This was private and personal, this grief, and I should

not stay and witness it, stranger as I was. Yet I could not tear myself from the scene. In my youth and ignorance I could not understand, yet I sensed that this was no ordinary sorrow, no ordinary loneliness.

The face was raised again, deeply, calmly sorrowing, accepting sorrow, strong in sorrow. "Thy will, not mine, be done!"

My heart burned with bewildered incomprehension. I had no notion what cup he referred to. Ah, with the years how I have come to understand the anguish which pressed upon the Lord Jesus that lonely night, the anguish it was my fate to witness that I might one day record for all men the scene no other witnessed. At the time I could not plumb the agony of submission and acceptance and relinquishment in those words, "Thy will, not mine, be done."

I sorrowed for his sorrow. But what I mainly felt was disappointment. By no means would this man set up a kingdom when tomorrow dawned. This man, for all his wondrous powers, was no Messiah destined to be the savior of the Jews.

Jesus rose, rubbing away the sweat and tears from his face. He crossed to where Peter and the sons of Salome slept. For a brief moment he stood looking down upon them, his face shadowed but his posture erect and ready. "The spirit is willing," he murmured gently, "but the flesh is weak. God strengthen you, my dear ones, for what is to befall you."

Perhaps his sharper senses had caught sounds I had not heard. Out of the dark came threading one of the disciples, Judas, who carried the purse for the company. One at least, I thought, was awake to stand with Jesus tonight. Judas crossed the clearing, spoke a greeting, kissed Jesus.

What they said to one another I did not hear because a rattle of arms and the stir of moving men was suddenly audible to me. This was something I had never thought to hear in our orchard. Soldiers entered the clearing, our Temple police

—our own Jewish soldiers—trespassing here, a sight as strange as the moon-cast shadows of the warped old trees through which they moved.

A cry escaped me as those Jewish soldiers laid hold of the rabbi. An officer bound a thong about his wrists to which a leading cord was attached.

Now the sons of Salome were awake, and Peter. Others came stumbling into the light, expectant that their master would by some miracle save himself from his enemies.

Judas implored, "Lord, Lord, call down angels! Smite your enemies! Proclaim your kingdom!"

Someone wrested a dagger from a soldier and brandished it. This was Peter, impetuous Peter, eager to put down the enemies of his rabbi's kingdom.

Peter shouted, "Lord, Lord, smite them with fire from heaven!"

The rabbi stood submissive, yielding to arrest. He said quietly, "Put up the sword, Peter. Those who take the sword will perish by the sword."

To the man who had bound him Jesus said, "I have been daily in the Temple. You could have taken me there."

Then I saw a terrible thing. The man Judas screamed and fled. Panic spread. Others ran, fleeing a terror neither they nor I could name. Someone laid hold of my coat shouting, "Here is one of them."

Terror overwhelmed me. Leaving my coat in the soldier's hands I fled through the orchard in my loin cloth, tears streaming. Branches raked my flesh. Twice I stumbled, but I leaped up and ran on. I knew no sense of direction, yet some instinct brought me out into the clearing where stood our strong, safe house. Sobbing, I ran to it, found the vine, began to climb. I fell headlong onto the roof. In the court below I heard the protests of women roused by the hasty arrival of panicky disciples.

By now, I thought, Mother knew the worst. I fell upon my bed beating the floor with my fists. The rabbi and healer who had promised so much had meekly accepted arrest, even after all the warnings, all the strange foreknowledge evidenced by that scene in the clearing. What kind of wonder-worker was he? What kind of leaders were the rulers of the Jews who had done this shameful thing, trespassing the privacy of our orchard to lay violent hands upon that humble, submissive healer, that gentle rabbi from Galilee?

My mother had been right from the first. Those confident, dependent folk who followed Jesus were wrong. Jesus would die. He knew it, and he made no effort to save himself for those who loved and needed him.

What kind of man was he, so to punish himself and those who had put their trust in him?

# CHAPTER 3

By the time I had wrapped a coat about my naked and shivering body, the court was in turmoil. Warmly clothed though I now was, I still shuddered with the terror which had sent me crashing through the orchard, and with fear of what was ahead for the rabbi whose love and sorrow and submission I had witnessed. With foreknowledge as mysterious as his healing powers, with a terrible dread of what was to happen, and profound grief at leaving his followers, who must suffer anguish on his account, he had nevertheless gone passively to meet a fate fashioned by the Jews who ruled the Jews.

"Thy will, not mine, be done," he had prayed. How could hatred of Jesus of Galilee by the rulers of the Jews be God's will? Yet how could such a man be so misguided, so wrong, as to submit to the fate he dreaded, calling it God's will?

Mother moved among the followers, quiet amidst their wild grief. Most of the twelve were here, perhaps because our house was near the scene of the arrest. Agabus limped among them, lighting lamps, while Damaris brought wine.

Into this tumult my kinsman Seth stiffly descended, wrapped in a gray coat, his bald head uncovered. "Be calm. Do not disturb the sleepers. Put your trust in our Sanhedrin. With what crime is he charged? If innocent, he will be set free."

Above the clamor rose the high, bright voice of Salome. "He promised us a kingdom. Listen, all of you! Listen to me! He gave us solemn assurances. Who knows where these promises will be fulfilled? Not in an orchard! How many times has he admonished us, 'Do not hide your light under a bushel measure. Set it on a lamp stand. Let your light be seen!' Why should he call down legions of angels into an orchard when by now he is in the midst of a midnight meeting of the Sanhedrin?"

"No!" The protest burst from me.

A few heads turned toward where I leaned across the parapet. My hands flew to cover my mouth. I had seen what no other had seen. The Lord Jesus in whom they trusted had abandoned them. Yet it was not for a lad to gainsay followers who had been with him during the years of his ministry.

Mother hurried to the roof, while the followers clustered about Salome. Mother urged, low-voiced, "Mark dear, go to bed. There's a good boy."

I shook off her anxious, protecting hands. "I was in the orchard. I saw the arrest, and I saw what went before it, while all these people slept. He knew the soldiers were coming. He expects to die." I spoke for her ears alone, not to those in the court, who now were arguing hotly, with Salome's penetrating voice rising above all.

Mother laid a hand over my mouth. "Let them hope while they can. Hope gives courage. They must go to him. If they desert him tonight they will be ashamed as long as they live. Jesus must be able to look out over the crowd and see his friends with the others."

I said with grief and bewilderment, "He is the greatest Jew since Moses, and our leaders will kill him, and he will not use his powers. He submits." The awful realization marked the end of childhood for me, whether Mother understood it or not.

We stood at the parapet and watched them go. Seth went grumbling to bed, having commandeered Agabus to carry his lamp. As soon as Seth was settled, however, Agabus hurried away after the followers. Mother laid her head against my breast and wept.

Anger swelled within me. Mother's grief need never have been if only the rabbi had used some common sense, if only he had taken warning and gone back to Galilee. He could easily have saved himself, had he wanted to do so. No legions of angels, no fire from heaven were required—merely an act of simple caution.

I longed to follow Agabus, to see how the Jews would go about convicting this Jew who had been rash enough to cross swords with Annas. I longed to see how he would bear himself when he stood bound before the Sanhedrin. For mingled with my anger was the faint hope that something might be said at his trial which would make sense of what I had witnessed. However, I did not ask Mother to let me go. I could not add anxiety for me to her poignant sorrow.

She dried her eyes. "When he was at table with Simon he said to the disciples, 'Set your troubled hearts at rest. My peace I leave with you.' I don't know how a man can die, yet leave his peace with those who mourn. Still, he said it, so it must be true."

"Take your rest." Unconsciously I repeated the rabbi's words to his friends in the orchard. "Take your rest, for you will need it."

"Oh, Mark, I am glad you are here. I wish you could have been spared this tragic affair. I wish you need never know of the evil men may do to one another. Yet it comforts me that you are here." She kissed me. "Go to bed, my dearest boy, and I will do the same."

On the hours of that night and the day which followed I will not dwell. They passed as a nightmare.

Not all our guests were involved in the trial and hanging of the Nazarene. For their sakes the Passover must be celebrated when the next sun set. As the hours of the day dragged by, our house was filled with the odor of boiling vegetables and roasting lamb and baking bread in preparation for the Passover meal. My memory of that dreadful day has been forever charged with the pervading odors of baking and roasting and boiling.

The rabbi's followers came and went, reporting the progress of the several ' hearings—before the Sanhedrin, before the Roman governor, Pontius Pilate, before the so-called Jewish tetrarch of Galilee, Herod Antipas, who had come to Jerusalem for the Passover season.

The Herod dynasty were called Jews, though they were originally Edomites whose ancestor Antipater had been forced by the Maccabees to be circumcised and to adopt Judaism. The family was notorious for incest, infanticide, and other detestable crimes, and the Jews would not own them, but certain Romans took pleasure in giving them the Jewish label. Antipas himself was half Edomite, half Samaritan, but there had been other Herods with Jewish, even Maccabee blood in their maternal heritage.

Since Jesus came from Galilee, Pilate sent him to Antipas, hoping to shift the responsibility for disposing of a difficult prisoner without alienating the rulers of the Jews. In this he got nowhere. Herod Antipas was unwilling to be maneuvered into killing another such Jew as John the Baptizer had been.

The charge brought by Annas against Jesus was conspiracy to overthrow the princeps, Tiberius Caesar. He had produced witnesses enough and the charge was one no Roman governor dared ignore. Moreover, the prisoner offered no defense, nor would this man whose words had moved multitudes speak a word in his own behalf. In the end, the Roman ordered the execution though he made it quite clear that the Jews were responsible, that he found no fault in the man he condemned.

At noon the rabbi was executed, together with a pair of thieves similarly sentenced. Mother went with Salome and Mary of Magdala to stand beneath the cross on which he was hanged. The hill of execution was suitably named the Place of a Skull.

I remained at home with the few guests who lingered there. I wandered about the roof, lonely as a ghost, numb with disenchantment. My mind would not let go of the unanswerable question, Why had the rabbi submitted? Why had he not taken a few simple precautions to save himself? Anger is easier to bear than grief, and as the day wore on I grew more and more angry.

The third watch began. Suddenly the world grew dark. Thick clouds hid the sun. A tremor stirred the city. I felt the house shiver. Later I learned that the quake was more severe in the northern end of Jerusalem. Some damage was done to the Temple and in the neighboring Antonia Roman soldiers fell on their faces in fear. In Bethany the quake was slight, yet I dropped to my knees, burying my face in my hands. Could this be the signal for Jesus to summon his legions of angels?

By now he had been upon the cross for five hours. Men died after twelve hours there. I thrust the foolish hope away. No legions of angels would be summoned, not now, not ever. What the legionaries would do with three half-dead men when sunset approached I did not want to know. They would be taken down and killed by some sort of hasty torture before Passover began, and buried out of sight of the setting sun.

Agabus returned before the others, limping drearily in

through the narrow door beside the camel gate. His mouth twisted as he came, and I knew he was muttering to himself. His mutterings, his hitching walk, the twitch of his shoulders, all were more expressive of exasperation than grief. This was ever his way, to blame tragedy upon the stupidity of men.

I followed Agabus as he resumed his household duties. By questioning I learned what he had seen. Jesus on his cross had cried out as the sun was darkened by clouds, saying that God had forsaken him. When the earth shuddered and the crosses swayed, he cried out again, commending his spirit into his Father's keeping. When they took him down he was dead. The thieves lived, but when their bones had been broken they were pronounced dead and carted off to the Hinnom ravine for burning.

Nicodemus, with Joseph of Arimathea, had taken Jesus' body to a nearby garden where Joseph had a new tomb. They buried him in haste, for the day was ending.

I followed Agabus as he hitched his way from the court to the tables in the pavilion, carrying up food Damaris had prepared. "Why did it happen?" The question was wrenched up from deep within me, not because I expected even Agabus to have an answer—after all, the whole tragic episode was Jewish, and Agabus was Greek.

Agabus turned upon me. "Why did your ancestors at Sinai cry out when God appeared upon the mountain, saying, 'Do not show us your face, lest we die'? Only the early Greeks were fools enough to think the gods can walk among men without starting some mighty conflagration."

I turned away. "If you're going to give me high-flown answers I can't understand there's no use talking."

Agabus gripped my shoulders in his bony hands. I saw then that even Agabus, who used exasperation as a cloak for grief, had been weeping. "What kind of answer do you want, Marcus?" His voice was gentle.

"I just want to know why he didn't go away. He knew Annas meant to get him killed. Why didn't he go back to Galilee?"

"Why did Socrates drink the hemlock? He could have slipped away into exile. Yet he took the cup in his own hands and drained it."

I gaped at him. In Agabus' view Socrates had been a Messiah to the Greeks. "You think Jesus is another Socrates? You didn't even know him!"

"I heard every public utterance of the last day of his life. It was enough. And you, Marcus. You saw him. You heard him speak. Don't ask me what he was or who he was. Judge for yourself."

Mother returned with the two women as the sun touched the walls of Jerusalem. Watching her come, I was wrung with pain that she had seen it all, that the sights I visualized were printed forever in her memory. Salome entered clinging to her son James. As long as Jesus remained alive upon the cross Salome had held to the expectation that at any moment he would turn upon his tormentors with bolts of heavenly fire and throngs of angelic warriors. When his enemies walked by, wagging their heads, gibing, "Come down if you be Lord," Salome had waited, expecting momentarily the miracle which did not occur. The Salome who entered our court was a woman bereft of hope.

A few guests partook of the Passover meal. I sat in the pavilion with them, but the food stuck in my throat.

In a corner of the court the disciples huddled together, a desolate group.

Presently Seth remarked, so loudly it carried to the farthest corner of the court below, "Those thieves—they weren't much to look at but at least they were alive when they came down from the crosses. This Jesus must have been a weakling to die in only six hours."

Every head in the little group in the court snapped up. Anger invaded faces apathetic with despair. Peter rose slowly. His arms knotted with the clenching of his great fists. His eyes were rimmed in red.

"You are an old man, sir, and strengthless," he said. "As for me, I fled when they arrested my Lord. I denied him when questioned by a servant girl. I will not add to my record of cowardice by tearing you to pieces, old man. But know, sir, that Jesus could walk farther, fast longer, speak and heal and comfort all who came to him long after the rest of us fell exhausted on the hillside or in the boats. I myself am a strong man, a fisherman, one who throws out the net over the sea, then dives to draw together the edges, fighting off fish as they lunge against the confining mesh and holding my breath for long periods of such struggle. I am strong, but the Lord Jesus was stronger. He gave all he had and it was not enough. He came to his own, and his own rejected him. He died as a criminal dies, between two criminals, while the Jews cursed him and spit upon him. He was a strong man, and he died of sorrow."

Peter sank upon his heels, rubbing his bearded face with his big hands.

John rose, a blade of Damascus iron, gentle yet strong, the youngest of the twelve, slender, disciplined from the labors fishermen endure. "He died of sorrow. He was a strong man, and he died of sorrow." Gentleness was in his glance, and tenderness like the tenderness of my mother. He looked over the group of his friends and asked, "Where is Judas?"

"Dead." Thomas spat out the word. "If he had not killed himself I would have killed him."

John said, "He knew not what he did. May God forgive him."

The rich voice of Mary of Magdala held a fathomless grief. "He betrayed our Lord Jesus with a kiss."

Peter said, "He broke bread with us and slept in our company. He traveled with us through the land for three years. He dealt with innkeepers and fishmongers for us. If he needed thirty pieces of silver he could have taken them from the common purse."

Andrew said heavily, "He was impatient for the kingdom. He loved our Lord Jesus but he was impatient. He hoped to compel Jesus to set up his kingdom then and there."

"Kingdom!" said Thomas. "What kingdom? There was never a kingdom for us and there never will be one. When the Sabbath ends I will go home to my father and my farm. I have neglected them these three years, for what? For an illusion. For abandonment. For—for this bottomless loneliness."

Peter rose. "We will go up into the orchard. We will take our desolation where we need not trouble these good people. Come, my friends." He led the way and they filed out of the court. I did not see them again until the first day of the week had dawned.

My mother occupied herself that Sabbath day with collecting linens, spices, and unguents for a final service to the dead rabbi, who had been hustled into the tomb without this final ministration.

On the morning of the first day my mother set out with Salome and Mary of Magdala to go to the garden of Joseph's tomb. From the parapet I watched them go, each with her mantle wrapped closely about her grief-ravaged face, each carrying an alabaster box or jar of myrrh, aloes, or nard. I watched them walk away down our road toward the Jericho road which skirted the shoulder of Olivet. I thought how the rabbi of Galilee had brought together three such different women, my mother, daughter of wealth and widow to a man of wealth, a woman who ordered her great house with the help of as many servants as she cared to bother with; Salome, wife and mother of fishermen, her hands hard with toil, a mother whose great desire had been to see her sons better themselves; and Mary, whose gifts had been beauty and a heart which understood men's needs. Her spirit had been so whipped by the lusts of men that in the end she was possessed by demons, till the rabbi drove them out and invited her to follow him.

In the fellowship of the Nazarene the three were bound together. When today's grim business was finished nothing would remain to unite them.

The garden was an hour's walk at their slow pace. They would not return, I thought, before midday.

Now the court was in a bustle, for our relatives were preparing to return to the provinces or to the lands of the Diaspora. My duty was to see them off in my mother's absence, to listen to the repetitious farewells and injunctions. I was relieved when Seth was finally on his way, after repeated warnings against association with criminals and questionable characters. When the court grew quiet at last I returned to the roof, where Agabus was busy with broom and mop. He muttered as he worked, not in the classical Greek of Plato and Sophocles and Homer, but in the Aramaic of our Galilean guests.

"Peace I leave with you. My peace I give unto you. Set your troubled hearts at rest. You believe in God, believe also in me. I go to prepare a place for you, that where I am, you may be also."

The pointed, pixy lips spoke with surprising tenderness. Seeing me stare, Agabus said gently, "Marcus, my son, I followed the rabbi for one day only. Had I followed him for three years I would not mope in an orchard as some do. I would be out on the roads, repeating his sayings to everyone who would consent to listen."

I said, past the pain in my chest, "He's dead. The Jews killed him."

"Is Socrates dead?" Agabus limped over to grasp my arms. He tipped back the big head with its fine eyes and twin fringes on chin and forehead and looked into my face with a strange grief all his own. "What a pity he had no scholars among his followers. For want of a Plato to record his sayings—his parables—his sermons—he may indeed be dead." He sighed deeply. "At least no Greeks had any part in killing him. The Jews and the Romans must bear the full guilt."

He was looking past me toward the Olivet road. I saw two women approaching along the track. They moved queerly, staggering and holding to one another. They passed out of sight under a jutting boulder. When they emerged onto our private road I saw that their garments were rent and their hair pulled down about their faces.

"Mother!" I raced down into the court and across to fling open our camel gate and draw them in. The second woman was Salome. She raised her arms in unspeakable grief and fled past me. Her sons and Peter were in the court. She was soon folded in the embrace of the elder son, James.

"He is gone! The tomb is empty! They have taken him to be burned in Hinnom."

I closed the gate with shaking hands.

Mother said, "I don't know what Nicodemus and Joseph will say when they learn that the tomb was violated." She took a box of aloes from Salome and laid it with the other alabaster vessels on a table. She came and laid her head against me in deep weariness. "They denied him even a decent burial. They are the rulers of the Jews, and their hatred followed him even to the tomb."

From the parapet Agabus declaimed, "Fear not those who kill the body but cannot kill the soul. Are not two sparrows sold for a penny? And not one of them will fall to the ground without God's will."

Mother repeated, "How can Jews do such things to one another?"

A cry came from outside the gate, the rich, full-throated cry of Mary of Magdala. "He lives! He spoke to me in the garden. He said to me, 'Tell my disciples to go into Galilee. I will see them there. Tell Peter I will see him in Galilee.' This he said! He is not dead! He lives! He lives!"

In the stunned silence I was chiefly aware of the pity which twisted my mother's face.

Salome turned stiffly from James' embrace. "The devils have entered into her once more. Go to the house of Simon. You will find him leprous. You will find that Lazarus is dead."

Peter swiftly girded his coat. "Come, John."

John kissed his mother. "If he lives, we will bring him here where you can minister to him." The two of them departed, running.

James, the practical one, the homely, sensible James, said, "He was on the cross only six hours. He always had great stamina. Mother, be comforted. Perhaps the hours of quiet rest within the tomb have restored him. If so, he must be hidden well and tended by the best physician. Miriam, whom can we trust to heal the Lord Jesus if he lives?"

Mary was laughing and crying in an excess of emotion. "James, foolish man, he was dead and is alive. He is radiant, transfigured. He needs no physician. Come, all of you. Gather your belongings. Make your farewells. We must hasten to Galilee. He will be there. He will not be seen upon the road, but we will find him in Galilee."

James repeated stubbornly, "I will find a physician to treat his wounds when John and Peter bring him here. Miriam, tell me whom we can trust."

"James, James, if he is indeed alive, he is himself the greatest healer ever known. We need no physician for him." Mother was torn between the longing to believe Mary's story and a sort of wry astonishment at the stodgy James.

When Peter and John returned, they reported that they had found the tomb empty and the stone rolled from the door, but they had seen no trace of the Lord Jesus in the garden or near it.

Before midday the Galileans from all over Bethany had set out down the winding Jericho road, their belongings upon their backs. I walked with them for an hour. Until the end they continued to argue concerning what had occurred in the garden. Some believed the worst and some believed the best. For myself I had no hope but that the Jews had taken him to Hinnom and burned his body there.

# CHAPTER 4

Three wretched weeks passed before Barnabas reached Jerusalem. Mother carried her head high, pretending all was well with her when I knew she was breaking under a burden, of grief. She went sometimes to visit Simon. I thought they wept together. Why did she not weep with me? Would she never realize that I was no longer a child? Could she not see that I also was weeping, deep within me? I had been away for half a year. Since my return I was out of touch with my mother. If she hoped to protect me from sorrow by her silence she understood me not at all, for I carried my burden of confusions unresolved, grief alternating with anger. I looked for Barnabas and waited for his coming, thinking foolishly that all my troubles would end when he arrived.

Barnabas was six years younger than my mother. He had been twelve when bandits killed my father on the Jericho road and made off with the bag of silver he had been carrying down to the lowland to buy wheat from the early harvest. Barnabas stayed with my mother and me for two years, but when he returned to Cyprus to begin his apprenticeship in our copper business at Salamis he took me with him. He had been active in the business ever since, traveling from city to city to promote the sales of our wares among metal dealers in forums and bazaars. He had made influential friends, including Sergius Paulus, proconsul of Cyprus. Barnabas knew cities and men in Syria and Cilicia, Galilee, Samaria, and Judea, and all over Cyprus itself. Barnabas often spoke of the stability and safety Rome had given the world. He usually wore his toga when traveling, and the sturdy, high-backed Roman sandals called the caligula. Nobody, I thought, draped a toga with more authority and neatness than did Barnabas.

He arrived at last. He came up the back way through the orchard. We had known he was on the way because he had sent a messenger from Bethany to say he was stopping at Simon's house and would arrive soon. Obviously he had heard the news of Simon's healing. What else had he heard on his journey south from Antioch? I watched at the parapet, impatient to welcome him. When Agabus first told me the legends of the Greek gods I had visualized Zeus, father of all gods, as Barnabas in his finest toga with crimson bands about the wide, circular hem; as Barnabas with his handsome beard rolled into fat curls, with the tip of the strong chin with its deep cleft peering between the curls; as Barnabas with his straight, handsome nose, and dark eyes like Mother's, bright with animation and appreciation of all things good and beautiful. When Barnabas appeared among the trees I scrambled down the vine to rush across and throw welcoming arms around him.

Soon we were on the roof. Mother settled on a rug nearby while I set about washing Barnabas' feet.

"Tell us about your journey," said Mother.

I glanced at her. Not once in these three weeks had she asked about my journey home from Cyprus.

"I came overland from Antioch by way of Damascus."

"You didn't take ship to Caesarea? It would have been quicker."

"My friend Paul of Tarsus joined me in Antioch. He had crossed the bay by ship and advised against further travel on the sea. The weather has been contrary this spring."

I said, "We had a bad voyage from Salamis."

Mother glanced at me. "You did? You didn't mention it, dear."

"You didn't ask me."

Barnabas glanced from Mother to me with amusement and affection. Damaris came wheezing from the court with a bowl of fruit. Agabus, who had been Barnabas' teacher before he became mine, laid aside the scroll he had been reading, a Hebrew scroll, the writings of the prophet Isaiah. He moved over to join us.

"It has been an unseasonable spring, sir. There was an earthquake in Jerusalem, and rain after the season for rains had ended." Barnabas was one of the few men who could draw deference from Agabus.

Mother asked, "Did you make the entire journey with Paul?"

Mother admired the keen-witted, scholarly Benjamite without really liking him. She considered him opinionated and didactic, impossible in an argument because of his ready flow of both logic and information. Tarsus had a fine university, one of the finest in the Hellenist world. After his graduation there Paul had come to dwell with a sister in Jerusalem. For two years he had studied in the School of Hillel, for Paul was a Pharisee. There he had been taught by one of the greatest teachers the sect had ever produced, the rabbi Gamaliel.

"Paul traveled with me as far as Capernaum." Barnabas took the towel from me and tousled my head affectionately. "So young you are, my boy, to have seen so much."

Mother said, "So you know what happened here before the Passover?"

"Before—and after. We had stopped in Damascus, where

I paid my respects to Mark's Uncle Seth. He told such a tale of criminals housed under my sister's roof that I made some inquiries. I soon realized that Seth spoke of the rabbi who had brought Lazarus from the tomb at the Passover season a year ago. I broke my journey at Capernaum while Paul continued south down the Jordan roadway. I searched out the rabbi's followers, desiring to hear their version of Seth's story. I knew you would be glad to have news of them, Miriam."

"How do they fare, poor souls?"

Agabus edged nearer. "It would not be easy to find a handful of obscure fisherfolk in a city of fishermen."

"I found them easily. I walked down to the sea to inquire for the sons of Zebedee, and there was Peter, bringing in a great catch of fish. His boat was deeply laden, and wind and waves were high. Yet he handled the boat as easily as in a summer zephyr, quite unwearied."

The coincidence of the meeting did not surprise me. Nothing that concerned the Galileans, I thought, would ever again surprise me.

"When I told Peter my sister is Miriam of Olivet he took me home. I spent a night and a day with him. I went with him to fish the whole night, hoping for a recurrence of an encounter he had had a week before, but nothing happened. However, I met his good wife Perpetua and his wife's mother, who was formerly afflicted by frequent seizures of the fever, until Jesus of Nazareth healed her. James and John, with their parents, Zebedee and Salome, came over and spent more than an hour at the house while I was there."

Barnabas laid his hand over Mother's two hands. "They tell some very strange stories, Miriam."

Mother reddened and shot a sidelong glance at me. "For any hysterical tales you heard in Capernaum I hold Mary of Magdala responsible. She imagines she talked with Jesus in

the garden of tombs where he was buried by Joseph of
Arimathea and Nicodemus—that he arose and somehow escaped from a sealed tomb. Barnabas, these are good people,
but they are simple-hearted. We hear these superstitious tales
from Syrians and Greeks and Romans—forgive me, Agabus. I
have listened to the legends you have related to Mark. So long
as one realizes they are only fables they do no great harm. But
when Jews begin telling similar tales as if they had happened
to the Lord Jesus, intertwining truth with myth, I find it—
well, embarrassing."

Agabus said, "My lady, I have no more belief in Greek
myths than yourself. I have been all my life a disciple of
Socrates, whose faith was in the one God who created and
rules all men."

Mother said quietly, "Of course. Else I would never have
entrusted Mark to your teaching." She turned back to Barnabas. "The Galileans had fixed great hopes in their rabbi. Do
not take it amiss if they repeat Mary's story of a risen Lord.
They were crushed when he died. They were utterly cast
down. Do not blame them if they seek comfort in one of the
Adonis stories now."

Barnabas looked at Mother rather queerly, his smile compounded of affection, pity, and a strange inner excitement.

Agabus said, "My lady, does it seem impossible that the man
who healed Simon's leprosy and brought Lazarus from the
tomb could himself return from death?"

Mother's hands plucked in agitation at the folds of the full
coat she held wrapped about her knees. "Truly, Agabus, I
cannot bear it when you mix the old fables with the pure
teachings of Jesus. I expect something better than superstitious nonsense from you, of all people."

Barnabas took the nervous, plucking fingers into his fine,
strong hands. "Miriam, hundreds—thousands—in Galilee

have recently seen Jesus alive. The incident I spoke of—a week before I saw Peter he had brought his boat near the shore as night was waning and dawn not far off. There on the shore a fire burned, and by the time he came in close enough it was only a bed of coals. The Lord Jesus was beside it, and had broiled some fish, and Peter came ashore and partook of the fish, and Jesus stayed and talked with him until the sun rose. Jesus has spoken with many others, and has taught them. The household in Nazareth, the kinsmen of Jesus who never believed in his mission while he lived—they have seen him, and have spoken with him during these recent weeks. The eldest of them, James of Nazareth, declares that Jesus is alive and is Messiah. The sons of Salome and Zebedee have talked with Jesus. Andrew, and Thomas, and Matthias witness that Jesus lives."

"Surely you do not credit the witness of ignorant fisherfolk?"

"My dear sister, they are excellent witnesses. They lack the imagination to invent the details they describe. But to make sure of what I heard in Capernaum I stopped to call on Simon the Leper after I came through Bethany. His healing, Miriam, is marvel enough for any man."

Mother said softly, "It is marvel enough. I am glad you talked with Simon."

"I told Simon what they say in Capernaum. Simon believes Jesus did indeed return alive from the tomb. Simon believes that Jesus is Messiah."

Mother cried, "No! Oh Barnabas, no. He was a prophet, a very great prophet. It is our eternal shame that Jews rejected him and connived to get him killed. But don't label him Messiah."

"Miriam, wait and see. When you hear the witness of the

Galileans you will know that Jesus can be no other than Messiah."

"When I hear—Barnabas, are they coming back to Bethany? Oh, I wish they would not. This can only embarrass all of us, and distress us."

"They will return before Pentecost."

Mother pushed back the full sleeves of her coat. Her movements were restless. She was deeply troubled. "I have never seen anyone like Jesus. I long to believe that he lives." Tears washed her dark, lovely eyes. "If he lives, where is he staying? Why didn't he come to us here? How did he get to Galilee? Does he dwell in Peter's house, or in Nazareth, or where? Is he fully recovered? Is he well? Did you see him? Six hours on the cross—it was frightful. But men do not die in six hours on the cross." Her voice rose. "Who opened the tomb? Even if he recovered in the tomb, he would be wounded, feeble, crippled in hands and feet. Who rolled back the stone to let him come out of the tomb?"

Barnabas asked quietly, "How did he cleanse Simon?"

Mother's eyes burned upon him, and he continued, "Miriam, this is a miracle or it is nothing. This is a man who died and is alive. The Jesus who appears to the Galileans dwells in no house. He appears, and he vanishes."

Agabus quoted solemnly, " 'A little while and you will see me no more. Again a little while and you will see me.' I, for one, believed the Magdalene's story. It had a ring of truth to it."

Mother exclaimed, "Agabus, fables are for the credulous. I suppose they will be saying soon that Joseph the carpenter is not his father—that Jesus was virgin born, sired by a god."

A startled look crossed Barnabas' handsome face. "It is being said now. Mary was betrothed to Joseph when Jesus was born. She married him afterward."

Agabus limped about the roof, shoulders twitching. "Your Isaiah and your Amos wrote prophecies which have been fulfilled in unexpected ways in the life and death of this rabbi of Nazareth. In the overlapping myths of other peoples I find evidence that all men seek for God, for the true God who created all men and who may choose strange and marvelous ways to make Himself known. Not only Jews have dreamed of a Son of God come to take upon himself the burdens of men. I suggest that certain myths may also be prophetic. This I declare, my lady Miriam . . ." He came to a halt directly facing her. "If Jesus is the Messiah of the Jews he is for all men! God is not the God of Jews alone. That Jesus was a Jew is only as significant as that Socrates was a Greek."

Barnabas' large, dark eyes were fixed brightly upon Agabus. "You speak a profound truth, Teacher."

Mother exclaimed, "Stop it, both of you. What am I to tell my son to believe? What am I to believe? All this mixing of our pure Jewish faith with pagan legends is dreadful. How will I bear it when they come with their ecstatic stories, when they sit in my house pouring out credulous nonsense about the greatest Jew since Moses?"

I ran from the house and out into the orchard. Mother called but I did not stop. "What shall I tell my son to believe?" Mother had said, as if I had seen nothing and heard nothing and had no thoughts or opinions of my own.

How many times had I run away to the clearing to stand beneath the tree with the twisted, hollow trunk, staring at the stone where Jesus of Nazareth had prayed while he waited for Jews to arrest him, waited for the betrayal of his friend Judas, for the panic and terror and desertion of those who loved him?

"Thy will be done," he had prayed. What had followed could not have been God's will! Jesus was wrong. Agabus was wrong. Barnabas and Peter and Mother were wrong. Yet how could they all be wrong? And how could Mother be so blind to my pain and confusion, to my longing to know what was true—to know how truth could be one thing, and all that Agabus believed and all that Jesus had promised be something completely different.

I crossed blindly to the mossy stone, not because I had planned it but because the pain within me drew me there. Whatever the stone had been to Canaanites long centuries ago, it was holy now. Whether the Nazarene was prophet or wandering wonder-worker, his tears had cleansed this stone. Suddenly I was kneeling, wrenched by soundless sobs, torn with longing.

"What is truth?" Pilate had asked Jesus this question during the trial, and had received no answer. Now I wept, my clenched hands softly beating upon the stone, and my heart cried, What is truth? What is truth? My heart cried, but found no answer.

A hand touched my shoulder. It was the maimed hand of Simon. "No need to weep, Mark," he said. "He is not dead. He is risen. He lives."

I took the hand, and looked at the pink flesh that grew over those stumpy, misshapen fingers. Simon had been my father's good friend. I had played in his orchard as freely as in our own, and in his courtyard had been fed many a choice sweetmeat until disaster made Simon a stranger to his neighbors.

"How did he do it, Simon? How did he heal you?" I clung to the thick, queer hand. I looked up into the strange face on which no hair grew. I saw only affection and kindness in his eyes, a kindness unchanged since my childhood.

He replied, "With God all things are possible. Come. I need your help. These hands must learn to handle spade and pruning shears. Come and help me, Mark." Then, with great warmth, "You have grown to resemble your father. He was a handsome man, and a good man. May he rest in peace."

We climbed to a clearing near Simon's house. He had a bundle of olive cuttings beside the gate. I took a shovel and fell to digging holes for the new little trees. When all were planted I brought water from his cistern to pour around them. I stayed with Simon until evening. We spoke of the care and nurture of orchards, and when we were silent I still felt the comfort of his companionship.

During the weeks between the arrival of Barnabas and the return of the Galileans before Pentecost, Paul of Tarsus paid us two visits. I was with Simon in the orchard the first time he came. When I entered the court, sweating, with earth on my hands and manure on my sandals, I heard Paul's harsh, incisive, rich, unforgettable voice.

"He made the Temple seem vile. He called the bankers thieves. Our rulers are answerable to Romans and to Jews. Their dignity must not be publicly shattered. A man with the following of the Nazarene should have spoken to our rulers with responsibility and discretion."

I left the court and went round to where the vine grew. By that route I could reach my room without being seen. When I had washed and changed I would be fit to present myself.

As I emerged after bathing, Barnabas was asking in a tone of amusement, "Why does a tentmaker call fishermen nobodies?"

A master coppersmith himself, Barnabas respected the manual trades. His challenge was legitimate.

"I respect the trade of those men," Paul answered harshly. "I do not respect their scholarship. Why should a man with the insight of this Nazarene fail to attract a single scholar into his fellowship?"

Agabus said, "He came not to call the righteous, but sinners to repentance."

Paul cried passionately, "We are all sinners, whether scholars, scribes, coppersmiths, or tentmakers. Annas knows his own imperfections, and those of his priestly sons."

Paul of Tarsus was a small man, no larger than Agabus. He was younger than Barnabas by three years, sallow, but with eyes as fiery as his voice. His Hebrew name must have caused him endless embarrassment as a lad, for he was of the tribe of Benjamin, named for the mightiest of all Benjamites, King Saul, who had stood head and shoulders above his people. Paul was shorter than most men by a span. As a fiery, impetuous youth he must have loathed his Hebrew name. His Roman name Paul, meaning small and beloved, suited him. Barnabas, who understood him and loved him, called him by his Roman name, and I did the same.

Agabus said, "I followed him from one hearing to another that day. I stood amongst the hirelings of Annas who screamed, 'Crucify him.' I tell you he went to his death because it was his destiny. Even as your prophet Isaiah foretold, 'He was despised and rejected, a man of sorrows and acquainted with grief.'"

Paul said angrily, "A gifted teacher and healer is dead, a man who loved righteousness. The Jews need their great men. This is a terrible loss, yet he brought it upon himself."

Agabus said, "Surely he has borne our griefs and carried our sorrows, and the chastisement of our sins is upon him."

Paul said, "Agabus, friend, you should have been a Jew."

"I am sure you mean that kindly," Agabus replied.

Paul said, "Yet your argument that God sent Messiah to the Jews with the purpose that they should reject and destroy him is specious. God would not so mock the chosen people." His fine voice vibrated with passion.

Agabus replied with equal passion. "The God of the Jews is the God of all men. He gives into men's hands the power to exalt or to debase themselves. How far it can go not God but men will decide. This God permits slavery. I do not know what else He might permit."

Mother exclaimed, "Agabus, do stop ranting about slavery. You are one of the family and you know it. How many times have I offered you your seal of manumission, and you refused?"

"What good is freedom to me while other men are slaves?"

I wandered away, dazed by Paul's argument, which exactly stated the staggering facts against which I had been beating my head ever since that night in the clearing. "God would not so mock the chosen people. God would not send Messiah that the Jews should reject and destroy him." Now that it had been stated for me I understood the real nature of the perplexity which had set me against those I revered and respected.

The lonely man in the orchard had been wrong when he prayed, "Thy will be done." His death was not God's will, and he had been wrong-headed in thinking it was.

Yet day by day in those spring months I saw the hands and naked face of Simon, and day by day the tormenting question recurred. By what power was he healed?

In the end, Paul suggested an answer for this question also.

Simon and I were in the orchard that day, anchoring the olive saplings by tying them to tough sticks thrust into the earth amongst their small, springing roots. Barnabas brought Paul to the orchard, and for a while they discussed the saplings, now a little wilted because the weather had turned hot.

But Paul was never one to waste much time on agricultural topics. He sent a sharp, inquiring glance into the beardless face of the older man. "You are one of those who believe that the crucified Nazarene is alive and has appeared to certain Galileans."

Simon smiled serenely. "You are a Pharisee. Do you find his resurrection so difficult to accept?"

"I find the whole idea blasphemy—a tale concocted to discredit the rulers of the Jews."

Simon extended his hands. "I was a leper. Jesus healed me. Death cannot hold a man with such powers."

Paul took the extended hands, examining them. "Tell me what the healer did, what he said. Tell me what you felt in your flesh at the moment of healing."

Simon looked directly into the intense, intelligent eyes. "The Lord Jesus commanded me, 'Say nothing to any man, but take gifts to the Temple for your cleansing.' I tell you only this—before it was done I had faith that Jesus was Messiah, the savior of the Jews. I had faith that the man who brought Lazarus from the tomb could heal me if he would. I asked Lazarus to bring him. The healing came from God. Many physicians had treated me. What men could not do, God has done, through the divine power of the Lord Jesus."

"Blasphemy!"

"When leprosy eats away his flesh a man comes to feel that he is no longer made in God's image. If my lips denied that I am cleansed, my hands and this beardless face would testify that Jesus touched me and made me whole."

"Healers come and go, Simon. This one is gone." Paul bent over the hands he still held. "This flesh did not grow here clean and wholesome in the flash of a moment, the beat of a heart. Years were needed to cover rotting stumps with such flesh. Simon, you are both charlatan and blasphemer. You were healed years ago by physicians, but until Jesus came to Bethany and called Lazarus from the tomb, you knew not how to persuade your neighbors that you were clean."

I was staring at Simon, distrust and suspicion eating away at the love I had for my father's old friend.

Simon's smile was compassionate. "Faith comes hard to a Pharisee. Only the mind of a little child, or of a man as lonely and despairing as I was, could open to receive the truth about the Lord Jesus. May God help you, Paul of Tarsus. May God open your mind to receive the truth for which you thirst."

I continued to work in the orchard, for I had to keep myself occupied, and this was work that needed to be done. But whenever I looked at Simon's hands thereafter I tortured myself with the silent question, What are you, Simon of Bethany? Charlatan or living miracle?

# CHAPTER 5

As I look back after so many years upon those seven weeks between Passover and Pentecost, it seems we stood upon the shore of a mighty sea. As the Hebrews at Sinai clung to memories of Egyptian hovels and Egyptian habits and the meager slave diet of Egypt, unaware that a great new faith was coming into being on the earth, so we clung to what we knew, looking neither forward nor backward. We had no prescient insight into the mighty meaning of what had come into the world with the life, the death, and the resurrection of the Lord Jesus.

This was true of Barnabas and Agabus, but it was especially true of my mother and of me. When a ripple of understanding washed over our sandals we leaped back, fearful that the wavelet might turn into a deluge which would wash us away from the familiar into the vast unknown.

The Galileans returned ten days before the Feast of Pentecost. Agabus welcomed them with wine, and with water for cleansing away the dust of their journey. Mother welcomed them dutifully, ignoring the air of glory they wore, inquiring about their journey. As for me, I escaped to the orchard, dissolving in labor and the sweat of my body the thoughts inspired by their troubling presence.

There was, however, no escaping their joyous stories about the appearances of the risen Lord Jesus to this one and that, sometimes in rooms but oftener upon the road, or a mountain, or beside the sea. They could not cease speaking of these things. The frequent recurrence of the phrase, "Before he was parted from us," I took to mean various disappearances, until a day when Peter and Andrew came with Simon into the orchard. Peter was carrying water from the spring to pour about the young saplings.

"The prophets foretold that Messiah should suffer, and on the third day rise from the dead, that repentance and forgiveness of sins should be preached in his name, beginning in Jerusalem. The Lord Jesus said, 'You are my witnesses. Behold, I will send the promise of my Father upon you. Remain in Jerusalem until you are clothed with power. Afterward you will witness to all these things, not only in Jerusalem, not only throughout Judea, not only in Samaria, but to the very ends of the earth.' "

Andrew echoed, "This he said, before he was parted from us. We had come all the way from Capernaum and had reached this very mountain. He said all these things to us here on Olivet, saying, 'You are my witnesses.' Then he was parted from us, vanishing into thick clouds. Yet we know well that he will return to dwell among us and to restore the kingdom to Israel, though we do not know his times or his seasons."

Thus I came to realize that the random appearances of the risen Lord were no longer expected, that the disciples' expectation was of a time when Jesus would return and remain among them in a kingdom to be established on earth. Thus I learned that the Galileans would not return to Capernaum after Pentecost, but had come for an indefinite stay.

Peter and James and John dwelt in the house of Lazarus. Others dwelt with Simon or in other Bethany houses. The

Magdalene and Salome were our guests, also Andrew and Philip and Thomas.

Because our upper room was large and airy the followers formed the habit of coming there daily, some three score Galileans plus others from Bethany and Jerusalem. The order of these meetings was to sing a hymn and pray, using a prayer Jesus had taught them. Following the prayer one, then another, would rise and witness.

"I remember how the Lord Jesus said when he was with us in the flesh . . ."

This was the opening formula, followed by some parable, or a fragment from a sermon, or perhaps an interpretation of Hebrew prophecy which had been applicable in one way or another to the life and ministry of Jesus. The recitals tended to be grouped by subject matter. To me it seemed the topic they touched on oftenest was the exhortation to become like the lilies of the field.

"Do not lay up for yourselves treasures on earth, where moth and rust consume and where thieves break in and steal, but lay up treasures in heaven."

"Do not be anxious about tomorrow, for tomorrow will take care of itself."

"Ask, and it will be given you; seek, and you will find. If you who are evil give good gifts to your children, how much more will your Father give good things to those who ask?"

"Take nothing for your journey except a staff; no bread, no bag, no money in your belts. Where you enter a house, stay until you leave the city."

"Look at the birds of the air; they neither sow nor reap, yet your heavenly Father feeds them. Consider the lilies of the field; they neither toil nor spin . . . If God so clothe the grass will he not clothe you?"

"When you fast, anoint your head and wash your face, that

your fasting may not be seen by men but by your Father, who sees what is secret."

If any of them fasted, I did not observe it. We daily fed more followers, together with newly made converts to The Way, which was the name they used for their fellowship.

The Day of Pentecost, so great a milestone for the seventy who met that morning in our upper room, was for me marked only by the changes which came after it. Thereafter Peter and James and the others preached the resurrection of the Lord Jesus openly in gates and squares and even in the Temple cloisters. Thereafter the followers of The Way were numbered by hundreds. From Pentecost onward, my mother's house was no longer home for me, but a public hostel, open to people of every sort.

For Mother, Pentecost meant far more. Her doubts were set at rest on that day. For her the resurrected Jesus became real, the Messiah of the Jews and the Son of God.

I was not at home that morning. But I have heard the witness of those marvels scores of times. As they prayed together in our pavilion suddenly the wind sprang up, a strong, driving wind. And there appeared tongues like flames of fire, dispersed among them and resting on each one. Then they were filled with the Breath of God, the Holy Spirit, and began to talk in many different tongues in a very ecstasy of joy.

I have since encountered inarticulate utterances (which seem to me an hysterical imitation of the phenomenon of Pentecost) in the ecclesias of various cities. Yet this has seemed an empty symbol of grace rather than the grace itself. I was not there, and perhaps should not pretend to authority about the event, content to record merely that Mother was there, and all her doubts were henceforth set at rest. Mother dated her joyous faith in the risen Messiah from Pentecost.

Barnabas and I had gone to the Temple that morning, carrying grain and early fruits, with loaves made from the wheat harvest of the Jordan Valley. We each brought also a gold coin for the Temple treasure chest. As I listened to the chants, the readings, the prayers, I remembered that our chief priests had haled Jesus before Pilate and with copper farthings had bribed the rabble to shout, "Crucify him! Give us Barabbas!" I had loved the Temple always, but now I wondered whether it would ever again seem truly God's dwelling place for me.

As we returned homeward we encountered a throng outside Damascus Gate. Someone stood upon the platform used by prophets and magicians and other entertainers, someone who was haranguing the crowd. As we drew near I saw with astonishment that the speaker was Peter, and that he spoke with boldness and with an authority that was new.

"Men of Israel, hear me. Jesus of Nazareth, a man manifested to you by God through mighty works and signs which God did through him in your midst—this Jesus you crucified. But God raised him up, for death could not hold him. Let Israel know that God has made him Lord and Messiah, the very Christos of the prophets, this Jesus whom you murdered."

I protested to Barnabas, "They'll crucify Peter also if he goes on like that."

"Listen to him!" Barnabas' eyes glowed. "Listen, and open your heart."

A shaft of loneliness shot through me. Barnabas was one with those people. I was not. I had lost my reverence for the Temple, but I was not one with the followers of Jesus as were Barnabas, Agabus, and Simon.

From somewhere a wail came, "I have sinned. What shall I do?"

Peter shouted, "Repent and be baptized in the name of Jesus of Nazareth for the forgiveness of your sins. You will receive the outpouring of the Holy Spirit, as have all who follow Jesus." He beckoned with great, sweeping gestures. "Come down to the Kidron. All who truly repent come and be baptized in Jesus' name."

We were swept along with the surging crowd down to the Kidron. There Peter and Andrew and James and Matthias and others were busy throughout that midday, baptizing those who came crowding down to them saying, "I have sinned. Jesus is Lord indeed," and other expressions of the sort.

Barnabas tugged at me. "Come, Mark. Come down to the Kidron."

From behind us came the harsh challenge of Paul of Tarsus. "Blasphemy. Barnabas, don't be a fool!"

I did not hear Barnabas' reply, for across the valley I saw Mother descending by the winding path. With her were neighbors I had known all my life, the sisters of Lazarus, Simon, and many others. They were streaming down to the spillway below the Gihon Reservoir.

Andrew baptized Mother. I did not hear what was said between them in the confusion of many voices. The rejoicing of those who came up from baptism formed a sort of choral background against which rose the sharp protests of Paul. After Barnabas went down, Paul continued to argue with others. Barnabas had pulled at me again as he moved down, but I jerked away.

Low-voiced I said, "I can't go. I can't!" Anger and pain were choking me.

He looked at me strangely. "I'm sorry, Mark." Then he plunged down.

I saw him as he rose from the waters. The fat curls of his beard were dripping runnels and his linen coat stuck to him with the wetness, but his lifted face was glowing and his mouth moved, forming words whose shapes were strange to me. And behind me Paul of Tarsus said, "Mark, you are wiser than they—wiser than I could have expected you to be."

Barnabas had found Mother. They embraced, their faces filled with glory. Then Barnabas lifted his wet, flapping skirts to ascend toward the Bethany road, and I saw Agabus standing off to himself beside the road. Barnabas spoke to Agabus in passing, but Agabus just shook his head without speaking. Mother had disappeared in the throng, and Paul had moved off and was haranguing those who still lingered on this side of the stream. I went round by the road and started toward home.

Because of the enormous increase in the number of believers after Pentecost, half a score of houses became centers for the common meals, some in Bethany but most of them in Jerusalem. Following the meal the ecclesias convened.

One of the disciples could be found in each house where believers broke bread together. Peter or Andrew was usually in our pavilion. John had gone back to Galilee, where he hoped to make his home in Nazareth and preach the resurrection to people who had refused to listen while Jesus himself dwelt there. Jesus had asked John to be as a son to his mother, and this was John's intention. Yet we still spoke of the disciples as the twelve.

From the day of Pentecost on, anyone could gain admission to the hospitable houses and sit at meat with the followers by repeating the password, "Jesus is risen," or the equally acceptable, "Jesus is Lord." To me the arrangement seemed an outrageous inducement to lying and hypocrisy. Many so-called converts were worthless men who had found a way to live that was easier than working. My appetite vanished as I looked upon the long tables in our pavilion, filled with men of every sort, whose wives and children were fed at long tables in the

court. I longed to stand and shout at them one of the neglected sayings of Jesus, "By their fruits you shall know them."
I am not mean by nature or training, but I grew mean as the
weeks of summer passed.

I protested to Mother, "My inheritance is dwindling. There
is no virtue for you or Barnabas in giving *my* heritage to feed
the poor. And there is no virtue in it for me, since it is done
without my consent."

Mother embraced me lovingly. "Dear Mark, they bring
what they have. Those who work give their wages. Many have
sold their possessions and given the money into the common
fund. Remember the words of the Lord Jesus, 'Inasmuch as
you help the least of these, you help me.' "

"Has Peter sold his boats and his nets?"

"They are his father's boats. Mark, when the Lord Jesus
comes to set up his kingdom there will be no buying and
selling, none who beg for alms and none who give alms."

That was the key, that conviction that the Lord Jesus' return was imminent. I would see them at the parapet, looking
off toward the Jericho road, faces alight with expectation, or
perhaps downcast with disappointment, when another day
and another passed, with no change except that the multitude
of those to be fed from the common fund increased.

Servants disappeared from these hospitable houses, or alter-
natively became guests by repeating the desired formula. And
guests helped with the work if so disposed, unless they felt
more like clustering in corners to talk about the coming kingdom. Ultimate responsibility rested upon my mother and
upon Damaris in our house, and I suppose there were women
of their sort in every house where the tables were spread.
Others worked at the ovens and the fires or washed and dried
utensils and bowls as volunteers for the day. Mother grew thin
and hard as whipcord, but her strength was the daily expecta-

tion of Jesus' return, the daily remembrance that she labored for love of the Lord Jesus.

"*When*," I demanded. "*When* will this kingdom be?"

The answer was by now terribly familiar. "It is not for us to know the times or the seasons. My son, my son, lay up treasures in the kingdom of heaven, for where your treasure is there will your affections be."

I replied darkly that I shuddered to think what would have become of us all if my father and grandfathers had been lilies of the field.

Damaris and Agabus ate apart from the Jews. The pattern was set on the day of Pentecost, when James had refused them baptism. The laws of common sense had been cast aside, but the restrictions of the Mosaic code had not. These two Greeks, who labored to serve the hordes which infested our house, could not sit at table with them unless they first became Jews, Agabus by submitting to circumcision, and both by subscribing to the whole burden of Jewish law.

On an afternoon in the month Tammuz, when summer's heat was at its height, I came from the orchard grimy and sweating and climbed the vine to the roof to avoid the clutter of the court. As I stepped over the parapet I stumbled into a scrawny child with matted hair and filthy face. She was licking at a fig cake with an expression of rapture.

"You are Mark." She spoke with a flat inflection and made no move to get out of my way.

I backed off against the parapet. "Excuse me. Yes, I'm Mark." I should have said, "Welcome to this house," but the civility would not come.

"I am Rhoda. We came today." Her tongue moved lovingly over the fig cake.

"Who came with you?" What we needed was a score more specimens like her.

"My father Ananias and my mother Sapphira. We have land in Bethlehem and a score of sheep."

She was the grubbiest and the scrawniest landowner's child I had ever seen. "Who will tend your sheep while you are here?"

"Who needs sheep in the kingdom of heaven? Anyway, I have some cousins. Maybe they will come too. I like it here." She licked the cake.

"You'd better go and wash," I advised her, and went to my room.

As I started to strip off my tunic to bathe I heard a sound at the curtain. Rhoda stood in the doorway, staring around with a curious, unwinking gaze. "Is it your room? Yours, all by yourself?"

"Not any more. Whoever wants to move in, does so." I wondered how a landowner's child could be so ignorant, so starved, so very dirty.

She eyed my basin of bath water, my soap and towels, the clean clothes I had laid out. "Are you a Pharisee?"

"No."

"The Pharisees are whited sepulchers."

"At least, they wash before they eat."

"Did you sell all you have to give to the poor?"

"Not yet. But I expect I will, before the kingdom comes."

"My father will wait awhile before he sells our land and our sheep. He says if the kingdom is delayed he might need it and we cannot know the times or the seasons. We slept in the orchard last night. I don't have any place to wash." She eyed my basin and towels and the clean clothing laid out with her unwinking stare.

"They're mine," I told her. "I haven't yet given them to the poor."

"We aren't poor! We have land."

"And sheep," I said. "Who invited you?"

She looked reproachful. "You don't get invited. You get baptized."

"Go to the court where the women are working. Ask Damaris to show you where to wash. Tell her I sent you."

Barnabas pointed out the child's father to me at the tables in the upper rooms. Ananias was a gaunt, stooped man, rather elderly to have begot a child as young as Rhoda. His mouth was pinched and mean within his stringy beard. His clothing was new, though his dingy flesh testified to years of uncleanness. He wolfed down his food and continued to pick at remnants of fruit and crumbs of bread even after others turned their attention to the witnessing.

Later I saw Rhoda, still grimy and uncombed, with a gaunt woman who was probably younger than she looked. From Barnabas I learned that Ananias had kept his family on short rations while he accumulated his holdings in Bethlehem.

"Now he will live at our expense, while his kinsmen tend his sheep," I said grimly.

Barnabas' bright eyes were fixed upon me with compassion. "How hard it is for the rich and comfortable to enter into the kingdom of heaven."

"I am not comfortable. Nor will I long be rich, at the rate things are going." I did not often show Barnabas so little respect.

"Leave him to Peter. Peter has his own ways of dealing with such cases. Meanwhile, let the child and the woman be fed. When the kingdom comes, the chaff will be winnowed from the wheat."

On an evening late in the month Ab, Barnabas went to Peter in the podium to lay in his hands a bag of coins for the common fund. A few brought gifts each evening to Peter or Andrew—usually no more than a day's wages, or the price of a tool or a garment sold in the city. Regardless of the admonition of the Lord Jesus to do their giving in secret, the followers made this public show, perhaps to encourage others to contribute to the fund upon which such heavy demands were daily made.

Barnabas said, "Today my sister and I sold a piece of land, our farm on Mount Scopus. Here is the price of it."

"Is this farm all the property you possess, my brother?"

"Not all. The produce of my sister's farms is brought to the tables of this company. We sold only the one farm."

"God will reward you, brother Barnabas."

Peter waited. The company waited. The meal could not begin until Peter took his place at table, after returning thanks in the podium, a spot visible in both the pavilion and the court. When no more gifts were brought Peter said, "Remember the words of the Lord Jesus, 'It is more blessed to give than to receive.' " His somber gaze rested on one man, then another. It rested longest on Ananias.

The next evening Ananias, looking green and distraught, went forward. Seeing his distress I knew this was no simple man, but a complex one, driven by strong desires. He wanted the best of both kingdoms. He laid a bag of coins in Peter's hands.

"I too have sold my land." He swallowed. "I—too. Here is the price."

He bulged strangely, a man underfed for years who had enjoyed a summer of gluttony. More ailed him than the sale of his property and the surrender of the proceeds. From his color I judged that his digestion was disordered. As a Levite I had been taught to observe the symptoms of common ailments.

Peter poured out the coins into one broad hand. "Is this the full price, my brother? Did you not receive double this amount?"

Ananias slumped. "You ask too much."

"Before you sold them, your possessions were yours. After you sold them, the money was yours. Is this the full price, Ananias?"

The man whined, "The followers are well known in the markets. We cannot command decent prices. We sell at a loss, but we sell and we bring you the money. Why do you accuse me?"

The house was utterly still. Not a soul had missed a word of this exchange. He is ill, Peter, I thought. Let him go. Leave him to his conscience.

"Is this the full price, my brother?"

"It is the full price." Ananias swayed.

"You lie, not to men, my brother, but to God, to the Holy Spirit who dwells within us, to our Lord Jesus, who died for us and rose again."

Ananias clutched at his middle, then at his chest. He gasped and fell. Peter knelt beside the twitching figure. When the breath no longer rasped and whistled Peter said in awe, "Our brother is dead. He lied to God, and God has smitten him."

I was one of those who carried the body out to the lower Kidron for burial. As we passed through the court with our burden bundled in his coat I saw a cluster of women about Sapphira, who was prone upon the pavement.

Mother walked with Rhoda, who followed us down to the burial. The child watched it all, more with astonishment, I thought, than grief. When we returned we found that Sapphira was also dead. We buried her beside her husband, and now Rhoda sobbed heartbrokenly against my mother's breast.

The common fund had never received so many gifts as in the weeks that followed.

Summer was drawing toward its end but nothing was said of my departure for Cyprus, though I often thought with longing

of the quietness of my home in Salamis. Yet when the witnessing began I had observed how intently Agabus listened, and
for his sake I delayed bringing up the subject. As for Mother,
she was much too busy to think of me these days. Rhoda was
incessantly beside her. Child though she was, Rhoda worked as
hard over the tables and the dishwashing as any of the women.
She was clean at last, with smooth, shining dark hair. Mother
had cut down two of my outgrown scarlet coats for her. She
was looking quite presentable these days.

Rhoda was on the roof one day as I came from the orchard.
I was sweating and covered with earth, and my fingers were
stained the color of ripe grapes. Rhoda slipped one of her
clean little hands into my stained one. "You are my brother,
now, Mark," she said. The smile she turned upon me held
pure affection. "Mother said so."

She had called my mother Mother! I jerked away from her
touch. The poor will be with you always, I thought, this
daughter of Ananias and Sapphira among them. Why did I
have to learn from Rhoda that Mother had adopted this waif?
Why hadn't Mother consulted me before making such an important decision?

I sat through dinner and the witnessing, wrapped in sullen
anger. When the people scattered I went into the court and
drew Mother away from the clutter of dishwashing. My heart
ached as I took her thin, dry, hard hand.

"How much longer will this continue?" I demanded.

"Until he comes—the Lord Jesus." She raised her face, and
the light of a nearby torch touched it, and suddenly I was
reminded of the suffering face of the man who had prayed in
our orchard. Her heart must often cry, "Let this cup pass from
me," the cup of endless labor and responsibility. The bitter
cup of being always, always, always surrounded by the hungry
and the needy. She had been pampered as I had been, a child
of wealth, the beloved wife of a wealthy husband.

Pity swept away my jealousy and self-pity, though it did not lessen my anger. I drew her close. My tears fell into her dark, smooth hair. "They are picking you clean to the bone. They consume your strength. They consume my inheritance, and they consume my mother."

She rested against me for a little while. Then Rhoda came running. "What's the matter with you two?" Her piercing voice must have carried to every woman at the fire, and to every lingering guest on the roof. "Mark! You're crying! What's the matter, Mark?"

I yelled, "Get out! Can't I have my mother to myself for two minutes?"

Mother exclaimed, "Children!" She gave a shaky laugh, and reached to embrace that obnoxious child. "I have two children now," she said softly. "I must expect them to quarrel. Ah, Rhoda, you must forgive your brother. He was rude."

Rhoda's chin quivered. "I forgive you," she murmured obediently, and fled.

Mother said, "Mark, you are suffering because you do not share our joy in the Lord Jesus. I pray daily that you will open your heart, accept baptism and the guidance of the Holy Spirit."

I slumped upon the nearest table. "You don't consult me about anything. You adopted that—that lump of a girl. You give away my inheritance to strangers. You fill my father's house with beggars and hypocrites. And you push upon me a stupid, disgusting girl and pretend she is my sister and give her your love while I work alone in the orchard, and for what? To produce more food to feed more beggars."

My voice cracked. I rushed to the stairway. I paused at the top to shout, "I'm going to Cyprus. This time I won't return." I raised my voice. "Agabus. We're going to Cyprus."

Mother rushed up the stairs. "Oh Mark. No, Mark!"

"Why not? You don't need me."

She caught my sleeve. "Do this for me, son. Go where Peter goes. Listen when he preaches. What I know, what I feel—I cannot explain as Peter does. Let Peter become your teacher."

"Agabus is my teacher." I was about to shout again for Agabus when I saw him coming from the pavilion.

Agabus said, "You are disturbing the guests in this house, Marcus."

I lowered my voice. "The guests are disturbing me." Then in a passionate outburst, "I wish Jesus had gone away, that night in the orchard. I wish he had gone to Galilee and left us alone. Everything would be fine, if only he had gone away."

"Talk to Peter," Mother said softly. "Peter understands."

"Talk to Peter, Marcus," Agabus echoed.

# CHAPTER 6

The next morning I did not go to the vineyard. The grapes were being harvested, and I was needed, but my mind was in a turmoil, and I followed Agabus about the house, persisting in the effort to make him leave off his labors and argue with me. He turned upon me presently in exasperation.

"I cannot answer your questions. 'Be as a little child,' the Lord Jesus said. Yet you, a child of fourteen, set up your opinions against those of the lady Miriam, of Barnabas, of me, your teacher. Why should faith come so hard at your age?"

I answered reasonably, "You rebuke me when I do not think. Now I am thinking, and you rebuke me for that. Do you suppose I enjoy being the only one who hasn't been baptized?"

"Baptized!" Annoyance filled the large eyes below the curling fringe. "They refuse me baptism. They insist I must first bind myself by all the strangling tendrils of the Mosaic code. I must first be circumcised! The Lord Jesus left profound truth in their care, and they bury it under the wrappings of a code designed for a nation of nomads wandering the desert. Yet if any man can make sense out of their confusion Peter can. He is the best of them. Follow Peter to your Temple. He preaches there, but I cannot go because I am Greek."

"You want to go to the Temple?"

"You ask that? What a failure I have been as your teacher. Do you think your God and my God are not one God? Marcus, I long to worship where our Lord worshipped."

I was accustomed to Agabus' rebukes, but today they had a special sting. If I could be baptized, I thought, perhaps Mother would sometimes look at me in the pleased, approving, joyful way she so often looked upon Rhoda.

Agabus said more kindly, "Peter is a faithful witness, though an ass in some respects. Go and learn from Peter before the follies of these apostles scatter them, and the knowledge of the Lord Jesus becomes ointment spilled in the earth and lost."

I said, "You speak as if it were *your* inheritance that is vanishing."

"Truth is every man's precious heritage."

"My inheritance from my father is consumed by these grasshoppers. My mother's strength is devoured with every loaf and every joint of roasted kid."

"Ah yes, that, too." He turned away. "Do you think because I am a slave I care nothing for my family, my own people?"

I embraced him. No matter how often he intimidated me with his "Lo, the poor slave" theme, it always moved me. "We belong to you far more than you to us. We are all at your mercy."

He limped about the roof angrily. "They are pigheaded men without imagination. 'Preach the good news to every nation, baptizing them,' the Lord Jesus said. I cannot think why Jesus chose such simple men as his witnesses."

Parroting the witnesses I said, "When he returns to restore the kingdom to Israel their work will be finished."

"I am not so sure about that kingdom. They twist the teachings to mean whatever will relieve them of responsibility. The

kingdom will not be an empire ruled by Jews from Jerusalem.
They are wrong about that. Yet here they sit, selling their
substance. How gladly I would go and preach to all men—to
Greeks, Syrians, Romans, and Egyptians."

He stared moodily out at the rising mount with its check-
ered pattern of fields and vineyards and orchards. He said,
"Follow Peter. He is wiser than some and a better man than
most. Learn while you can, before their follies destroy them
and the dream collapses and all the Lord Jesus brought to the
earth of wisdom and understanding is dissipated with your
mother's health and strength and the heritage left to you by
your father."

Peter had a habit of going daily to the Temple in mid-
afternoon, at the hour of prayer. There he caught the crowds
as they departed. In the cloisters he preached, accusing them
and their rulers of murdering Messiah. For some reason Annas
ignored him.

I began haunting the Temple at the hour of prayer, though
I found little in Peter's preaching that I had not heard many
times. His message was dynamic. "This Jesus whom you killed
is the hope of Israel. Repent. Be baptized. Be filled with the
Breath of God. Jesus is risen, for death could not hold the
Holy One, the Messiah for whom the Jews have waited so
long."

Peter was a passionate speaker. In that one thing he reminded me of Paul of Tarsus, who no longer frequented our
house. No giant, Peter was only average in height. But I have
never seen a man, not even a gladiator, with better chest and
shoulder development. Even among fisherfolk Peter's great
arms and shoulders would be noticed. His neck was short, and
one got the impression that the sunbaked face peered out from
between the great shoulders, an impression heightened by the

way he gestured with his shoulders and upper arms as well as with his hands.

Peter's command of ideas and language was limited. From first to last he was a witness, not a theorist or an innovator. I never saw him with a book in his hands. When, in years to come, Peter was pitted against Paul in the council of believers, only his stubbornness and his repeated, "This I saw. This I heard—" could check the fiercely intellectual Pharisee.

Often I saw young Pharisees from the School of Hillel in Peter's audience. Paul had said that Gamaliel's method was to give each new cult a hearing, and to thresh out in open discussion, with open minds, all theories which arose amongst the Jews. Gamaliel was sending his students to hear Peter just as he had sent them to give Jesus a hearing.

On an afternoon in late summer, I was overtaken on the Jericho road by Peter. He spoke of what the Temple means to a man like himself, a provincial who saw the holy place rarely. "Until our company began coming here for the Passover feast I did not see the Temple often, or think of it much. Now that I have lived for a time on Olivet and have gone daily to the Temple I know what the captives felt in Babylon six hundred years ago, when they sang their homesick song:

> 'How lovely is thy dwelling place,
>     Lord God of Hosts.
> If I forget thee, O Jerusalem,
>     let my right hand wither.' "

Peter's quotations, and his accurate references to the writings testified to his excellent memory. I thought of him as untaught, but he was not. He must have been very attentive to the rabbi when he attended synagogue school as a boy. He had listened to the teachings of the Lord Jesus during his entire

ministry, and remembered much of them. He was no scholar,
but he was not ignorant.

Peter asked, "My son, what did you hear when you listened
to our Lord during those last days?"

"I heard no discourses, except for a few fragments on that
day when Mother anointed him with nard."

The hazel eyes within the abundant auburn hair softened.
"She knew he was to die. She did what was fitting."

"I heard Jesus pray in Gethsemane before his arrest. He
tried to waken you. 'Could you not watch with me?' he
said."

"No man ever made a sorrier spectacle in time of crisis than
I did, that night. Yet Jesus called me Peter. I believe he called
me Rock for what I will become, through grace, if I live long
enough. In the same way he called James and John, who were
timid and self-seeking, Boanerges, Sons of Thunder, to show
what they could become. Ah lad, as long as Jesus was with us
we did nothing but lean upon him."

I continued, "He said, that night, 'Sleep on, dear friends.
You will need your rest before the night is over.' "

Peter said, "In all the witnessing, no man has ever explained
what it means to a simple fisherman to walk the roads of
Galilee with Jesus of Nazareth. Did he choose us to show what
God can do with even the most ordinary men? I have often
wondered."

"In Simon's house that day he said you would do greater
works than he had done if you believed in him," I said. "Will
you, Peter? Will you cleanse lepers? Will you cast out evil
spirits? Will you cause the lame to walk and the blind to
see?"

What drove me on to such talk I do not know, except that I
was deeply troubled, and willing to spill trouble over onto
others. Wonder-workers came and went in Jerusalem. I did

not understand their power, nor believe half the explanations I had heard, or indeed half the miracles, for that matter.

"Lad, you jar a man." Peter turned upon me a look of pure amazement. "He said it. I forgot it long ago. He said much which passed me by, for I was confident that he would set up a kingdom, asking nothing in return from us except our joy to be with him."

"Then you will do mighty works?" I asked. He probably would not, for he did not seem the type who worked wonders. Jesus was wrong about that, as he had been wrong in believing that God willed him to die.

Peter's answer came slowly. "If I believe. If I have faith, so much as a mustard grain. Such faith comes hard." His face twisted with pain. "I have preached repentance. Now my time of penitence has come."

We passed through Damascus Gate into the city. Peter spoke as if to himself. "He was one and we are eleven. If we go our ways, each a beacon on a hill, how much we could accomplish. Instead, we linger here, drawing comfort from one another, waiting for our Lord to come back to us, to lift all responsibility off our shoulders."

We entered the triple gate, ascending into the Court of Gentiles. Peter mused, "I have seen those who need help. I have seen many Jesus would have helped, had he been with me. Yet the Breath of God is locked within my being. Oh, I have longed to stretch out my hand. But I feared to make the attempt, lest I fail, and be ashamed. My faith is small, less than a pinprick, less than a mustard grain."

He stumbled. I took his arm. His lips moved as I guided him into the shadows among the rows of pillars called Solomon's Cloister. He murmured, "Lord Jesus, give me faith, or the willingness to try, and become a fool in trying."

Between the cloister and the Court of Women was the

Soreg, a low curb on which words were engraved: "Let no Gentile enter within the Soreg. Whoever is caught shall have himself to blame for his consequent death." This was the point beyond which Agabus, for one, could never penetrate.

I gripped Peter's arm, lest he stumble as we stepped over the Soreg.

The Court of Women was enclosed. Supplies of wood and water filled two corner rooms. Booths in the other corners were provided for Jews defiled who awaited examination by priests. Beyond this court, ascending ever upward toward the mountain's top was the innermost court with its altar and lovely sanctuary. Only adult male Jews who were ritually clean could ever venture there.

Fifteen steps rose to the handsome Nicanor Gate which Jews proudly called the Beautiful Gate. On those steps absolution was given. There also women came to kneel after childbirth, that priests might pronounce them clean, fit once more to be joined with their husbands.

Halfway up these steps lay a beggar named Korah. His relatives brought him daily to lie there, his bowl beside him, his stick legs exposed. He could not have begged there had he been unclean or afflicted with the running sores of so many beggars. He could not have begged there without a franchise from Annas. Korah had been begging in this choice spot before I was born. Few were the Jews who had not given him alms.

Korah raised his bowl. "Alms, good sirs, in God's holy name."

Charity is as essential to sanctity as cleanness. Here, where Jews passed in to pray, Korah gave an opportunity to sanctity. My hand went to my scrip. Then I remembered that I was giving alms in my own house to my ruin.

Peter also paused. Would he give from the common fund to

this man? He said, "You were here when Jesus of Nazareth came to the Temple, my brother. How is it he did not heal you?"

Pain filmed the dark eyes. "I am dependent upon—those who accused him. I dared not ask him for healing."

Peter's voice deepened. "Silver and gold I cannot give." I felt power, like heat, emanate from him. "Jesus is risen. Rise in his name. Rise and walk."

People were clustering about us. At this hour traffic through the gate was a tide. Korah looked at the people, and shrank into his pallet. "Go your way, sir. Leave me."

Peter gripped the thin hand. His voice rang through the court. "In the name of Jesus of Nazareth rise, Korah. Rise and walk."

Above us priests filled Nicanor Gate. Shame filled me to be part of this humiliating spectacle, though I had certainly brought it upon myself.

Peter tugged at the thin arm. "Rise, Korah. Rise. Walk."

Something dawned in the thin, bearded face. Longing, hope, belief. Peter tugged, not enough to lift the man though he could easily have done so. A sigh of amazement went over the massed watchers when Korah rose. Holding fast to Peter's big hand, Korah took a step, stiff, tottering, for he had never stood upon his feet or learned balance as a child. He took another step, and another, descending toward the pavement, moving with growing confidence down the handsome granite stairway. Step, lurch, step, lurch, and all the while Peter followed, his hand gripping Korah's bony hand.

When Korah reached the pavement he shook off Peter's grip. He moved stiffly out toward Solomon's Portico, making his way through parted worshipers. By the time he reached the Soreg tears were streaming down his face. Someone gave him a hand over that obstacle. Then he began to leap. With every leap he shouted, "Praise! Praise!" We followed, staying near him. When he reached the end of the portico he turned, running, leaping, shouting, while tears streamed down his furrowed, narrow, bony face.

When he reached us this time he knelt and kissed the hem of Peter's coat. His voice rang through all the Temple. "Praise! Praise!"

Peter's face glowed. He lifted his arms amongst the pillars. His voice rang out. "Listen to me, men of Israel. Why do you marvel? Why do you stare? Do you think it was our own power or piety which made this man walk? The God of our fathers glorified Jesus of Nazareth, whom *you,* when Pilate would have released him, delivered up and denied, shouting, 'Crucify him!' *You* denied the holy and righteous one. *You* demanded the thief Barabbas, when Pilate would have given you Jesus. *You* killed the Son of God, the Author of Life, whose name has healed this man."

Peter's voice grew soft, persuasive. "Faith in the Lord Jesus has restored this man, to whom you have given alms these many years. To his healing each of you is witness."

He paused. Oh, it was a powerful dose he was giving these righteous Jews, as their stricken faces testified. And for now I was all on Peter's side, forgetting my confusions and doubts.

"Now, brethren, I know you acted in ignorance, as did the scribes and priests, your rulers. But what the prophets foretold, that the Lord Messiah should suffer, God has fulfilled. Repent, therefore, and turn again, that your sins may be blotted out, that times of refreshing may come from the presence of God, that he may send the Lord Jesus to establish the kingdom of God among us, and to accomplish all that God spoke to our fathers through the prophets. You are sons of the prophets, sons of the covenant, and God sent the Lord Jesus to bless you in turning you from wickedness."

How rich with kindness was his voice on the last line, "To bless you in turning you from wickedness." I shared the longing in all those crowding faces, longing for righteousness, for a share in the confident joy of believers, that the kingdom of heaven would come, and that they should have a part in its coming.

Peter was luminous in his joy, in joy over what he had done, joy for himself and joy for Korah. I loved Peter in that hour, loved him because of the charismatic mark that was upon him, the evidence that he was well pleasing to God. This was one mighty work about which I never had a moment's doubt. Korah was healed, and by God's power, working through Peter. I loved Peter because I witnessed not only the healing, but the struggle. I knew with what effort he had risen above his natural fears to this peak of faith and power. I loved Peter then, and I loved him from that day forward.

Korah held Peter's feet all the while, his tears wetting the pavement. When Peter ceased speaking the cry broke from Korah anew, "Praise! Praise!" All about us people were entreating Peter to baptize them in the name of Jesus, whose power had healed the crippled beggar.

Into the midst of this clamor two men entered, crowding down from the upper court. One was the officer who had bound Jesus in our orchard. Alexander was with him, youngest son of Annas, and the only one never named to be high priest.

Alexander shouted, "Silence! Jesus of Nazareth died a criminal's death. You know the saying, 'Cursed be he who is hanged on a tree!' " He reached the foot of the steps. He shouted, "Go about your affairs, all of you. Clear this court. Officer, arrest these two rabble-rousers."

The people dispersed, some up into the inner court, others out through the cloister. Among them I had seen a few who daily sat at our table, and knew the event would soon be related in Mother's hearing. Korah remained, rising stiffly to stand before Alexander, proof of a power no bluster could banish.

"Sir, you know me." He spoke humbly, as he must have spoken to men of the Annas faction all the years of his life. "Tell me, wherein did this man sin, seeing he made me walk who have been lame from birth?"

Alexander swung on him. "Get out! Or stay and share the scourging with your friends if you prefer. Tomorrow you will appear with them before the Sanhedrin. See that you get there."

Korah's thin face glowed. "I will walk into the presence of the Sanhedrin." He took a few steps toward the cloister, then paused and turned back to look earnestly upon Peter. "Do not fear men, even the rulers, for God is with you."

Alexander said contemptuously, "Go home, Korah. See how your wife and brothers will welcome you, now that you have lost your livelihood."

Peter said, "Sir, this lad is Mark, son of Miriam of Olivet. He has not spoken so much as a word throughout this affair. Send him to his mother. Do with me as you will, but send the lad home."

"Be silent!" Alexander stalked up to Nicanor Gate and disappeared.

The officer tugged on the thongs and we followed around to a narrow door in the inner wall of the court, behind the stairway. This door opened into the caves which honeycomb our holy mountain. Here were the dungeons where prisoners of our Jewish rulers were confined. I had heard of these dungeons, but had never imagined I would one day be confined there.

# CHAPTER 7

Surely no dungeon ever held two of such contrasting moods as ours that night. Peter has said it was the happiest of his life, while I was never more wretched. Scourging was the least we could expect. If Annas trumped up a blasphemy charge we could be stoned—the only death sentence legal for Jews to execute upon one another. Annas could even turn us over to the Romans if he could stretch the healing of Korah and Peter's remarks about the kingdom of God into a charge of sedition and insurrection. Knowing how likely Peter was to stand before the Sanhedrin tomorrow and charge our rulers to their faces with murdering the Lord Jesus, whose name had healed Korah, I could not exclude that possibility, with beheading or crucifixion to follow.

I was terribly afraid. But Peter was full of joy in his triumph over his own fears, and in the grace which had touched him and through him had healed Korah.

The cell door was a heavy wooden grill, reinforced with iron strips. When we had been bolted in Peter said, "Fear not, Mark. There are many witnesses to swear that you were only a bystander in this affair today."

Outside the grating guards were casting dice. By the ghostly

flicker of their torch Peter's happiness was visible, and it was
audible in the fervor of his voice. "Neither of us is worthy to
share Jesus' suffering. My ministry is only beginning, and
yours is not yet begun. There is work we must do, my son.
Scourging is the worst that will befall us. 'With his stripes we
are healed,' said the prophet Isaiah. I will count it joy to share
the sufferings of our Lord, for within me today a new and
deeper faith was born."

"I do not aspire to wear the stripes of the Lord Jesus, any
more than I have aspired to sell my heritage to feed the poor
who infest our pavilion."

Peter hunkered down beside me. "The common table has
become a stumbling block to others than yourself, Mark. If I
could take your hand and say, 'Believe,' I would, and gladly.
For the grace of faith is a greater miracle than the healing of
Korah. To believe that Jesus is Lord and Messiah, that he rose
from the tomb, that he lives—this faith makes all other questions shrink to minor importance. But faith comes to every
man in his season, and it does not come with the laying on of
hands."

My world was falling apart. The least I could expect tomorrow was public scourging by order of our own elders—I, a
Levite, obedient to the law in every picayune detail from
childhood. And Peter sat here on his heels talking as if we
were safe in my mother's house. I was suddenly overwhelmed
with longing to find comfort and safety in my mother's arms.

I wept for a time. Presently I remembered Nicodemus.
Among the seventy elders surely others besides Nicodemus and
Joseph of Arimathea were sympathetic toward the followers of
the Nazarene. Yet Nicodemus was a prudent man. He came to
visit us, as he had come to visit Jesus, only at night, lest he be
observed by toadies of Annas. With Nicodemus prudence was

a virtue ranking with piety, charity, and cleanliness. Would Nicodemus find it prudent to take a stand on my behalf?

Peter inquired, "Why were you in Gethsemane that night?"

I roused and began to speak of that night, of the brilliance of the Paschal moon, the restless night-noises of our guests on the roof. As I spoke the prison darkness and the dank prison smell fell away. I was in the orchard, drawn by dreams of a kingdom restored miraculously to Israel. I stumbled over a sleeping body and went on into the shadows, drawn by muted, human sounds higher up the hill.

" 'Could you not watch with me?' " I repeated. The lonely sorrow of the man who faced arrest, prison, buffeting, mocking, scourging, denial by those dearest to him, rejection by the people who had hailed him King of the Jews—and afterward the hideous agony of crucifixion and slow death—all were upon me, a sorrow and loneliness so great I forgot personal anxieties.

"He said, so lovingly, 'The spirit is willing but the flesh is weak.' "

The guardroom had grown still. Whether the soldiers slept or listened I did not know. "He prayed for you," I said, "saying, 'Deliver them from the evil that is in the world when I am no longer with them.' "

Peter rubbed his face with his big hands. "You alone witnessed that scene. Nobody but you can tell the story. Mark, why have you never stood up to witness?"

Unwilling to admit even to Peter that I would never willingly witness before the company which ate at our tables, I evaded the question. "I wanted to watch with him. But I was a stranger. I dared not intrude on his sorrow."

"No man was ever a stranger to the Lord Jesus, my son."

The words burst from me in a torrent. "He did not need to suffer. He could have gone away. He knew the Temple Guard was coming for him." Presently I continued more quietly, "When they came he stood like a lamb. They bound him. You wakened then. You saw the rest. I did not see the trials, or the crucifixion, or the death and burial."

"Nor did you see the risen Lord."

Peter prowled about the cave, running his hands over the rough stone walls. "My first prison. It will not be my last." He turned again to me. "Many believe who have heard our witness, though they did not see the risen Lord Jesus. What holds you back? Why have you never been baptized?"

The words burst from me. "If he had loved the Jews he would not have laid upon our rulers the guilt for his death."

"So that's the problem."

"He prayed, 'Thy will be done,' meaning that God also hates the Jews."

"For a Levite, taught in the synagogues of Jerusalem and Salamis, you are strangely ignorant of the meaning of innocence and guilt."

"Then explain it to me. Explain how it could be God's will that the Chosen People should reject and crucify Messiah."

"If you want theory, go to Gamaliel. Jesus rose from the tomb. That I know, and it is enough."

From some other cave in this labyrinth of misery came a growl. "Shut up. Let a man get a little sleep."

Peter said kindly, "We will be silent, my brother."

The torch beyond the gratings flickered, giving off a stink of bitumen. Snores came from one of the guards near the door. Peter lay down on the rough stone. I crouched near him, my head upon my knees. The thongs chafed my wrists, and my hands were numb with the tightness of the bonds. The cold of the sunless crypt seemed to penetrate my bones. Peter stirred often, but presently his breathing told me he slept.

I wept for my mother then. Afterward I slept to dream of

frightful punishments. The torch flickered out and darkness was complete. I slept again, to be wakened by the screech of our prison door. Morning had come, and we were to go before the Sanhedrin.

We wound through narrow corridors of stone. From one of the gratings came a voice. "Tell them I am still here—Simeon of Bethel." Another voice said hoarsely, "Remind that old goat Annas that Jacob of Jericho waits to be heard."

"What a warren of misery honeycombs our holy hill," Peter said. Then, "You are a Roman citizen, Mark. They cannot scourge you."

"I am not a citizen."

"But Barnabas is?"

"He is my mother's brother. My father was not a citizen."

"Fear not, my son. You are only a lad. They will not hurt you."

From beyond a grating came a low voice, infinitely sad. "Remind Annas that I am here—Joses of Anathoth."

We emerged into blinding sunlight. The Temple was behind and above us. Overhead arched the bridge which connected the Temple with the opposite hill, called the Upper City. There the house of Caiaphas stood, with its judgment hall. We climbed the steep stairway carved into the valley wall to reach a narrow door which entered the judgment hall from the rear.

Most of the seventy elders were already present, standing in little groups among the handsome pillars of the portico or within the triple semicircle of benches set for them. They were colorful in the robes of their several callings, alike only in their dignity. Among them were the feeble and the strong, the calm and the excitable, young men like Nicodemus, whose age was not yet two score years, and old men like Annas and Gamaliel of the house of Hillel. Among them were the judicious and the zealous, the scholarly and the practical. Among them were some who would have saved Jesus had they been able, and those upon whom rested the guilt for his crucifixion.

As we approached the prisoners' box I caught a glimpse of Mother's pale face in the court of spectators. The sight was well-nigh my undoing. I was rumpled, unfed, unwashed, and my hands were numb and purple from the tight binding of my wrists. The court was thronged. Our case was obviously attracting all Jerusalem.

The guard whisked the thongs off our wrists. I rubbed the aching flesh, my hands behind my back. The pain was terrible, yet I controlled my face as I flexed my throbbing fingers. Peter had no such trouble. He had explained to me the trick he used of gripping his fists to swell the wrists while the thongs were tied on.

"It is well to be prepared for these indignities," he had said.

Most of the elders were in place when Annas entered, followed by his five sons in priestly robes, and Caiaphas in the brilliant apparel of the chief priest.

Annas was a small man and spare, with forked, white beard, high cheekbones, and a jut of jaw and set of the thin, ascetic lips which testified that here was a man of mighty will. Nicodemus had said of him that the principles he served were founded upon God's purpose for Israel, as revealed in the sacred writings. Israel's covenant with God, and God's covenant with Israel had been his guide. But somewhere along the way self-will had for Annas become confused with God's will. And the need to prove both to himself and to all men that the original purpose still guided him had driven him to terrible deeds. As surely as Judas had betrayed Jesus for lofty reasons —the hope of forcing Jesus to call down legions of angels and immediately set up the kingdom of heaven on the earth—so Annas had contrived Jesus' crucifixion to protect the Temple, its officers and rulers and priests, from accusations which undermined their effectiveness. Yet in these months since that event the light of holy purpose had gone out of Annas, replaced by the ruthless gleam of a man who must spend the rest of his life proving that he had done well, when his associates and even his own heart dared tell him he had sinned grievously.

Annas sent a cryptic glance toward the witness box, which was empty. The key figure in our drama had not yet appeared.

Those elders had not come primarily to judge Peter and me. The jostling crowd in the open court was not here on our account. Korah was known to every pious Jew in Jerusalem, certified a cripple by Annas himself. These people had come to see Korah walk. Would a man so long dependent upon Annas' goodwill put in his appearance? Would he walk into this judgment hall? Or would he yield under the pressure which had surely been applied during the night, and come borne on a litter by his brothers?

I looked out over the benches where sat most of our seventy rulers. We Jews had these men to thank that we were policed by our Temple Guard, not by legionaries. My grandfather had sat with the Sanhedrin. My father would have done so, had he lived longer. I had expected some day to be one of this august body. These were familiar faces, the faces of men I had been taught to revere. The twenty-four heads of the twenty-four courses of the priests were here, together with lawyers and rabbis, bankers and merchants and land-owners. I believed in the honesty of these men. I could not do otherwise.

Nicodemus was among them, a tall, pale, spare man, a little stooped and hollow-chested for all his youth. Joseph of Arimathea, twice as old and half as rich as Nicodemus, was beside him. Gamaliel sat behind Annas and to his right. The serenity of wisdom and an orderly mind peered through those keen old eyes.

A shout went up in the court. Korah had entered, walking. He moved less stiffly than yesterday. Had he been awake far into the night, walking, walking—practicing the wondrous gift? His eyes were fixed on Peter as he advanced. I seemed to hear the echo of his shouted, "Praise!" with every step.

Erect, calm, Annas watched Korah's advance. Was he not surely hoping the beggar would fall flat upon his face ere ever he reached the witness circle? Whatever his thoughts, Annas contained them.

"Korah, son of Ezekiel, stand forth." The voice of Annas was not loud. It was firm and strong, reminding all present that in this court all things were done decently and in order. At the sound of it the watchers grew still.

Korah did not stop at the witness box, but proceeded to stand directly below the throne of judgment. In a voice now personal and paternal Annas said, "Korah, speak the truth! Have you deceived us these years, begging alms as a cripple when you were in fact no cripple at all?"

So this was the line he would take.

Korah said simply, "My lord, you appointed the physician who examined me year by year, whenever my franchise to beg was renewed."

Annas gathered the white, forked beard into one thin, transparent hand. Nothing in his expression acknowledged that the power he had once had over this man was gone. He said, "Simon Peter, son of Jonah, stand forth."

Peter moved down to the foot of the throne.

"You are a Galilean, a fisherman of Capernaum?"

"That is true, sir."

"Are you a physician?"

"I am a fisherman."

Annas glanced at me. I stiffened under the eyes of this strong-willed old man. "John Mark, son of Levi, stand forth."

There was strength in Peter's nearness. In my rumpled coat, unwashed, I stood tall beside him, tall as ever I had stood before the holy altar in the Court of Israelites.

Annas eyed me, taking in my youth. He sent his son Alexander a glance of blistering contempt. "How old are you, John Mark?"

"Old enough to enter the Court of Israelites at the hour of prayer, sir." I knew fiercely that I would never ask mercy of this old man on the grounds of my youth. I knew fiercely that if Jesus had called him hypocrite, that was what he was, whether he knew the truth himself or not.

The old eyes dismissed me as of no consequence. Annas leveled a veined finger at Peter. "By what means did you heal this cripple?"

Peter's stature seemed to swell. "Rulers of the people and elders—keepers of Israel, upholders of the righteousness of the Jews—if you question us about help given to a lame man, and ask by what means he was cured, here is the answer: in the name of the Lord Jesus of Nazareth, *whom you crucified,* and whom God brought back from the dead, by his name this man stands before you fit and well. This Jesus is the stone rejected by the builders which has become the keystone—and *you* are the builders. No other name under heaven can bring salvation save that holy name, the name of Jesus."

The rulers stirred, glanced at one another and at Annas. The boldness of this weathered fisherman and the sheer effectiveness of his argument astonished them.

Annas' keen eyes appraised Korah, then rejected him. Korah's bearing was proud. I remembered that pride had marked him even as a beggar. Annas is only a man, I thought, for all his power. He made a fearful error last Passover. Now he must spend his remaining years proving he was right.

Annas rose. The power of his will was in the glance which swept the audience. "Men and women of Israel, this is a case for your rulers to settle in closed session. Go hence. Officer, clear the audience court."

A hubbub of protest rose, as soldiers descended upon the court, driving the people before them. Annas' strong old face showed anger only in the narrowing of the eyes, the tightening of the thin mouth within the white, forked beard. While he still watched the people's departure a soldier came and bound my wrists, and Peter's, and hustled us back down the long flight, across the valley, and so to the labyrinth of the Jewish prison.

Voices from the caves marked our passing. "You'll never see daylight again." "Did you remember me to Annas?"

Peter began to speak, and continued speaking all the way down the dark corridor, as we followed the flickering torch. Eyes appeared at the gratings wild as wolves' eyes in the midst of matted hair.

"Fear not those who kill the body. The soul is immortal. Jesus of Nazareth, whom they crucified, rose from the tomb. He lives, and he is our hope and our salvation. He was innocent of any evil, yet they hanged him. On the third day he walked forth from the tomb, alive, strong, radiant. I myself spoke with him beside the Sea of Galilee after he rose. I saw him again on Mount Olivet before he vanished into thick clouds to be seen by us no more. Yet he will return to establish Israel's kingdom, the kingdom of heaven upon earth. Repent in Jesus' name, my brothers. Believe on Jesus, for he is Messiah. He lives, and his kingdom is forever. Fear not your rulers. Their guilt is heavy upon them. Forgiveness of sin is for you and for all men who repent in Jesus' holy and blessed name."

As we went on it seemed to me the guard with the torch moved more and more slowly. When we reached our cell he removed our bindings and sent his fellow guard to bring us meat and wine. Then he asked, low-voiced, "Where did you see him, afterward? How did he look? What did he say to you—afterward?"

# CHAPTER 8

When our guard led us out into daylight again I saw by the sun that a day's full cycle had passed since I set out yesterday to go to the Temple at the prayer hour. We climbed from the valley to the judgment court, finding comfort in the sun's warmth after the dank chill of the caverns.

Fewer than twenty rulers remained, perhaps because this was the hour of prayer. As we passed down toward the prisoners' box I searched the faces of the few remaining rulers. Nicodemus was gone, but I caught the eye of Joseph of Arimathea. He nodded pleasantly. My spirits rose. Joseph was satisfied with the verdict. We would not be scourged.

Annas stood beside the throne of judgment. Only one of his sons remained. Annas was speaking calmly, in friendly fashion, with Gamaliel. When we stood directly under the dais he turned from Gamaliel saying, "Peace go with you, my brother." He gathered his skirts in one hand and tucked the other into the arm of his son. He seemed about to step down from the dais, but paused to say, "Simon of Capernaum and John Mark of Olivet, the mercy of your rulers has been extended. Go hence with this injunction: Speak no more in the name of the crucified malefactor from Nazareth."

He stepped down. He had taken perhaps four steps toward the exit when Peter made his reply. "Whether it is right to listen to men rather than God, you must judge. As for me, I cannot cease to speak of what I have seen and heard."

I tugged at Peter. What ailed him that he could not let well enough alone?

Annas turned impatiently. "Disobey at your peril. You have been warned, Galilean." He moved off at a purposeful, dignified pace.

Our guard was busily unbinding Peter, then me. "Come out through the side entrance. Make haste." He was as eager to be rid of us as I of him.

I tugged Peter out onto the portico, impatient to reach Olivet and my mother. Again Peter halted, this time as we stood at the top of the broad, marble steps. Peter looked back toward the judgment hall. "We stood before them with courage, Mark. The Lord Jesus had no cause to be ashamed of the first to witness in his name before this Sanhedrin."

Impatient as I was, I shared his pride. "You spoke well, Peter—to the rulers, and also to the prisoners and our guards. I was proud to be your companion. But when you stand again before the Sanhedrin I hope you will not call them murderers."

"I will speak as the spirit moves me. Come, lad."

Never before had I appeared in the city streets rumpled and unwashed. Yet people turned to stare after us, not because we were dirty, but because Peter was recognized. "He healed the lame man." "The rulers arrested him, then let him go free." "He is Peter. He called Annas murderer, and was not punished."

The comments followed us through Damascus Gate and on along the Jericho road. When we reached the turn-off to my home I watched Peter go on down the Bethany road, a man untroubled by doubts, filled with joy that he had at last proved himself worthy of the trust placed in him by the Lord Jesus.

The camel gate stood wide open. I entered a court bustling with preparations for the sunset meal. I marvel still that all my memories of that first ecclesia are so permeated with the odors of food, the kitcheny bustle of women.

Rhoda saw me first. She rushed at me, screaming, "Oh Mark, were you scared?" Before I could disentangle myself, "Oh Mark, we prayed for you. All last night we prayed, and again today, till Nicodemus came and said you would not be hurt." In a rush she inquired, "What was it like when Korah began to walk? Did it make you go all shivery? Did you help? Can you heal people, Mark?"

Mother embraced me tenderly, and I fought off a childish impulse to burst into tears.

Nicodemus sat on the parapet, looking gravely down upon the tumult. Korah was near him, walking, walking, as if he could never get enough. I broke through the women and went to the roof.

"Nicodemus, thank you for coming to relieve Mother's anxiety." I made no mention of the fact that he had not come to our house by day since we became notorious as a center of the sect of believers. I turned to Korah. "Welcome to my mother's house. Did your wife come with you?"

"My wife, my two brothers, my five children."

Alexander had said, "See whether your brothers will welcome you, now that you have lost your livelihood." They need not be troubled, I thought, as long as there is food in the house of Miriam, widow of Levi of Olivet.

I pushed the churlish thought away. My paternal heritage was gone. My life and my person had been in jeopardy because of the crucified Nazarene. Now I relinquished my Olivet property in his name. I would never stand in the ecclesia and lay gold in Peter's hand, but the relinquishment was real and definite, nonetheless.

Nicodemus said, "We have come, Korah and I, to be baptized by Peter. Will you consent to be baptized with us, Mark?" The warmth of his concern poured over me. I wanted to cry out in protest against this pressure from a new source.

I shook my head, unable to speak.

Nicodemus said, "You conducted yourself well before Annas, my son."

I said, "Now I suppose you will sell your goods and give all the money into the common fund?" If Nicodemus became a fool, there would be no foundation left in my world for simple prudence.

"No, my son. My season for that is past. Two years ago, before the Passover, I went to the house of Lazarus by night to question the Lord Jesus. 'Good rabbi, what must I do to win eternal life?' I asked him. 'Keep the commandments,' he replied. When I assured him that I had scrupulously observed the law from childhood he looked upon me with love, saying, 'Sell your possessions. Distribute the money to the poor. Then come and join my company.'

"I refused. I could have been with him daily for two years, hearing his teachings, conversing with him as a friend. I missed the greatest opportunity ever given any man. I refused."

The harsh voice of Paul of Tarsus echoed in my memory. "Why did this rabbi choose only fishermen and farmers?" Had there been others of Nicodemus' quality who had been asked, and had refused?

Nicodemus said, "I chose to keep my possessions. I made myself their steward. The income from my possessions will be used to help remedy the errors these good people have made in selling their property, lest we all become paupers together."

Korah had been listening intently. "I will not sit idle, a beggar among the followers," he said. "I will find work to do, and my brothers also, and we will bring our wages to the common fund. I am the steward of the strength restored to me in the name of the Lord Jesus."

We were surrounded by the gathering ecclesia but I had not yet washed or changed into clean clothing. I went to make myself fit to sit at table. Never had I felt so homeless, so orphaned, so lonely and apart.

Nicodemus had saved a place for me beside him at the table. "This is a fearful burden Miriam carries," he said. "Is every day like today in this house?"

"Every day since Pentecost."

"She's aged ten years this summer. Are the apostles blind?"

"Mother thinks it will all end soon. Whenever she has a moment free she sits on the parapet, looking off toward the Jericho road. She has pinned all her hopes on Jesus' return."

Nicodemus laid down the fig in his hand. "I cannot partake of food which has cost Miriam such infinite labor."

Across the table someone hiccuped. "They scorched the fish," he observed to his neighbor. "I'll speak to my wife about that."

"Your wife was gossiping with my wife while the fish were broiling. Speak to Miriam. She's in charge."

Nicodemus leaned across the table. "Speak to both your wives, that they lend a hand in this house so long as you are fed here."

"You give orders to your wife, friend. I'll give orders to mine."

The second man said, "You have no standing here, Lawyer. You have not even been baptized."

Andrew entered the podium, or I know not what discourtesy I might have committed.

"Brothers and fellow believers, we rejoice that the dangers

of this past day have, by God's mercy, been averted. My brother Peter is with the brethren at Simon's table, and John Mark, son of this household, is safe among us once more. Korah, a cripple from birth, walks in our midst, healed in the blessed name of the Lord Jesus—the first miracle of healing performed by one of us since our Lord was parted from us. Rise, brother Korah. Walk up to stand beside me and witness that the power of God is in our very midst."

When the people had rejoiced over Korah, Andrew called upon Nicodemus. "Tomorrow Korah and our brother Nicodemus will be baptized by Peter. It is fitting that Korah be baptized by none other. Meanwhile, Nicodemus sat with the Sanhedrin today. He can witness to the power which moved them to release Peter and Mark."

A grunt of discomfort came from one of the men across the table as Nicodemus walked gravely across to the podium, where witnesses stood to be heard both in the pavilion and in the court.

"My brothers and sisters in the Lord Jesus, many of you saw this morning how courageously Peter and the lad John Mark stood before the rulers, and with what boldness Peter answered Annas. Of what was said after the court was cleared and only the seventy rulers remained I will speak now.

"The Sanhedrin is split three ways concerning the followers of Jesus. Men of the stripe of Alexander bar Annas declare, 'This pestilential doctrine of the dead Nazarene is spreading in too many quarters. These men stand in the Temple and accuse their rulers of the blackest crimes. They must be destroyed.'

"The opposite faction, to which many rulers subscribe, Joseph of Arimathea and myself among them, declare, 'Jews are free to form sects and follow cults so long as they keep the law and bring their gifts to the Temple. The followers of the Nazarene are exemplary Jews. Moreover, the healing of Korah was a notable miracle. How can we accuse men who have wrought such a mighty work?'

"Caiaphas holds a third view, and the majority of the rulers take this middle course. To their view you should listen, my brothers, for it contains practical common sense. 'A movement which makes a virtue of improvidence will soon collapse. We can ignore it. As for the leaders, should they prove troublesome, we will arrest them next time on less controversial grounds. We can wait. Time works against them.'

"In the end, Gamaliel stated the case for all. 'Be cautious in deciding what to do about this new cult. Other men have arisen, each claiming to be the savior of the Jews. Other men have done mighty works and attracted a following. They died in due course, and their followers scattered, and their movements came to nothing. Keep clear of these men. If their teaching is of human origin it will collapse. If it is of God you cannot stop them, nor would you care to be found fighting against God.'

"Now my brothers, the malice of fanatics has been turned aside for a time. But the danger remains. You yourselves will destroy this movement unless you take thought for tomorrow. Surely never has there been a community as hare-brained as this, where men deliberately beggar themselves, become lilies of the field, dependent upon the labor and the liberality of a dedicated few. This community is doomed if it continues as it is. Give over the common tables. Go to work, you who live in idleness. Feed your own households, then come together to witness and to worship."

Cries rose from everywhere, recitals of land sold, animals sold, tools sold, money given into the common fund. Other cries rose against Nicodemus' assumption that the Lord Jesus would tarry. "We wait for the kingdom," was the ultimate answer.

Andrew quieted the dispute by starting a hymn. The ecclesia closed with a prayer, after a brief reminder of the baptismal service at Gihon Spring tomorrow morning, and an invitation to all not otherwise employed to attend.

Andrew and Nicodemus remained. Barnabas and Agabus and I joined them. Presently Mother came up to sit with us. Andrew said, "I am reminded how the Lord Jesus said to us, 'I send you as sheep among wolves. Be wise as serpents, therefore, and innocent as doves. Beware, for men will deliver you up to councils and flog you in synagogues; and you will be dragged before governors and kings to bear witness.' This is a hard saying, and we have set it aside. Yet it points toward the possibility that many years will pass before our Lord's return. We must consider then—"

Mother protested, "He will not tarry! He will surely come."

Andrew's voice was gentle. "So say we all in our deepest hopes. However, we must consider all the possibilities. We have been innocent as doves. We have not been wise as serpents. What can we do to amend our errors?"

Mother was weeping softly, a new thing for her, for she had never been one to lose her composure. "I will agree to nothing which means we no longer expect our Lord's return." She buried her face in work-roughened hands.

Nicodemus said, "My dear girl, nothing we say will hasten his return, or delay it. Let us acknowledge that we could have erred, and prepare for whatever is to come."

Agabus had been limping about restlessly. Now he halted, facing Andrew squarely. "I am convinced that Jesus will not return until we have gone into the cities of the world to preach and teach. Let us be honest. He may not come in our lifetime."

Mother cried, "No! I will not listen!" She clapped her hands over her ears.

Nicodemus said, "You are worn out, my dear. You have a right to be unreasonable. Nobody will blame you for it."

Andrew said, "The disciples will discuss it, and you, Nicodemus, must meet with us."

Agabus said, "My lady, may I go now to Cyprus?"

"Oh Agabus, what will I do without you? Why do you want to go?"

"I burn to carry the good news to the Greeks. Here in this house I am willing hands and an aching back. In Salamis I can bring words of life to thousands. The Greeks are ripe for new truth, a new voice. I long to bring living waters to thirsting thousands."

Andrew exclaimed, "Send a man uncircumcised to carry our witness into the world? It is unthinkable!"

Barnabas said, "We cannot hold him if the spirit moves him to go."

"We cannot license this Greek as our spokesman unless he first becomes a Jew."

Nicodemus said, "He does not ask license, Andrew. He will preach in a city where the good news has never been heard. If this ecclesia, which lays incredible burdens upon its women and rewards hypocrisy and improvidence, would redeem its errors, every man who is capable of witnessing will go to preach and teach and organize ecclesias in other cities. Our brother Agabus is a man of wisdom and vision. Do not despise wisdom, brother Andrew, even when it is found in a Greek."

Mother moaned, "But I cannot do without you, Agabus."

Barnabas said, "Have we become so ill-organized that we value the setting of tables above spreading the good news of the Lord Jesus?"

All the half-formed resulutions I had made in the prison

and since returning to this house suddenly fell into place. I knew what I must do. "Mother, I will go with Agabus to Cyprus. I am going to learn the trade of coppersmith. Will you give me your blessing?"

Andrew interposed, "First we must consult with Peter."

Mother rose, pressing her weight upon my shoulders, for she was swaying with exhaustion. "Andrew, my brother, this is a family matter. The decision is ours to make. Mark, my dear son, Agabus has excellent reasons for going to Cyprus. You also, who might have been—scourged today—by our rulers—" She threw herself against me, weeping against my breast. The words came from her brokenly, "But oh, if only you would be baptized before you go."

"Mother, mother, I will be baptized when I can, if ever I can. But I must get away from the winds that buffet me in this house. I am filled with resentment. I cannot find my way to truth while I am here. And I can no longer stand by and watch what I am powerless to prevent."

Nicodemus said, "Miriam, he has a right to make this choice."

Mother took my face between her hands. "Go then, Mark. God keep you."

Within three days Agabus and I were off for Caesarea and a ship to take us to Salamis. My last act before I left our house was to kiss Rhoda good-bye.

"I am your sister!" she cried. "You have to kiss your sister good-bye!"

I kissed her. The taste was on my mouth long after we got beyond sight of Jerusalem's towers. I did not see either Rhoda or my mother again for five years.

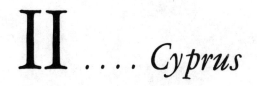

II .... *Cyprus*

# CHAPTER 9

On the journey to Cyprus Agabus no longer muttered Greek as he limped about the deck. He muttered Aramaic, quoting the witness of the apostles. Sailors followed him, as if hearing a tale of some new Jason, some new Heracles or Odysseus. For Greeks love nothing so much as a tale of a god-sired hero, an adventurer somewhat larger than life. When they saw that this new story did not follow the familiar pattern, they listened the more closely, crowding Agabus in growing numbers. Before we reached Salamis he had them singing hymns, and had taught a score of them to repeat the Lord's Prayer.

As we neared Salamis we saw to the north the bony finger of rocky ridge which points off twenty miles across the strait toward Antioch. On a golden autumn afternoon the ship nosed in toward the sandy crescent of our beach. Sailors leaped over the side and drew the boat in, snubbing a line about a battered post. I left Agabus to see to the luggage and set out briskly toward home.

Salamis was a city of great beauty, combining Greek architecture, Roman engineering, and the prosperity which Jewish commercial acuity brought. Salamis climbed steadily from sheds which lined the beach to fine homes and temples on the heights. The long, double-arched aqueduct brought in water from the mountains sufficient for a hundred thousand souls, for Salamis was the largest Cypriot city. Half of our population were slaves, from Macedonia and Thrace, from Pontus and Gaul, from Africa and the distant land of Britain—from wherever Roman arms had prevailed. Slaves were the tangible fruits of victory, slaves to be sold in the markets of every city from which soldiers for the armies of Rome had been recruited.

Of the fifty thousand free inhabitants, more than half were Jews. There was a synagogue for every temple to the gods of Greece and Rome. In the bazaars which lined the agora seven merchants in ten were Jews, the others Greek.

The agora was pure Greek, square in shape, for it dated back to a time when Greece ruled Cyprus. Roman-built forums were oblong, affording a better arena for combat, with gates for gladiators and ramps for beasts at one end. I am glad to say that these brutal affairs, so popular in Roman cities, never caught on in Cyprus. If they had, perhaps our square forum would have been elongated to accommodate them.

The temple which occupied the south end of our forum was originally a Greek temple to Zeus. The Romans converted it into a temple to Jupiter by the practical expedient of erasing the Greek names beneath the statuary and substituting Roman ones. In the paved square of the forum a score of Greek statues and busts on tall pedestals had become Roman by erasing the names of Greek athletes, senators, and philosophers, and replacing them with the names of Roman generals. Homer's bust became Cicero's when he was governor of Cyprus, by changing the name and painting the blind eyes with ocher.

The north end of the forum held official buildings, where causes were heard, citizens voted, and officials met in council.

The lower or eastern booths were occupied by merchants in the food trades—bakers, cheesemakers, grain dealers, fishmongers. Dealers in clothing, jewelry, leather, furnishings, metal wares, and imports from over the empire had the upper or western side. Amongst these was our family business, the House of Aaron's little shop.

I wandered through the forum, happy to be back in the familiar, Hellenist world, greeting acquaintances. I answered inquiries for Barnabas with a brief and unsatisfactory, "He has been detained in Jerusalem."

Our shop had a simple portal decorated with a pair of copper scales. Old Omar was dozing amongst his cooking pots and harness hardware. He opened one eye, then both, struggling to get his feet under him as he recognized me.

"Marcus, lad, welcome!"

Omar had grown obese, sitting in this shop for forty years. Much of our business was transacted at the house, and no wonder, with Omar dozing his days away here in the shop.

Omar embraced me with his one arm. Half the other had been destroyed under a spill of molten metal forty years ago. As a child I had been fascinated by the whitened scars of Omar's stump, and his colorful tale of how he acquired it. Omar was rumpled and smelled of sweat and garlic. We ought to pension the old man off, I thought, and get someone with more hustle into the shop. I looked about at the dusty jumble of copper wares while I answered questions about Mother, Jerusalem, and the voyage.

Omar's old eyes grew shrewd within their folds of fat. "You are meditating that it is high time Barnabas returned to oversee the House of Aaron. You are thinking that hirelings cannot be trusted when the owner stays too long away. And you are quite right, Marcus. Moreover, Romans ask to see the owner. They do not care to transact business with an employee. I hope Barnabas came with you?"

"He was delayed." The evasion was not good enough. The truth would have to be presented to each member of our household—to Kyros, who ran the shop and foundry, to Phoebe, who was Agabus' wife and our housekeeper, to Omar and his four grandsons and their sharp-tongued mother, to each artisan who hammered out copper wares, and the old Greek who delivered charcoal for the furnace. All over Cyprus there were shopkeepers who were accustomed to receiving visits from Barnabas. They would have to be told why he came no more.

Omar inquired, "Business?" His face grew merry. "Marriage?"

"Not marriage."

"Too bad. Barnabas should marry a wife and beget sons. The House of Aaron has only one heir, and you, lad, are in Jerusalem half the time, two years past the age to begin your apprenticeship, and nobody knows whether you will be a coppersmith on Cyprus or a farmer in Judea."

He had grown serious. No doubt every member of our household wondered what the future held for the House of Aaron. Omar concluded softly, "The House of Aaron is an old and honorable establishment. It deserves better of the owners."

Nothing less than the truth would satisfy our own people. They must all be called together. Agabus could open his first ecclesia in Salamis by telling everyone at the same time why Barnabas remained away from the business.

I said, "Come to the house at sunset, Omar. Bring your grandsons, even the youngest ones, and your daughter-in-law. Agabus will explain about Barnabas to all of you at the same time."

"Agabus? Not Marcus?"

"This is a tale fit for Agabus to tell."

"Good, good, good, good." Had he had two hands, Omar would have been rubbing them together. Instead, he rubbed the one hand across his vast belly, back and forth. Our people were never happier than when listening to Agabus tell his stories.

I said, "Tomorrow I will help you clean up this place and see whether we can rearrange the wares. After that I shall go into the foundry to begin my apprenticeship as a coppersmith."

"Good, good, good, very good." Omar was beaming. "The lady Miriam consents that you shall learn her father's business. Good, good."

As I turned to go he said, "Now I have all day to puzzle over what detains Barnabas, and what has happened to Marcus. You wear a strange look, lad."

I paused in the doorway. "I've got a new sister." Seeing the wild conjecture that leaped into his eyes I laughed. "Mother adopted an orphan."

"Ah, good, good! A woman needs a daughter. A son is precious, but a daughter is a companion when the son is away." Omar twinkled. "Serving his apprenticeship as a coppersmith."

I left the forum feeling oddly justified. I would not want Mother to miss me too much. Yet the idea that Rhoda could take my place was humiliating.

I wandered on through streets of mixed architecture. Most Jewish homes present a blank face to the street, with a single inconspicuous door. Romans make much of portals, with painted frescoes above, often in bas relief. The fine homes had statuary beside the door. As a Jew I find much of the statuary objectionable, perhaps because graven images are forbidden to us. I especially dislike painted statuary, and the way the Romans have of adding decoration upon decoration.

I passed a small but exquisite theater, its fluted columns forming a circle of beauty. Between the columns I could see the pit with its paved stage, and rising above the stage the hemicycle of the cavea. How many times had I sat upon those stones with Agabus, enjoying the dramas of Sophocles and Euripides or the comedies of Aristophanes. Salamis was devoted to the Greek dramatists. The farces and pantomimes of Roman playwrights were seldom seen, however, and poorly attended.

Now I was nearing home. Originally built in the Jewish fashion, our house had been altered by the generations of copper merchants who dwelt in it. My great-grandfather had built a foundry behind the court, then a shop, to get all metal working removed from the court.

My grandfather had opened a portal on the street and transformed the court into an atrium by roofing it, leaving the pillared central opening above the pool. The pool was sunk into the earth to receive rainwater and serve as a supplement to the cistern. All this thrift with water in a city served by the excellent Roman aqueduct seemed foolish to me, and I often thought that one day I would stock the pool with goldfish, as many Romans do. The pool was paved in a handsome mosaic depicting a palm tree with cherubs plumply perched in the branches, all a-shimmer under the water. Low benches were set near the pool, where the light was best. Instead of statuary or paintings to ornament our portal my grandfather had planted a vine, which had long since overgrown and completely covered the plain stone lintel.

Omar's eldest grandson, Ken, a chunky, good-natured youth three years older than I, answered my knock. We embraced joyfully, for Ken had been my friend and companion from the times long ago when it was his duty to keep me from falling into the pool. Ken grinned broadly. "Welcome, most welcome, Marcus." He jerked his head toward the atrium. "Strange things happened in Jerusalem, huh, Marcus?"

From somewhere came the voices of Agabus and Phoebe in argument, blending with the familiar tap-tap of hammers from the shop. Phoebe exclaimed, "Barnabas is needed! Why do you make a mystery? Is the lady ill? I was her nurse for sixteen years. I have a right to be told—"

Agabus said, "The lady Miriam is well, wife. Would Marcus be here if she were not?"

The kitchen opened off the atrium, also a large family dining room, two small reception rooms for business consultations, and some family bedrooms. A stairway rose to the roof, where quarters had been arranged for slaves and employees. Baggage was piled near the pool. Afternoon sun poured in, a square of brightness just east of the pool. The voices came from the kitchen.

I shouted, "Phoebe! I'm here."

She came, arms extended. Phoebe was a tall woman, stately, and today a little red-faced. She would have made two of Agabus. I always supposed he had married her hoping for athletic sons. But no children had been born to them. It was another of his frustrations.

Phoebe welcomed me with warmth and dignity. She was as fond of me as was Damaris, but her way of showing affection was not the same.

Kyros, the bearded, booming giant who had in charge our foundry and shop, appeared, wearing his leather apron. One eye had caught a cinder years ago. He wore a black patch over it. His black beard was singed. He clasped my hands and boomed, "Welcome, Marcus. Is Barnabas with you?"

Agabus emerged from the kitchen, sampling some fruity concoction of Phoebe's. He nodded his greeting to Kyros.

I said, "We must get along without Barnabas for a while. Agabus will explain."

Phoebe protested, "Agabus will explain to Kyros but not to his wife?"

"Today at sunset Agabus will explain to all the household, with their families. I have invited Omar. This story cannot be told in bits and pieces. Kyros, pass the word to all the men in the foundry and the shop. Phoebe, circulate the news amongst the servants."

The pixy smile twisted Agabus' lips. "You don't give me much warning."

"You've been rehearsing the story all the way from Jerusalem."

Phoebe looked baffled. Kyros boomed, "If Barnabas is ill, or has business, or is courting a wife—what takes so long to tell?"

Agabus headed toward the stairway. "It is none of those things. Invite the neighbors with their servants, wife. Invite as many Greeks as can squeeze into this atrium. Let them all get the story straight at first hearing, for it will circulate." He started up, leaving the luggage where he had dropped it.

Phoebe followed him to the foot of the stairway, protesting, "Husband, where are you going? I have a thousand things to do if this atrium is to be filled with guests at sunset."

Agabus hitched his way steadily upward. "I am going to my room. To meditate and to pray."

Phoebe looked stunned.

I said, "It is a religious matter."

Kyros blinked his one eye. "A religious matter which involves a Levite of the Jews and a Socratic Greek?"

Phoebe protested, "Agabus is no mystic."

"Tell that to the neighbors, when you invite them. Make it as mysterious as you like. Agabus has a remarkable story to tell. It deserves a large hearing."

Kyros' heavy beard opened in a smile. "Ah, a story. I have only to say that Agabus has a new story. They will come flocking in, more than the place can contain." He vanished into the shop. I heard him booming, heard the metal tapping stop, then a confusion of comments, laughter, questions.

Phoebe looked around with an appraising eye. The atrium looked ready, to me, but I was sure she saw a score of tasks to be done.

"Ken, don't stand gaping! Put away the luggage. Get out the mop. Marcus, lad, you give me little warning. We will need to get in wine. Cakes must be baked. So much to do, with no time for preparation."

"Bake no cakes, Phoebe. Serve a little wine if you like, but prepare no food for this ecclesia."

"You invite your household and your neighbors with their households, and offer no cakes or dainties?"

I said soberly, "My mother daily feeds more than five score people. In Salamis we will start the ecclesias as we mean to continue, without the labor of women. On second thought, Phoebe, we will serve no wine. Let the people come to hear Agabus and for no other reason. This ecclesia will survive on its own merits, without the labor of women or the gluttony of men."

"This is a private affair, yet twice you have called it ecclesia. Marcus, this seems unduly mysterious. How can a public meeting be held in a private home—with the lady Miriam serving food to all who come?"

"I have asked the same question, and have found no answer. Mistakes are sometimes made, Phoebe, by good and wise people who mean only the best. You will understand, Phoebe. Meanwhile, serve no wine. Bake no cakes." I took her hands affectionately and kissed her cheek. She had been a second mother to me during all the winters I had spent in Salamis. "Don't be anxious. All will be well. Trust Agabus."

Subdued and doubtful, Phoebe headed toward the kitchen. Important and expectant, Ken busied himself carting away the luggage.

My room adjoined the atrium. I bathed and changed into clean clothing. I went to the kitchen to learn what kind of supper Phoebe was giving me. I found myself wondering what sort of sermon Agabus would preach—the first sermon about the rabbi of Galilee ever preached to Greeks or by a Greek.

The atrium overflowed into adjoining passages. I was one of those who perched upon the stone flight which led to the roof. The benches about the pool were so crowded I expected some-one to topple in before the evening ended.

Agabus had kept a small space cleared beside the stair. He wore the simple white tunic of a slave, though his wardrobe was rich and ample. He used the spoken Greek dialect called Koine. The message, geared to minds which had never before heard the story, spoken in Koine instead of the Aramaic com-mon in Galilee and Judea, struck upon my ears with fresh impact.

"I come to you, fellow Greeks, in the name of Jesus of Nazareth, the Messiah of the Jews, the son of God and the son of man." Agabus had long been a spinner of tales. I had seen him hold listeners spellbound much as blind Homer must have enthralled the households of kings where he was a guest. But this was not a tale like the others. This was witness. The attentive Greeks were soon aware of the difference.

"I saw this Jesus. I listened as he taught and preached. I saw him die a criminal's death, upon a Roman cross, charged by Jews with treason and inciting to riot."

A low sigh went round the room. Agabus had told the end-ing before he told the story. Kyros' face mirrored the disap-pointment in all these Greek faces.

Agabus hitched across his bit of rostrum, turned and looked earnestly into the massed faces. "But death could not hold him. He rose from the tomb and appeared afterward to hundreds in Galilee. 'Preach the good news of the kingdom of heaven to every nation,' he commanded. Yet he also said, 'I must go to my Father in heaven, but I will return, for lo, I am with you always.'

"His followers forgot the injunction to preach to every nation. They remember only the promise, 'I will return.' They wait in Jerusalem for the coming of their Lord. They preach in the city and witness to one another at sunset each day in their several houses, breaking bread together as a memorial of the times when they broke bread with the Lord Jesus. Barnabas is one of them. He will come here one day and give you his witness. Meanwhile, I will tell you all I know, all I heard from the witnesses and saw for myself, for this Jew was more than the Messiah of the Jews. He came to bring the kingdom of heaven to all sorts and conditions and races of men, throughout all the earth."

Kyros boomed, "Why did they kill him?"

Agabus paused in his hitching pace. "I will tell you of the death and resurrection of Jesus of Nazareth, Messiah and Christos." He glanced up to where I sat upon the stair. A pixy smile twisted his pointed lips within the curling beard. "But first Marcus, son of this house and the only witness to Jesus' arrest, will tell you what he saw. Come, Marcus. Give your people your witness."

Agabus had sprung the trap neatly. I had refused to witness in my mother's house. I could not refuse here. I was totally unprepared. Yet as I climbed over the children on the steps I remembered that Peter had said, "I will speak as the spirit moves me to speak." I felt an odd surge of confidence. These Greeks had served me from infancy and my mother and Barnabas before me. The words came readily. Before I finished the words were a tide I could not check, a tide to which every troubled doubt of the past months became tributary.

"We reached home before the Passover. Mother was at the house of a neighbor, Simon, called the Leper. Damaris told me the rabbi of Nazareth, who had been coming to Jerusalem for the annual Jewish feasts and had done mighty works of healing at various times, had healed Simon of his leprosy. When I reached Simon's house I found Simon at the table with his guests. My mother was among the women who served them, and all Bethany was crowded at the gate, watching in awe and amazement.

"At first I could not see the rabbi or Simon because of the crowd in the gate. But I saw Simon's hand, maimed by leprosy but with pink flesh growing over the stumps of the fingers. That hand had dipped in the common dish."

A wind seemed to pass through the atrium. This was the sort of tale they loved to hear, these Greeks—a tale of mighty works performed by a demi-god.

"I heard the rabbi say, 'Greater works than I do you will do, if you believe.' He also said, 'Love one another as I have loved you.' "

Love one another. This admonition was no part of Greek hero tales. Justice, yes. The destruction of evil doers. But never the simple injunction, Love one another. Omar's fat face was a moon of astonishment.

Kyros boomed, "Why was such a man killed?"

"The rabbi spoke truth so sharp that those who did not love him hated him. He rebuked men in high places because they were grasping and unjust. He called chief priests whited sepulchers, glittering outside but within full of the bones of dead men."

These Greeks nodded solemnly. Each shared the pleasure

most men feel when they see the powerful and the pompous rebuked, the smiter smitten. The story of Jesus was greatly to their liking, something they understood and applauded.

I told how my mother had poured spikenard on Jesus' head, how the neighbors complained of the waste, but Jesus defended her. " 'Wherever you tell of me, tell how Miriam anointed me for my burial.' How fitting it was," I exclaimed, "that he was so anointed while he lived, since death could not hold him."

Caught up in the tale, buoyed by the absorption of my audience, I rushed on, describing the scene in the orchard. "He knew they were coming to arrest him. He knew they would ridicule him, scourge him, and in the end crucify him, for nothing less would appease his enemies. He prayed, 'Let this cup pass from me.' "

I paused, overcome by memory of that pitiful, human cry.

"Then he prayed, 'Thy will, not mine, be done.' For he had come to teach and to preach and to heal, but he had also come to die, for he came in love, and unless he died, how would men measure the fullness of his love and the meaning of his admonition, 'Love one another as I have loved you'?"

I described the coming of Judas with the soldiers, told how Judas betrayed Jesus with a kiss. I told how the followers fled, I with them. "Agabus will tell you of the three hearings, two in Jewish courts and one before the Roman governor, Pontius Pilate. Pilate wanted to free Jesus, but the rabble shouted, 'If you free him you are Caesar's enemy.' He came to his own, and they rejected him. Yet I think if he had come to Greeks they would have killed him as they killed Socrates. For wherever such a man comes there will be those who listen, and leave everything they possess to follow him, and there will be those who shout, 'Away with him! Crucify him!' "

It was strange to see tears roll from both Kyros' eyes, the

good one and the eye under the patch. It was strange to see Phoebe look upon Agabus, her face soft with love. Many wept, and I was astonished to find that my own eyes were brimming.

"Agabus will tell you of Jesus' burial, and of all that happened afterward. I have only one more story to tell—of an event I witnessed only three days before we left Jerusalem to return to Cyprus."

I told of the healing of Korah, of my arrest with Peter, our night in prison, our hearing before the Sanhedrin. "Peter healed Korah in the name of the living Jesus. In his defense before the rulers Peter accused Annas of murdering Messiah. Annas could not deny that Peter had wrought a mighty work in Jesus' name. He had to set us free, lest the very people he had bribed to shout, 'Crucify him!' turn and inform against him. Thus you see that the power of Jesus endures, and lives, that the promise, 'Greater works than I have done you will do, if you believe' is fulfilled in Peter."

Utterly overwhelmed by the tide which had poured from me, I looked for a place to sink down and rest. Finding nowhere to sit, I leaned against the stairs, wanting only to cover my face, to be left alone with my emotions.

Agabus said, "Tomorrow at sunset, friends, I will tell you more about Jesus of Nazareth, which is a village of Galilee. But before we part I will teach you the prayer Jesus taught his followers."

He repeated the prayer in full, then line by line, with the Greeks joining in. At the end, all in the atrium were speaking the prayer together, I with them. "Forgive us our sins as we forgive those who sin against us. Deliver us from evil. Thine is the kingdom, the power, the glory, in Jesus' name."

So ended the first ecclesia in Salamis. Others followed. The people learned the songs sung by the Bethany believers, and other songs with familiar Greek melodies to which Agabus set words he chose from the teachings of Jesus. Winter passed. When the rains ended we went out to meet upon the hills, for a house could no longer hold all who came to hear Agabus preach, and to sing the hymns, and pray together the Lord's Prayer.

I never witnessed again. That first night, tossing in troubled sleep, I seemed to hear Paul's harsh voice saying, "God would not send Messiah to the Jews to be killed by the Jews. God would not so mock the chosen people." All my doubts came flooding over me as I jerked awake, humiliated and shamed that I had been such a charlatan as to proclaim as truth what I did not myself believe. I lay awake till dawn, wondering how I could explain to these Greeks that I had lied to them and betrayed their faith in me.

# CHAPTER *10*

I wakened next morning after a wretched night to the rasp of metal, the acrid taste of smoke. It was late, and I had overslept. I found Phoebe in the kitchen with two of the servant girls. They were talking animatedly of the Christos of Nazareth but fell silent when I entered, though they watched me with bright, excited glances.

Phoebe said, "Marcus, lad, your story touched our hearts. I have never seen Agabus so proud."

So Agabus was proud. After fourteen years of me, Agabus was finally proud. I could never face the people of our household with my doubts of the witness I had given, but Agabus would have to hear the truth.

The truth? What truth? That I had been carried away! I had said only what I yearned to believe. Perhaps that is how myths begin.

Fruit and cakes had been laid out in the big dining room. Here I would take my meals in solitude until Barnabas came. What a bother was the Jewish law which forbade a Jew to break bread or dip into the dish with Gentiles. How many times had I wished I could invite Agabus to share my meals. Not even in my earliest childhood, when he had guided my uncertain spoon, had we dipped into the dish together.

"Where is Agabus?" I might as well get my confession over with.

"He is on the roof. He forbade me to disturb him, Marcus. He is writing down the witness of the apostles as he remembers it."

He had lost no time starting the job he had set himself to do. Well then, I must launch my own projects.

I reached the forum before midday. But Omar, with his grandsons, Ken's three brothers, had been at work for hours. The copper wares were gleaming, nor could I find fault with Omar's new arrangement of the wares. He wore a clean brown coat under the dusty apron. His scrubbed and glowing face reminded me of a bust of Socrates in the forum—a bust renamed for Germanicus, though to the Greeks it would be forever Socrates.

Omar beamed, rubbing his dusty hand across his stomach. "Marcus, lad, you are second only to Agabus as a spellbinder. You must not waste your time polishing brass." He looked about the shop proudly, then fondly at his grandsons. "You see there is no need. Ah, Marcus, you must tell that story in your synagogues, and here in the forum, and down at the docks—wherever men gather. That is a story that touches the heart." Tears stood on the plump cheeks. "You are a Levite of the Jews, Marcus. You must become a rabbi."

I walked home through the warmth of midday, scarcely able to bear my guilt. I found Kyros at the furnace. An apprentice had slopped a bit of molten bronze on his sandal. The injury was not too serious, and I told Kyros my decision to enter upon my own apprenticeship as a coppersmith.

It was soon clear that Kyros and Omar had talked together since the ecclesia last night. I had thought Kyros would rejoice to hear of my plans. Instead he said, "Apprentice metal workers we can find, but last night as you spoke it came to me,

'That boy must be a rabbi. He has the spiritual gift of the best of his people.' Lad, I scarcely slept for thinking of your Messiah, and what it could mean to men if all the world knew of him as you and Agabus told the tale to us. Marcus, you had us all in the palm of your hand. I wept as I listened. I confess it—I wept. Be a rabbi. Be a teacher of men."

"Barnabas has become a sort of rabbi. One from the House of Aaron is enough."

He raked his fingers through the great, scorched beard, looking troubled and perplexed. I said, "I discussed this with Mother and Barnabas before I left. They have agreed that I shall serve my apprenticeship with you, Kyros." I glanced about, found one of the leather aprons, and tied it about my middle.

Kyros started me to making charcoal. The work hours were long, and the interest I had in every phase of the business of my maternal ancestors eased my troubled mind. Soon Kyros had me firing the furnace, where the object was to produce maximum heat without waste of fuel. I knew the worth of the fuel by that time. The months passed, and I performed each operation with absorption and thoroughness. I learned to handle the heavy crucibles and pour molten metal into molds without spilling. I learned to gauge the hardness of the bronze, varying the proportions of tin and copper to get bronze of various hardnesses suitable to many different uses. I burned my hands a score of times and have scars to prove it. My hands became tough and discolored, and muscles bulged in unexpected parts of my body. My beard was sprouting, and it was scorched more than once, and my face blistered as well. But I learned the basics of the trade as no other man of the House of Aaron had learned them since my great-grandfather, who laid the foundation of our business. When Barnabas came in the spring I had moved on into the shop, where I was learning to hammer and shape the vessels we made.

Barnabas brought me two letters, a brief one from Mother and a smudged and blotted rag from Rhoda. He drew them from the bosom of his toga.

"Rhoda worked on this letter for weeks, toiling by firelight long after she should have gone to bed." His bright eyes smiled as he rumpled my hair affectionately. The cleft peered from his chin, between the fat curls of his beard. "She is terribly fond of you, Mark, for some obscure reason. She wept because the letter looked such a mess and she had no time to rewrite it. Miriam says she learned to write for your sake, in order to send letters to you."

"Nobody asked her to." The moment the churlish words were spoken I was ashamed of them. Rhoda was such a busy little thing, rushing about the court at home in her hand-me-down tunics and long, well-brushed hair.

"Miriam says the child never rests so long as there is work to do. She had little time to practice writing, and nobody seemed to want to bother to teach her. Well, the next letter will look better than this one if I know Rhoda, and I rather think I do."

Strangely enough, Rhoda's letter told many things Barnabas had not thought to mention, things Mother did not take time to write about.

"We sleep in your room on the roof now that spring is here again. Mother likes it there. 'If the Lord Jesus should come suddenly in the night,' she says, 'I would know of it sooner here than shut up inside the house.' How she longs for his coming! Sometimes I waken to find her weeping. She is not as she used to be, but weeps often. I think she does it because she exhausts herself too much. When Nicodemus or Damaris tries to make her give it up and live more easily she always says,

'Whatever I do for the least of these, I do for the Lord Jesus.

"Once when she was ill I heard her say to Nicodemus, 'If he does not come soon, perhaps I will see him in the heavenly kingdom.' Nicodemus wants her to marry him and come and live in his house, where there is no ecclesia. But she wants to keep everything just as it was when Jesus went away.

"Nicodemus is often here. Sometimes I am lonely, as you used to be, Mark, when Mother did not have time to sit and visit with you. A daughter can at least be useful. For this I am glad. I remember how it was when I lost my other mother, and I think, What if I lose this mother also?"

Something else was written and smudged out. I held the parchment up in the light and made out the words. "If that happens, can I come where you are? I have nobody but my mother and my brother."

I rushed away to find Barnabas. He was on the roof, delightedly examining the document Agabus had spent the winter writing. "You have captured so much of it," Barnabas exclaimed. "How did you contrive to call it all to mind?"

Agabus lay flat upon his back, arms under his head, staring moodily up at the clear, blue sky. "I have forgotten more than I have remembered. And some of it comes out far from clear. Especially the parables. I think even the witnesses did not always understand them well enough to tell them right."

I laid hold of Barnabas' arm, shaking him. "Is Mother ill? I want to know the truth. Are you concealing something from me?"

He turned from the scroll, his fine eyes alight with the pleasure he had in it. "Why no, Mark. Certainly not. Where did you get that notion?"

"Rhoda said something in the letter."

"Oh? What was it she said?"

"Mother says if she were to—die—she would not have to wait any longer to enter into the—the kingdom of heaven."

Agabus exclaimed, "That is what comes of huddling there and just waiting! Why don't those men do as the Lord Jesus commanded them—scatter out and preach in many cities, to all peoples?"

Barnabas said, "Put your trust in the Lord, Agabus. These good and devoted men will be set upon the right path, if they are in error. Meanwhile—" He took my hand in a reassuring grip. "I think you are homesick for your mother, Mark. It is spring—the season when you have always gone home. Don't you want to return with me and see for yourself that Miriam is in good health?"

I said stiffly, "I have my work here. I cannot go running off like a child just because the seasons change."

"Miriam is well. Don't fret, my boy. She is not the only one to grow weary of waiting for our Lord's return."

Anger with Rhoda rose within me. Why had she written what could only frighten me into making a fool of myself? Didn't she know what it means to a son to be so far from home?

I read Mother's letter again. It was short. The community of believers had grown since the healing of Korah and Peter's bold defense before Annas. Many men now brought their earnings to Peter, having turned from idleness to some form of daily employment. In this change Nicodemus had played a part. Hellenists complained that the Hebrews did not give enough from the common fund to their widows and orphans. It was a pity to find believers bickering amongst themselves. One could not imagine where it would lead, unless the Lord Jesus returned soon to set everything right.

She often pictured me in the home of her childhood. What a peaceful place it seemed, in retrospect, and how lovely were the hills of Cyprus. She found comfort in knowing I was safe. In Jerusalem one never knew when Annas would again take action against the believers. I was to give her love to dear Phoebe, and her warm affection to all the household in which the quiet years of her childhood had been spent.

I sent letters to both Mother and Rhoda by Barnabas when he departed. I urged Mother to deed over our property on Olivet to Peter to be used for all the believers. Mother herself should marry Nicodemus. "Let them have our property, but let their own wives serve them. You have been working too hard. You owe it to Nicodemus and all of us, and to yourself, to give up this strenuous life."

To Rhoda I boasted of my growing facility in the copper works. I also thanked her for the trouble she had taken to learn to write for my sake.

Summer passed, and in the autumn Barnabas came again, and the following spring also. So the years passed, with Barnabas bringing news to us and carrying news back to Jerusalem.

On his fourth visit Barnabas reported that Peter had twice been arrested, and the second time scourged. Rhoda wrote, "The Lord Jesus stood beside him while they scourged him." Her tears spotted the parchment. No witness could have painted for me a more vivid image of Peter's triumphant courage.

Barnabas reported the cleavage between Hellenists and Hebrews. They no longer met together, but had formed separate ecclesias. The common fund was divided, with a committee of Hellenist elders to administer their share of the fund. Chief of this committee was a preacher called Stephen, who taught daily in the synagogue of freedmen.

Annas continually harassed believers. Nicodemus declared that the continuing growth of the ecclesias was exasperating him more and more. He urged the apostles to go and preach in other cities, lest Annas in a sudden move seize them all and bury them in the caves beneath the Temple and thus destroy their witness forever. On this subject Mother disagreed bitterly with Nicodemus. She wanted to keep everything unchanged until the coming of the kingdom, for which she continued desperately to wait.

Rhoda's letters brought me much pleasure, for as her writing skill grew, so did her ability to describe events vividly. In return, I reported my growing skill in fashioning utensils and ornaments of copper and bronze. I wrote of how I spent my free time looking for improved or new uses for metals, seeking ways to beautify the familiar without loss of utility. Only to someone young like myself could I write of my hopes and ambitions. Kyros and Omar were content with things as they were, and smiled over the foolish dreams of youth. But when I wrote to Rhoda of my hopes I knew there was nothing impractical or extravagant in them. On just such dreams had my great-grandfather built the House of Aaron.

So while Omar dozed in the forum and Barnabas gave all his energies to the new movement, Kyros competently turned out the same articles in the same way, and our storehouses grew crowded with goods we were unable to dispose of, since Barnabas no longer went to our agents in the cities of Syria and Cyprus to promote the sale of our wares.

Soon after I became a coppersmith I made a pair of handsome spools, upon one of which I rolled my next letter to Rhoda. I had decorated them with a wreath of palm leaves. I had etched her name, "Rhoda, daughter of Miriam of Bethany" upon the rim of each spool. Thereafter her letters came to me rolled upon one of the spools, with Mother's letter rolled over hers, and the whole thing wrapped in linen. I in return sent back my replies upon the same spool.

Barnabas carried money to Jerusalem, whatever profit was made by the business, both his share and my own. I knew the money I sent would no more buy comfort for Mother than if I had taken it out and flung it into the sea. Yet it eased my mind to give my income to the poor, though I firmly believed that the particular poor here involved would be better off if forced to provide for themselves.

Every Jew knows that charity is part of righteousness. But I could not then, nor ever since those years, justify the promiscuous charity practiced in those first ecclesias, except in the light of early misinterpretations of Jesus' teachings. So eager were the believers for the return of the Lord Jesus they could not wait to shuck off earthly possessions in the hope of hastening his coming.

Yet that first ecclesia, misguided as it was in many ways, laid the foundation for what was to come. In sharing their witness over and over, the followers codified their memories. When events finally scattered them, they went out grounded in their common witness. I heard the apostle John preach in Ephesus many years later, and was struck by the difference his witness bore to the witness of those who tarried in Jerusalem. John did not share those years. He was in Nazareth, dwelling in the house of Joseph the carpenter. I suppose his witness was no less accurate than others. But he seemed to remember different events, and to see different meanings in some of the teachings.

Agabus made the first written record of the Jerusalem witness, and I, even I, unworthy though I was and have always been, made my written record also, though not until years later, after I had spent a winter with Peter in a Roman dungeon. To me these events seem to show how God turns even the blunders of men into good.

When Barnabas came to Salamis the fourth spring after I became an apprentice coppersmith, the apostle Andrew brought him home to us. Barnabas had been scourged in Caesarea. His back was frightful to behold, and he was light-headed from the fever of his festering wounds.

# CHAPTER *II*

Although I was a Levite trained in the application of remedies and unguents, I had never before seen the back of a scourged man. Agabus ministered to Barnabas while I stood by with oil and clean linen, shuddering with horror of what I saw.

Phoebe moaned, "If you had worn your toga, sir, they would not have dared."

"More wine, wife." Agabus was calm amid the cluster of horrified viewers.

Andrew said with a deep anger, "They took him from the synagogue. They scourged him without a hearing. Alexander had pursued us to Caesarea, bearing the Sanhedrin's warrant to arrest all who preached in the name of the Lord Jesus, to bring them back to Jerusalem for trial."

"Alexander!" He was the hotheaded son of Annas who had arrested Peter and me, and had suffered public humiliation when the Sanhedrin released us. I said, "No wonder he scourged Barnabas on the spot. He will not be in a hurry to take his prisoners before the Sanhedrin again."

Andrew said, "He is hot-natured as well as a fool. He did not bother with formalities."

Agabus calmly continued to press exudations from the

bursting wounds and lay on anointed linen strips. That such a thing could happen to the kindly, conciliatory Barnabas made no sense at all.

I asked Andrew, "Where were you, sir, when this happened?"

"I was preaching in another synagogue."

Phoebe repeated, "You should have worn your toga, sir."

Nobody replied. Phoebe knew as well as any Jew that the tasseled tallith was worn in the synagogue, that no Jew would wear a toga there.

Barnabas moved painfully. "Tell about Stephen."

Andrew sank onto a bench. He was short of stature, but seated he looked tall, for his shortness was in his sturdy legs. His kindly face was bleak in the autumn twilight. "Stephen is dead. They stoned him."

Agabus paused a moment in the midst of his ministrations. "He is in the heavenly kingdom with the Christos."

"He was the best preacher among us all. He had eloquence and learning. His witness will be sorely missed."

Barnabas said with feverish excitement, "He was worthy of martyrdom. Most of us are not." He struggled into a sitting posture. "Phoebe, bring me a tunic and coat. I must go to the forum and tell our Jewish merchants how they dragged Stephen from the hall of judgment before his hearing was concluded. They stoned him before sentence was passed! Our good Rabbi Gershon must be told of this. I must show my stripes to the Jews of Salamis. They think because they are Hellenists they have no responsibility for the administration of our Jewish elders in the homeland. They must hear of the outrages committed by Annas and his sons."

His face burned with fever. His eyes were wild. "My friend Paul is among the zealots who follow Annas and do his bidding. He enters homes and makes arrests in the name of the

Sanhedrin. God knows how many of our brothers are now buried and forgotten in the Temple dungeons."

Remembering Peter I said, "There are men to hear their preaching even in those dungeons."

Agabus said, "Lie down, Barnabas. Rest today. Be healed. Afterward you shall speak in the forum and the synagogues."

From Phoebe Barnabas took a draft of wine. Then he lay down with a long sigh. "Agabus, show your 'Sayings' to Andrew," he mumbled, and drifted off into troubled sleep.

Phoebe covered him warmly and went away, one hand pressed tightly over her mouth. I sank onto a bench near where Barnabas lay face down in the atrium. Agabus led Andrew to the roof, where the light was best, telling of how he had come to write down the witness as he had heard it given in Bethany.

The stoning could have happened to anybody—to Peter, to Barnabas. I bent to adjust his covering, for he was twitching and groaning as he slept.

"How can Jews do such things to one another?" Mother had said when Jesus was arrested. In my anger I thought, None of it would have happened if only Jesus had gone away to Galilee that night.

Slowly I got out the letters Barnabas had brought. Both were on the little bronze spool, Mother's over Rhoda's, so I opened hers first. She of course knew nothing about the scourging of Barnabas. By the time she learned of that, his back would be healed.

She wrote, "I will not speak of Stephen's death. It is too painful to dwell upon. Yet we know that for him the kingdom has come and the waiting is ended. Ah, my dearest son, no pains are too hard to bear since we know our Lord Jesus will return in the day and hour when we least expect him. Yet the house seems an echoing, empty place, for the apostles and all our leaders who escaped prison have fled. Nicodemus is gone, I know not where. Annas hates Nicodemus more than any of the others. Annas called him traitor in the very midst of the Sanhedrin. We miss our dear friend, yet we do not grieve that he has sought a place safer than this in which to dwell and give his witness.

"Those who remain no longer break bread together. Sunset became a favored time for our enemies to burst in and carry off our men to scourging and prison. The ecclesias meet in various places, at irregular times. The faint of heart have fallen away. Those who came only to be fed come no more. The chaff has been winnowed out, yet good wheat was lost in the winnowing.

"Damaris and Rhoda and I find ourselves with idle hands. And when I am idle I miss my beloved son more than ever. Yet I cannot wish you here where danger is never absent from us."

Rhoda's letter was so neat I knew it had been copied from an earlier draft—eloquent testimony that she now had time enough on her hands. Her account of Stephen's martyrdom was vivid.

"He kept rising out of the stones as if nothing could hurt him. Nicodemus had sat with the Sanhedrin that day. He saw it all. At the end, Stephen saw the Lord Jesus in glory, and praised God, witnessing to the vision which blessed his final moments of life. Paul of Tarsus was there. He is a bad, bad man. He goes storming into houses to drag people away to the dungeons. I do not see how Barnabas could ever have been his friend. He is fearfully wicked.

"You must not think the apostles fled because they fear death. To die is to be with the Lord Jesus forevermore. They fled to preserve the witness. Wherever they go they preach the good news. Imagine ecclesias in every city of Judea and

Samaria and Galilee—even in Antioch and Damascus! And all
because Annas tried to stamp out the fellowship of those who
believe!"

All because Annas tried to stamp out the fellowship of those
who believe! Awe gripped me. Could it be that God used even
the wrath of a strong-willed, hard-headed man like Annas for
His unknowable purpose? I was swept by a longing to hear
Peter speak on this subject. Where was Peter? In Samaria? In
Galilee? Wherever he was, he would be preaching, and people
would raise their faces to him, and listen, and repeat, and
believe, and become new people because Peter came to them,
preaching the good news of the Savior and Messiah.

To believe! Oh Lord God of Jacob, how I longed to believe!
"Let me know what is true, what is right and true," I prayed,
there beside the feverish, muttering Barnabas, who had been
scourged for a faith I could not share. "Is this Jesus the Holy
One? Let me know the truth!"

Andrew and Agabus were descending the stairs. Andrew
said, "Stephen's death brought home to us the injunction, 'Go
into the world. Preach the good news everywhere.' "

Agabus said stiffly, "The exact quotation is, 'Preach the
good news to every nation.' You misquoted our Lord Jesus,
Brother Andrew. The written records have value if only to
prevent such garbling and confusion."

Andrew said mildly, "I am only a fisherman turned
preacher. Written records move me less than the spoken witness. Moreover, when our Lord returns to rule his kingdom we
will have no further need of written records."

Barnabas moved painfully and managed to prop himself up
upon his elbows. "My dear Andrew, you who followed him are
eleven. The written witness could be copied and recopied, and
carried to scores of ecclesias where you will never go. To me it
seems that a complete, authentic, written record is beyond
price." He sank down on the mat, groaning. "Our brother

Agabus has given us a record which preserves the spoken witness as it was given that first summer in Bethany."

Andrew's heavy face was bleak. "I cannot believe we will need it. I cannot believe the Lord Jesus will tarry longer. Surely—soon—" Suddenly tears spilled out of the honest eyes of this fisherman. "Forgive me. I so long for my Lord's return. We were so—so unready for the responsibility—the decisions."

Agabus said inexorably, "Your companion who killed himself—the traitor Judas—was guilty of one thing only. He wanted to bring in the kingdom before the Christos was ready. I find it hard to be patient with men who do not trouble to obey the injunctions of the Lord Jesus to preach to all nations, yet refuse to see that until they have obeyed all his injunctions he will not come."

Andrew took no offense. He merely looked bewildered. "But we are now preaching everywhere, Brother Agabus."

"Only in the synagogues. Into whatever city you go, you preach to the Jews. This is not preaching to every nation."

Barnabas started to roll over, then thought better of it. "Our brother Philip, a Hellenist who was the companion of Stephen before Stephen was stoned, was in Caesarea with us. He told how he had encountered on the way a eunuch who serves Queen Candace of Ethiopia. This man was reading aloud as he traveled down the road in the queen's chariot. Philip heard, and recognized the reading as coming from the prophecies of Isaiah. And Philip told the eunuch how all that prophecy had been fulfilled in the life and death and resurrection of the Lord Jesus. The Ethiopian believed him, and was baptized by Philip."

"Baptized!" A look of utmost longing dwelt for a moment on the face of Agabus. "An Ethiopian baptized?"

Barnabas looked from one to the other, each so devout, so dedicated, so devoured with longing for something beyond the work to which they had devoted all their powers. In spite of his fever and pain he sat up.

"Agabus, I think you know that our brother Andrew was the first, with Peter, to leave his boats and his nets to follow Jesus. Andrew was standing beside the Jordan on the day when Jesus was baptized by John the Baptizer. He went, then, to his brother Peter to tell him that the Holy One had come. When others were called by Jesus, saying, 'Come, follow me,' there were disciples with Jesus, but when Peter and Andrew left all that was familiar and dear, Jesus had no followers. And they were with him from that early beginning of the ministry to the very day when he was parted from them as they approached Bethany, forty days after the resurrection. There is no other witness with so rich and abundant a store of memories as our brother Andrew."

Ill and suffering as he was, Barnabas had again played the peacemaker. Agabus turned to Andrew. The pointed, pixy mouth formed a bow of pure love. "Forgive my churlish tongue, my brother."

Andrew took the slight figure into an enveloping embrace. "Forgive the blindness of my spirit and the ignorance of my mind concerning your book, brother Agabus. For those who never knew the Lord Jesus it must surely have great worth."

"We Greeks keep the First Day of the week as our day of meeting together to worship," said Agabus. "Will you give our ecclesia the blessing of your rich and vital witness, brother Andrew?"

"I will joy in witnessing to the first Greek ecclesia, my brother. But before I stand and preach to Greeks I must right the wrong we have done to you, Agabus. Will you accept baptism at my unworthy hands?"

Agabus did not reply for some little time. He did not speak at all, for he was weeping.

# CHAPTER *12*

Those were the years of my alienation. I was neither Jew nor Greek. I did not follow The Way nor could I rid my mind of it. On the Sabbath I attended synagogue. But when our sacred writings were read I listened always for the prophecies of Messiah's coming. Whenever an elder rose to harangue, I seemed to hear the voices of the scattered apostles preaching in the synagogues of Syria and Samaria, of Judea and the cities of the Diaspora. When I attended the First Day meetings of our Greek ecclesia I longed to believe as our Greeks believed, as my mother and Rhoda and Barnabas and Agabus believed. But I could not.

Agabus was gone, having been called to Antioch to preach to the multitude of Greeks who dwelt in the warrens near the docks. The good times were when Barnabas came, brown and healthy from his travels and wearing the special aura of joy which he called the indwelling Breath of God. He brought news of the ecclesias which were springing up everywhere, and he brought letters from Mother and Rhoda. James had remained in Bethany, a bulwark of authority in the midst of the sadly shrunken body of believers there. Peter, however, moved from city to town to village, preaching everywhere. I longed for Peter to come to Cyprus in his travels, but he never did. Nicodemus dwelt in Joppa, the ancient Jewish harbor south of Caesarea. It was a poor harbor compared with that the Romans had built, yet it survived, and Nicodemus dwelt there, doing business with the seaports of the world. Wherever his ships went they carried messengers of the good news of Messiah's coming.

As my hands learned the skills of their trade, my spirit accepted loneliness and doubt as inescapable. More and more I sought peace in the exercise of my trade. More and more, however, I became convinced that my hands would never acquire 'skill enough to execute the ideas my mind conceived.

On an autumn afternoon Ken summoned me from the shop. I found in the atrium the last person I would have expected —Paul of Tarsus. His face was livid. His body shivered with an ague. He was scarcely recognizable in his tattered tunic, with his hair and the thick, curling beard all matted.

I exclaimed, "What brings you here?" Then, because he was ill, I motioned to a bench. "Sit down, Paul."

He sank onto the bench. "Barnabas sent me, Mark. I fled the Sanhedrin. On the way I fell ill—the fever. Every second day it returns. On the ship I was robbed of everything—even my poor coat. It will pass, but—" He clutched his head in his hands, doubled over, and fell to the floor.

Ken and I carried him to the room kept ready for Barnabas. His body was very hot, and his utterances grew increasingly incoherent. We wrapped him in coats. As the shuddering worsened we held him to keep him wrapped and prevent him from injuring himself. Phoebe brought hot stones which we laid against him, since the extremity of his suffering would continue until the fever broke. Through chattering teeth came sounds of anguish with occasionally recognizable meaning.

"Blind! I cannot see! Who are you, Lord Jesus? What do you want from me? I cannot see! I cannot see!"

The noise he made brought peering faces to the doorway, but Phoebe shooed them away. Fever is a familiar enemy in our world. Both my maternal grandparents had died of it. More than half of all so afflicted die, for often it goes into ague and dropsy, or into the black fever, that stinking horror when all emissions are black as pitch.

I had some knowledge of the ancient medical lore of the Jews, both how to heal and how to prevent certain ailments—blains, poxes, and the like. I had learned a little Greek medical lore from Agabus also. Nothing can be done for the fever but to keep the patient warm until the fever breaks. When that happens, the patient must be bathed and provided with dry clothing, for sweat pours in drenching rivers while the fever leaves the body.

Paul's attack had begun as he approached our house. For six hours he threshed and shuddered and muttered in delirium. Ken and I had our hands full keeping him wrapped, small and slight as he was. I could have wept with pity as I thought of his helplessness on shipboard during those attacks. What sort of creatures would rob a man suffering in the throes of fever I cannot think.

Whatever he suffered, I told myself, he deserved to suffer, for he had done great evil to good men. Yet as he continued to cry out, the unthinkable conjecture returned again and again.

"Blind! My spirit blind, Lord Jesus. Let my eyes be dark but let my soul know the light of truth." And I remembered his original statement. "Barnabas sent me. I fled the San-hedrin."

I hate you, Paul of Tarsus, I thought, even as I wrapped the cloak close, holding him against the warmed stones to hasten the breaking of the fever. If you had never come to our house, if you had never spoken words which expressed my confusion and doubts so very clearly and convincingly, I might have been one with my mother and Barnabas in their faith all these years.

So you fled the Sanhedrin, I remarked silently to the unconscious, suffering, undersized figure between the warm stones. Annas must be hot against a convert to The Way who once served his purposes as you did, Paul of Tarsus. You were wise to flee to Salamis, but not alone! A man subject to these attacks should never travel alone.

The night was half gone when suddenly Paul grew quiet. Sweat beaded the fine mouth, trickling through the matted beard, the tangled forelocks. I dipped a towel in warm water and began washing his face. Paul's eyes opened. The cracked lips muttered, "Love your enemies. Bless you, Mark, for I have been your bitter enemy. I do not deserve your care." With that he fell asleep.

We stripped away the rags to wash the sweating body. That was when I found the brazen spool hidden in his breast. The parchment was blackened with sweat. Of all the possessions with which he had fled Jerusalem, this thing only had been left, tied inside his tunic. I doubted the letter on the spool could be read, after repeated soakings in his sweat. I continued bathing him, Ken helping and Phoebe hovering over us, bringing fresh water and clean towels, until he had ceased to sweat. At last he slept quietly, clean, and clothed in clean garments. Then Ken stumbled off to bed. But I sat under the flickering light of a copper lamp and opened the letter.

Mother's letter was rolled outside of Rhoda's. It was hopelessly blurred. But Rhoda's letter was mostly readable. "Greetings, brother Mark. May peace and grace be with you."

How formal that hooligan child had become! Imagine her putting on airs with me, who had seen what she was when Mother took her in and cleaned her up.

"You will be astonished to see our brother Paul, as I was when he knocked upon our door. Morning had dawned, after a late night of talk upon the roof, for both Barnabas and Peter had come to spend the night. When I opened the needle's eye in the little door beside the gate to see who knocked, behold, Paul stood there, flushed with fatigue and dusty from a long journey.

"My heart stood still, for I thought surely he had come to drag Barnabas away to prison. I shouted, 'Go away! There is nobody here you'd care to arrest! We are three women only.' But Barnabas came, for all the while Paul had gone on pounding upon the door. When he made sure Paul was alone, he opened to him.

"I write in haste, dear Mark, for after two weeks in this house Paul must flee the city. He is a stubborn little man. In spite of all Barnabas and Peter say to warn him he preaches in the synagogue where Stephen used to preach. Now he must be smuggled from Jerusalem as he was smuggled from Damascus. He will tell of his conversion, so I will not spoil the story with hints, except to say that Mother is greatly excited, knowing Paul has seen the risen Lord Jesus. She is more confident than ever that Jesus will come soon—any day, any hour."

The spool dropped from my hand to trail away across the floor. It could not be true. Scores of true believers longed to see the risen Lord Jesus—Mother most of all—yet here was this renegade, this cynic who had transformed all my early confusions into a wall of doubt I could not breach—this persecutor of believers—and he alone of them all had seen the risen Lord.

I recovered the spool, feeling sick at such injustice. I had longed, I had prayed to believe. Yet here was Paul, henchman of Annas—

I rerolled upon the spool as much of the letter as I had read, and read on. "Paul was not evil, only zealous. He did what seemed to him right, with all his soul and being. Alas, I hope he does not read this letter on the road. If he does, well then, Greetings, Brother Paul. Peace be with you."

From there on I made out only fragments. "Paul and Barnabas will go to Caesarea, decked out in their togas and every Roman trapping they can lay their hands upon . . . Mother is often ill. Her former physician will not come to a house as notorious . . ."

I could read no more. How ill was Mother? When had ever a physician refused to call at our house on Olivet? Twenty physicians had broken bread there in the old days, and been glad of the invitation. I tucked the coat about Paul when he turned in his sleep, and leaned my head against the wall, nursing my anxiety and anger. I must have fallen asleep, because the next thing I knew Phoebe had come in and was extinguishing the lamp. Dawn was faintly pink outside the high, slitted windows.

By noon Paul was up and about, weak and pale but impatient to begin the task which had brought him to Salamis, which was to read and perhaps make a copy for himself of Agabus' book, the "Sayings of the Lord Jesus." Peter and Barnabas and James had spent two weeks teaching him, but Barnabas had insisted the book would be the best source. Moreover, Paul was one who loved and trusted books.

On the following Sabbath Paul went to the synagogue of Rabbi Gershon, which was the synagogue which regularly received the tithes and offerings of the House of Aaron. I went with him. We sat where the men of our family had sat for four generations. There I heard for the first time the full story of Paul's conversion. For when the readings and prayers ended, the service became a forum. Any man who desired might rise and speak. Paul arose.

"Men and brethren, I am Paul of Tarsus, a Roman citizen by birth, graduate of the University of Tarsus, a Pharisee and for two years a student of Gamaliel in the School of Hillel in Jerusalem. I want to speak to you concerning the sect of Jesus, the Nazarene, who was crucified by Pontius Pilate during the Passover season four years ago. He was executed at the behest of our chief ruler Annas, who since that time has persecuted many who preached that Jesus rose from death and came forth to appear to thousands in Galilee. These followers have since preached in his name throughout Judea, Samaria, and Galilee."

The introduction caused no great stir. Barnabas spoke in this synagogue whenever he was in Salamis. Yet Paul's scholarly background, together with his splendid voice and diction, caught the interest of the men.

"In my blindness of heart I opposed these believers, arresting some to take before the Sanhedrin for punishment. And now hear what befell me. I had set out for Damascus with letters from the Sanhedrin empowering me to arrest certain followers who preached there and bring them to Jerusalem for trial. As I neared Damascus, suddenly a great light flashed around me and I fell from my horse. Then I heard a voice saying, 'Saul, Saul, why do you persecute me?' I answered, 'Who are you?' 'I am Jesus of Nazareth, whom you are persecuting.'

"My companions saw the light but did not hear the voice. I said, 'What shall I do, Lord?' for I was filled with awe, nor doubted for a moment that the radiant figure which stood over me in the road was indeed the risen Nazarene. And he replied, 'Rise and go to Damascus. There you will be told of the work you are to do.'

"Now when I arose, I was blind. My companions led me by the hand, and so we came to Damascus. There a believer who had also had a vision concerning me encountered us in the street. He took my hand and led me to his house. He it was who said to me, 'You must witness before the world.'

"Now for three days this good man expounded to me all his faith and all his knowledge of The Way preached by Jesus, and when, after three days, my sight was restored to me I was baptized in Jesus' name. Afterward I preached the risen Lord Jesus in the synagogues of Damascus till I was driven from the city. I fled to Jerusalem and there preached in the synagogue of freedmen. Again I was obliged to flee from the wrath and vengefulness of Annas, and so I have come here. I will rest here for a season, and learn more about the Lord Jesus and so prepare myself to go forth and preach in his holy name, for of a truth I am convinced that he is the Holy One foretold to us through many centuries to be sent by God to redeem the Jews and all men and establish a kingdom of heaven on the earth."

Paul's first witness in Salamis created no great reaction. When he returned repeatedly, however, to preach in all the synagogues of Salamis, using the sacred books of prophecy as introduction to his talks, the Jews turned against him, for they had come to regard the cult as Greek superstition, a bastard faith built upon a Jewish framework. After all, Greek ecclesias had been flourishing in Salamis for four years, setting forth the very doctrines now preached to them by Paul. Soon Paul was forbidden to speak except in Rabbi Gershon's synagogue, and there only out of deference to the House of Aaron, where Paul was lodged as a guest. On the First Day, however, Paul found ready audience in the Greek ecclesias.

Paul's copy of the "Sayings" was even more handsome than Agabus' original. Paul made marginal notes in his strong, handsome script. Far from cluttering the margins, the notes appeared to decorate them. In these notes Paul quoted from the law, the prophets, and the wisdom writings fluently.

Paul used our meals together to harangue me, or to question me. "Where was Jesus when he spoke this parable? To whom was he speaking? What event led up to it?" Then, impatient at my ignorance, "What we need is a record of the movements of Jesus, some inkling of the circumstances surrounding the various sermons."

One afternoon I delayed going to the sunset meal, caught in an argument with Kyros over a sketch I had made for decorating a pair of bronze scales. As we argued, I with some heat, Kyros with the patient superiority of experience, Paul rushed into the atrium, afire with a new concept.

"I see it clearly," he exclaimed, unmindful of our argument. "The Cross is everything—the symbol, the meaning of his life. The apostles make much of the resurrection. But that is only another of his mighty works, another proof for men who find faith hard to come by. His mission was the cross—death suffered by a sinless man for the sins of all men—the shameful death, the degrading, shocking, frightful death of the cross. Death for the sins of Jew and Greek, of slave and free. Death by which men may know God's mercy and forgiveness, may put away sin to become new creatures in the Lord Jesus. This is my message. This I will preach."

He strode about the atrium, afire with excitement. "Now I am ready! I will preach in Cilicia. My ministry will begin where my life began, in Tarsus. I will preach this good news to the rabbis who taught me in my youth. I will preach to the learned men who taught me in the university in Tarsus. But first I will take ship to Antioch, greet Agabus, and thank and bless him for this book he has written, this book beyond price. I will show him my copy, with its marginal notes. From Antioch I will travel up through Syria and around the crescent into Cilicia and so to Tarsus."

I protested, "You mustn't travel alone. If you were to fall ill of the fever you would be robbed again. You might lose your copy of this book."

Kyros said, "Our neighbor Mnemos is going to Antioch. Agabus will find someone to accompany you from there."

Paul exclaimed, "Mark, you must go with me. Go all the way, remain with me. You have the hands of a physician, and you have a background of acquaintanceship with the early followers. Share my ministry, Mark."

The sheer effrontery of the suggestion stunned me. Paul's eye was too sharp to miss my indignation that he could assume that nobody but himself had affairs of any significance. He smiled and turned, for Phoebe had signaled that our meal was served. "Mnemos will do very well as a companion as far as Antioch," he said, and walked quickly into the dining room.

Phoebe had laid out a meal of roast young kid (for Cyprus abounds in goats more than in sheep), with fruit and bread and some stewed vegetables. Paul picked at his food, for he was never a hearty eater. Presently he shot me a sharp glance across the table.

"You are not over fond of me, Mark."

The words I had dammed up all winter burst forth. "When I hovered between faith and doubt that first spring and summer, you came amongst us, argumentative, supremely confident in your opinions, and oh, so logical. You said the Lord Jesus did not heal Simon, but merely provided a means whereby he could convince his neighbors of the healing which actually had occurred earlier."

Paul made to interrupt but I rushed on, "When I was troubled that the rulers of the Jews had contrived the death of a man many believed was Messiah, you declared, 'God would not so mock the chosen people.' All these years I have been alienated from Mother and Barnabas because of what you said in my hearing."

Paul wiped his fingers on a napkin. "Mark, you were in the soul and center of great events. You heard from the lips of witnesses what Agabus has recorded. You witnessed Jesus' agony in Gethsemane; you saw the prophecy fulfilled, 'As a sheep before the shearers is dumb, so he opened not his mouth.' For the conclusions you formed you are responsible, Mark. I am guilty of much evil, for which I have been forgiven through God's infinite mercy. Yet I say to you, my son, that your season of faith will come. When it comes, faith will be the more precious to you because it did not come easily."

I muttered, "Do you believe Simon was healed in a day, by Jesus' power?"

"If he was, it is a measure of Simon's faith, for the powers of the Lord Jesus are infinite. Do you believe in Simon's faith?"

I exclaimed, "Certainly I believe in Simon's faith."

"You know the man. You have answered your own question."

"Does God—hate the Jews? Did God send Messiah only to mock them?"

"Mark, how can a cousin of Barnabas be such a fool? God sent His son to the Jews first. This is the great gift. It is for the Jews to pass on the supreme gift, the supreme message to all men. Remember, Mark, for every Jew who shouted, 'Crucify him' there are twenty ready to lay down their lives to spread the good news that Messiah has come."

I left the table. If this was truth, it had come too late. I could not twist and bend my mind as Pharisees do to change what I had harbored therein at such great personal cost.

After Paul departed, the dining room was lonelier than ever. Moreover, I had concluded I would never be craftsman enough to satisfy my critical taste. We had three Greeks in the shop who could better execute my ideas than I could. We were out of contact with our dealers. The yearly orders we received from them, and from our proconsul, Sergius Paulus, came no more, for it was Barnabas who had brought their business to the House of Aaron.

Sergius Paulus had his palace in Paphos, eighty miles away at the opposite end of our island. I determined to make the journey to Paphos, taking a donkey or two with a sampling of our wares. I would stop to visit our dealers in the market places of the villages and cities of the central valley which crosses Cyprus. I would remind them that the House of Aaron was still making copper wares and articles of bronze to sell.

I was ripe and ready for some personal bewitchment that spring when I met Sergius Paulus and fell in love with his daughter Malnor.

# CHAPTER 13

On Cyprus everything runs east-west. Two mountain chains follow the northern and southern coastlines, with a fertile plain between. As you follow the road westward you see the heavily forested peaks rising to both right and left, with the great massif called Mount Olympus sometimes on your left, though often, with the winding of the road, dead ahead. Once you have rounded Mount Olympus you descend to Paphos and the western coast. The road follows two rivers, both rising on the slopes of Olympus. The longer river flows east to empty into the sea near Salamis. The western river makes a seaport for ancient Paphos.

Travel on Cyprus is safe, for it is a quiet land. The caravans of Asia and Africa invite robbers to the highways of the mainland, but no great caravans traverse our island. I traveled to Paphos as Barnabas did, with no protection beyond that of the five youths who led the donkeys, Ken among them. Each was armed with a short sword, but none had had experience with these weapons, so it was as well we had no need for them.

Roman law and Roman legions protected the traveler on Cyprus and indeed throughout much of the empire. The Pax Romana, established by Caesar Augustus before I was born, looked to last out my lifetime and beyond.

The hills of Cyprus are a patchwork of vineyards, orchards, grainfields, and meadows, crowned perhaps with forest. For me the disciplined beauty of our hills is linked with the tireless industry of our sturdy Cypriot women. One saw them everywhere, pruning grape vines, sowing grain, leading a score of goats to market by a sheaf of tethers, or leading donkeys laden with wares of their making or grain of their harvesting, or wine of their treading. One saw them on the roads, walking behind donkeys ridden by their men, spinning as they walked, spindle high in one hand, wool skillfully paid out by the other.

Our journey was broken by villages and by two cities, Tamassus and Idalium. The House of Aaron had business in cities and villages alike, since there is use for copper lamps and copper pots in any house that can afford something better than earthenware. Merchants in even the meanest villages take pride in the use of copper scales, enjoying the prestige accruing to their little shops because they weigh out grain or vegetables as testimony to their honesty.

Our journey was delayed by flocks upon the road. Men drove the flocks to shearers in the market towns if they had wool to sell, for shearers were provided by merchants who bought the wool. There in the town the men could drink the sour Cypriot beer with other farmers while their goats were shorn. One saw men in the fields with the women also, but my image of a typical Cypriot sight is a man riding sidewise on a donkey, both heels drumming in the rhythm of its walk, slumped confortably and greeting all who passed with smiles and shouts, followed by the industrious wife, well wrapped in her coat and mantle, her spindle whirling as she spins woolen threads for the insatiable family loom.

Every village has its tombs, some neatly kept, others fallen into ruins. Amongst these latter we saw the weathered limestone votaries, vine draped, with lizards running across the pixy mouths and curling beards. Their smiles seemed to hint that death had shared amusing secrets with them. I know not for how many centuries these vine-shrouded figures had stood guard over ancient dead. Perhaps they were there before the Greeks came. I suppose nobody will ever know, for stone keeps its secrets well. Before the Greeks came, Phoenicians and Syrians and Egyptians and God alone knows who else had found this rich land hospitable and inviting. I suppose men have dwelt on Cyprus ever since they first learned to travel upon the sea in ships.

Paphos has always been the capital of our island. The old city, where dwelt our former rulers, lies perhaps an hour's journey south from the new city. Every Roman denarius of Cyprus coinage has stamped upon its back a likeness of the temple of Aphrodite for which old Paphos was noted.

The new Paphos is pure Roman, unlike any other city outside Italy which I have seen save only Caesarea. Elsewhere Romans took over what others had built. In the new Paphos the forum, theater, three thermae, two temples, and the palace of the proconsul, as well as the villas of officials, are Roman in architecture and decoration. Paphos is a handsome, colorful city, spacious, without huts or hovels such as cluster about the skirts of other cities.

I found an inn where I left my donkeys and my Greeks. I changed into a clean coat and headcloth, put on new sandals, and went to the forum.

Our Paphos dealer was a Jew called Amos whose grandfather had been awarded citizenship when he established his business in Paphos. Amos affected Roman curls and the toga, and lost no time hustling me to the merchants' thermae. Amos was a vigorous, outgoing, clever young man. The fingers of his left hand were webbed and he kept them tucked inside his coat. It was strange to see so animated a man talk without gestures. He busied himself introducing me to the merchants, those in the forum and those in the baths. He explained to one and all that I was cousin to Barnabas of Salamis. This proved to be identification enough. To every man I had to explain why Barnabas had been so long away. I had planned something brief but conclusive, but found that repetition made even this statement tiresome.

I was glad to bathe away the dust of the journey amid the frescoes and decorative urns of the handsome baths. But I found the ministrations of the heavy-handed masseur less welcome. After walking eighty miles in nine days I felt no great need of either massage or exercise. I squatted against the wall while Amos drove his wiry body through the grotesqueries which pass amongst Romans as healthy exercise.

Amos made our appointment to see Sergius Paulus the next morning. I enjoyed the evening with his family, which included a widowed sister and her four little ones. We talked mostly about the copper trade and I departed early for the inn and a good night's rest. Next morning I rose at dawn to look over the wares I had brought and choose what to take along to the palace of the proconsul. Amos joined me in the task. Then we set out, Amos glowing with health and cleanliness and wearing a handsome toga of white linen with bands of blue along the garment's straight edge. I wore my best crimson coat. My beard was short, but thickening nicely, the brand of my youth yet a brand of which I was not ashamed. Amos compromised with the Roman custom of shaving the face by keeping his beard short. As beards go, there was little difference between us.

The stout, granite walls of the palace were topped by battlements, and towers rose at the corners and over the gates. Four legionaries passed us through promptly. The palace portal was impressive with a fine statue of Mercury wearing winged sandals on one side and on the other Orpheus with a painted harp and curling hair. Above, in bas relief, was a fresco of a mother wolf suckling twin boys, with a suggestion of Tuscan hills in the background. Blues, ochers, and greens glittered in the morning sun. The figures were strong, a credit to the Greek slaves who had chiseled them.

An elderly servant admitted us. "You are expected," he told Amos, and led us to the atrium. His body was bent like a bow, yet he moved briskly.

The atrium was spacious, with pillared promenades on all sides. The central pool was very clear. Its handsome mosaic paving showed Neptune on a mossy rock, with ducks and nymphs and a colorful sea serpent filling a background of rich blue. A score of fat, lazy fish swam in the clear water. A large peristyle adjoined the atrium, with a formal garden filling the area within its galleries.

An elderly Jew with gray forelocks and the roughest of raiment paced the atrium—a strange figure to find in such a place. The servant disappeared through one of the doors and Amos introduced me to the other guest. "Elymas bar Joshua, magician and prophet, formerly one of the community of Essenes near Jerusalem."

Amos had told me about Elymas. He was a sort of traveling magician, and an object of the proconsul's bounty. He had been cast out by the Essenes for reasons unknown to Amos, and came and went as he pleased. Now that he was under the proconsul's protection, he resented all comers welcomed in the palace, especially Jews.

Elymas said sourly, "The proconsul is late."

Amos was genial. "No hurry. A handsome atrium, eh Mark?"

Statuary was grouped everywhere, both in the atrium and in the formal garden of the peristyle. The family lares and penates were grouped under a handsome tile roofing of the red ocher one saw so much of in Roman buildings. A painted background of this red, with trailing vines of yellow and green, enhanced the statues of the family deities.

Elymas said, "I do not trust any Jew who wears the toga." Then to me, "You are a Jerusalem Hebrew, not a Cypriot." His sour, censorious examination of me did not sit too well, especially as I was facing the first major encounter whereby I hoped to take Barnabas' place in our business.

I replied reasonably, however. "My mother's ancestors have been Cypriot for four generations. My father's have dwelt at Jerusalem since the time of Zerubbabel." He was a stiff-necked, self-righteous old man, this so-called prophet and magician who pandered to Romans while looking down his nose at his fellow Jews.

Sergius Paulus did not keep us waiting long. He was hand-some in the Roman manner, with hair a mass of gray curls, face shaved, toga neatly draped over a lean figure. His eyes had the burning intensity which expresses itself in religious zeal in the Jew but in a Roman may find outlet in devotion to law and order, or in adoration of the emperor. I suppose Sergius Paulus had been sufficiently devoted to Tiberius Caesar and his predecessor, the great Augustus, to advance him politically, but certainly he could have felt no admiration for Caligula, who had climbed to the throne over the murdered body of Tiberius, his benefactor and foster-father.

Sergius Paulus clasped wrists with Amos in the Roman style, nodded in friendly fashion at Elymas, and shook hands with me in the Jewish manner. I was to learn to my sorrow that Elymas usually managed to drop in at the palace whenever the proconsul was receiving Jewish guests.

Seeing my confusion at his handshake, Sergius Paulus said, "My grandmother was a Jewess. She taught me many things."

He motioned for us to seat ourselves. "Barnabas has been absent from Paphos for five years. We have missed him. Tell him so, for me, Marcus." The austerity of his manner bordered on loneliness. He really cares for Barnabas, I thought.

The euphemism I had prepared would not serve. "Barnabas is involved in a new religious cult. He gives all his time to it. So does my mother."

"A new cult." Sergius glanced toward Elymas, who seemed to be simmering. "The cult of the Nazarene who was executed?" A veil covered the large eyes. Suddenly it struck me. Those eyes were a heritage from his Jewish grandmother.

"The crucified Nazarene," I agreed. Amos moved restlessly beside me on the bench. He had not come here to discuss with Sergius Paulus the eccentric cults which rose now and then amongst the Jews.

The proconsul said, "Elymas and I have discussed this cult. Pontius Pilate was profoundly impressed by the man. He has said the Nazarene could have been freed had he made any effort to defend himself from the charges brought by the rulers of the Jews."

Elymas emitted a noise of contempt. The proconsul silenced him with a sharp glance. "You have spoken your mind to me, my friend. Now I want to know why Barnabas follows the cult."

I swallowed and plunged in. "Barnabas believes Jesus came from the tomb after three days. So do thousands of others. They say he lives, that he is Messiah, even though our rulers rejected him."

"Why did your rulers reject him? Pontius believed the charges were trumped up to fit Roman law and to conceal the true objections they had to this man."

"My mother said Jesus accused the rulers of hypocrisy—not all of them, but Annas, chief of the rulers, who has many adherents. Jesus preached a searching and convincing truth, and he attracted a very large following."

Sergius said, "Public disputes are part of Jewish tradition. If the Romans had to hang every man who rose to harangue the Jews on the shortcomings of their rulers there would not be crosses enough in Palestine."

"Jesus also did mighty works. He was able to teach people to live at peace with their own conscience. His interpretation of—righteousness—was compelling. He had a strange power to rouse and hold the love of his followers."

Sergius frowned, his penetrating gaze fixed upon me as though he saw beyond me, visualizing certain scenes which had occurred in Jerusalem. "His death was the measure of his influence. Many harangue, but not so many attract a following. Yet Barnabas did not follow this Nazarene before his death."

"Barnabas believes that Jesus came forth from the tomb on the third day. Hundreds—thousands—witness that they saw him, in Galilee. These people believe that Jesus has ascended to heaven but will return any day, any hour, to set up a kingdom on the earth."

"If this is the teaching, Romans would have to take an interest in the cult. I would not want to see Barnabas become an enemy of Rome."

Elymas could hold his peace no longer. "It is an evil, blasphemous cult."

I could do nothing but sit there, red-faced, tongue-tied. This was what came of making myself a spokesman for a faith I could not share.

Amos burst out, "I know nothing of this faith, but I know Barnabas. He is reasonable. He is proud to call himself a Roman."

Sergius Paulus bent his intense, intelligent eyes upon me. "Well, Marcus?"

It is fortunate indeed that out of the void in that moment came a memory of the witnessing of so many years before. "It is not a subversive faith. It is concerned with righteousness, not with politics. When someone put a similar question to Jesus himself he took a denarius and asked his questioner who had struck off this coin, and the man answered, 'Caesar.' Then Jesus said, 'Render to Caesar what belongs to Caesar, and to God what belongs to God.' "

Elymas was sputtering again, but Sergius Paulus turned to him. "If this conversation troubles you, friend, return some other day. Marcus is my guest, and I have asked him to speak of this matter. I am already aware of your views." Turning back to me he inquired, "What does this cult call itself?"

"Followers. Believers. The Greek converts in Antioch have begun calling themselves Christians."

"For the Greek term for Messiah, the Christos. Ah, Marcus, you must not think that only Jews have prophecies of a Christos. Our gifted poet Virgil wrote of a golden age which would be ushered in by the birth of a child. I have been taught that the literature of even the most ancient peoples contains similar prophecies of a savior who will bring to men the supreme good they have failed to achieve for themselves."

"So my teacher told me."

"Your teacher? A rabbi?"

"A Greek. He is now a Christian. He preaches in Antioch. He has founded Greek ecclesias both on Cyprus and in Syria."

"My grandmother used to say that Messiah would come from Bethlehem. Nazareth seems an unlikely home town for the Christos."

"So I was taught." I was becoming increasingly uncomfortable. Amos was restive. He had come here to sell copper.

Sergius said, "And you, Marcus. Are you a Christian?"

From the shadow of the balcony a figure emerged, a slight girl whose bright hair was arranged in the masses of curls affected by Roman women, with scarlet ribbons threading in multiple strands amongst them. She wore a sleeveless linen tunica girded high under delicate breasts, and soft scarlet sandals with matching cords twined about her slender ankles. She had her father's eyes, but the high-bridged nose was all her own. There was something about the Jewish eyes in the midst of the Roman curls which sent waves of pure happiness surging through me. I could not take my eyes from the perfection of the lovely face, the rounded arms, the dancing lightness of her movements.

The governor beckoned the girl to him, and she stood beside him as he said "My daughter Malnor, who has probably been listening behind that curtain for some time." His face glowed with love for the girl. "This young man," he told her, "is Marcus bar Levi, heir to the House of Aaron and cousin to Barnabas. Amos you know, and Elymas is our old friend."

Malnor's voice was strangely deep for so slight a creature. "You did not answer my father's question, Marcus." Amusement danced in her dark eyes, and I realized that I had not stopped staring at her from the moment she appeared. Yet the sight of her filled me with a throbbing happiness. I could not tear my gaze from her face.

"What question was that?"

Amos stood. "We are wasting the proconsul's time. As you know, sir, we came to show you some copper wares. They are outside the portal with a young man who will bring them in and spread them here for your inspection whenever you like."

Malnor laughed. "You are too young, Marcus, to take Barnabas' place."

Amos said, "My lady, this is a young man, but he has served his apprenticeship in the shop. You will find him knowledgeable."

I was suddenly aware of my stained hands. They could not be hidden, not unless I copied Amos' manner of tucking them into my sleeves, so I extended them. "Kyros taught me to make charcoal and smelt ores before he let me go into the shop to mold and shape copper wares. I have much to learn. In fact, I made this journey in the hope of learning more about what people want."

Malnor's eyes were upon me with amusement and delight in my embarrassment. I could not go on. I could not find anything further to say.

Sergius Paulus glanced from Malnor's delighted face to my scarlet one. He said with a smile, "So you are not a Christian, Marcus."

I glanced from Sergius Paulus to Elymas, who was staring at me with hatred, his mouth working though no sound came. I was in an agony of embarrassment, for I could not witness against the faith of Barnabas and Mother and Agabus and Peter in the presence of this fanatic, this cast-off prophet from the Essenes, nor could I speak falsely of my own views about it.

Malnor said with a quick shift from amused raillery to sweet seriousness, "Father, you are embarrassing Marcus. You are too personal."

I looked at the proconsul, ashamed to appear childish. "I am torn between two opinions, sir. More than anything in the world, I long to be a Christian."

"I am sure it creates great difficulties to find yourself at odds with your mother and Barnabas." He rose. "I confess I am more eager to discuss this Nazarene than look at copper wares today. Amos, you are a busy man. If you will return tomorrow I will be ready then to discuss business. As for you, Elymas, your views are already formed. I will not discomfort you further by asking you to be silent during this discussion. Come another day. You are always welcome."

It was smoothly done. I breathed a sigh of relief as the bowed old servant showed those two out. I felt no hesitation about speaking freely to this Roman and his delightful and lovely daughter. In fact, I longed to do so. But it had been impossible with Amos so restless and Elymas so antagonistic.

The proconsul asked, "Did you ever see the Nazarene, Marcus?"

I told of the night in our orchard. As I spoke I was caught up in emotion. The happiness I felt in Malnor's presence was transmuted into pity for the lonely rabbi.

Malnor exclaimed, when the story was told, "But you were so young!"

"I was fourteen." Deeply mired in my emotions I could not say more.

Malnor asked, "Did Romans arrest him?"

"Jews. The Temple Guard."

Sergius Paulus cleared his throat. My story had moved him. "Pontius was never able to get at the root of the matter. As you must know, our former princeps Tiberius demanded a strict accounting from us who represent Rome. The surest path to oblivion for an official was to line his pockets at the people's expense or render injustice in the courts. Tiberius could overlook a judgment which was too liberal, but not one that was too harsh. This applied to all crimes but one. He had a terrible fear of plots against his person, and rightly so, considering that in the end he was murdered. We never dared be lenient when the accusation was conspiracy against the person of the princeps. This was the accusation your ruler, Annas, had brought against the Nazarene. Witnesses swore that he had preached sedition. The accused did not deny it, nor defend himself in any manner. This was the most puzzling aspect of the case."

"Jesus expected to die. For days he had been telling his followers how to conduct themselves after he was parted from them."

"People of many races have legends of a god who dies to bring good to men. This is part of the Messianic legend. If Jesus believed himself to be Messiah, he must have considered this sacrificial death to be his destiny."

I exclaimed, "He looked much like Barnabas, and his way of speaking also reminded me of Barnabas. I saw them bind him. The disciples, who would have defended him, panicked when they knew he would not resist. They had seen his mighty works. They expected him to call down legions of angels. They were utterly terrified. So was I."

Malnor said softly, "I wish I had seen him—a man willing to die for the sake of other men."

The words were torn from me. "He laid upon the Jews the guilt for his death. Messiah, when he comes, will redeem the Jews. God would not mock the chosen people by sending Messiah, only to lay upon them the guilt for his death."

Sergius' eyes held a burning intensity. "This argument smacks of the Pharisees. Now let us assume that Jesus was Messiah. God is One, as every Jew knows. God is One, as all intelligent men know. Yet God sent His son to the Jews—to the Jews, yet to all men, since He is God of all men. When the Holy One dies for love of all men, at whose hands should He die? Would you have God say, 'The Jews are chosen, a people apart. To them I send My son. But the Romans I detest. They shall bear the guilt for killing him.' Is it not enough, Marcus, that the hands of Romans drove in the spikes, that Romans lifted the cross with its precious burden and dropped it with a thud into the earth?"

All my views and values were tumbling about me in disorder. The question had to be put by a Roman, in the presence of this Roman girl with the Jewish eyes, for me to comprehend its full significance. Doubts may begin in the mind, but faith is born in emotion, and my emotions were already deeply stirred that morning.

"I must have known this all along," I said, and choked. "But I did not know I knew it until now. What Peter and Paul and Barnabas could not do, nor Agabus, nor my mother, you have done, sir. Messiah has come, even Jesus of Nazareth."

"I almost believe you," the proconsul replied.

And Malnor nodded, her face wet with tears, nodded and nodded but did not speak.

# III .... *Jerusalem*

# CHAPTER *14*

I returned across Cyprus in a tangle of shifting moods. How pleased Mother would be to learn that I was ready at last for baptism! I must send a letter telling the good news. Better still, I should go home to her and be baptized in her presence. But I couldn't! I had had a gratifying business trip. I had disposed of the wares I carried west, and had collected a sheaf of orders, including a large one from Sergius Paulus.

"I govern a copper island, named for the ore its mountains abundantly yield," he had said. "To my eyes bronze is handsomer than gold. Why should I spend my people's tax money on golden accouterments when bronze is stronger and more durable?"

His order included many things for Malnor—ornaments for her sandals, boxes for her treasures, fibulae to pin her palla at the shoulder, metal clasps (she called them knots of Hercules) to fasten the girdle which confined her tunica about her little waist. I longed to supervise each of these in the making, perhaps even make some of them with my own hands. When they were ready I would take them immediately to Paphos.

The underlying echo throughout the journey was Malnor, Malnor, Malnor. How reverently would I touch each buckle and box destined for her use! Malnor, Malnor, how can I feel what I feel when you are Roman and I a Levite of the Jews?

I veered between delight and anguish as I followed the Cyprus roads at donkey pace or ran ahead to stretch my legs. When I slept I dreamed of the dainty little creature who had twice been unexpectedly yielding and soft within my embrace, though usually so elusive and tormenting.

"You are funny," she had giggled, the last afternoon I spent with her. "Marcus, why do you look at me this way?"

"I am happy when I look at you." I longed to explain that for me her piquant, lovely face had made all the peoples of the earth the children of God. I ached to pour out in words all my churning emotions. But how could I? For I was a Jew and she the daughter of our Roman governor.

She had taken my face between her little hands. "I also am happy when I look at you, Marcus. Mark." She savored the Hebrew form of my name, then rose on tiptoe and lifted her face. Before I could reflect on my folly, I was kissing her.

When I let her go she gave my beard a fierce tug. "You look so foolish with all that hair upon your face. My Roman husband will shave his face each morning. There will be no ridiculous whiskers to tickle me." She rubbed her cheek against my beard, then, giggling, dodged out of my arms and sped out of the atrium into the peristyle. I caught her in the midst of the blooming shrubs near the arching roof which sheltered the family lares and penates from the rain. What might have happened next I do not know, for I was aflame in all my senses. But Elymas bar Joshua appeared at the doorway.

"Quite the Roman," he said mockingly. "Playing games with the governor's daughter! You must know this girl is destined for the bed of some sycophant of Caligula."

Nothing could have jerked me more brutally back to reality. Even in the provinces we had heard of the dissolute youths who surrounded Caligula. I had to get away. I must find a place where I could recover my senses and subdue my flaming emotions. I rushed into the atrium, wild with frustration and pain. Malnor was not for me!

She followed, her bright amusement quenched. She greeted Elymas with a womanly dignity and directed him to the stable, where her father was examining an ailing horse. When he was gone she stood before me. "Why did you run? He has nothing to do with us. I would never hurt you, Marcus. And you would never hurt me."

I seized her shoulders. "You must never marry into the Roman court."

"Of course, Marcus. My father will never take me to Rome again, if he can avoid it. When first these stories about Caligula began to reach us, he said he would never go to Rome while Caligula ruled."

I would never, never hold her again. I stood near her, within touching distance, gripped by the pain of renunciation.

A change of mood swept her, one of the enchanting changes so typical of Malnor. Tweaking my ear she said in a smother of giggles, "Maybe I will not marry a Roman. Maybe I will marry a whiskery Jew. Like you, Marcus, but with a bigger beard."

I stepped away from the teasing hands. "I must return to Salamis tomorrow," I said stiffly. "When we have got together all this plunder you require I will—I will personally bring it." The prospect eased my pain a little. "See that you behave yourself till I return." I marveled at the control I had mustered to take a light tone on the concluding line.

The bright face clouded. "Oh Marcus, I'll miss you." The tender, Jewish eyes searched my face. Suddenly she turned and ran from the atrium. Her hands covered her face as she vanished under the gallery.

That night I dreamed that Malnor was in Rome. I pursued her about the atrium and across the peristyle. When I caught her she turned her laughing face to me but it was a painted face, a wanton face, the face of a girl degraded. I wakened in a sweat of horror and did not sleep again. A score of times before dawn I was ready to curse Elymas to his face for the torturing images he had planted in my mind.

When morning dawned I went with Amos to the thermae; then, in my best scarlet coat, went to bid the proconsul farewell.

He shook my hand in parting. "Tell Barnabas I want to hear more about this Nazarene for whose sake he has forsaken the copper trade."

"I will tell him, sir." I left the palace and the city without another glimpse of the girl who would thereafter haunt my waking thoughts and my nighttime dreams.

On the homeward journey I was torn between duty to Mother and my wild longing to return quickly to Paphos. When I reached Salamis I learned that the choice was not mine to make. Phoebe conveyed her anxious message. Barnabas had been there soon after I set out for Paphos. He had left a letter:

"Greetings, dear Mark. Miriam is quite ill and yearns for the sight of you. I will see you at Olivet before Passover. Meanwhile, I have urgent business with Paul in Antioch. I hope you got on well with Sergius Paulus. He is the best Roman I know."

I read the letter to Phoebe. "Mother can't be very ill," I said, to comfort Phoebe and perhaps myself also, "or Barnabas would have said more about her and less about other things."

The truth was I had been hearing that Mother was ill for a long time now, and had not taken the reports seriously, having convinced myself the illness was merely a sort of listless longing for the return of the Lord Jesus.

I turned over the orders to Kyros, gave him so many verbal instructions concerning those for the governor and his daughter that he ceased to listen. Then, with Ken, I took ship for Caesarea.

Ken had never been off Cyprus. He was goggle-eyed when the low shore of the maritime plain came into view. The westering sun shone on the glowing marble and formidable towers of Caesarea, and on the endless reach of the double-arched viaduct which wound all the way north to Mount Carmel to bring its fresh springwater down to the sand-girt, seaport city.

The Jerusalem road wound south through the Sharon Plain to intersect the ancient road from Joppa harbor and thence up through crowding hills to the heights upon which Jerusalem had been built so many centuries ago. We walked swiftly, I setting the pace, Ken panting from his efforts to miss no sight and yet keep up with me, discussing and exclaiming and questioning. As we drew on toward Jerusalem he chattered ever more about his eagerness to meet other men who, like Andrew, had known the Christos in his lifetime.

For me the sense of homecoming begins when I reach the hilltop from which the Temple's gleaming dome bursts upon the view. We crossed the city, jostled by pre-Passover pilgrims. We left by Damascus Gate. Beyond the Kidron, amongst the trees, was the familiar granite shape of home. When we turned onto the Bethany road which skirts the mountain I began to run.

The camel gate was bolted, and so was the narrow door beside it. "We'll surprise them," I said. "Come. I'll show you the way."

I dashed round to where the vine rose to the parapet and began to climb. And the intervening years dropped away as I set my feet upon the familiar knots and bulges. I was over the parapet, and it was as if I had never been away.

Not a soul was in sight, either on the roof or in the court. Almost I shouted the old greeting, "Mother! I'm here!" But the silence slowly quenched my joy. I had left this house overrun with scores of believers. The emptiness and the silence chilled me. I looked down into the deserted court, expecting Damaris to materialize beside the dying fire, nibbling at a fig. An empty pot stood on the pavement near the stove. The pitcher at the cistern had been overturned. Even Ken was silent beside me. From somewhere came a low sob.

I moved slowly down the stairway. A tall young woman emerged from the corridor which led to my mother's quarters. She brushed both hands over her face, a distracted, helpless gesture. Rhoda! She was almost as tall as I. Her soft tunic of yellow linen had once been mine.

I called her name as I ran down the steps. She flew to me, relief and grief struggling in a face grown strangely mature yet somehow, strangely, the same. She threw her arms about my neck. "Oh Mark, she is so sick! Everyone says, 'Do this! Do that!' but they disagree and I don't know what to do. Praise God you have come."

She kissed me. I felt the wet tears against my cheek. "Mother may not even know you, Mark. She is next door to death. The physician—I don't trust him, but nobody else will come, and so I don't dare send him away. I just don't know what to do. She is so terribly sick."

There was comfort in holding her close while the terrible news slowly took on shape and meaning. The strong, lean body and big, bony hands were dear because of the reminder that she had shared all Mother's labors of those years when our house was a hostel for believers. She's very young, surely not yet sixteen, I reminded myself. Probably she is hysterical. If Mother were as sick as all that Barnabas would not have gone to Antioch to see Paul. He would never have come even to

Salamis. Poor little gamin, she had grown up so fast. I would get the straight of it from the physician, or from my own observations. After all, I had some knowledge of medicine.

I said kindly, "You have carried too much responsibility, dear sister. Now take me to Mother."

The dark eyes were almost on a level with mine as she drew back to look at me. "I'm not your sister, Mark." The full lips tightened in a strangely unchildish way.

"No sister could be kinder. Or dearer."

Her searching glance shifted. "Come," she said.

I followed her to the bedroom I had shared with Mother until my seventh year. Ken was busy at the fire. He was a good servant, and would do what needed doing.

Mother's room was crowded with apathetic, weary, tear-stained women. The air was stale. Beyond the bed sat a corpulent figure wrapped in a dirty coat, his dirty hands busy at Mother's thin, extended arm. I went cold with horror at sight of the sluggish ooze of precious fluid from the gash above her wrist. That face could not be Mother's! That inert, emaciated body, the hollow cheeks, the lifeless, white-streaked hair, the dry and pallid flesh could not belong to my lovely, blooming mother! Ah, she was even nearer to death than Rhoda realized.

I shouted, "Close that wound, sir. Bleed her no more."

The fat face jerked. The dirty coat dragged at the dish, spilling blood. But he left the wound to continue oozing the pale, precious fluid onto the floor. Now I recognized him as a brickmaker who had sold his tools and given the money into the common fund during the ecclesia's first summer.

I leaned across to press my thumb upon the vein below the cut. Mother's flesh was dry and hot. I exclaimed, "When was bleeding ever a cure for exhaustion?" All about the bed the

women were murmuring, agitated, some horrified, others relieved that I was here.

The man exclaimed petulantly, "Take your hands from my
patient, sir! I am the attending physician. You have no authority here." He pulled at my hand to loose my grip on
Mother's wrist. She moaned, turning her head from side to
side.

"Brickmaker," I shouted. "Ignoramus! You have probably
killed my mother."

He rose hastily. His bluster changed to a whine. "Then you
are Mark. Well, we will close the wound, for now, and leave
the lady Miriam to the care of these good women. Come. I will
explain the disease to you, and the treatment. And you will
pay me the three silver sheckels which are owing."

Rhoda touched his shoulder. "Please go, Ben Eli. Mother
must be quiet. We can speak of all these differences later."

Martha of Bethany moved in beside Mother and began to
bind up the wrist. I had known her for a competent woman,
and at her touch Mother grew still again. Ben Eli came round
the bed. He plucked nervously at my sleeve. His eyes reminded me of the eyes of children I had seen who had been
trained to beg in the streets. "So Mark is home, after many
years. Ah, my young friend, we have sought by every possible
means to restore our sister, yet God has not seen fit to reward
our labors. The best Greek physicians bleed the sick, and
when all the Levite remedies had failed I sought this desperate
means—"

"The worst Greek physicians bleed for epileptic seizures." I
tried in vain to keep my voice low. "The best Greek physicians
bleed nobody. Look at those arms—look at the cuts, unhealed,
putrifying, yet you have gone on butchering, hacking. If you
ever lay your filthy hands on Mother again you will be publicly beaten, by me. Get out of my sight!"

He scuttled away, leaving on the floor his bloody knife, to which clung the scum from previous usage, leaving also a filthy bundle of indescribable junk, fish scales, lizard skins, and I know not what else. I gathered it up and carried it out to Ken to be burned.

The women were quieter when I returned. Rhoda knelt beside Mother's bed, weeping. "Physicians would not come. Ben Eli was one of us, a believer, a Levite. I did not know what to do, Mark. I did not know which way to turn."

Martha said briskly, "Don't cry, child. You did your best."

"That's right," I said. "Come, we'll take Mother to the roof where the air is cool and fresh. Damaris, prepare a gruel. We'll see whether we can get something into her to replace the blood she's lost." I turned to the women. "Come again tomorrow—or a few days hence, when Mother is better. Accept our thanks for all your love and care."

I carried Mother to the roof. She was so light a burden it broke my heart to lift her. I laid her on the bed Rhoda had rushed to make ready. I must waken her if I could. I must try to get some wine or other nourishment down her throat. I kissed her cheek, brushed back the sweated hair, touched her softly, speaking to her, begging her to open her eyes, yearning to see the old love alight in them.

Damaris brought wine. "Marcus, welcome home. Most welcome, lad. Do drink a little wine to strengthen you after your journey, and the trouble you found waiting in this house." Her kind old eyes were swimming in unshed tears.

I drank from the cup she brought, wiped my mouth and kissed Damaris' moist cheek. "Our own wine is best. It is always good to get back to the faces, the rooms, the wine we know and love. Now bring a spoon and let's see whether we can get Mother to swallow a bit of this good wine."

Damaris held the spoon to Mother's lips. I touched her throat, working my fingers downward. Damaris poured wine but it ran from the corner of the flaccid mouth. I crooned, "Mother, swallow. For your Mark, who is home again, swallow the wine. Please swallow." Then in desperation, "Lord Jesus, help her. Just a little, small miracle. Just to swallow a little wine."

The thin throat contracted. Mother swallowed three spoonfuls of the wine. Her eyes opened. Her hand moved weakly. "You're here." A tear slid from the corner of her eye. "I dreamed—but it's no dream." The words came blurred, as the sight of her thin, pallid face was now blurred for me.

"Swallow, Mother. We'll talk when you are stronger."

She swallowed several spoonfuls. "How beautiful is my son." Again her hand moved. I laid my face against it, overwhelmed. Mother drank half a cup of wine before she drifted into sleep with my hand holding hers. When I looked up again I saw that Rhoda knelt at the opposite side of the bed. Her face was radiant.

All that night Mother slept while I watched beside her. One wick only burned in the small bronze lamp. Twice Mother wakened to swallow broth Ken brought from the fire he kept burning. In the corner of the room Damaris slept deeply. Rhoda slept on a mat beyond Mother's bed. How many nights, I wondered, had those two kept their vigil?

About dawn Mother's eyes opened. Her hand groped for mine. "Do not grieve, dear Mark, when I am gone. I will be in Jesus' kingdom. Do not sorrow for me."

How clear it was—the years of exhaustion and labor, the longing to find rest in the promised kingdom, a longing doomed day by day to disappointment. Could I call her back to life?

"Mother, you must wait to enter the heavenly kingdom. You must wait at least until you see your son baptized."

She smiled tenderly. "I know. I heard you pray. It seemed a dream, when you called upon the Lord Jesus. But I knew I must swallow, and somehow it was not at all difficult. Why did you ask for only a little miracle? Great or small are the same with the Lord Jesus."

Rhoda sat up suddenly, sparing me the need to find an answer. "Mother! Oh Mother, I thought I had killed you, bringing that awful man, letting him deceive me with his prattle about the lore of the Levites and the lore of Greeks and Egyptians. I am so ashamed."

"My two children." Mother took Rhoda's big, rawboned hand and laid it in mine. "Take care of one another, when I am gone. Rhoda loves you, Mark. Very much."

Rhoda's face was scarlet in the dawn light. I said quickly, "Rhoda is a dear girl, a dear sister, and we will take care of one another. But we will both take care of you. Don't leave us, Mother. Please don't leave us."

"I will wait, if I can, to see you married."

Rhoda's dark eyes met mine steadfastly. "Her heart has been set upon it for years."

"And yours, Rhoda? Is your heart set upon it?"

"Only if it—pleases you, Mark—to want me." The touching truth was in the quiver of the full lips. Rhoda's mouth and eyes, I realized suddenly, were very handsome. A memory of the little ragamuffin she had been flashed in my mind and was gone. Rhoda had changed indeed. In some men's eyes she would have seemed really attractive. I loosened my hold on the work-roughened hands.

Mother's eyes were closed. "My two children. You will cherish her, Mark. You cannot do otherwise. She is the dearest girl in the world."

"I have never deserved the love squandered upon me." I stumbled from the room. I stood at the parapet looking off over the shimmering, silvery green of the olive trees toward the clearing. There Jesus had prayed, "Let this cup pass from me." The rising sun slanted across the trees and I felt myself a Judas as the name Malnor, Malnor, Malnor vibrated within me, as the dancing vision of a delicate figure in high-girdled linen tunica with ribbons threading the bright curls sent shafts of longing through all my senses. Malnor was the girl I would have chosen in my folly. Mother was wiser. So my mind argued, while all my senses yearned for the delightful little creature so unlike Rhoda in every particular.

A scrape of sandals, the swish of a skirt, and Rhoda was with me. Her eyes searched my face, and she moved a step away. "Mother sleeps so peacefully. For the first time I believe she may recover. Without you—I do not think she would have lived through the night, Mark." The dark eyes met mine, holding self-containment and reserve.

Desperately wanting to do what was right I took one of the hands—so unlike Malnor's soft little hands. I smiled. "The first time I saw you, you stood just where you are now."

"The years have changed me. I used to feel ashamed of what I had been, what my parents had been, how we must have looked to you, Mark. But Mother healed me of shame. I could never have loved the poor, the outcast, the forlorn—yes, even the self-seeking deceivers of the world—had I not once been such as they are. Jesus loved and pitied them. For his sake Mother loved and pitied me. Mark, how will I bear it if she dies?"

"She will not die. The Lord Jesus touched her, last night. I prayed—my first real prayer to the Lord Jesus—and in that moment her healing began. Rhoda." I moved closer, put my arm about her. "I am a metal worker now. My business is in Salamis. Are you willing to live in Salamis?"

The steadfast eyes did not waver. "Where my husband is content, I will be content. But it sticks in my mind that you should marry a wife who can bring you a dowry. Your inheritance here has been scattered, as the wind of persecution scattered those who formerly frequented this house."

"My mother chose you, Rhoda. I am content with her choice." I detested myself that I could find nothing warmer or kinder to say.

Her eyes searched my face. "Are you indeed content?" She drew away. "Come. We will see whether Mother is awake."

We found her avidly drinking goat's milk from a cup held by Damaris.

# CHAPTER *15*

The news that Mother was mending spread through Bethany. Before midday callers began arriving, singly, in threes, in clusters. I wanted to shout at the good creatures, "Go away! Give Mother time to gain strength."

I was not obliged, however, to deal with them. Rhoda was gracious without relaxing the firm position that Mother must not be disturbed. I watched from the parapet while this tall young girl quietly kept the tide of callers under control.

"Dear Martha, thank you for the broth. Mother will enjoy it as soon as she wakens . . . Matilda, Mother will be glad to know you came. We must see that she sleeps a great deal these next few days. Soon she will be right here in this court, having a lovely visit with you—with all of you . . . Yes it is a miracle. The Lord Jesus surely laid his healing hand upon her. Do pray for her when you are at home again."

She touched one and another with warmth and affection. I turned from the parapet. These good creatures were Mother's friends. She loved them. Yet the reminder that these women had had free access throughout her illness angered me.

Before I escaped to the orchard I went to look at Mother, who had slept soundly all morning. Her flesh was tinged faintly with returning color. The serenity of her sleeping face restored to me the happiness which the bustle of visiting women had disrupted.

Damaris sat nearby, contentedly nibbling a fruity concoction. I broke off a wedge of the sticky stuff and found it delicious. "You did not weep over me when I came home, Damaris. I have stayed away too long, and you forgot to greet me properly."

With my help she got onto her feet. We went to stand where the roof overlooked the orchard. "God be praised you came in time, Marcus. The Lord Jesus surely touched my lady Miriam, but not until after her son lifted her in his young, strong arms, and carried her away from those who molested her."

"I am at fault for this illness. I stayed away too long."

"A man must be about the family business—what remains of it—or how will hangers-on survive, and who will feed useless old servants who clutter the house?" Her little eyes within the fat folds of flesh held their old twinkle.

"Bless you, Damaris." I kissed the moist cheek. "Now I am going up to the orchard. Send Ken if I am needed."

"That orchard! You will find it in shameful condition. An orchard can die of abuse and neglect." Damaris looked darkly toward the court, whence came the muted chatter of Mother's visiting friends. "Listen to that Martha! She is called a good woman. But I could not tell you how many times she sat beside the lady Miriam, pouring out complaints against her sister Mary and her brother Lazarus, when my lady was too ill to listen to the quarrels of her friends. And nobody to send her away! For how can an elderly Greek housekeeper or a young daughter cope with such as Martha?"

"Rhoda is coping today. She is doing an excellent job."

"I will tell her you have said so. She knows she must answer to you if she falls short. A man in the house gives assurance and courage. Yet she is a good girl, Marcus. She will bring joy to her husband." The bright eyes probed my face as sharply as when I was a lad.

"I do not doubt that." I swung over the parapet where the vine clung. The touch of the rough bark and the creak of the swaying stem brought back a night when I climbed in panic after watching the arrest of the Lord Jesus. Ah, it was a comfort to know at last that his submission that night had been right, and wise, and courageous. Perhaps, if I went to the clearing and prayed beside the alter where Jesus had prayed, I would come into possession of the kind of grace and joy and peace which others had found.

I believed in him! I had seen the change which faith in him had wrought in so many others. Yet no change had been wrought in me. What good is faith if grace does not come with it? Would I never know the joy of my own Pentecost? Would I never sluff off the contempt I felt toward the hordes who had infested our house? Would I never be rid of the disturbing vestige of contempt which I felt toward Rhoda? Would I ever feel for Rhoda—this was the crux of the matter—what a man ought to feel for the girl his mother has chosen for him?

As I moved toward the trees the teasing, mischievous face of Malnor rose before me. I longed to hold her, to conquer her veering humors and make her truly mine. This was what a man ought to feel for the bride he was to take. You get a poor bargain in me, Rhoda, I thought. And then, I also am cheated of the joy a bridegroom has a right to expect.

As I approached the edge of the clearing Ken came racing, calling, "Marcus! Wait!"

I paused, one hand grasping the dead branch of a gnarled old tree, a branch which ought to have been pruned away.

"That physician is in the court. He takes credit for the lady's healing. The lady Rhoda says—"

"Send him to me here. Hurry! Get him out of the house!"

Had that charlatan disturbed Mother's rest? At the least she would be embarrassed to learn that his fees had been argued in the presence of her friends. My fists knotted with the impulse I felt to speak to Ben Eli in a language he could not twist to serve his paltry vanity. Then he appeared, a corpulent, dirty old man. He rushed across the clearing. His beard bobbed joyfully.

"Praise be to God for His gracious goodness to the lady Miriam and to all of her household! I am humbly thankful for the part I had in this wonderous cure. Surely God uses the physician in working His inscrutable will."

I strode into the orchard, ashamed that this wretch had been baptized into the fellowship of believers, had shared the common tables denied to Agabus and Damaris. This creature was one of hundreds who had devoured Mother's strength with my inheritance these years. I rushed up-slope among the twisted trees, and Ben Eli panted after me, babbling.

"The question of my fee remains, my boy, and also there is a packet of potions and tinctures I left behind in the haste of departure."

He chuckled. "You were difficult, Mark. You were remiss in the courtesy due a physician, a man of learning. I had given laborious hours to a lady whose son remained away for five long years. Alone she was, with neither husband nor son, but only the young girl Rhoda and a housekeeper who is Greek. Her loneliness touched my heart! Only God took note of my labors on her behalf.

"Yet the softness of my heart is my undoing, for I do not ask gold, as a physician should after so notable a cure, especially in a house of wealth. Three silver sheckels, this is my paltry

fee, which will never be missed in the abundance of such a
household. Three silver sheckels, and the restoration of my
little packet of remedies."

I swerved to evade his touch as I turned upon him. "You are
a Levite. You know such filthy rubbish brings only harm to a
patient. The poisons you call your potions and tinctures were
burned, with all the other filth of the sickroom."

With a screech of rage he rushed at me. A broken branch
tangled in his gray, greasy locks. "Look at this orchard," he
shouted as he struggled to free himself. "A man born to possessions is their steward. A man who neglects his inheritance
will naturally neglect his mother also."

Now at last I looked about me. The dead and dying branches
of these old trees had not been pruned away in years. In
consequence the new branches which come on to keep a tree
bearing fruit for generations were spindling, tangled in dead
or dying limbs. Tares had sprung up about the roots, robbing
the trees of nourishment and killing the new shoots old trees
send up before they die to make an orchard eternal. Broken
branches testified that gleaners had been overzealous to reach
fruit left by the beating poles of the harvesters.

"Neglect is wicked! Waste is wicked!" Ben Eli was sobbing.
"Had I been born to property, how I would have cherished
every tree, every vine, each inch of precious soil."

He had finally worked free of the branch. He rubbed his
head, rearranged the soiled headcloth, then turned to examine
the branch as if it had been a man's broken arm. "What
waste," he mourned. "What wicked waste."

He turned upon me a face in which anger mingled with
anguish. "Nobody will call Ben Eli to heal the sick since I
have been thrust hence from the house of Miriam. I am not
like those who, having sold their goods to give to the common
fund, turned to beggary when the common meals ceased and

the hospitable houses closed their doors and the common fund vanished with the fleeing apostles. I was never blessed with property, but I sold the tools of my former trade. I gave the price to our leaders. It was all I owned. Now I have not even the respect of the Bethany believers. My remedies you destroyed, a wanton waste by a man who makes a practice of waste yet refuses to pay his honest debts. There is a curse upon me. Those God has blessed with possessions have no compassion."

He made a pitiful spectacle. I rushed away, climbing toward the clearing which had been my goal from the moment I left the house. Ben Eli panted after me, muttering accusations all the way.

The clearing was littered with broken branches and tares. Trees had split their ancient trunks, and nobody had cleared away the rottenness to save the wholesome wood on which these ancient olive trees can survive for decades. Vines had sprung up, a further burden to the neglected trees. The altar stone was buried under vines. The oil press had not been cleansed last fall after harvest ended.

I could not blame anyone. This land was never Barnabas' responsibility; Mother and Rhoda had their hands full. There should have been a steward of the farm, but in a community where the ideal is a lily of the field and treasures on earth are suspect, who could be held responsible for the lands my father had left to me?

I crossed to the stone and pulled away the vines, tearing their roots from the earth. Five years had passed since Jesus knelt here on a spring night. I had meant to kneel here myself, to pray the Lord Jesus' prayer in this place. But I could not, with that detestable old man prowling the clearing, muttering accusations.

The midday sun beat down. I thought of moonlight on a lifted face, and love for the Lord Jesus swept through me.

Love one another, he said, as I have loved you. Inasmuch as you show mercy to the least of men, you show mercy to me. I bent and laid my hands where his tears had wet this stone. Inasmuch as you despise the least of men, you despise and humiliate me.

From somewhere Ben Eli had got hold of a knife. He was digging out rottenness from the split trunk of the tree under which Peter and James and John had slept while Jesus prayed. I went over and gathered the rotten stuff in my hands to add to the pile I had prepared for burning.

"They seized and bound him in this clearing," Ben Eli said. "What a disgrace, that this holy spot should have fallen into ruin. What want of feeling it shows!"

As if the stone itself spoke to me came the challenge. This is not a beast. This is a man. Talk to him as a man. I exclaimed, "Jesus had no respect for fakes, for charlatans, deceivers, hypocrites!"

Ben Eli shouted, "The Lord Jesus dined with publicans. He was a friend of sinners. With bankers and rulers he had no patience, for unto them much had been given and they abused their privileges. With the poor he showed compassion."

From the altar came the voice of my conscience, Love one another.

I turned from Ben Eli, girded my skirts, and began pulling up vines and tares to add to the bonfire. I could not love that man. Yet something drove me to make the effort, to talk to him. Men talked even to their donkeys and their sheep. I could make the attempt.

"I will send Ken with fire to burn what we gather. I appreciate your help, Ben Eli."

He grunted and fell to sawing with his knife at a dead branch.

I said, "I was here, that night. I was a lad, only fourteen."

Seeing the sharpening of his glance I asked, "Were you in Jerusalem when they crucified Jesus?"

His face twisted as if with some terrible memory, but he answered, "I was in Jericho." He turned his back to me. "Pentecost—that was the time. I heard Peter preach in Damascus Gate. I went down with hundreds of others to be baptized in the spillway below the Gihon Reservoir."

I said, "Many of the seventy who had followed the Lord to Jerusalem were in our house. I had heard Salome and Mary declare that Jesus would set up a kingdom with Bethany as headquarters before the Passover season ended. That night I lay awake on the roof, and heard their voices in the orchard. I came to listen, for I thought they were plotting how to overthrow Rome with legions of angels. Jesus was here, kneeling at this stone, praying. Peter and James and John were asleep under that tree where you stand. I stood in the shadow of that hollow tree yonder with the three trunks twisted together and listened while the Lord Jesus prayed for the disciples. He knew they expected only glory, and he knew what would happen—his death, and all that went before it. I was intruding but I could not go. Jesus said to the three sleepers, 'Could you not watch with me?' When they did not waken, he said, 'Sleep then, for you need your rest.'

"I wanted so much to say, 'Let me watch with you, Rabbi.' But I dared not. Then Judas came and saluted him and kissed him. Soldiers rushed in and bound Jesus, and everyone woke up and—and then they fled, and I also fled. I saw it all, and I felt their terror."

I choked on the memory. Ben Eli stood with his face bowed against the great, gnarled trunk of the split olive tree.

I said, "When I reached home they were in our court. Salome insisted that Jesus would call down legions of angels when he was in the midst of the Sanhedrin. So they all took heart, and went to attend the hearings. But I knew Jesus would not save himself. I knew he would die." I paused again, swallowed, and said, "I saw nothing more. My mother would not let me leave home. She was afraid there would be rioting."

"She did well not to let you see that sight."

Which sight he referred to was not clear. His manner more than his words should have informed me as to the state of his mind, but I was absorbed in my own vivid memories.

"Because I saw the agony of Jesus here in this clearing, and knew he was powerless to save himself or avert what he dreaded, I could not believe it when the disciples declared he was risen, and was indeed Messiah. I was at odds with Mother and Barnabas and went to Cyprus rather than remain among those dear to me. When my doubts finally vanished, when I could honestly believe that Jesus is—Messiah—" The words came hard, even now. "When that time came I returned to my mother. Yet now I know it is not enough to say, 'Jesus is Lord.' For honest faith should change a man, and I am as—self-righteous and as pig-headed as ever I was. I long to experience my own Pentecost, but I cannot change myself."

Ben Eli's heavy breathing finally drew my attention from my own preoccupations. His face was dark above the scraggly beard. His mouth snarled within the white locks. "That Judas! What an evil fellow! Yet he was daily with the Lord for years. What I would not give for such a privilege as was given him! As for the others, we yield them veneration and obedience, though they were cowards of the worst stripe when the Lord Jesus needed them most. That must have been the loneliest hour of his life, and they took their ease within sound of his voice and ignored his plea for the comfort of their love."

He kicked the earth beneath the tree. "Here he lay, that James, snoring. From this clearing he fled in terror. Yet he sits in judgment upon us. He tells us to abstain from this and give him that and do thus and so, and we obey as if he were an angel of light."

Something unimaginable was at the root of the twisted nature of this man. He could not bear, I thought, to look into his own heart for fear of what he would find. I said, "When you sold the tools of your trade as brickmaker, to whom did you give the money?"

"To James. To the righteous and saintly James." He hitched up his coat and fell to hacking savagely at the heavy branch which he had earlier set about pruning away. "Do you think he thanked me? He rebuked me! He ordered me to redeem my tools and work at my trade and bring him my wages. I, a new convert, thirsting to sit amongst believers and learn of the healing love of the risen Lord. Why should I work while others sat together talking of those things? The apostles had left their farms and their boats to be with the Lord. Jesus himself left his carpenter's bench to walk the hills of this land and teach and heal the people. 'Lay up treasures in heaven,' he said. But James wanted me to spend my days toiling for his enrichment. I lack strength for the brickmaker's trade. It is heavy work, doubly heavy for me since I am afflicted with obesity. But what would a soft and elegant youth like yourself know of heavy work? So I gave my all—little enough, but all God had seen fit to bless me with. For James it was not enough. For this gift I gave he rebuked me."

I was strangling on my rage. "For such as you my mother wore herself down till she lay at death's door. But you were not content. Pretending a knowledge you do not possess, you laid your filthy hands upon her and bled away the little strength left in her. I will never let it be said that I acknowledge your standing as a physician—or as a Christian! If you were honest you would confess your ignorance to those you have deceived. Be glad you were not here that Passover of Jesus' crucifixion. Had you been here you would surely have taken from Annas the copper farthing he offered those who shouted in the court of judgment, 'Away with him! Give us Barabbas! Crucify Jesus!' "

The face he turned upon me then was so terrible I backed well out of reach.

He shrieked, "What do you know about men born with no heritage? Keep your paltry sheckles, since they are all-important to you." He jerked at the dead branch at which he had been hacking, and it broke, and he fell to the ground but I did not go near to offer him a hand up. He scrambled somehow to his feet. He looked about wildly, but slowly the change came over him, as he looked at trees all but ruined by neglect. He said softly, "I would give half the few remaining years of my life to have for one year the stewardship of this orchard, to return to fruitfulness this neglected place of holy associations."

Without waiting for me to reply he moved out of sight amongst the trees. I heard him hacking, heard a branch crack off.

I was halfway to the house before my disgust with him had drained away. The sense made by Ben Eli's suggestion was debatable. He probably knows as much about trees as about medicine, I reflected. Yet a persistent wish to do right nagged at me. What could I lose by giving him an opportunity to redeem himself? I could think of nobody else to leave in charge of the orchard. If I gave my goods to the poor—this orchard, at least, for a single year—Ben Eli was poor enough—about the poorest specimen I had ever encountered—poor by every definition of the word . . .

Still I walked on. Whatever decision I reached, it would not be reached in haste.

I came in sight of the house. Rhoda stood at the parapet,

one hand shading her eyes from the midday sun. She called, "Mark! James is here, and Mother is awake, and is asking for you."

I shrugged off the impulse I'd had to turn back to Ben Eli with my crack-brained offer. No matter what Jesus had said about giving your property to the poor, there could be no virtue in a gift given in contempt.

# CHAPTER *16*

James sat beside Mother's bed, a plump, comfortable man with a weathered face and gentle eyes. One lid drooped, adding a humorous touch to the round, homely face. The beard was short, grizzled, round as the face. James looked to be two score years of age, though I knew he was younger than he appeared. His handshake was warm and firm. It was testimony to his judgment and influence that the women had vanished. The court was quiet and Mother, fully awake now, was rested and content.

Mother said, "I hope you have paid Ben Eli his fee, Mark."

"I have not. He did his best to kill you, and would have, had I arrived a day later."

"He did his best. We cannot know whether he helped me. I would not want to add to his troubles by humiliating him."

"Nor would I." I sat beside her, wishing that goodness of heart came to me as readily as to her. "But I cannot support his pretensions. He is a quack and a charlatan."

James said, "So you leave him stranded in this small and intimate community, with no way to save his dignity."

"Does he deserve to save his dignity?"

"He has helped more people than he has hurt, my son."

I said in wonder, "He calls you his enemy, James."

"He is his own enemy. That is trouble enough for any man."

I exclaimed, "How could you baptize such a man and admit him to the common tables and refuse Agabus and Damaris?" James, more than anyone else, had been responsible for the division between Hellenists and Hebrews in the community of believers. He was responsible for the long struggle to lay the burden of Judaism and the law upon Greek converts. James had never been contentious, but there was a rockbound firmness in his character which would not yield.

He said, "When a Jew casts aside the precious heritage, the law, he shows himself thankless. God chose the children of Abraham. The law makes us Jews and keeps us Jews. I cannot cast this gift back into the teeth of God. The law is our strength, our covenant, our seal."

Rhoda entered while he was speaking. She carried a steaming bowl. "Your second breakfast, Mother. This is broth Martha brought."

She settled herself to feed Mother and said to James, "Jesus said he came to fulfill the law. What did he mean?"

"He was a Jew, and we are Jews, and we must all fulfill the law in every respect. We who have taught in Jesus' name since he was parted from us must be especially careful in this regard. We who knew him must not wander from the road along which he led us, since it was our special privilege to walk beside him and hear his teaching with our own ears."

I said, "If we had Agabus' book we could be sure we knew exactly what he said."

"It sticks in my craw that a Greek wrote the book." James rose to look off toward Gethsemane, as if that spot could speak of Jesus to him. "Your point is well made, Mark. Our memories are less accurate than records written on paper. Yet who could have believed our Lord would tarry so long that we would need written records to verify what he said to us?"

He turned back to sit with us. "Tell me about Agabus. You know him better than most men do."

I spoke of our voyage to Cyprus, of how Agabus tramped the deck of the little freighter muttering in Aramaic, of how sailors listened. "Before we reached Salamis he had taught the Lord's Prayer to many."

The drooping eyelid rested on the weathered cheek. "Let a Greek teach Greeks. This I can accept, since the Lord Jesus commanded us, 'Teach all peoples.' I would have liked to join my voice with the voices of those Greeks when they prayed the prayer our Lord taught us."

I told how we called the Greeks together in Salamis, of how the ecclesia began and how it flourished. But when I spoke of Andrew's visit, and of how he had baptized Agabus, James paced about the roof, hands knotted in agitation.

I said, "Andrew had heard in Caesarea that Philip baptized an Ethiopian. And Agabus longed for baptism."

"The Hellenists have their own views. Philip is Hellenist, but Andrew—I dread what we may become as we move farther from the years when the Lord was here among us. We are fallible men, but Andrew was of my temperament as none of the others were. I trusted in Andrew to hold fast our basic doctrines."

I asked curiously, "How did so careful and conservative a man as you find himself able to leave family and living and go among the zealots and adventuresome types who followed when Jesus said to them, 'Come, follow me? Had you no sleepless nights of wondering whether you had been rash?"

James's homely face was sober. "Second thoughts I had, and often. I justified the folly—the seeming folly—with the excuse that I must look out for my young brother John. Yet the true reason is very simple. I loved the Lord Jesus."

"Andrew gave the same explanation. So did Peter." It was not the first time I had wished with all my soul that I had paid more attention during those last few days when Jesus was living.

Mother said, "We all loved him. Forgive me, my dear children, for the wish I have so long kept in my heart to leave this earthly home to dwell in the kingdom where Jesus new dwells. I was selfish. Worse, I was foolish. The wish is gone now. I am content to wait for the time and the season which the Lord Jesus shall appoint." She kissed first Rhoda's hand then mine.

James said, "You are not alone in the wish, Miriam. How many times have I yearned for the old days, when we took every puzzling question to our Lord for answer. He spoke a truth more profound than anything I had ever heard before or since. No matter how crafty were the questions men brought to him, he cut through to the core of truth at the heart of every situation. Had we been able to bring all our questions to Jesus, how many mistakes of these past years we could have avoided. When the Lord Jesus was parted from us he left to us a work far beyond our collective wisdom. We have erred often since that day when he was parted from us on this Olivet. He had already given us the keys which would unlock the gate into the kingdom of heaven. But we sat here in our ignorance, waiting for him to return and open and lead us in. The marvel is we did not lose the truth he gave us in a sea of free food and free wine. It is as well Agabus wrote down the witness of that first summer, while all was so fresh in our memories—Greek though he is."

"If you heard Agabus preach you would forget he is Greek. If he were a Jew we would call him prophet. He is a remarkable scholar. His memory is unusual. Paul was deeply impressed with his book. So was I, though I am not much of a judge in such matters."

I described Paul's winter at Salamis. Then, plunging ahead because of the urgent sense that James was blocking growth in the movement along natural and necessary lines, I told of my visit to Paphos, of Sergius Paulus, who had set my doubts at rest with one simple and obvious question.

"He asked for Barnabas to come and tell him more. Do you believe Romans can become Christians?"

James sighed. "Mark, Mark, I am ashamed that you need even to ask me such a question. 'Teach all nations,' our Lord said. Yet I was a Jew before I followed Jesus, and I am a Jew today, and many things trouble me."

Mother said, "We are all Jews. One day our Sanhedrin will acknowledge that there is room within the hospitable arms of our ancient faith for all who love God, even for Christians." She had finished the soup. She lay back, comfortable and content. "Martha makes excellent soup. She is a good neighbor and a good woman."

"But she has wasted your strength when you had none to spare. Rhoda did well in keeping the tide of your friends from washing over the threshold of this room."

Color rose in Rhoda's cheeks. "You must not think I am always as foolish as when I brought Ben Eli here."

Mother said warmly, "Rhoda does many things well. How often have I praised God for sending me so dear a daughter. James, my brother, rejoice with us. These two are to marry and give me grandchildren."

"Surely your cup overflows." He turned a penetrating glance upon me. "And yours, Mark. A day of wonderful joy this must be, for all this household."

"A day of wonderful joy." I infused as much enthusiasm as I could into the words. "I came home meaning to ask Mother to choose a wife for me, and she had already done so." I looked for some response from Rhoda but she gazed down at the cup in her hand. I added, "The wife my mother chose pleases me." I wished heartily that it were true, and resolved to make it so if I could.

The sudden silence was an accusation. It was broken by a knocking at the gate, the grind of an opening door, then Damaris' joyful greeting, "Nicodemus, sir! Ah, most welcome to this house!"

A startling change came over Mother. She seemed almost to lift from the bed. Her face was filled with color and brightness.

James said, "Lie still, Miriam. He will come to you."

I rushed to greet Nicodemus. He crossed the court in great strides, wrapped in a hooded robe of unbleached wool. Encountering only welcoming smiles he exclaimed, "This is no house of mourning! God be praised! Where is my beloved?"

I said, "Come to the roof, Nicodemus, or she will come tottering to meet you, weak as she is."

"God be praised! I am not too late! I have sent for Peter to come and lay healing hands upon her."

He started stairward with a rush, paused, kissed Damaris on the cheek. "How blessed it is to see the faces of those we love."

He sprang up the stairs, embraced me in passing, kissed Rhoda, greeted James. When I reached the bedroom Mother was in his arms, her face above his shoulder illumined with joy. Her arms twined about his neck in spite of the voluminous coat. She murmured, "You were missed. Oh my beloved, you were missed."

"Miriam, you will come with me to Joppa after Passover. Or I will remain here at whatever risk. I will never again dwell in a city apart from you."

Nicodemus sat down near James, still cradling Mother's slight, wasted figure in his arms. "They brought me word that you were at death's door. I never thought to find you still living. Forgive me, Brother James. I am overcome with the joy of this reunion."

He kissed Mother, and she returned his kiss. I could not take my eyes from them. Mother's happiness stirred me to joy that was mingled with pain. Be happy, Mother, with this good man, my heart implored. But my eyes met Rhoda's and I thought, I want to be happy also, with a girl I could love as Nicodemus loves my mother. I want to know the kind of joy they have in one another.

James said, "It is splendid to know that Peter will be coming for Passover. So few of our old company return here nowadays, for they are scattered afar. I keep hoping to see Andrew, but he does not come."

Mother said, "Mark will be baptized when Peter comes. And Nicodemus, when you and I go to Joppa Mark and Rhoda will marry and—go to Cyprus, I suppose. Is that what you are planning to do, Mark?"

I nodded. "I have served my apprenticeship, and I have made a journey across the island to Paphos to sell our wares as Barnabas used to do. I am a copper merchant now."

Nicodemus said, "I am delighted to know the matter is settled, Mark."

Presently Mother said, "I lived beside the sea as a child. It will be a joy to me to dwell in Joppa with you, my dear one." She reached a hand across to Rhoda. "And Salamis and Joppa are, after all, only a short sea voyage apart. I will see my children, and my grandchildren, often. I have so much—so very much—to live for."

James rose. "Come, Mark. We will go to the pavilion. Come Rhoda, my child. We are not needed here."

The pavilion echoed with the witness of the far-scattered believers. James said, "This is becoming a Passover of reunions. I wonder whether Andrew may find his way here. Perhaps that is asking too much. Yet I miss the dear companions of those blessed years when we walked the hills of Galilee and Samaria and Judea with our dear Lord Jesus. Of them all, I miss Andrew most. It was a shock to learn that he had baptized Agabus. Deserving as Agabus is, the barrier remains. Agabus should accept the law. He should be circumcised."

"Do you feel no compunction over baptizing a scoundrel such as Ben Eli?"

"We attracted to the ecclesias many such men. The way to the kingdom is straight and narrow, but we offered the broad path which leads to destruction. May God forgive us for bribing hungry men with bread and wine to speak our simple credo. Of Ben Eli I can only say that he is hiding something in his inmost heart—something so terrible he cannot bear to bring it out into the light of truth and righteousness."

"I accused him of being one who took a farthing to shout, 'Crucify Jesus! Give us Barabbas!' "

Rhoda had been utterly silent all this while. Now she said softly, "Oh, no!" Whether she meant the act itself or my callous accusation I could not tell.

James said, "He would not be the only such man to join our company. We offered far more than a copper farthing to men for saying a good deal less. That would be a fearful burden for a man to carry in his soul. How I long to lay my responsibility upon Jesus. I am often at a loss. I have an indescribable longing just to lay aside my burden and be with the Lord. I grow terribly impatient for his return."

Rhoda exclaimed, "But he did return! He did not tarry! That first Pentecost he came! He has come among us every time a believer received the gift of the Breath of God. I have felt his presence many times. He was with us when Mark tried so hard to get Mother to swallow the first spoonful of wine. Mark prayed, 'Lord Jesus, help!' I *felt* him with us, when I saw her throat move as she swallowed that very first time."

She ducked her head, a childlike motion. "Forgive me, James. I should not speak to you in this way. But you who knew Jesus as a visible companion do not always realize how truly he is with us, how truly the kingdom comes among us whenever we believe in him and love one another. 'I am with you always,' he said. Do you think he lied when he said that? Oh no! Jesus returned at Pentecost. He never left our company since that day. He is with us here, and he is with Agabus in Antioch, and with Barnabas in his journeys. He is with Peter and John and Andrew and Philip and Thomas and all the others, and with the ecclesias wherever people meet together in his name."

James' round face was very ruddy. The drooping lid gave a sinister cast to the displeasure he turned on Rhoda. "I cannot think we have all been such blind fools as to mistake his meaning completely. Wisdom comes, my child, if ever it comes at all, with age and experience."

Rhoda's chin lifted. "I have had experience. I watched Mother yearn all these years for the physical presence of the Lord Jesus. I have wakened many nights to hear her sobbing with the longing to rest her cares upon him, the burdens which the ecclesia in its ignorance had let her bear alone. Yet all the while—all the while Jesus was with us. He was among us, waiting for us to solve the problems our own mistakes had created."

Rhoda rose, a tall, strong girl with hard, capable, willing hands and heart enough to carry any burden. Her voice was deep, vibrant with emotion. She looked toward the top of Olivet with its crown of shimmering, silvery green. "He was among us all the while. He did not deceive us, for he was with us all the while."

Now the dark eyes looked directly into mine. She laid her hands on my shoulders, stooping because I was seated on a rug. "Do not worry, Mark. Everything will be all right. I will go to Joppa with Mother and Nicodemus. You will return to Cyprus. It will be all right. We have seen today how a man greets his soul's beloved. I think there is a girl somewhere whom you might—love—and greet—in such a way. We cannot change what we feel, nor pretend what we do not feel. I am your sister still."

The heavy, smooth, dark hair swung all about me as she stooped to kiss me softly, sweetly, on the lips. Then she walked swiftly away. I heard her descend the stairway. Her pace quickened as she crossed the court. I looked over the parapet. She was running as she vanished into the corridor.

I turned to James, bewildered, humiliated. "She refuses me."

"She does indeed, my son. Her price is above rubies. And she refuses you."

# CHAPTER *17*

"James, my brother, I must tell you how Peter raised from death a woman called Dorcas in our Joppa community."

We sat in the pavilion, Nicodemus, James, and I. Mother slept and Damaris and Ken were busy in the court. Guests would be coming, more each day, as the Passover approached. As for Rhoda, she had vanished into her room and had not reappeared.

A profound wistfulness filled the homely face of James. "From the dead! That would take a mighty faith. I longed to lay healing hands on Miriam, and on others, in the past. But I have performed no mighty works."

"Most of us have not," said Nicodemus.

"Was this woman in the tomb when Peter brought her back to life?"

Nicodemus told us that Dorcas had been laid out in an upper room of her own house. The court was filled with widows who held up little coats and tunics Dorcas had made for their children, for she had been constantly occupied with good works. Then Peter came. The widows crowded the doorway as Peter approached the couch. Peter took Dorcas' hand, saying, "Dorcas, arise," and she arose.

"Did you see it?" My doubts angered me. Peter had faith enough to do the impossible, but I could not muster faith to believe in what he had done.

Nicodemus said, "I did not see the event, but I heard the story from twenty witnesses. In the Joppa ecclesia it was told over and over. You can appreciate my emotions when news came of Miriam's illness three days after Peter departed for Caesarea. A centurion called Cornelius had sent for him."

Nobody commented on the centurion's action, strange though it was. The raising of Dorcas so far overshadowed it. James mused, " 'Dorcas, arise!' It would take a mighty faith."

It had taken a mighty faith for Peter to stand before Nicanor Gate and say to Korah, "Rise. Walk." I had seen that miracle. Why did I doubt this one, having seen that?

I moved about the pavilion restlessly. I was beset by problems—what to do about this Olivet property after Mother went to Joppa, for one thing. As for Rhoda, she was impossible. I had consented to the marriage. What ailed the girl? I had tried to do the right thing. I had said I was pleased with the choice Mother had made for me. What more did she want?

I said, "I hope Peter comes to no harm in Caesarea. Barnabas was scourged there."

"Barnabas was scourged by Jews. The Romans have nothing against us, Mark. Cornelius has a reputation for honor and piety. Peter is safe with him."

James asked, "What is Joppa like, these days?"

While Nicodemus described the ancient seaport, sunk into stagnation since the Romans built a better harbor at Caesarea, I prowled the parapet, wishing Rhoda would come out of that corridor. Bread was baking in the court. Ken was cleaning vegetables. Damaris had gone to the women's quarters. Maybe she would bring Rhoda out. Maybe Mother could talk sense to the silly girl. Rhoda was fond of me. Why should she be contrary and flout Mother's wishes? The prospect of returning alone to Salamis was not inviting. Why must I dwell alone? When Mother married Nicodemus, Rhoda's duty to her was done!

"I work side by side with my lightermen," said Nicodemus. "Miriam says I am brown as any sailor, and no wonder, for I am out in that choppy harbor in all weather, shifting cargo. I've never enjoyed better health!"

I glanced at him. He certainly looked well. The scholar's stoop and the old pallor were gone. He was as brown as Peter or Andrew.

"We have in our Joppa ecclesia mostly Jews, but with them also a mixture of Egyptian, Libyan, Greek, Cappadocian, Cyrenian—freedmen and men of property as well as slaves— all sorts and conditions of men. We meet in the house of a tanner called Simon, a Jew. The house holds the stench of half-cured leather, but it is on the hill above the harbor, and it catches the breeze. The roof is commodious enough for all the Joppa believers to assemble upon it."

James said, "You teach all nations, yet you pursue your own business also. You are fortunate. How do you manage the memorial supper with mixed peoples?"

I missed the reply. Three men had left the Bethany road to turn up the track to our house. One was Barnabas. I flew to the camel gate and on out to meet and welcome them. I could have shouted for pure joy as I embraced Barnabas. The life he now led, far from aging him, made him grow stronger, yes, handsomer. His face glowed with the joy believers called the peace which passes understanding.

Paul was with Barnabas, and a stranger, an Antioch Greek called Titus. All three were carrying bundles on their backs. Titus led a laden donkey.

By the time we had unburdened the donkey and laid out the bundles in the court Barnabas had explained to James that these were gifts to the Jerusalem believers sent by the Christians of Antioch.

James looked about at the grain and dried fruits, the cloth and leather. "God has prospered our Antioch Jews. They are indeed our brothers in the Lord Jesus to remember our need in this manner."

Barnabas took from his scrip a small bag of coins. "The money is the gift of Agabus and his Greek ecclesia. The project originated with Agabus, and the gifts came from both ecclesias, Greek and Jewish.

James looked at the money in his hand. "May God reward our Greek brothers."

Ken was washing Barnabas' feet. Barnabas looked across at James with the glowing smile which combined affection, understanding, and a trace of amusement at the quirks of men's minds. "Brother James, Agabus would welcome a sign of your love and blessing. Can you send some personal message, welcoming these Greeks into the body of the believers?"

James stiffened. "If the gifts were sent as the price of my blessing, you must carry them back to Agabus. Andrew baptized him, though Agabus refused circumcision. Do not ask me to condone the breaking of our precious law."

Titus said simply, "There is no price upon these gifts. No return is required."

Barnabas said gently, "The gifts were sent in brotherly love. Send your blessing in brotherly love, James."

Perhaps the matter would have ended then and there, and much heartache and dissension avoided, had Paul kept silent. But Paul was never one to whom silence is a virtue.

"Don't be a stiff-necked fool, James! God looks upon the heart. The Breath of God has entered into these Greeks. Why judge by externals? 'By their fruits you shall know them,' as the Lord Jesus said. These Christians bear the fruits of the kingdom. While the Jerusalem ecclesias diminish, choked by narrowness and error, the Antioch ecclesias flourish. You had years of intimate association with the Lord Jesus. You should lead us all in brotherly love. Yet with or without your blessing the Greek ecclesias will grow and prosper."

Nicodemus joined the altercation. "In Joppa men of many nations worship together in the ecclesia. Whoever has carried a burden on his back or in his heart may find comfort in the fellowship we share—whatever floatsam the sea has washed ashore in our little backwater. For Jesus said, 'Come unto me, all who labor and are heavy laden. Learn of me, and I will give you rest.' Brother James, this is the meaning of Jesus' injunction, 'To the Jew first, but also to all peoples.' "

I winced at the misquotations, for I had heard the sayings as Agabus wrote them. The worth of written records grew clearer as I listened while these men argued. Of them all, only Paul quoted Jesus' sayings accurately, as the witnesses had first reported them that summer after Pentecost, and as Agabus had recorded them. The altercation sharpened, with James standing alone against Paul and Titus and Nicodemus, while Barnabas tried to make peace among them. When Damaris beckoned from the balcony I went up to Mother.

"Carry me down," she said. "I will welcome these guests and kiss Barnabas. Then I will go to my room, where the sounds of contention will be muted. Poor James, he is wrong. But if he yields he will be left without a foundation. He lacks the imagination to change. He is very dear to us. The constancy of his views has been our rock of security. Oh, I do wish Paul were less outspoken."

Rhoda was still in her room when I carried Mother in there. She rose, self-possessed. "I will help Damaris serve the meal. Rest well, Mother dear." She kissed Mother. With only a glance at me she left the room.

I covered Mother with an extra coat. "Rhoda is going to Joppa, Mother."

Mother looked at me searchingly. "Have you had a lovers' quarrel?"

"We have scarcely spoken to one another. Certainly we have not quarreled."

Mother said tenderly, "Confide in me, Mark. Perhaps I can mend matters."

I said bitterly, "She complained that I did not greet her as Nicodemus greeted you. She says we cannot help what we feel, that she will be my sister. Ask James. He heard it all." Deeply humiliated, I concluded. "It will do no good to talk to her. I do not want an unwilling bride."

"I see. Nor does Rhoda want an unwilling husband. So pride comes between you. Ah, Mark, it is a sad thing to be so young."

"Be happy with Nicodemus, Mother."

"I will, Mark. Truly."

"It will be strange when this house is no longer home. Shall we deed it over to James for the use of the ecclesias here?"

"No, dear. This house will always be our home. We will return to it, one day. The Jews cannot fight their own forever."

"We must find a steward, meanwhile. Do you have someone in mind?"

"Nicodemus will attend to all that."

I said stiffly, "It is my heritage. I will attend to it. I am not a child, Mother. I do a man's work at Salamis. There I am treated as a man of business."

"You were a child when you went away. And now you are back, and it seems as if you had never been gone. Kiss me, my dearest boy. I find all these discussions and arguments exhausting. Nicodemus will take care of everything."

I went out wondering how long it takes a mother to learn there are some hurts she cannot kiss away.

Peter had come, and the argument had moved up into the

pavilion. Peter had gone first to Bethany, and Simon, with his steward, a young Jew called Silas, and other Bethany Christians had arrived with Peter. Now Peter's voice was added to those in contention against James.

"God is not willing that any should perish, but desires that all men may reach repentance. Let us therefore grow in the grace and knowledge of our Lord Jesus," Peter was saying as I crossed the court. "Let us not be carried away into error."

James shouted, "Indeed, let us not be carried away. If we cast aside all we have been taught from our youth, where do we begin to build anew?"

Paul was answering with considerable heat as Peter saw me, and turned to embrace me, his great arms holding me against his chest. "Mark, my son, how joyful I am to see you once more."

"Peter, I am ready at last for baptism. I want you to administer the sacrament." Would my problems vanish away then? Would the Breath of God make me a new creature, wiser, kinder, better than before? Would I find the wisdom and grace and the glowing joy I needed to solve my problems and become the kind of man I longed to be?

Peter soon returned to the altercation, though without rancor. Soon he went to the podium, lifting his arms, calling that he had a story to tell, an experience to relate, which had a bearing upon this very discussion. And now everyone sat down to listen, turning to Peter their confident attention. How mellow Peter appeared, how settled into the harness of leadership. Tranquillity and confidence marked him. All my love for Peter was renewed and strengthened as he told his story.

"I tarried in the house of Simon, a tanner of Joppa. As I prayed upon the roof, I fell into a trance. I saw a rift in the sky, and a thing came down which looked like a sail-cloth slung by the four corners. It was lowered till it opened before me there upon the roof.

"In it I saw creatures of every kind, whatever walks or crawls or flies. A voice said, 'Up, Peter, kill and eat.' But I said, 'No, Lord. I have never eaten anything unclean.' Then a voice said, 'Do not call unclean what God counts clean.' "

A gasp from James did not serve to interrupt the story.

"While I puzzled over this vision, messengers came, asking for me. Cornelius, a centurion, had sent for me. I went with these men to Caesarea. Rufus will bear witness that we found the atrium with adjacent rooms and even all the adjoining corridors filled with people, the family and household and even the soldiers of Cornelius, Romans mostly but with some Greeks among them.

"Cornelius came himself to welcome me, and bowed to the ground before me."

Paul said sharply, "A Roman bowed to a Jew?"

"Rufus will bear witness. He bowed to the ground. I raised him up saying, 'I am only a man, like yourself. Do not bow to me.' Then he led me to a place in the atrium where I could see and address all the company he had brought together. 'We are here before God,' he said, 'to hear all that you will say to us.'

"I had never before preached to such a company, yet the meaning of the vision was plain. God has no favorites, my friends, but in every nation the man who fears God and does right is pleasing to Him. God sent the good news of the kingdom first to the Jews, yet the good news is for all men.

"I told these Romans and Greeks of the ministry of Jesus, of his mighty works, of his death and resurrection. I told how Jesus appeared to hundreds after his resurrection, myself among them. 'Jesus commanded us to proclaim him to the people of all nations, and affirm that he is indeed the Christos, the Son of God, judge of the living and the dead. To him the prophets testify, and everyone who trusts in him receives forgiveness through his name.' All this I said, and much more, and as I still spoke, the Breath of God moved among them. Rufus will bear witness. We were astonished that the Holy Spirit should come upon these Gentiles. Then I asked for water to be brought, and I baptized all who desired baptism, from Cornelius himself to the lowliest slave."

As James listened a strange pallor came over the browned, homely face. "It is not possible," he exclaimed. "The Breath of God, and the sacrament of baptism—these belong to the Chosen, not to Romans. Certainly not to a Roman centurion."

Paul said, "We have seen such things in Antioch, James. Open your mind. Open your heart. God has no favorites!"

Before the contention grew noisy again Peter silenced them with lifted arms. "I tell you only what happened, and Rufus will bear witness that all is just as I have told you. We remained in the house of Cornelius for three days, preaching and teaching all the household, Cornelius with the others. I suppose I would be there still, had not our brother Nicodemus sent for me, summoning me here with the sad tidings that our sister Miriam was ill unto death."

A stillness of shock had settled over James. That Peter preached to Romans, that the Holy Spirit came upon them— that was bad enough. That he had baptized them was even worse. But that he had dwelt in that Roman household, had sat at table with Cornelius, and had dipped into the common dish, this was beyond astonishment. This was shocking. This was incredible.

Slowly James rose. "Peter, my brother, do I understand that you broke bread with this centurion?"

"Could I condemn those whom God had blessed?"

"You have flagrantly broken our law. Taking God's name as your shield, you have cast aside your heritage as a Jew."

"My dear James, God gave them no less a gift than He gave us at Pentecost. God had sent me a vision, just before the messengers from Cornelius arrived to summon me. God had commanded that I accept what God has blessed as clean and uncondemned. Do you ask me to act contrary to such a vision?"

Paul exclaimed, "God has granted repentance and salvation to Gentiles. Don't be a fool, James. Are you better than your Lord, who ministered to Samaritans and broke bread with publicans?"

James' face was ashen. "Shall we cast aside the law and the prophets, and wait for the guidance of visions?"

Paul cried, "I will never condemn what God has blessed."

Now indeed the clamor was renewed, with voices shouting "Amen," and others shouting, "Sacrilege!"

Barnabas went to stand beside James, who by now was surrounded by half a score of the Bethany believers who saw all things as he did. "My dear brothers," Barnabas began, "these differences we have among ourselves witness to God's greatness. For God, who made heaven and earth and all that is in them, God, who made the incomparable firmament of the heavens and the smallest crawling creature, is far greater than our minds can grasp."

His eyes were warm with affection as he looked about from one flushed face to another. "My brothers, this is our faith: God, who reads the heart, finds in us even when we differ amongst ourselves that which is well pleasing to Him. God knows our frame. He remembers that we are fallible. If we sometimes err in knowing one another's hearts, how much oftener do we err in interpreting the meaning of some of our Lord's teachings. For we see all things with the limited vision of men, rather than the infinite understanding of our father God. Our very misunderstandings, our very limitations, then, witness to the infinite greatness of God, and to the longing within each of us to be righteous and judge with wisdom.

"Let us remember first of all that Jesus said, 'Love one another as I have loved you.' Let us remember that great gifts have been given us, and upon us great responsibilities have been laid. Let us pray in perfect faith for wisdom to guide us in all these decisions, remembering that we each long for what is righteous and what is just, and what is well pleasing in God's sight. Let us believe that God, whose spirit dwells within us, will use us each in our diverse ways."

James and Paul had lost their truculent air during this discourse. James put a hand affectionately upon Barnabas' shoulder. "We will speak no more of the things which divide us. Tomorrow at the hour of prayer let us all go up to the Temple. Now, my brother Paul, if you will dismiss us with a benediction, we will go our ways for tonight, knowing that we part from one another in brotherly love."

There were no references to fools in Paul's closing prayer. We separated peacefully enough, for which we had good cause to be thankful. For when Peter and James went together to the Temple early the following morning they were arrested by soldiers of Herod Agrippa, whom Caligula had made tetrarch over Judea and Galilee and also the trans-Jordan. Before the passover had come, James was beheaded.

Peter remained a prisoner. We had no hope at all but that he would suffer a like fate when the passover season had ended.

# CHAPTER *18*

Passover week had brought the usual throngs to Jerusalem, seething with the usual rumors that this year would bring to the Jews their savior and Messiah. Our house had its full quota of guests, all Christians. My father's uncle Seth was one who no longer visited us. I encountered him in the Court of Gentiles one afternoon. He undertook to chide me on the subject of consorting with criminals and harlots, but I made my escape.

I was much in the orchard and vineyard those last days, pruning away branches, securing tangled tendrils, fighting the discouraging battle to restore in days the devastation of years of neglect. I would not be here long. None of the Christians would remain long, now that Herod had revived the persecution. We could not go till we knew Peter's fate. Yet we all knew we must keep out of sight, and when the end came for Peter we must manage to get away unobtrusively.

James was dead—good, dependable, honest, beloved James. Nobody cared to be reminded of our last evening with James, when every voice had been raised against him, except those of a few Bethany believers. James must have felt his worth as a leader slipping away that evening. What his thoughts were during the final hours of his life I could not bear to think. Now his death, coming when it did, had confirmed the Bethany Christians in the stand he had taken. Simon and Lazarus kept to themselves, avoiding Paul and Barnabas.

James of Nazareth had come for Passover and was lodged in Lazarus' house, in the room James the apostle had occupied these five years. He was one with Lazarus and Simon in their views. There were rumors that he would remain in Bethany, a bulwark to the ecclesia when these other leaders, Barnabas, Paul, and Peter, had taken their departure. Certainly James would add his influence on the side of the faction which enforced Mosaic law upon all Christians.

Occasionally I encountered Ben Eli in the orchard. I found evidence of his labors everywhere. The press was clean. The clearing was as neat as hands could make it. Once I found him kneeling at the altar stone, staring moodily off toward the tree with the split trunk. When he noticed my approach he fell to scrabbling about as if he were still cleaning the area.

Determined to make peace with him, I crossed the clearing. "I thank you, my brother, for your labors." In spite of my good intentions I spoke with stiff formality. "Let us agree upon the wages I owe you for your excellent work in this orchard."

He stared scornfully past me. "You owe me my physician's fee, three silver sheckels. I take no pay for the rest. I work here for love of the Lord Jesus, in memory of his sufferings in this place."

Stung by his scorn I inquired coldly, "Do you still detest our brother James?"

"I envy him. He longed to be with Jesus. He is with Jesus."

"So now James is added to the long list of those you envy."

I walked rapidly away, fearful of what further cruelties

might escape my lips if I remained in the presence of this man. Where does one turn to find Christian charity for a man one loathes?

Herod Agrippa, the childhood friend of Caligula, was blamed by many for the contempt for traditional Roman virtues which cursed Caligula's reign. Antipas, Agrippa's uncle, had beheaded John the Baptizer after John charged Antipas with incest. But Agrippa had beheaded James for no reason except the desire to curry favor with Annas and his clique. Persecution of believers by Annas had quieted down after the Jerusalem ecclesias shrank in size and vigor and the most aggressive leaders scattered. But who could say what turn the powerful Herod's persecutions might take? With all Palestine and even the trans-Jordan under his rule, where could the apostles hope to preach in safety?

Nicodemus learned, through Joseph of Arimathea, that the witness who had testified against James had denied any knowledge of Peter's preaching. Herod had sent to Joppa and to Caesarea for witnesses, and when the Passover ended, Peter would be brought out for his hearing, and beheaded.

No other disciple had been as close to our Lord Jesus as had Peter. He had preached all over Judea, Samaria, and Galilee, and his death would leave wounds in uncounted scores of souls. This was surely a time when we ought to comfort one another, yet petty dissensions separated us. The Bethany people met with James of Nazareth in Simon's house, while in our house believers with Hellenistic leanings gathered daily to comfort one another. We kept our own sad vigil, and in Simon's house other believers kept theirs.

Passover day was a day of mourning for us. The believers gathered, as they had been doing each day. The long day passed and night fell, but nobody went away, for in all our minds was the fear that tomorrow would bring Peter to his death. Tonight, while Peter still lived, we remained together, weeping, praying, finding comfort in one another. The pavilion was filled with Christians, and also the court. Occasionally Barnabas or Nicodemus or Paul would step into the podium to lead the people in a prayer or to exhort one another to be strong and courageous in this hour of darkness. There was witnessing also, reminiscences of Peter's life and ministry.

Ken rose toward the end of the first watch to repeat a story he had heard from Andrew of how Andrew brought Peter to Jesus on the day after Jesus was baptized in the Jordan River, and of how Jesus called Andrew and Peter first of all his disciples. Others related incidents in which both Peter and the Lord Jesus figured. I told the full story once more of the healing of Korah as I saw it, and of the things Peter had said in the prison, to me, to the guards, and to other prisoners as we passed through the corridors.

"I am not worthy of martyrdom," Peter had said that night. "My work is not yet finished." And as I repeated those words many fell to weeping, I among them.

We prayed for comfort for ourselves, and for Peter to find strength to endure his ordeal. We prayed for help in the time of troubles which lay ahead for all ecclesias in the wide-flung provinces over which Herod Agrippa ruled. Had Peter been among us, and the prisoner some other man, Peter himself might have suggested that we pray for the deliverance of the prisoner. But none of those present had either faith or imagination enough to suggest such a thing.

As the first watch ended Barnabas raised his fine voice in a hymn in which all joined. Then Nicodemus came to the podium and warned us not to sing, lest we attract enemies to our vigil, and others besides Peter die on the morrow.

As the second watch began, Mother came from her room to

sit with us, nor could Nicodemus persuade her to return to her room. "I have slept," she said. "I will not sleep again. Do not deny me the comfort of this fellowship." And she remained with us, and Nicodemus, Barnabas and I came down to be near her. With Rhoda we formed a family group.

Paul was in the podium, witnessing to Peter's forgiveness and kindness on the occasion when he came to Jerusalem following his flight from Damascus. As he spoke there came a knocking at the gate. "The terror begins," said Paul with a kind of fierce courage. "Passover is ended. The new week starts. Let us be strong in danger, my friends. Let us not flinch or draw back."

The knocking continued, loud as thunder in our sharp silence. Mother nudged me. "Go to the roof. Run. Be ready to escape by the vine to the orchard."

Nicodemus said, "Rhoda, go and see who knocks, my child."

Rhoda, straight and courageous, opened the peephole. "Peter!" she screamed. "Peter's angel is knocking!" She rushed to bury her face in Mother's lap.

A voice cried, "Peter's dead!" and another, "His guardian angel is knocking."

The sound came again. I threw the door open.

Peter, dazed, strange as a ghost, entered. His wild, unbelieving stare was fixed upon us as he turned this way and that. Yet there was about him an odor unforgettable, the prison stink of lice and human excrement and unwashed, human flesh.

I threw my arms about him. "Peter!"

With that the whole place burst into clamor. Peter's big fists beat upon my shoulders. "Are you real, lad? Or is it a vision?"

Paul shouted, "This is the living Peter."

Peter gazed in wonder about the court and up at the crowded parapet. Every soul was pressing forward, whether on the roof or in the court. Mother touched Peter's cheek above the bushy, uncombed beard. "It is no vision, dear Peter. You are among us. How did you get here?"

Rhoda pressed against me. "Is it Peter? Are you sure?"

I pulled the silly creature close. For all her virtues, she was just a foolish girl who surely needed looking after.

Peter said, "I was asleep, chained between guards. I dreamed I was here in this house, and as I dreamed an angel touched me."

Rhoda breathed, "An angel touched him."

On the balcony Paul called, "Come to the podium. Let all hear your story."

We all trooped to the roof with Peter in the midst of us. He went to the podium. His face glowed with joy as he gazed upon one and then another, upon all these rejoicing friends who surrounded him.

"I was sleeping, chained between guards. Two more guards kept watch outside the dungeon's door."

"A strange precaution," said Nicodemus, and was echoed by other voices.

Peter's eyes crinkled with amusement. "Whenever I have talked to one guard alone strange things occur. Mark will bear witness to the interest of the guard on a night in the Temple prison five years ago. Herod ordered that no less than four guards should stand watch at all times, two in the cell, two outside the door. So I slept, and I dreamed I was with you all in this house. As I dreamed an angel, wearing a hooded coat of gleaming white, wakened me. 'Rise, Peter,' he said.

"The chains that bound me fell away. I sat up, but the two men beside me slept on, heavily, as if drugged. The door stood open. One of the door guards was snoring beside the open door. The angel beckoned and I followed, stepping over the sleepers. All up the corridor as we moved I heard the sounds men make in sleep. This white-robed figure moved swiftly along the winding corridor, up two flights to other corridors, and so to the entrance. Save for torches which burned dimly at stair wells and corridor turns, the prison was dark. Yet the figure glowed as he moved swiftly before me through the winding way. When I stumbled on the rough pavement no voice was heard, either of guards or of prisoners.

"The whole world sleeps, I thought. Nor did this seem strange, for I considered it all a vision of the night.

"We found the great entrance door ajar and the guards asleep upon the broad stairway. I followed my guide past the wailing wall and around past the Temple walls. When I reached Damascus Gate my guide was gone, but the narrow door we call the needle's eye stood ajar. So I left the city and came to this house. I knocked and knocked, and I knew you were within, and afraid to open lest soldiers of Herod be found at the gate waiting to seize others of our company and hale them off to prison and to death. Then this little maid—" he smiled at Rhoda—"this little maid peeked through the slot and cried, 'It's Peter's angel.' "

Rhoda's cheeks grew scarlet as a gust of laughter swept the pavilion.

Peter continued, "Indeed, I thought she was right, until Mark opened and drew me in."

Rhoda exclaimed, "Oh Peter, I could not have borne it if they had beheaded you."

Nicodemus stepped onto the podium. "We have rejoiced long enough. When the guard changes they will find the prisoner gone. This is the first house where Peter will be sought. When they come, the house must be dark and all within asleep. Paul, Barnabas, you and I must be well away before dawn. You, Peter, must go beyond the bounds of Herod's domain and swiftly. This will not be easy."

We had indeed rejoiced long enough. Peter had been restored to us, but all the dangers we had dreaded remained with us, and on all the sobering faces this awareness was apparent. Peter's face also sobered. "Our brother James will be sorely missed," he said, then, "Where is Lazarus? Where is Simon? I must find them, for we share an abiding sorrow for our brother James."

"They are at Simon's house. James, the Lord's brother, is with them."

"I must see them before I depart. We must comfort one another."

"I will go for you," Barnabas said. "You must be on your way, Peter. I will go to them with the news of your return, and tell them how you longed to bid them farewell before departing Jerusalem."

Mother said, "Peter, where can you go to get beyond Herod's reach?"

"My feet will be set upon a safe path. The angel did not bring me from prison to abandon me now."

"The angel," Rhoda breathed. "Was it really an angel?"

Voices rose on all sides. "Of course it was an angel."

Rhoda said softly, "God has not forgotten us. The Lord Jesus is with us, here and now. He is with us still."

Peter kissed her. "He is indeed, my child."

He turned to me. "Come with me, Mark." His eyes held mine.

All the affairs, the anxieties, the problems of recent weeks fell away. "Of course." I turned to Mother. "I'm going with Peter. I was with you only these few days. I will return to you when I can."

"You will find her in Joppa," Nicodemus said.

Not far away, staring at me strangely, Ben Eli stood. Naked longing was written large upon him till he caught my glance and concealed his emotion. He was alone, apart, even in this warm and loving company. He was with us, but he was not one of us. Casting aside caution—for would I not become a lily of the field when I went forth in Peter's company?—I extended a hand to Ben Eli.

"Will you be steward of this property for me, my brother?"

Out of the personal darkness which dwelt within him, Ben Eli said loudly, "If ever again I work for you there must be a written contract between us."

"Nicodemus will draw a contract. Mother will sign for me."

"You are of age. I accept no contract unless you sign it."

"Nicodemus is my lawyer. He will make it legal and binding. Let these friends witness that I am bound by whatever contract Nicodemus makes with you. For Peter's sake, Ben Eli, consent, for I go with Peter, and he must be away before dawn."

Grudgingly Ben Eli yielded. "For Peter, then."

I cannot say that I felt any glow of virtue in the act. I needed a steward. There was a chance that this one would serve.

Peter's farewells were drawing to an end. One farewell remained for me. Yet when I looked about, Rhoda had vanished.

A senseless anger swept me. She picked a queer time to run off! Then I saw her. She held in her arms my bed, rolled around a bundle. Left to myself I would have gone out into the dark without even a clean tunic or a change of sandals. The sight of Rhoda with my belongings all neatly ready for me to carry brought a strange sense of well-being coupled with grief. A wifely gesture—or perhaps only sisterly? She was having trouble reaching me through the people, with her bundle. I moved to meet her. When I would have embraced her the bundle was firmly between us.

"You will need this," she said.

I looked at her dumbly, unable to find expression for all my emotions.

Her smile was too bright. "Peter takes nothing, neither money nor sandals nor coat, since a teacher is worthy of his hire. But your faith is small. You pray for small miracles only. You will need these things, and money. Here is your purse, Mark." She managed to extend it, still gripping the bundle in both arms. And when I took it she turned me about and tied the bundle upon my back.

"Come with us, Rhoda," I said. I turned back to embrace her but she was kissing Peter good bye.

"God go with you, Peter," she said, then, to me, "God go with you both."

She had not heard my foolish, impulsive invitation. It was well she had not. In a flurry of blessings we were gone into the dark that comes before dawn.

"Take Peter to the house of Agabus," Paul had advised. "They won't look for a Jew in a Greek household."

"Take Peter to Salamis," Mother had said. "He will be safe on Cyprus."

Nicodemus had said, "Follow the wadis directly north. Peter will be sought among the pilgrims returning along the Jericho roadway."

Take him, they said. But I knew from the start that Peter would go where he chose, and I would follow. If he was arrested and executed, I would witness his death, perhaps share it. Yet there was no terror in the thought. Peter had not come from prison to die on a Judean highway.

"I am not yet worthy of martyrdom," he said in parting from our company. He had said the same thing five years ago when we shared a dungeon below the Temple. I did not believe him then, but I believed him now. His work was not yet done. He would take me where he willed to go, for I was his disciple. The thought was warm with promise. I knew, at last, why James and Andrew and John and Peter had left their nets when Jesus said to them, "Come, follow me."

We passed throught the silent street fronted by the houses of Bethany, and down the eastern slope of Olivet and on down the winding, swiftly descending highway toward Jericho. Long ago, while I was still an infant unweaned, my father had died at the hands of thieves who infested this road. But I felt no fear. The eastern sky was flaming with the promise of dawn.

Peter said, "What a pity I was unable to baptize you in the Kidron, with your mother standing on the brookside as witness. Now I shall have to do the next best thing, and baptize you, without witnesses, in the Jordan."

In the press of events I had forgotten the delayed sacrament. And so had Mother.

Peter said, "You have had a change of heart. Tell me how it came about."

I began with the arguments between Barnabas and Paul. "Paul said, 'God would not so mock the Chosen People as to send Messiah with the intention that the Jews would reject him and kill him.' When I heard him say that all my conflicts and doubts were crystallized, fixed, and I could not by any means reason them away."

"So you said, when we were in the dungeon. I knew there was an answer, but I could not produce one. I am not a theorist, as our brother Paul is."

"After Paul's conversion, when he fled to our house in Salamis, I taxed him with the question, but he had no answer then, except to call me a fool for entertaining doubts after all I had heard and seen."

Peter laughed. His laughter rang through the hills. "Our

brother's many virtues do not include tolerance." Then, soberly, "If Paul did not answer your questions and your doubts, who did?"

I told of my visit to Paphos, of the discussion in the palace of the proconsul. "He had a Jewish grandmother," I said. "He knows a great deal about our sacred writings and our beliefs. He said, 'Let us assume that this Nazarene is the Son of God, the Christos. God sent His son to the Jews, yet surely also to all men, since God is One. When the Son of God died for all men, at whose hands should he die? Would you have God say, 'The Jews are my beloved, my chosen. To them I send my Son. But the Romans I detest. They shall bear the full guilt for his death. Is it not enough that the hands of Romans drove in the spikes, and lifted the cross against the sky?'

"As he said these things I looked into the face of his—his daughter Malnor—a beautiful young girl with strangely Jewish eyes in the midst of Roman curls twined with ribbons—and I knew then that God is God of all men."

Peter said, "May God's blessing be upon that good Roman —and upon his daughter with the Jewish eyes. And upon you also, Mark. I have been deeply troubled to have wounded James in speaking out concerning these problems we have as Jews preaching to all nations. Yet he was wrong to set bounds upon God's mercy. I wish you could have told him this story just as you have told it to me. There are many things a man feels but cannot explain, and this preaching of our Jewish Messiah to all nations does not come easily."

The sun was well up and the road filled with pilgrims before we reached the Jordan River. And before that I had unburdened my heart of all its perplexities.

"I long for some deeper change within myself. I long to be better than I am. Agabus recorded a parable spoken by the Lord Jesus of seed in stony soil, which sprang up meagerly, with small yield of grain. I must be the sort of Christian he had in mind. I confess that I examine and question every vision and every miracle. When you spoke of an angel coming to you to release you from the prison, the thought leaped into my mind that Cornelius with his legionaries must have escorted Herod Antipas from Caesarea up to Jerusalem for the Passover. Any man with enough authority to have access to the prison keys, and dinarii to buy drugged wine for the guards could have put on a white robe and delivered you."

The rich, red hues of Peter's beard were bright in the slanting rays of the rising sun as he replied, "Wherever angels are spoken of in our sacred books they are called God's messengers. Surely I left Herod's dungeon in the company of God's messenger, Mark, whether that white robe covered a seraph's wings or the trappings of a soldier."

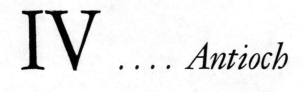

IV .... *Antioch*

# CHAPTER *19*

I had never before broken bread with Agabus. We had lived together and traveled together. I had accepted his authority from the time I was a toddler. But we had not dipped together in the common dish. Now Peter sat at his table, and I with them. My hand went out but was withdrawn, so strong is habit.

Agabus turned upon me his pixy smile. The twin fringes had grizzled during these three years of his Antioch ministry, but the hair was still thick and curling, a handsome adornment for the large head above the spindling body. Smiling his challenge, Agabus took bread and broke it, dipped a piece in sop and offered it. I opened my mouth to receive the morsel.

"Eat well, my son," said Agabus. The fine, large eyes were warm with love. "Eat well in the house of Agabus."

I swallowed. "I never tasted better." I added, "Agabus, my brother."

When I spoke those words they became true. A man may love his slave, and I had loved Agabus, admired, obeyed, respected him, even feared him at times. Now we had broken bread together, and Agabus was my brother. It was another step toward the Christian perfection for which I longed.

Baptism had not been for me a Pentecostal experience. Seeing my depression when the longed-for miracle did not occur,
Peter said, "There are men who are transformed into this
grace in the twinkling of an eye. Our brother Paul was such a
man. Our beloved James was as you are. The years passed,
while we followed our Lord, and he learned to accept each
step into grace as earnest of what he might hope to become."

That had seemed a poor substitute for the joyous experience
Mother and Barnabas had known on the day of their Pentecost. Yet when I looked back I was able to count many steps of
my progress into grace, though still oppressed by the abyss
which separated what I was from what I hoped to become.

We had arrived at the house of Agabus at midday, Peter
and I. We had spent the afternoon hearing the news of the
two Antioch ecclesias, and telling Agabus of the summer-long
journey we had made of the three hundred miles from Jerusalem.

We had stopped to visit ecclesias along the way. In Capernaum we remained three weeks in the house of Peter's wife's
mother. I protested the delay, daily expecting a squad of
Herod's soldiers to appear and carry Peter away to prison and
death. But Peter's serene confidence was justified by events.
Not till Paul and Barnabas reached us in Antioch late in the
autumn did we learn that Herod had died hideously soon
after his return to Caesarea, that his vendetta against the
Christians had perished with him.

For Peter the weeks in Capernaum had been a deeply happy
time. His wife Perpetua longed to travel with him, but she was
bound to Capernaum by her invalid mother. The Lord Jesus
had once healed Perpetua's mother of the fever, but the unfortunate woman had fallen a victim at about the time of the
Lord's death to a wasting illness which continued intermi-
nably. Perpetua was bound to Capernaum, and Peter was

bound to his ministry. Yet their mutual love outwore the necessary separation.

As we walked the miles through Galilee's hills and up between the twin ranges of snowy Hermon and Mount Lebanon, Peter learned from me all there was to tell about Mother's marriage plans for me, and of the turmoil of my memories of Malnor which had mangled and destroyed them.

"You will go to Joppa, to Rhoda, when your season for it comes," he said. "But before that you must return to Paphos. You must see this little Roman maid again, lest a boyish dream of love mar the mature love a man has for his wife."

I had witnessed this mature love between Peter and Perpetua during the weeks in Capernaum, and would never forget it. I had seen their glances, their hands when they touched one another. I had heard the timbre of their voices when they spoke to one another. I had talked with the steadfast woman, the strong, gaunt, weathered woman, who had married Peter when both were young, and who had never said to him, "Stay!" when the Lord Jesus said to him, "Come!"

When we had departed Capernaum and he kissed her good bye, she said, "Every breath is a prayer for my beloved."

"God blessed me when He gave my wife to me," Peter replied. "I have no claim on further blessing."

The querulous voice of Perpetua's invalid mother had called from an inner room, and we had departed. There were no tears. Each was as strongly serene as if Peter were going out for a day's fishing.

Midsummer had brought us at last to Antioch, to the house of Agabus. At sunset that day Peter blessed the meal, and I broke bread with Agabus.

Before Agabus had come to Antioch to enter upon his ministry he had asked for his freedom. "Lest my ministry be disrupted by my seizure as a runaway," he said.

I took him before the Praetor in Salamis for the brief cere-
mony. Afterward, Agabus rolled the pileus into his luggage,
tucked into his scrip the metal tablet certifying his manumission, and he sailed from our low and lovely harbor. Now I had
broken bread with Agabus, and he had become my brother.

Antioch the Beautiful, capital of Syria and of all Rome's
eastern empire, had been built three centuries earlier by
Seleucus Nicator. The site was remarkably favorable. Here the
Orontes River burst through between the Lebanon ranges and
the Taurus mountains. A score of miles down-river the
Orontes entered the Great Sea. From the harbor city of Seleu-
cia river boats brought the products of the whole world to the
teeming docks of Antioch. Antioch spread from an island
above the docks across a plain embraced within the river's
bend and on up the slope of Mount Silpius, which was topped
by the acropolis of a very ancient city, an acropolis toppled
into ruins by some forgotten earthquake but evoking still the
chastening consciousness of times long gone.

Antioch surpassed all cities save Rome itself in size, prosperity, and the beauty of its palaces, temples, civic buildings,
theaters, baths. Two intersecting avenues of magnificent
colonnades divided Antioch into four quarters. The finest
buildings were on the island and the adjacent northeast quarter. The dock area occupied the oldest part of the city, its
northwest quarter. Here Agabus dwelt, and here he preached
to men of all nations whose livelihood came from ships and
commerce.

Four miles down-river from Antioch was Daphne, a pleasure
resort of shady groves and waterfalls and running streams. In
the midst of these rose a temple to Pythian Apollo fine enough
to grace any street of any city. The precincts of the temple
were endowed with the right of sanctuary. To these groves had
fled the outcasts of the world, so that this place of surpassing

beauty was the haunt of runaway slaves, thieves, cutthroats—
outlaws of every stripe.

At first Peter preached in Antioch, in the Beroea Gate and
the River Gate, beside the bridges and under the acropolis, at
palace doors and the doors of the public baths built long ago
to honor Caesar Augustus. I translated his Aramaic into Greek
that all who would listen might understand.

One day he preached in the Daphne Gate. On a sudden
impulse he went striding west along the marble-paved road
which Herod the Great had built to Daphne. Thereafter he
preached daily in Daphne, where nature is at its loveliest and
men are most evil.

They listened, perhaps out of idleness and boredom. The
holes and huts they had found for themselves concealed so
much one could not determine how many dwelt there in sanctuary. Often as many as two score came to roost upon the
broad, marble steps of the temple and amongst the magnificent pillars of the porch. Peter preached to them, standing
upon the base of a nearby fountain.

As long as he gave them narratives of the life, death, and
resurrection of the Lord Jesus they were more or less attentive.
Their leader was an enormous, hairy fellow called Philetus,
who had served seven years in the Roman galleys. He set the
tone for these hearings, together with his lieutenant, Onesemus, and a woman called Thekla who must once have been
handsome, and who at thirty still possessed fire and intelligence.

Onesemus was of Germanic origin, and had been a slave in
the Gallic settlements called Galatia on the northern slope of
the Taurus mountains. When Philetus, Onesemus, and
Thekla listened, all listened. When they heckled and howled,
all did. They were most offensive when Peter preached on his

favorite theme, "Love one another as the Lord Jesus loved you."

Preaching through a translator was troublesome enough. The emotional impact of his deep sincerity was lost when I translated in my direct, unornamented fashion. Yet Peter might have failed to win these outcasts in any case, since his warm-hearted concern did not penetrate the thick hides of men so brutalized.

Peter turned to narratives, drawing upon his inexhaustible store of memories. He spoke of how the people of Capernaum thronged about the Lord Jesus until he was driven to preach from some hillock, or from a boat held near the shore. He told of the miraculous feeding of five thousand Galileans, told how the sick were brought to Jesus till they could not attain to his presence. He told how one man was let down through the roof into a house where Jesus sat with those who questioned him.

The stories they liked best were of the sea, of Jesus stilling a storm or walking upon the water. These tales held their attention, though they won no converts. Peter's only convert after three weeks of preaching in Daphne was a man called Xenophon, who had fled his debts, his ailing wife, his seven children. After Xenophon was baptized, he went home to pay his debts. He returned after two weeks, bringing a sickly girl of fourteen who was, he said, his eldest daughter. His back was raw from scourging.

"My wife is dead," he reported to Peter with more resentment than grief. "My children are scattered. I had meant to sell the children as slaves to pay my debts, and hereafter live a righteous and godly life. But my wife's relatives had made off with the children, all but this puny creature. My creditors had me flogged. My intentions were honest and I have suffered unjustly, and your Christos did not come to my aid."

Xenophon relapsed into a state worse than before, for he

sold his daughter for a night to this man or that, whoever had the few copper farthings which were his price for her.

Evil sets its stamp in idleness, in cruelty, written into the faces of these people with their matted hair, crusted flesh, grimy garments. As we saw them day after day I remembered what Rhoda had said about compassion for the outcasts, the forlorn, even the self-seeking deceivers of the world. As autumn rains sifted into their booths of boughs and tent-cloth scraps, I longed for grace to feel something more for them than exasperation and disgust.

Barnabas and Paul arrived, bringing Titus and Rufus and Ken. They had gone to Joppa, where Barnabas served as friend of the bridegroom for Mother's wedding. They traveled north by the caravan route, passing through Caesarea and the cities of Phoenicia. Paul had preached in Antioch for more than a year, but never in Daphne. Now he could not wait to preach to Peter's outcasts. Paul's passionate, penetrating voice drew the people from their damp hovels to listen as he drove home his central theme, the meaning of the cross of Christ.

"An innocent man, without evil or guile, suffered death upon the cross between men who might have been any two of yourselves. He died this shameful death for you—for *you* and *you* and all of you!" He pointed to one and another, repeating, "for *you*. Turn then. Leave your sins at his cross. Put evil forever away from you. Accept God's pardon, the forgiveness Jesus earned for every living man. All men are lost apart from God, even the princeps in his palace, the governor on his throne. But whosoever turns from evil to God discovers that what was wrong within him somehow becomes right."

So intent had I been on Paul's magnetic voice and impassioned appeal that I did not notice at first how closely these tough and hardened creatures were listening. When I looked out at them, ranged upon the marble magnificence of the temple's portal, I knew Paul had gotten through to them. Faces were lifted, spellbound, naked with longing. While the passion of Paul's splendid voice filled the area, suddenly I was caught by the yearning face of Philetus. A miracle, I thought. A true miracle.

Paul preached again the next afternoon, and the next. On the third day, Thekla and Onesemus came down from the pillars to the lowest step, nearest to Paul's station on the fountain's base. Thekla, it was, who first cried out, "What must I do to be saved?"

On the day when Onesemus and Philetus were ordained elders in the Daphne ecclesia, I sailed with Ken for Salamis, carrying orders for copper wares from Antioch merchants. Peter had been called to preach in the Jewish ecclesia which met under the shadow of the acropolis which crowned Mount Silpius. He no longer needed my services.

I had in mind a double mission. I must go to Paphos, and I had excellent reason to go, for by now surely the wares were ready to deliver to the cities of Cyprus and to the governor. I must go, but I did not mean to go alone. My plan was so simple, and in a sense so childish, that it amazes me still to reflect that in the perspective of the years it turned out to have more far-reaching results even than the original scattering of apostles from Jerusalem following the stoning of Stephen.

The plan was an outgrowth of Paul's splendid success with our Daphne outcasts. I wanted to make up to Peter for his failure in Daphne. I was confident I knew how this could be done, hence my hasty crossing to Salamis to make sure all was ready there for a return journey across Cyprus.

I had determined to persuade Peter and Barnabas to go with me, and to preach to Sergius Paulus. Let Peter preach to the proconsul as he had preached to the centurion Cornelius of Caesarea, let him convert so notable a Roman to The Way, and the Christians of Antioch would forget his failure in Daphne. So I went to Salamis to make sure the business side of the venture would be ready, when I had persuaded Peter and Barnabas to make the journey.

I carried letters from Agabus, such as he had been sending to Salamis from time to time, exhorting Christians to stand fast, to comfort one another in adversity, and promising to visit them soon. I returned within a month, with bundles and hampers of wares from our bulging warehouse for the Antioch merchants, and with the assurance that Kyros had everything ready for the cities and villages of Cyprus and for the governor and his daughter.

I found Agabus engaged in the homely occupation of mending a sandal.

"You never did such things when you were a slave," I remarked.

"I am a slave of the Christos now." His pixy smile flashed. "A lily of the field."

He said that Peter and Barnabas were in the Jewish sector and Paul was at Daphne. "One of the Christians of Daphne was arrested in Antioch—a runaway slave from Colossae. He has been bound and sent down to the harbor. He will be returned to his master in chains."

The slave was of course Onesemus. I could not doubt that the Daphne community was in ferment, yet I reflected that Peter was better equipped than Paul to persuade those men to meet adversity with courage.

Agabus continued, "Your neighbor Simon of Bethany has come with his steward, the youth Silas, bringing messages from James of Nazareth. You will find them on Mount Silpius, and Barnabus and Peter with them."

The Jewish ecclesia met in a house high on the mountain slope, a house built much like our own spacious and comfortable home at Olivet, with a pavilion on the roof which caught the breeze. I found them there, Barnabas and Peter with Simon and Silas. Peter was telling of the patience with which Onesemus had submitted to brutal handling by legionaries. He would be dumped into the hold of a vessel bound for Perga in Pamphylia, from where he would travel inland over the Taurus Mountains to Galatia. His owner, a man of wealth called Philemon, would pay well for his return, for he valued Onesemus and moreover wanted to make him a warning to others who might attempt to escape to freedom.

"Even as I grieved for Onesemus," Peter concluded, "I rejoiced that our Lord Jesus will now have a witness to his grace and love in the heart of that land to which no other witnesses have penetrated."

"Is it true," I asked, "that he was betrayed by Xenophon?"

"The Daphne Christians will know how to deal with Xenophon," said Peter.

Simon handed me a letter Ben Eli had sent, a letter which began, "Brother Mark," and reported in tedious detail all he had accomplished as steward of the Olivet property. Silas assured me Ben Eli was doing well, that he had asked advice both from Simon and from Silas. Early in the autumn Ben Eli had gone to James of Nazareth. They had talked together for an entire afternoon, and Ben Eli had come from the interview as one who had found peace. Whatever he had confessed to James was known only to them and to God.

While we still spoke of Ben Eli, Paul arrived. Agitated as he was, over the evils in the world which led even men of good will into outlawry, he had no call to vent his distress upon Peter and Barnabas. Yet he did.

"My brother Peter, it pains me to see how you leave off dwelling with Greeks when our brothers from Bethany arrive.

Do you hope to conceal the true situation in Antioch? Do you expect to hide the fact that you have been breaking bread with Gentiles and living under a Gentile roof? This is not something which can be hidden."

Peter's first reaction was astonishment. "That I have broken bread with Greeks and Romans is well known. I disputed the matter with our brother James just before he was beheaded, as you did yourself." Peter laid a hand on Paul's thin shoulder. "My brother, this is a time of trouble in Daphne. Let us not vent our griefs upon one another."

"You suggest that I speak out of some personal pique? How unworthy!"

Peter said quietly, "I will remain here with these friends for a short while. Soon they will return to Bethany. Paul, my brother, Barnabas and I shared with Simon and with Silas that last Passover week when our Lord was still with us. We shared the anguish of his death. I slept in Simon's orchard those three dreadful nights while our Lord lay in the tomb and we had no hope with which to comfort ourselves or one another. Do not darken this reunion with baseless charges of duplicity."

The reminder that Simon and Silas had been joined with Peter and Barnabas in The Way while Paul still persecuted believers did nothing to conciliate Paul. He exclaimed, "I warn you, Peter, and you also, Barnabas. Do not deceive yourselves. Your motives are your own, but self-delusion is unworthy of you!"

Barnabas laid an affectionate arm about Paul's narrow shoulders. "Our friendship goes back many years, Brother Paul. These visitors also are my friends. Do not look for evil in this friendship."

Suddenly I sensed that this was not the first quarrel to arise between Paul and Peter. They ought not to work in the same ecclesias, I thought, since neither can submit himself to the other's leadership. My plan for Peter was even better than I had realized.

Simon of Bethany exclaimed, "Brother Paul, I never expected to hear any man address the chief of apostles as you have addressed our Brother Peter."

Paul said hotly, "I also am an apostle, by appointment of our Lord Jesus, when he spoke to me on the Damascus road. Let me tell you, Simon, it is time a man of education became one of the leaders in our movement. Do not ask me tamely to submit to the authority of farmers and fishermen!"

Simon's face reddened. "Do you include carpenters in the category of those from whom you do not accept authority?"

"I am a tentmaker! Do not twist my meaning!"

Now deeply angry, Simon said, "Why not add the great lawgiver Moses to your list, since you take meals with the Greeks? My brother, our Lord Jesus was specific. 'I did not come to abolish the law,' he said, 'but to fulfill it.' The Jews of Antioch find you a stumbling stone. You cannot win Jews to The Way if you flout the law."

Paul retorted, "Peter dwells with Greeks, except when men of Bethany are here. Those who hide hypocrisy under a cloak called friendship should take a fresh look at the double-edged blade of truth. Let us beware lest we become unfit instruments for the ministry by calling vice virtue when we find it in ourselves."

Peter rose. "When we can speak together with less heat we will discuss these things again." He left the pavilion.

Silas was the youngest of them, with a sweetness about him one finds oftener in women than in men. He could not have been much past fifteen when he became steward of Simon's farm. Now he said with his warm, affectionate smile, "Brother Paul, I have longed to hear more of what the law should mean to Jews who are also Christians. You are the one man who can discuss the matter with intelligence and without prejudice. Will you enlighten me?"

Paul's anger ebbed under the sunny smile. He sat down with Silas and Simon. As they fell to discussion of a problem which never failed to challenge Paul's full attention, I beckoned Barnabus out to the open roof where Peter had gone. From it we had a breath-taking view of the magnificent spread of the great city.

Standing beside the parapet I broached my plan for the Cyprus mission. I concluded, "The conversion of the proconsul would make of Cyprus an asylum where persecuted Christians could always find refuge."

Peter looked at me keenly. "So you are going to Paphos. Excellent. Greet the little Malnor for me."

I reddened under Barnabas' quizzical glance. I had never mentioned Malnor to anyone except Peter. I said, "Greet her yourself. You will go with me. Surely you will go! Barnabas, you like the plan!"

Barnabas said, "The plan is very good. Mark will attend to business, Peter, while you and I attend to this mission. I have wanted to tour Cyprus, and visit Sergius Paulus. He is the best Roman I know."

"It is a good plan," Peter agreed. "Only one thing is wrong with it. Paul must go with you. He is a Roman citizen, and he can speak to Sergius Paulus on his own terms and in his own Latin. He is our best evangel. You must make this journey, but Paul must make it with you."

"You are the best!" I exclaimed. I was sick with disappointment at the turn of events Peter suggested. "Paul has not healed a Korah or raised a Dorcas from death. Paul has not walked from prison, led by an angel. You are the best of us all, Peter. I planned it all with you in mind."

"No more arguments, Mark. We've had enough of those for today. Paul deserves a wider field. He has been more than a year in Antioch. He smarts under authority. He should carve out his own ministry, unhampered by lesser men whose only claim is that they have been longer in The Way. Barnabas, you are Paul's friend. You know this mission is right for him."

Barnabas agreed. "When he works with the older apostles, and especially with you, Peter, he constantly remembers that he was, as he says, born out of season—a latecomer to The Way. Also, I believe his style of preaching would appeal to Sergius."

"And I am longing to preach to Jews," said Peter. "Agabus can handle the Daphne ecclesia. As for you, my son, you will find that when you have come to understand and appreciate Paul, and to love him as a brother in the Lord Jesus, you will have taken a long step toward the goal you seek. Go then, my son, and God go with you."

I was overruled.

On the next Lord's Day the elders of the two Antioch ecclesias laid their hands upon us, Barnabus, Paul, and my unworthy self, and blessed us and the mission upon which we were to embark.

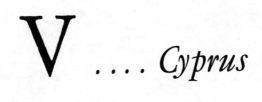

# V ..... Cyprus

# CHAPTER 20

The Antioch elders called our expedition Barnabas' mission to
Cyprus. Later it was known as Paul's first missionary journey.
Barnabas may have realized from the beginning that Paul
would direct the enterprise. He must have learned at an early
age to yield to Paul's decisions. I was not happy with the plan
after Peter refused to go, but my faith in Barnabas blinded me
for a time to the turn affairs would soon take.

The first major clash came the day we reached Salamis. This
had been a happy time for Barnabas, as his reunions with our
household always were. We both had followed Phoebe about
most of the day, Barnabas describing Mother's wedding and
Nicodemus' house in Joppa, and I discussing Agabus' needs
with her, and planning a liberal wardrobe which she could
make ready and send to Antioch by the next boat. We were
still following her as she set the two tables for the evening
meal.

Paul came in at sunset. With a warm and winning smile he
said, "Phoebe, my sister, we are all one in the Lord Jesus.
Among us it is the custom that all believers take their meals
together. There is no need for this extra bother of the two
tables."

Phoebe glanced at Barnabas, who was bent over a financial statement Omar had sent up from the forum. Her face was a little pale in the glimmer of the copper lamp she held. "Sir, what is your wish?"

Barnabas laid down the pad of papyrus sheets. "My dear Phoebe, we have all been eating at one table in the house of Agabus. However, this has led to some dissension between Hellenists and Hebrews, and has caused trouble when we go into the synagogues to preach to Jews. Since I hope to preach in Salamis synagogues, it seemed wiser—"

Paul's voice rose in protest but Barnabas overrode him. "A moment, Paul. Phoebe, I intended during this visit to ask the Greeks to admit me to the breaking of bread when they next celebrate the Lord's Supper. Perhaps this is an unfair compromise. I can see that for you the burden would be easier if you did not prepare two meals and set two tables. Let us arrange things in the easiest way."

Phoebe's back was stiff with disapproval. "We do not all have the same preferences in food, sir. The shell fish I have prepared for the Greek table has never been served in the dining room. Greeks take cheese and roasted kid together, but this is contrary to your dietary custom."

"Agabus serves a simple cuisine. We each take what we like. Yet if this will embarrass or trouble you, Phoebe—"

"Hypocrisy," cried Paul. "You are evading the issue. Phoebe, my sister, you need only lay three more places at the long table and set upon the table the food you have prepared." He shot a challenging glance at Barnabas. "Unless you fear trouble with your Rabbi Gershon, my brother."

"I hope to preach in our family synagogue next Sabbath, and then set out for Paphos after celebrating the Lord's Day with our ecclesias here. We will get a better hearing, more open-minded, in Salamis if we follow our former custom here. Yet if the change will lighten Phoebe's labor—"

Paul exclaimed, "Do as you like! I shall sit at meat with our Greek brothers. Phoebe, I will bring my plate from the dining room to the kitchen table. And I hope to be invited to invoke God's blessing on the first meal ever served to both Jew and Greek in this household."

Phoebe's back was stiff. She stood waiting, her eyes on Barnabas.

With a smile he said, "We will eat at the long table all together." Phoebe set the girls to moving everything from the dining table to the long table which filled one end of the kitchen.

For myself, I had long ago determined to make some such change at home, or at least to invite Kyros and Phoebe and Ken to keep me company in the dining room. Paul was right in principle. Even at the risk of offending so good a friend as Rabbi Gershon, one ought to abide by one's beliefs.

The meal would have been a subdued affair, had Paul not begun at once to describe the Daphne ecclesia. Everyone asked questions about the outcasts of Daphne, and in particular what changes conversion to Christianity had made in their community.

Had any of the debtors gone home to find ways to pay what they owed? Had slaves returned voluntarily to their masters? Had murderers surrendered themselves to the penalty of the law?

When Paul replied that so far the most notable result was that the people were cleaner, and kinder to one another, a dispute arose over what Christians should do about making restitution for past errors. It was an engrossing exercise in Christian theory, until one remembered Onesemus traveling in chains to Galatia.

Kyros boomed, "Righteousness sounds fine in theory, but just what is it, in fact? To what extent should unjust laws be obeyed? Is a debt owed to a usurer a just debt and binding? Slaves are slaves because of a war won or lost two generations ago. Has a slave no right to escape a wicked and cruel master and make a better life?"

Barnabas replied, "The answers can be found in the sayings of Jesus." He glanced at Paul.

"Not even Peter and James always understood Jesus' meaning," said Kyros. "Andrew told us so. Then how are simple Greek workmen to interpret what even the apostles did not understand when they heard the words from Jesus' lips? I confess, I have pondered this matter, and in our ecclesia we have discussed it. Jews have their Mosaic code and we Greeks have our ethics, but Jesus went beyond both. Who is to tell us the meaning of righteousness?"

Barnabas replied, "When our Lord Jesus comes to establish his kingdom, he will give us all these answers." Seeing the glances the Greeks exchanged, he continued, "Or if he tarries, we will find answers, through prayer and heart searching, and through the preaching of men with trained minds and devout spirits." Again he glanced at Paul.

Paul sighed, as if a weight had settled upon his narrow shoulders. "It will take more than preaching. A man could spend a lifetime searching out the meaning of righteousness in all its particulars, and writing it down to be sent to the churches. But while he was so occupied, who would be going throughout the world to preach the good news?"

Barnabas said, "God will provide the men, and will make sure they find time for the labor. We are an infant movement. We will grow. We will learn."

When the meal ended Kyros rose. "I for one enjoyed sharing this meal with the family which employs me, and with you, Brother Paul."

"I also," said Phoebe. "God bless you, Brother Paul, for suggesting it."

"Yes," said Paul abstractedly. "Yes indeed." He rose, frowning. "Preaching the good news is only a beginning. We who have cast aside the Mosaic code as our foundation create more problems, and more, and more. Much can be said for the views of our brother James. Yet righteousness goes beyond the law of Moses. How far beyond? If a man spent a lifetime studying the teachings of our Lord Jesus he still could not fully determine the meaning of righteousness."

Barnabas said, "You are one, Paul, who will at least make a beginning."

On the Sabbath it was Paul who preached in the synagogue of Rabbi Gershon. No other synagogue would receive him, nor would our own until after Barnabas went to talk with our rabbi. So Barnabas preached elsewhere, and I went with Paul to the synagogue which had received the tithes and offerings of the House of Aaron for three generations.

At the proper time Rabbi Gershon rose. "We have with us today a notable scholar, who has studied with Gamaliel in the School of Hillel. Paul of Tarsus, if you have an exhortation for us, speak, and we will listen."

Paul rose, be-tallithed, be-tasseled, his forelocks neatly curled, his beard handsome with oil. He had not been ill for more than a year, and was brown and healthy for all his small size. He went to stand near the ark, and his fine voice filled the building.

"Men of Israel, and all you who fear God, listen. The God of Israel chose our fathers and multiplied our people during their enslavement in Egypt. With a strong arm He led them out through a parted sea. For forty years He bore with them in the wilderness. When He had destroyed seven nations of Canaan, God gave our fathers the land as an inheritance.

After about four hundred years He gave them judges until the days of Samuel the prophet. When they asked for a king, God gave them Saul, son of Kish of the tribe of Benjamin. When God had removed Saul He gave them David, of whom God said, 'I have found in David a man after my heart who will do all my will.' Of David's posterity God has brought to Israel a Savior, Jesus of Nazareth, as He promised through the prophets."

Someone behind me shouted, "He was condemned by Jews and by Romans, and died by crucifixion. Cursed be he who hangs on a tree! This man blasphemes in calling a condemned criminal our Messiah!" The voice had a familiar sound, zealous, self-righteous. I had heard it before, but not in Salamis.

"Let him speak on," said Rabbi Gershon. "Give him a hearing."

Paul's eyes rested on the spot from which the voice had come. "This Jew has followed me from Antioch. I will answer him at an appropriate time. Men and brothers, let me continue. Before the coming of Jesus, John the Baptizer preached in the wilderness of the Jordan repentance and the baptism of repentance. As John's ministry ran its course John said, 'Who do you suppose I am? I am not Messiah! But after me comes one whose sandal cords I am not worthy to untie.'

"Brethren, sons of the family of Abraham, to *us* has been sent the message of this salvation! For those who live in Jerusalem and their rulers, because they did not recognize Jesus as Lord and Messiah, because they did not understand the utterances of the prophets which are read in our synagogues every Sabbath, fulfilled these prophecies by condemning Jesus. They could charge him with nothing worthy of death, yet they asked Pilate to crucify him. And in the end they prevailed. When they had fulfilled all that was written of him, they took him down from the cross and laid him in a tomb. But God raised him from the dead on the third day. For many days he appeared to those who came up with him from Galilee to Jerusalem, and these men, hundreds of them, are now witness to this event before all men. We bring good news, my brothers. What God promised to our fathers He has fulfilled to *us*. Messiah had come. The Kingdom is at hand! Let it be known, brethren, that through Jesus forgiveness of sin is proclaimed to you. By him every one that believes is freed from everything from which you could not be freed by the law of Moses. Beware therefore lest there come upon you what is said in the prophets: 'Behold, you scoffers, and wonder, and perish; for I do a deed in your days, a deed you will never believe, whoever declares it to you.' "

Paul returned to his place beside me. A disturbance rose behind us, but Rabbi Gershon raised a hand for silence. "We will ask our brother of Tarsus to address us again, for our minds are open. We do not reject out of hand the opinions of sincere and scholarly men. We listen, we learn, and in the end our understanding and faith are greater because we do not shut our ears, even when we do not fully agree. Every man in this congregation longs for the fulfillment of the prophecies."

Longing suffused the old eyes set deep in the devout and scholarly face. "We have awaited Messiah so long! The generation to whom he comes will be blessed indeed! Would God he might come in ours! Therefore, let us give all men who have traveled about the world a hearing, lest great events occur and pass us by in this island, far from holy Jerusalem."

As we were leaving the synagogue one of the elders took Paul's arm. "You will come again and speak to us?"

"I will wait upon the Lord in all things."

The elder's eyes were troubled. "We hear rumors that you sup with Greeks." Anger welled up within him. "I do not understand how a scholar trained in the School of Hillel can present and defend some new rule of conduct as more binding upon Jews than the Mosaic code."

I drew Paul away from the growing tumult about us. Within the synagogue I heard the harsh voice of the man from Antioch addressing the rabbi.

As we walked briskly homeward I said, "Paul, we set out Monday for Paphos. When we return these men will be ready to hear you with cooler minds."

"I will not return this way. I must finish my mission in Salamis before we go hence."

I protested, "Barnabas and I are ready. The wares are packed for loading. The donkeys and donkey boys are hired. We must leave Monday."

"I will wait upon the Lord for guidance."

I had been dreaming of Malnor ever since the plan for this journey was formed. That night I dreamed of her again. As I embraced her the voice heard in the synagogue, the harsh voice of the man from Antioch, shouted, "Whore of Caligula! Harlot of Babylon!"

I woke in a sweat. The mysterious enemy who had followed Paul from Antioch was Elymas bar Joshua, friend of the pro-consul.

I spoke to Barnabas early that Lord's Day morning. I described the character of Elymas and the influence he had with the proconsul. "We must get to Paphos ahead of him. We must go at once, and wait until we are returning to do business along the way and to preach in the villages and cities."

"Paul is not returning, Mark. He is going to Pamphylia, perhaps to Galatia. He has in mind to go to Colossae and preach to the Gaul, Philemon, who owns Onesemus. He also wants to learn how Onesemus has borne up under his sorrow and suffering, and strengthen him in the faith."

"So he told me. But you and I can complete the Cyprus mission. Above all, we must get to Paphos quickly. I want Sergius Paulus to hear you preach. After that I think Elymas can do us no more harm on this island."

Barnabas broached the matter to Paul, but Paul refused to budge. Three weeks passed, while Paul preached all over the city, returning daily at the hour of prayer to dispute with the men in our synagogue, and with Elymas, who came there daily. I never saw so many Jews at the synagogue at the hour of prayer as during the three weeks of this contention.

Repeatedly I protested, "Why does Paul make the decisions? We are two and he is one."

Barnabas eyed me keenly. "Is there something—or someone—in Paphos you are itching to see? The little Malnor, perhaps? She must be quite a young lady by now."

I exclaimed, "She is a Roman!"

"So she is. And a very pretty one, I expect."

When I cast down my eyes and did not reply he said, "So that is where Miriam's marriage plans for you went wrong."

I no longer hid my profound emotion. "Peter said I must see her again, then go to Joppa to make things right with Rhoda. Let's get started. This delay is torture. You have no idea what fearful dreams haunt my nights."

He stood quietly, this handsome, well-set-up man with his beard in fat curls between which peeped the tip of the strong chin with its deep cleft. Mother's eyes could not have been kinder than his. "Peter is wise, and it is well that you confided in him. Yet Paul is also a very great man, Mark, and Paul must function in his own way. For if there is one man in our wide scatter of ecclesias who can build us into a movement which will endure, which will survive lightning and fire and the sword, Paul is that man. Not Peter, nor James in Jerusalem. Don't get in Paul's way, Mark, or you will bear the track of his chariot wheels upon your body ever after."

On the third Friday of our stay in Salamis Paul came late from the synagogue. His coat was torn, his headcloth gone. Dirt clung to the luxuriant beard. "They do not come to learn but to mock," he said angrily. "We will leave this place. We will leave tomorrow."

Barnabas said, "Tomorrow is the Sabbath. The ecclesias meet on the First Day. Monday we will leave."

"We'll leave today, and camp tonight upon the road. They would have stoned me! That man from Antioch has so wrought upon the Jews that they were ready to drag me outside the city and stone me! The rabbi stopped them, saying, 'He is a Roman. You dare not stone a Roman.' They never came to learn, but only to entrap me. I curse this place. I will shake the dust of Salamis from my sandals and never return!"

Barnabas said, "You can shake the dust from your sandals if you like, but Mark cannot. We vouched for you in that synagogue. Permission to speak there was given you as a favor to us. Mark will one day bring his wife here to this house. His sons will go for their education as Jews to that synagogue. You are a stubborn man, Paul, and would not go after that first Sabbath's dispute though Mark and I strongly urged you. So now, shake off the dust of Salamis if you like, but not until Monday."

Paul sat down to mend his coat while daylight held. Phoebe tried to help him but Paul, a tentmaker by trade, did not like her way with a needle and did the job himself.

We took a winding route west, passing from village to village. Wherever a handful of people gathered, Paul and Barnabas preached. It was an unhurried journey, and we did not reach Tamassus until Thursday. We went to the inn, for the plan was to remain here through the Sabbath, perhaps longer. Tamassus was a city perhaps half as large as Salamis, and nobody as yet had preached the good news of the Lord Jesus here.

In the forum on Friday morning I was occupied with our agent, but Paul's passionate preaching filled the square, and presently the merchant joined the crowd who listened. I went then to find Barnabas. He was at the river, preaching to women who had gone down to do the family laundry. Three of the women, Greeks, cousins to one another, invited him to leave the inn and dwell in the home of the youngest of the three, a buxom, handsome woman no older than I but with three children clinging to her skirts. Her name was Illani. That evening Paul and Barnabas moved from the inn to her house. Her husband was a vintner, and prosperous enough to afford an upper room for guests. I remained at the inn with our donkey boys.

On the Sabbath Paul spoke in the synagogue. There was a considerable uproar when he rose to speak, since it was known by now that he dwelt in a Greek household. On the following day at the hour of prayer he returned to the synagogue, bent on continuing his dispute. I was in the forum when Ken came running. Tears streamed down the chubby face.

"Mark!" he shouted. "They're stoning Paul."

I began running, Ken beside me. "Find Barnabas. Try Illani's house."

I had seen the place of stoning outside the north gate, on the way to the river. But the cries emitted by a crowd of lynchers would have brought me there in any case. Once I was outside the gate I stopped running. They were fifty or more, howling with the blood lust, and I was one. I could do nothing.

They blocked my view with their arching, agitated backs. But I knew what was beyond. Twice I had seen women stoned for adultery. I would carry in memory forever the image of a young woman's crushed face, blood bubbling from the open, screaming mouth. The victims died quickly.

No sound came from Paul. He was already dead, no doubt. A single stone, well cast, striking head or throat or chest will kill. O Paul, we have lost you, and your work all unfinished. You are our best evangel, I see it now, and there is no man who can take your place.

Roman law permits Jews few forms of punishment. But the Mosaic code demands stoning men for blasphemy and women who are taken in adultery. By a special concession Roman law permitted to Jews this exercise of ritual duty. The code, I thought. I hate the code. Thank God I am free of it. And I remembered with a deep and terrible sorrow that Paul, as much as Agabus or Peter, had set me free of the code.

Barnabas was beside me now, gripping my arm. Tears wet his cheeks and lodged in the fat curls of his beard. "We needed him! He was the best of us all!" The Greek women had come with Barnabas, and Ken with them. The women wept and clung to one another with horror and grief.

Eventually the thud of flung stones ceased. A harsh voice shouted, "Evil has been punished! The code is fulfilled. So be it, wherever men blaspheme the sanctity of the law God gave us through Moses."

A rabbi climbed upon the platform beside the gate. "Let there be no rejoicing. You were instruments of justice. Now put away violence. Return to your work. Go in peace."

The Jews departed, more or less quietly, and the field was revealed, empty and dusty with its scattered stones, and at the far end a heap. Paul's coat, the one he had mended in Salamis, was deep in dust, with a few stones atop the heap. Most of them had rolled off. Paul's feet were drawn up under his body and the head was drawn in and under, protected by encircling arms which ended in bloodied things which must have been Paul's neat and skillful hands.

The women ran first. Ken, Barnabas, two of the donkey boys, and I followed. Barnabas prayed aloud as he went, a heartfelt, repetitious cry, "O God, O God, O God."

Then we were all about the heap, lifting off stones, straightening the dirtied, bloodied coat. As I bent for a stone which lay in the cleft between Paul's richly curling hair, now thick with dirt, and the circling arms, I caught sight of his face. Where the face was there was nothing to see but blood. I turned aside to vomit, and my foot touched one of the hands.

The hand moved. It laid hold of my ankle. A woman screamed.

Barnabas said, "Hush. You will bring them back."

He bent to grip Paul's shoulder. Paul's voice came clearly. "Touch me not. Be my shield. Stand near, on all sides, but touch me not." He raised his face. It was a horrid sight.

I leaned down my hand to him and he shifted from my ankle to lay his bloodied hand in mine. A moment, and he was on his knees.

"We will fetch a bier. We will carry you to Illani's house covered with a coat and they will not know you live."

Perhaps Paul did not hear the warning. Perhaps the force which sustained him was too potent to heed. He stood, and we made a shield around him. There amongst the stones he stood. One fiercely stubborn eye was open. The other was covered with blood from a gash above it.

"Let it be said that Paul rose from the stones and walked

into the city." Gripping my hand he moved, and we moved with him. Surrounded by weeping women, fiercely gripping my hand on one side and the arm of Barnabas on the other, he walked, limping heavily, back into the city which had dragged him out to stone him.

# CHAPTER *21*

Sunset came before all Paul's wounds were cleansed and anointed. A fearful cut over his right eye would have killed most men and would leave a scar as a permanent memorial. A laceration on his right thigh would have prevented a less stubborn man from walking. But Paul was determined to continue the journey on foot, setting out at tomorrow's sunrise. I offered him a donkey, but he would not pamper himself.

"Let it be said that Paul continued his journey on foot," he insisted, as if he were writing a history of the incident. He seemed exhilarated by the gravity of his injuries. "The marks of my apostleship," he called them. "I have shared the sufferings of our Lord Jesus."

"They are the marks of your fanatic zeal in forcing your views on Jews," said Barnabas. "Jews are a stubborn lot, and none more so than Paul of Tarsus."

"You may be right," Paul replied meekly.

While we bound up his wounds he embarked upon a new theme. "I see it now—why the promise of Messiah was not fulfilled until this age. This age is the perfect age for Messiah's coming. The world is united and at peace. We speak a common language—Greek in the eastern empire, Latin in the western. A man who has mastered those two tongues could preach anywhere in the world. We travel on the best roads the world has ever seen, and we travel safely because of Roman law and the unparalleled Pax Romana. These conditions combine to make it possible for a man of zeal and persever-ence to preach to every nation."

Barnabas interposed, "As to that—whenever we preach to slaves or to freedmen, we are preaching literally to every na-tion."

"Our Lord Jesus meant far more than you seem to realize, friend. Your interpretation is too easy by far. We will preach to the polyglot peoples of the waterfronts of our cities, of course. But we must also go literally to the far-flung nations of the earth. The nations are ready to give us a hearing. The old myths are dead. The ancient mysteries are discredited. Philosophy and a spreading belief in one supreme God have destroyed the Homeric tales except as pretty legends. Greeks in particular are ripe for a new faith. Socrates and the philos-ophers who came after him have prepared them. With the Romans the deification of Caesar Augustus brought faith in empire as a substitute for the old beliefs. But the Greeks are a subject people. With the Greeks there is this further advan-tage: They bear no guilt for the death of the Lord Jesus. The Greeks will give us a hearing wherever we go. This applies also to other subject peoples, slaves and freedmen brought to our Mediterranean lands from the borders of the empire. If we left our familiar Mediterranean world to travel amongst the Gallic people to the north or the desert peoples of Africa we would find them ready and willing to hear the good news we preach."

Barnabas must have shared my view that Paul's wounds had made him giddy, for he said with an affectionate smile, "It is a splendid vision, but first let us preach to the Cypriots."

Then Illani and her cousins, who had been staring at Paul with open mouths, smiled at one another, while Illani's husband helped Paul to his bed.

Already I was looking forward to stopping at this house on my return across Cyprus. Barnabas organized the new ecclesia in the conventional way. Ten Greeks were baptized in Jesus' name. They chose the vintner, Illani's husband, as their elder. Barnabas blessed him with the laying on of hands, and gave into his keeping a small scroll on which selections had been copied from the 'Sayings.'

"We will preach to you again as we return," Barnabus told the little group of believers.

Paul interposed, "But if God calls us to go on from Paphos, do not be anxious. We will send word to the Christians in Salamis and in Antioch that in this house in Tamassus an ecclesia exists. They will send teachers to you when possible. God will bless you and keep you."

Go where you will, Paul, I thought. But do not expect us to be bound by your decision after the Cyprus mission ends. Yet all the while I knew we were bound to this determined, courageous, wounded man, this man who could not be left to travel alone, if only because he might at any time be stricken again with the fever. How unfair of him, I thought, not to warn us of his wide-ranging plans before we left Antioch. We could have brought someone else, Titus, or Silas, or some other volunteer who was competent and willing to go wherever Paul might choose.

We set out before dawn the next morning. Paul put on Ken's striped linen coat and wore his headcloth in the Bedouin fashion to hide the bandage over his eye. He led a donkey. The coat of the chunky Ken would have wrapped twice about Paul's spindling frame, but made all the better disguise by its bulk.

Ken stayed in Illani's house. He would slip away after a few hours and hope to overtake us by nightfall. Thus, when we left the city, the count of our party was one man less than when we arrived. We had managed, we were confident, to conceal from Paul's enemies the knowledge that he had survived stoning.

Thus we shook off (so we thought) the zealot, Elymas bar Joshua.

Paul maintained the pace of the beasts we led. He was in pain, but found strength in quoting from the sacred books. "My strength comes from the Lord, who made the heavens and the earth." "He shall bear me up in His pinions and under His wings will I trust."

Our leisurely journey continued, day after day, with preaching in the villages and in Idalium, the other city of the central plain. The people listened, but no more ecclesias came into existence. "After we preach to Sergius Paulus—if he is converted and baptized—" said Barnabas, "we will find the way opening more and more until every village in the island has its ecclesia."

"After we preach to Sergius Paulus," he said. And I thought, After I see Malnor again . . . The nearer we came to Paphos the more I dreamed of Malnor. Oh God, heal my heart of this sickness, I prayed.

Paul and Barnabas talked as we journeyed, and Ken and the donkey boys listened avidly. I tried to fix my mind on their conversation, but found my attention constantly diverted, constantly veering from the longing to see Malnor to dread that I would again make a fool of myself, this time in the presence of Paul and Barnabas. I was haunted also by a growing longing for the future Barnabas described in saying to Paul, "Mark will bring his wife to Salamis. His sons will go to the synagogue to receive their education as Jews." Would I some day make journeys like this across a Christian Cyprus, accompanied by sons who were learning the copper business?

Paul must have read my thoughts, for he began haranguing me. "A man called to our holy mission has no room for the lusts of the flesh," was his theme.

"I am no missionary," I answered. "I am a copper merchant, and the House of Aaron needs heirs."

"If the lusts of the flesh become a hindrance," Paul said darkly, "by all means marry, lest the body become a burden and a distraction. It is better to marry than to burn. But it is better still to live above the flesh, as Barnabas and I have disciplined ourselves to do."

No good could come of reminding Paul that family life was the core of our Jewish heritage. He had been stoned by Jews. Yet when he railed against Jews as a stiff-necked and self-righteous breed, Barnabas reasoned with him.

"Elymas bar Joshua is one kind of Jew and Annas is another. Yet Jews conceived of one God, a spirit of might and majesty, when their contemporaries were serving Moloch and Astarte. A Jew is the author of our faith, and Jews are its messengers. Whenever God comes among men, whether they be Jew or Greek or Roman, men hide their faces and cry out, 'Begone, lest we die,' as did our forebears on Mount Sinai. Amongst whatever men the Son of God might walk, some would follow and others would drive him from their temples. Wherever he appeared, some would cry, 'Crucify him!' while others would glory in sharing his dangers and his sorrows and his agonies. Wherever and to whomever he appeared!"

So we came at last to Paphos: preachers, donkeys and drivers, and I, Marcus, a Christian with no value in the missionary enterprise and no vocation for bringing the good news to strangers; I, Marcus, whose body burned with the lusts of the flesh whenever I thought of Malnor, which was by now most of the time.

We went to the inn. We had sold a donkey in Tamassus and another in Idalium, after disposing of the wares they carried. The six donkey boys were with us, however, and would return together to Salamis when our mission in Paphos was completed. I hoped I would be returning with them, though I dreaded the pressures Paul could bring to bear to accomplish his will.

"Rest here," said Barnabas to Paul, "while I greet old friends in the forum." He put on his toga, oiled his hair and the fat curls of his beard. We went directly to the shop where Amos would be found at this hour.

The booth was buzzing with Jews who, when we appeared, fell oddly silent. Sibilant whispers died as they turned, one then another, to eye us with a peculiar mixture of distrust and regret.

Amos embraced Barnabas first, then others who remembered him. "You will never know how I rejoice to see you, friend," said Amos. A mist was in his eyes.

A loose-jointed leather merchant, to whom clung the stink of the tannery, inquired, "Did you come by way of Tamassus?"

At the question every head jerked about to stare intently upon Barnabas.

"We did indeed."

Someone said, "There was a stoning in Tamassus. You must have heard of it."

"A stoning? Terrible. We Jews ought to give over such brutality. Some unfortunate woman, I suppose?"

"A man. A cultist. A—"

Amos said quietly, "The charge was blasphemy."

"A Nazarene," said the tanner, staring fixedly at Barnabas.

Someone shouted, "Stoning is too good for them. They

teach that the law of Moses is worthless! They predict that the Temple will be destroyed till not one stone—"

Barnabas said, "Nonsense. You've been woefully misinformed. You know me, Ezra. Most of you men know me." His eyes went from one to another, renewing old friendships in the warmth which passed from him to all men. "You must know that I am a follower of the Nazarene. When you learned of the stoning, you probably thought I was the victim. For your concern, I thank you. Will you permit me to explain our beliefs in the synagogue?"

Amos broke the little silence which greeted the question. "It would be dangerous for you, friend, while the zealot is here. We want no trouble between you and Elymas bar Joshua."

"Elymas bar Joshua!" The voice was Paul's. Wearing his threadbare toga he had followed us. His head was bare, the bandage gone. The half-healed cut was plain to be seen above his eye. "That son of Belial!" cried Paul.

Now indeed the men in the crowded shop did not know what to think. For here was another Nazarene, a companion of Barnabas, mauled, wounded, but living.

Barnabas gripped Paul's shoulder, and Paul heeded the warning and fell silent. He must have known, as I did, that Barnabas planned to present this version of the stoning first to the proconsul before it became common gossip in the forum.

Barnabas introduced Paul to Amos, then with a wave of his hand to the others. "Old friends of mine, merchants of Paphos." Smoothly he continued, "They were speaking of a stoning in Tamassus, whose instigator was our acquaintance, Elymas bar Joshua. He has come here, and we will encounter him soon enough."

Amos turned to me. "Mark, my friend, the little Malnor has been asking for her bronze and copper trinkets. We expected you three months ago."

"I was delayed. My mother's illness called me to Jerusalem."

Someone muttered, "They do sicken, then, these Nazarenes, in spite of the mighty works attributed to their founder."

"She recovered," I said stiffly. The mention of Malnor's name, the knowledge that she had been asking after me, left me fussed and bothered, and angry with myself that it should be so.

Amos said, "I will send to inform Sergius Paulus that you are here. Meanwhile, come. We will go to the thermae. You will want to bathe away the dust of the journey." His position as host to Nazarenes was making him increasingly nervous. He thrust the webbed hand into his sleeve, withdrew it, rubbed his hands together, then quickly crossed his arms, covering them.

Barnabas said heartily, "The baths. Excellent!"

The tanner had hold of Paul and was questioning him. Was he a copper merchant? How did he get the cut above his eye? Would he be long in Paphos?

Barnabas drew Paul away before he could burst out with something which might lead to rioting. We followed Amos across the square and down the street to the thermae patronized by merchants.

Amos' messenger reached the thermae ahead of us. Sergius would receive his friend Barnabas and party at sunset. Tomorrow at the midday watch he would receive us with Amos to attend to our business affairs.

"Excellent," said Amos.

We entered, Barnabas greeting old acquaintances on every side, calling each by name. We began disrobing. Amos watched with growing agitation as Paul stripped down to the cuts and bruises his toga had concealed. The bruises had grown darker instead of fading, and the cut on his thigh was not closing properly.

The attendant exclaimed, "Body of Zeus, what happened to you, sir?"

Paul lowered himself gingerly into the hot bath. "I fell from a horse."

"Must have been a big one. A kicker? Or did he drag you?"

Paul settled back with a groan of pure pleasure. "Neither." Then, seeing the astonishment of the attendant and the nervousness of Amos' furtive regard, Paul said, "You could say I was dragged." He closed his eyes contentedly and splashed water over himself with his hands.

At least he had not lied. A fall from a horse on the Damascus road had surely led to his present condition. He had managed to save the truth for Sergius Paulus.

The masseur's heavy hands were too much for even Paul's superb courage. We soaked for a while, then dressed and departed. I think Amos was greatly relieved to see the last of us for that day.

Of my emotions as we stood before the splendid portal, the less said the better. I have never been proud of the follies of my youth, nor do I enjoy speaking of them even now, after the passage of so many years.

The same elderly servant with the bow-bent body received us. When he had seated us in the atrium and sent a boy for wine he went to announce us. Malnor came skimming over the bright pavement at once. She flung herself upon Barnabas, who kissed her warmly. Then he held her off, saying, "Really, young lady, you are getting too grownup for such romping."

Stiff with jealousy I watched, while Paul's disapproving glance passed from Barnabas to me, then to the little Roman in her flowing green linen tunica with green ribbons banding her curls.

Malnor turned to me sedately. "Marcus, I have been expecting you for three months. Had I known it would take you so long to contrive my simple little fibulae, I would have bought them from some other merchant."

I gazed into the tantalizing face, tongue-tied with the longing to greet her as Barnabas had done, but helpless without her cooperation.

Barnabas presented Paul. Malnor asked politely, "Are you in the copper trade?"

"I am a tentmaker. And you are the young lady Mark has been itching to lay eyes upon ever since we set out from Antioch to come here. He has pushed us along at a merciless clip, my child, for the sight of your pretty face. Nor do I blame him."

Malnor had heard too many pretty speeches to share my embarrassment. She moved toward Paul. "You have been hurt. How were you hurt?" When Paul did not reply she turned to Barnabas. "How was he hurt?"

Pity gave place to a kind of incredulous astonishment as Barnabas did not answer. She had heard of the stoning. From what I knew of Elymas I was sure he had mentioned no names, but had made his story an outraged account of blasphemers who spread the teachings of the crucified Nazarene.

Malnor glanced from Paul to Barnabas and back again. "You are the one! You preached in Tamassus, and you are the one! But you live! Elymas said you died. Men always die of stoning. Don't they? Barnabas, they do die of it! Tell me!"

"Almost always," Barnabas said softly.

"Oh." The word was a sigh. Malnor's eyes were tender with wondering pity. She touched Paul's cheek softly, lifted his hair to look closely at the wound. "You are alive. It is incredible." She was still looking upon him with awe and womanly pity when Sergius Paulus entered.

He embraced Barnabus, greeted me kindly, then turned to Paul, hand extended.

Malnor said, "Father, this is Paul of Tarsus. Father, this is the man Elymas told about, the man they stoned. He——" She put her hands to her face. "Oh, why do people hurt each other?"

Sergius looked at Paul closely. "This is true? You are the one?"

Barnabas said, "Paul was stoned. He arose in the midst of the stones. He walked with us into the city. He has walked all the way to Paphos."

The proconsul beckoned his doorkeeper. "Send for the magician, bar Joshua. Command him to me at once." He turned back to Paul. "Do sit down. Will you have more wine? I want to hear your version of this affair, but first of all I want to clarify my understanding of the teachings of this Nazarene. I am at a loss as to why he was executed, why his followers are persecuted. I had always assumed that the cloak of the Mosaic code and the Hebrew prophets was broad enough to shelter the many sects which arise amongst your people. Barnabas, will you explain to me this faith to which you have dedicated yourself?"

Barnabas glanced at Paul, who with a small gesture turned the initiative back to Barnabas. The strangeness of such a gesture coming from Paul passed me by in the turmoil of my emotions. Malnor sat close beside her father. She had slipped one hand into his, but her whole attention was upon Paul. All her pretty, flirtatious ways had vanished without trace. How very nice she is, I thought. How sweet, how womanly, how kind. While Barnabas spoke, amazing even me by the ready and accurate memory he had for the Sayings, I watched Malnor to my heart's content, as she watched Paul.

I know not how much time had passed when the realization came. "You must see her again before you marry Rhoda," Peter had said, from his profound, prophetic soul. I would always feel the warmest affection for Malnor but my hunger to hold her and possess her was gone. I was free. Now she will be hurt, I thought. Poor little creature, how she will agonize if she fixes her heart upon Paul. My attention was finally caught as Barnabas concluded a recital of the Blessings Jesus had pronounced in his famous sermon upon the Mount of Blessings.

" 'How blest are you, when you suffer insults and persecution and every kind of calumny for my sake. Accept it with gladness and exultation, for you have a rich reward in the kingdom of heaven; in the same way were prophets persecuted.

" 'You are light for all the world. A town upon a hill cannot be hidden. When a lamp is lit, it is not put under the meal tub, but on the lamp stand, where it gives light to everyone in the house. You, like the lamp, must shed light among your fellows so that, when they see the good you do, they may give praise to your Father in heaven.

" 'Love your enemies. Pray for your persecutors; thus you become children of your heavenly Father, who sends rain on the honest and the dishonest, and makes his sun rise on good and bad alike. Treat others as you want them to treat you. Enter by the narrow gate. The gate is wide that leads to perdition. There is plenty of room on that road. But the gate to life is small and the road narrow. Those who find it are few.' "

Tears stood in Malnor's eyes. She looked upon Paul as if he had spoken the words. "They could not stone a man who preaches such things."

Sergius also was moved. "Why would your chief priests condemn such a teacher? And by what means could they persuade Pilate to crucify him?"

Paul exclaimed, "When self-righteous men are held up to the public view in the glare of simple truth, they cannot bear it. The crookedness of the shadow they cast in its glare is plain for all to see. They could not destroy Truth. So they destroyed the man who preached it. Now when we dare to rise and preach that the man they murdered lives and that his kingdom is eternal, their chagrin and their hatred are boundless."

Elymas bar Joshua charged past the servant who was about to announce him. "You!" he shrieked, "Demon! Dead man! Devil! Back, while I exorcise you, child of hell! Back to the devil's domain from which you sprang!"

Sergius Paulus strode across the bright pavement to face Elymas. "You dared to stone a citizen of Rome!"

Elymas shrank within his white, hooded robe. "He said nothing of citizenship! He sat at meat with Greeks and dwelt in a Greek household. He preached the destruction of the Temple—by Romans, if you please. He preached a kingdom to be established by legions of angels, and heavenly fire which would destroy the lawful rulers of this empire."

"Elymas, you are a fool. I have suspected it for some time. You came to me for protection. Because I respect zeal in a man I gave you not only protection but friendship. You repay my friendship by repeating the kind of lying nonsense other zealots used to get the Nazarene convicted by Romans and hanged on a Roman cross. Do you think to use me as those men used Pilate?"

He turned toward Barnabas. The flush of anger ebbed. "So you pray for those who persecute you." He crossed back to his seat. " 'Thus you become children of God, who sends rain on good and bad alike,' " he quoted softly. Then, strongly, "Sit down, Elymas. Let us see whether you are capable of finding that narrow gate which leads to life. Sit, man! I will be obeyed by you, this one time. Sit and be silent, while these men give me their witness, for I will not rest until I have learned the whole truth about the prophet of Nazareth."

Elymas had turned toward the shadowed area beneath the

balcony, but at the term, "Prophet of Nazareth," he jerked about. "I tell you that man is a demon. He is not flesh and blood."

Paul threw back his toga. "This flesh you wounded. My blood you spilled. But I live, and these are the wounds you laid upon me." He lifted his tunic. Perhaps the hot bath had affected the wound upon his thigh. At any rate, blood oozed from it now. "This is my living flesh," said Paul. "My blood still flows."

Elymas pulled the hood over his face and huddled down on a rug in the shadow.

Paul said proudly, "I preached the good news of the coming of Messiah. The Lord Jesus delivered me from the malice of this evil man."

Elymas threw back his hood. "They base it all upon the mighty works they attribute to the carpenter. I myself know something of magic arts. You have seen me perform wonders, Sergius. When Messiah comes he will not come as a traveling magician."

"If you speak again I will lock you in a dungeon," said Sergius. "You are in trouble, man. You would be in worse trouble if this Roman of Tarsus had died. Now thank your God that he is alive, and be silent."

Malnor had remained quiet through everything, except for a little cry of pity when Paul's toga was thrown off and the extent of his wounds revealed. She was watching him with a kind of adoration.

Sergius said, "Can you state in brief the essence of the faith you preach?"

Barnabas paced the handsome pavement of red, yellow, and black stones, his wine forgotten, all else forgotten.

"The lost man is the man out of place, out of right relationship. Like a coin in a dark corner, a sheep off in the hills, a son among strangers, so is such a man out of step with men, with God, with himself. The relation with God is fundamental. Make that right and the rest will come. To that end a man must first see differently, feel differently. As the Lord Jesus illustrated by many parables, the man must come to himself. He must repent."

"Repent. How does he define that?"

"Repentance is sorrow for past misdeeds and mistaken attitudes, but it is more. It is a total change of mind and will. There must be faith—the faith which enables a man to put his hand in God's hand as simply, as confidently as little Malnor has put her hand in yours. The faith which turns heart and will toward God. Jesus said of such a change, 'Today is salvation come to this man.' "

This was where I had gone astray. I had thought if I walked with Christians and repeated the Christian words it was enough.

Paul burst out ardently, "He summed it up, 'You shall love the Lord your God with all your heart, mind, strength—and you shall love your neighbor as yourself.' "

Sergius said doubtfully, "The theory has a beautiful ring. It is what all men long to do, to be. But we are human and frail. How can you win followers with precepts which set so difficult a standard?"

Paul replied, "God so loved the world that He sent His son to men, to lead them into Truth, saying to them, 'Love one another.' Jesus so loved men that he gave his years to healing and teaching them. In the end he died, a sinless man suffering degradation and agony, that men who believe can say, 'My sins are forgiven. Through faith in the Lord Jesus I will sin no more.' "

Barnabas said, "Death could not hold him. He came from the tomb alive. Afterward he said to his followers, 'Preach to every nation. Bring the good news of God's love and for-giveness to all men, whether Jew, Greek, or Roman, whether slave or free. Preach repentance and God's forgiveness of sins. Tell men who believe and are baptized in token of repentance that the Breath of God will enter into them. By this grace are men transformed!"

It is true, every word, I thought in wonder, and the joy which had been building within me could be nothing less than the Breath of God for which I had waited and longed, blind to the blindness in myself which had shut me away from it, and from those to whom it had been given.

Sergius said, "No wonder you devote your lives to spreading these truths. How simple they are, and how beautiful."

Paul said, "They are not simple. They merely sound simple. But they change men's lives. These simple truths are more powerful than all the might of Rome."

Malnor was softly weeping. "I believe it," she murmured.

"I, too," said Sergius Paulus.

At this Elymas made a great outcry. "We have a saying, 'Cursed is he who is hanged on a tree.' They distort every-thing, Sergius. They lie with every breath, meaning to deceive and persuade you."

Paul cried, "We glory in the cross! How else could God's love for men be made known?"

"The Nazarene was an imposter! The Jews rejected him. The Romans crucified him. He is accurst."

Paul and Elymas were outshouting one another. Paul shouted, "The Jews rejected Jesus. The Jews stoned me. I reject the Jews. Henceforth I shall preach only to Gentiles."

"Now this is blasphemy indeed! I call you to witness, sir, that this Jew will henceforth preach to Gentiles the Messiah of the Jews."

Paul rushed upon him, seeming for all his slight stature to tower over Elymas. "You son of Belial, you enemy of righteousness, full of deceit and villainy, will you never stop making crooked the straight path laid out by our Lord Jesus? Now behold, God's hand is upon you. Your heart is blind. Your mind is darkened. Let your eyes also be blind. You shall see sunlight no more."

Elymas shuddered, clapped his hands over his face, and fell headlong. Paul stood over him, rigid with anger. "Learn what blindness is. Then let faith heal the darkness of your spirit and of your eyes, and the black darkness which is in your very soul."

Elymas screamed, "I cannot see! Thick mist covers me. Bring light! Sir, a lamp, I beg of you." He felt about with flailing arms, grasped the hem of Paul's toga, pulled so frantically that the worn cloth parted with a rending sound.

Paul said, "You will see when you will see. I have nothing to do with that."

Sergius bent over the frothing figure. With a gesture he turned Elymas over to the steward. Servants brought a blanket in which they rolled the writhing magician.

When they had carried him out, the room seemed terribly still. Then Malnor crossed to Paul and laid her hand upon his arm. "You cursed him, Paul. He is your enemy. You did not pray for him. You cursed him."

Slowly Paul came back to himself. "I have never before invoked the mystic powers of our Lord. Content I was to wield the blade of truth. How this happened I do not know."

Remembering Peter's first miracle I could have wept for Paul. But tears for Paul would have been wasted.

"We zealots are a strange breed," he said with a shake of his head, a small, wry smile. "For men of our sort a few days of blindness may be the only way God can find to open our hearts. It was so with me. God grant it may be true for Elymas. I would like to see his zeal turned into profitable channels."

"Then you don't hate him?"

"Why no, dear child. Whatever made you think I did?"

# CHAPTER *22*

Sergius and Malnor were baptized three days later, together with a handful of palace servants, including the steward who had taken the smitten Elymas to the Jewish dwelling where he lodged.

The ritual of baptism was performed in the palace atrium. Barnabas said, "If you go publicly to the river to be baptized, Sergius, a hundred Romans will be asking for baptism tomorrow. Let us build on a sure foundation in Paphos."

The precaution made no difference. The news spread. Moreover, the blindness of Elymas became as great a wonder amongst Jews as was the baptism of the proconsul amongst Romans. Barnabas and Paul preached daily in the forum, the barracks, the city gates, the portals to theater and thermae. Even I was witnessing as a part of every business transaction, and business had never been better. Soon, I thought, every vessel in Paphos will be of copper, and no alabaster will be seen. Even the prized Alexandrian glass was less prominently displayed. I was not ashamed of the pleasure I found in the pursuit of business. Yet now at last I found so great a pleasure in giving my witness that a vision of what my destiny could be was taking shape.

A man of business could witness wherever his travels took him. As steward of his possessions, a man of business could dedicate his wealth to the kingdom of God in the earth.

Paul and Barnabas were now dwelling in the palace. When my wares were sold I moved in with them, leaving Ken in charge of the donkey boys at the inn. Sleeping rooms in the palace opened off the balcony above the atrium. Except for the painted murals, the room assigned to the three of us was no finer than my own sleeping quarters in Salamis. The meals became occasions when Paul and Barnabas instructed Sergius and his guests in the Christian faith. Wherever they preached in the city the proconsul was among those who listened. Sergius was soaking up a reserve of knowledge against the time when Paphos would be left with its new ecclesia and no preacher.

Malnor went wherever Paul preached. Whether she went to learn or to adore I could not tell.

A day came when we had news that a ship bound for Perga in Pamphylia was in the harbor of Old Paphos. Paul ordered me to buy passage for three on her.

"I will buy passage for two," I said. "Business calls me to Salamis."

"This is the business of the Lord Jesus. Come with us." His eyes compelled, as did his voice. We were in the forum, and I was reluctant to argue.

I found Ken at the inn and instructed him to take the boys and return to Salamis. Into his keeping I gave the thick sheaf of orders for copper wares. "Tell Kyros I will return when God wills. For now I will go north to Perga with Paul and Barnabas."

Ken's eyes were merry. "I think you will go to Joppa before you come to Salamis, Marcus. When we see you again, I think you will bring your wife with you."

I said stiffly, "I wish I knew as much about my plans as you seem to."

I gave him a few denarii, enough to feed and shelter the boys on their journey. Ken was delighted to be the bearer of news of our eventful mission. Had I returned with him, I would have been the witness. Now it would be Ken.

At the sunset meal Paul opened his plans to Sergius Paulus. "We will go by ship to Perga, cross over the pass to Antioch in Pisidia, preach there and throughout the trans-Taurus provinces."

Malnor cried, "Those places are so far away! The passes are dangerous, Paul. Not even the legions can guard all the passes from bandits."

Sergius Paulus shot a keen look into his daughter's stricken face. "Why not remain in Paphos for a few weeks? Meanwhile, I will send letters to the governors of the provinces, ensuring you hospitality and protection."

Malnor pleaded, "Paul, let Father help you. Let him make sure you will not—not—" She choked, unable even to speak of the stoning at Tamassus, and the danger that it might be repeated.

Sergius and Malnor, I thought, had discussed this subject before. Does Sergius imagine, I wondered, that Malnor in her pretty Roman sandals might also travel the dusty and dangerous roads Paul would choose? Would it ever occur to Sergius that a man on whom his daughter set her heart might reject her? He must have given considerable thought to ways by which he could smooth the path they took.

Paul said sternly, "You are a woman, Malnor. Play a woman's part. Do not use your pretty wiles to block God's will." He turned to Sergius. "Our ship is in the harbor. We sail tomorrow."

Barnabas said, "We will send by Ken a message calling for

someone to come from Antioch to preach in Tamassus and here in Paphos, Sergius."

Malnor cried, "Paul! You will be killed by bandits in those mountains!"

I said, "If Paul encounters bandits he will preach to them."

Malnor fled, her hands pressing her cheeks.

Sergius laid a hand on Paul's sleeve. "Her heart is fixed upon you, Paul. Have you another commitment?"

Paul's eyes were bleak. His face was deathly pale. "I am committed. I am firmly committed—for life."

I did not wait for more, but rushed out to find Malnor. She had fled through the peristyle into the atrium and stood weeping soundlessly in the shadow where the balcony stairway backed against the wall. I pulled her curly head against my chest and held the slight, shuddering body.

Her arms went round my neck. "Oh Marcus, I love him so much."

"I know. Thus I loved you, this past year. I know how much it hurts."

She raised her wet face. "You did? But that was all just for fun. Did I really hurt you with my foolishness? You are so very nice, and so serious. I was such a little noodle I could not resist teasing you."

"It was good for me. I needed to begin thinking a man's thoughts and feeling a man's emotions. You were very good for me."

She caught a wavering breath. "Will this be good—good for me, Marcus?" Before I could frame a reply she had buried her face against me and was sobbing. "He won't ever love me. He won't ever marry me." The words were shaken from her between sobs. "Ever, ever, ever."

"Only Paul can answer. I cannot speak for Paul." I held her close while she wept. One or two servants entered, then quietly departed, and still I held her, remembering nights when I had awakened from dreams of her to weep into the sleeve of my coat. Then, as if Barnabas were speaking through me, I said, "If one must love, it is well to love the best, the greatest. It is well to know that the driving force of a tremendous mission is what separates your love from you."

Her arms tightened. "How good you are, dear Marcus." She looked up. "Do you—still love me, Marcus?"

"My mother has chosen a wife for me." I told her about Rhoda. "When I leave Paul and Barnabas I will go to Joppa and try to persuade her to marry me and come to Salamis."

She said sadly, "All this trouble you had, because of me. I was wrong to play at foolish little love games with such a serious boy. I deserve—I deserve to lose my—my love."

"I loved you before you flirted with me. I loved you when I first saw you. I could not take my eyes off you that first day I saw you in this atrium."

Her smile was wan. "I remember. I thought you were so funny. I did not know how much loving can hurt."

Voices from the dining room had been muted. Now they grew louder. The meal had ended. Paul and Barnabas and Sergius Paulus were in the peristyle. They were coming toward us. Why hadn't I managed this better? Malnor would be humiliated to be found here crying her heart out. Any girl would.

She had heard them, and suddenly she was gone from our shadowed retreat, running to meet them. Her head was up, her voice under control, however much her tearstained face might betray. She ran to Paul, hands out. "Oh Paul, I will pray every day that God will keep you safe."

For a moment Paul was speechless. This was something I had never expected to see. He faced her, looking inexpressibly sad. "You are a woman, and you play a woman's part," he said at length. "Our Lord Jesus said, 'Whoever loves father or mother, wife or brother more than me is not fit for the kingdom of heaven.' The ministry comes first, Malnor. This I have known since I was struck down by blinding light on the Damascus road."

He must have misquoted deliberately. Paul never misquoted by chance.

He kissed her forehead, released her hands, turned to ascend to the balcony. He stumbled on the stairway. Malnor turned to Sergius Paulus. "His hands are feverish. Is he ill?"

Paul stumbled again at the top of the stairs, then pitched forward on the balcony floor. Barnabas reached him first, but Paul was on his feet again, moving steadily toward our sleeping room. By the time he reached it Malnor was beside him. "Paul, you cannot leave us if you are ill."

"My child, the fever and I are old enemies. It comes and it goes. Now leave me. I cannot bear for you to see me in my extremity of pain."

Malnor moved blindly to Sergius, who had joined us on the balcony.

Barnabus said, "We know what to do for him. We have nursed him through fever before. But I think this will pass. The fever has not troubled him for more than a year. A night's rest will restore him. Do not be anxious."

We spoke our goodnights and parted. When Paul had bathed and lay upon his bed he looked normal enough, except for the pallor, and a terrible sadness written plainly upon his pale, pinched face.

That night I dreamed of Rhoda. She was with Mother in another room, apart from me, and she wept for me, as Malnor had wept for Paul. When I went in and sought to comfort her she turned from me. "I hope you will find a girl you can greet as Nicodemus greeted Mother," she said. "We cannot help what we feel." She threw herself into Mother's arms, shuddering with silent sobs.

I woke in a sweat of despair. How could I go to Rhoda with the lighthearted announcement that a year ago I had cared for another girl but now she was the girl I wanted for my wife?

I lay awake the rest of that night while memories of Rhoda thronged my mind. Even the little gamin who had first entered our house had a quality all her own. For what she had been before Mother adopted her I felt a sweep of compassion. For what she became after Mother took her in hand I felt thankfulness and love. She had become Mother's constant companion and comfort. Yet she was no more a copy of Mother than she had been a copy of Ananias and Sapphira. And she had loved me with all her generous and deeply affectionate nature.

I saw her toiling by late firelight over her letters to me. I recalled her description of the nights when she wakened to hear Mother sorrowing with the longing for the return of the Lord Jesus. With what sure insight had she found the meaning of Jesus' promises, the promises the apostles had taken as a literal fulfillment of their own deep longing. In spite of all that the Jerusalem ecclesias had shared and heard, it was Rhoda who first declared that Pentecost fulfilled Jesus' promise, "Lo, I am with you always."

I longed to talk with Rhoda, to know all the sweet mysteries of her strong and loyal spirit, her quick mind, her disciplined body. My children would be blessed to have Rhoda for their mother, I thought, and wept as I had never wept for Malnor. Rhoda, Rhoda, Rhoda, I need you. I want you with all my being.

The very strength of my longing warned me that I could not go to Rhoda with all my follies upon me. I had kept in mind, when I bought those three tickets for Perga, the fact that coasting ships sail right around the curving shore, calling at Ephesus, at Rhodes, at Perga, Tarsus, Antioch, at Sidon, Tyre, Caesarea, Joppa, and on around to Egypt. As we cross to Perga, I had thought, I will find a way to explain to Barnabas and Paul that the mission they have chosen is not for me. In the light of my dream and of my own strong feelings it seemed I could not confess to Rhoda the folly of my feelings at that Passover season when I was last in Bethany. I could not say to her, I did not want you then, but now I do.

Suddenly from Paul's bed came a groan, then the cry, "O God, will I never be delivered from the body of this death?"

Barnabas was up instantly, and bending over Paul. "Fever. I thought yesterday it might be coming on."

"Get me to the ship. Quickly! That child must not see me today. She has found enough to pity. Mark! Find the steward. Arrange to borrow horses to take us quickly to the harbor. God give me strength to walk aboard that ship!"

He prays for a little miracle, I thought, as I changed into a street coat and tied on my sandals. Why does he never pray to be healed of fever? I rushed downstairs, found the steward, then had a private word with Sergius Paulus to explain the haste of our departure.

We got Paul aboard safely. He walked along the weir clinging to us for support. He boarded the ship. The owner was too busy to notice us, beyond accepting the three wooden tabs given to me when I bought our passage. A Greek had come aboard, bringing a score of bundles and bales, and the owner was attempting to collect double fare because of the space his belongings would occupy.

Over by the mast the captain was in a hullabaloo with two sailors. The lines had been tangled when last the sail was lowered, and the captain sought by a combination of invective and main strength to hoist sail. So we were able to get Paul below deck into the passenger cabin in the stern without being stopped.

The cabin was empty of passengers, though half a score had been there to preempt their chosen space with beds and bundles. We found a crowded corner, the corner farthest from the grating which let in light. By the time we got Paul's bed spread and him on it, he was raving.

Every ship has its smell. This was not, praise God, a galley or a sheep ship. The stench of excrement, whether human or animal, seems to me the least endurable of all stenches. Ships which sailed west as far as Rome carried the sour smell of grain awash in the bilge. Our ship smelled of the tannery. Likely she had hides as part of her cargo.

The Greek with the bundles was in the hatchway, shoving in his baggage, bale by bale and parcel by parcel, and cursing the captain, who evidently had refused space in the hold for his belongings. The cabin promised to be very crowded, a small matter in ordinary circumstances, as no right-thinking passenger will linger in the cabin if the weather is fit to go on deck. But it would certainly increase the difficulty of giving Paul the proper care.

The Greek was now shoving his bundles in beside us. Absorbed as he was by his own problems he did not notice Paul till a hamper filled with strong-smelling cheeses slid off the pile onto my back. He shrieked, "Fever!" and rushed from the cabin.

Before I had got the hamper balanced back where it belonged the owner was in the cabin. An Alexandrian he was, with tremendous eyebrows and a great belly above short, stocky legs. "You cannot keep that man aboard. Fever is bad luck on a ship! Get him ashore."

Barnabas said, "Fever is bad luck for the patient. I cannot speak for the ship." He wrapped Paul's coat about his flailing arms. "Sir, this man's home is in Tarsus. He wants to reach the mainland. My cousin and I are Levites. We understand medicine and will care for him, and before we have crossed to Perga he will be on deck in the sun. Can you provide us with heated stones?"

The Alexandrian shouted, "Get off! The cabin is overcrowded, and a sick man cannot remain. I won't have a fever patient stinking up the cabin and dying aboard. Get him off!"

At that moment we heard the crack of the filling sail. The ship lurched, then moved out into the quiet water of the harbor. The owner slapped his leg with a stream of Egyptian curses and rushed to the hatch. Barnabas called after him, "The patient will recover overnight, sir, if you will provide us with heated stones."

Now we were alone with our patient. Presently a sailor appeared with three warm stones slung in a cloth. We tucked them against Paul's back.

"He's torn open the wound in his thigh, with all this threshing about," Barnabas said. "God help him."

"Amen," I said. "What a pity Peter never laid healing hands upon him."

"Not all who suffer are healed—not even by Peter. This is a mystery I do not pretend to understand."

"I wonder whether Dorcas, in Joppa, has had an attack of fever since Peter restored her?"

Barnabas glanced at me in the dimness. "When you go to Joppa you can ask."

"When I go to Joppa." I averted my face.

"I am glad you are here, Mark. I will welcome your company if it is your desire to continue the journey with us. What is your desire?"

"Rhoda. Only Rhoda. She is all my desire." I glanced about

the cabin. Thank God all the passengers were on deck, watching the little ship beat its way out of the harbor toward clear water and the passage north to Perga. I would not have many chances to talk with Barnabas, whether in this crowded cabin or on deck after Paul was able to be moved out into the sun. "I've been a fool. Now I cannot bear to hurt Rhoda further by going to her to say, 'I want you now. I did not want you then.' "

Paul was rolling so we both had to hold him down. In the midst of our struggle he cried out, "The lusts of the flesh! Be not led into evil by passion."

"Oh," I exclaimed, outraged, "what I feel for Rhoda is greater than you know, Paul of Tarsus! You shame me by reducing it to such terms."

"He speaks to himself, not to you. What do you feel for Rhoda?"

"So much I cannot take her such a tale as I would have to tell. I have humiliated her once. I cannot humiliate her by speaking to her of what I felt for Malnor."

"Rhoda would not be humiliated to learn that you love her, Mark. She was humiliated by a sense of her own follies. She would be glad to learn it was Malnor, not her traffic with Ben Eli, which caused your coldness."

"Ben Eli? Why, I understand all that. I found her follies endearing. She is so—so remarkable that a little folly—a little folly—" I buried my face in the coat I was holding tight about Paul's writhing legs. When I had mastered my emotion I said, "It is well I am here now, for you need me. How will you manage Paul when the next bout of fever comes, and I am gone?"

"We will not be alone. We will never be alone."

" 'Lo I am with you always, even to the ends of the earth,' " I quoted.

"That too. I was thinking of the converts. The prospect is glorious, Mark. I do not know how you can bear to miss this journey, even for Rhoda's sake. Think of converts, believers, ecclesias in cities whose names we have scarcely heard. An ecclesia, perhaps, in the household of Philemon in Colossae— with the slave, Onesemus, as an elder. Others will come later, Mark, but we will be the first."

I longed to share the great adventure. But I could not go. I must first put my affairs in order. "Perhaps my season for such a ministry will come," I said, but with no real hope that it ever would.

For a time we were occupied with Paul. A rain began to fall. Our fellow passengers crowded into the cabin. Between Paul's suffering and the complaints of fellow travelers, it was a bad evening. Around midnight Paul's fever broke. The cabin grew very quiet after that, except for the snoring of the man next to us. But on the following day the sun was shining and Paul was able to go up onto the deck.

Perga is a harbor built on swamps, sixty stadia upstream from the mouth of the river Cestius. Rising beyond the low houses and harbor sheds is a temple to Diana. Beyond the town, shadowing all the landscape, rise hills beyond hills beyond hills, till in the distance, overshadowing all the landscape, stand the forbidding, serrated peaks of the Taurus Mountains. The Lebanon Range, through which I had walked with Peter last summer, is gentle in comparison. The tops of Lebanon and Hermon are snowy in all seasons but the valley between them yields a natural and beautiful passage.

A skinful of bones, pallid, bruised, with a reopened wound upon his thigh which refused to heal, Paul would require a miracle to get him across that terrain to Antioch of Pisidia, a hundred miles away. Yet his will was inflexible. He would reach Antioch, or he would leave his bones in the pass.

We waited at an inn in Perga while sleep and wine and broth slowly restored in Paul some small part of his former vigor. I haunted the harbor, waiting for a coasting vessel on which to book passage for Joppa. After ten days such a ship docked. She was scabby and sour and stank of fermented grain. The owner, a Syrian of Antioch, wore a clean coat over a filthy tunic. I have learned that the worse a ship, the higher the price the owner will demand. I dickered with him for a while, then turned away with a shrug. He shouted a reasonable fee before I was beyond hearing, and I returned and bought my passage.

When I reached the inn Paul was propped in the thin sunshine in front of it, gazing toward the mountains. In later years, whenever I heard some new report of Paul's travels, or whenever I encountered him as I traveled with Peter, I was to remember that vaporous, swampy seaport, and Paul, pallid and emaciated, with his unhealed thigh wound, looking at those menacing peaks.

"Give it up for now, Paul," I urged, as I sank down beside him. "Go to Tarsus. When you are strong—in the spring—go north into Galatia from there."

"When I have used the strength I have, God will give me more."

"There is a coasting vessel in the harbor. Go aboard, Paul, and go to Tarsus and be healed. Or go to Antioch. The ship sails round the coast all the way to Joppa." I had meant to say Egypt, but my own destination slipped out.

Paul's eyes grew bleak and accusing. "You are deserting this mission."

Barnabas emerged from the inn. "You speak harshly, Paul. God does not lay upon every man the same mission. Mark has his own obligations."

Paul said sharply, "You pamper him. You, Miriam, Phoebe,

Kyros—all of you! Oh God, had I his strength what could I not achieve! No man has any obligations which outweigh the debt he owes to the Lord Jesus!" He struggled to rise, but could not. His whole body seemed to yearn toward those mountains.

"The field is white for harvest. The laborers are few. And this one, with his excellent education, his fine strength, his pleasing way with men—this one cannot go with me because he must first marry a wife."

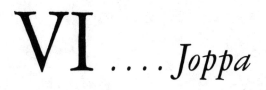

# VI .... Joppa

# CHAPTER *23*

Joppa harbor must look today much as it looked when Jonah took ship there for his rendezvous with the whale. Unlike other harbors, Joppa has no facilities beyond those God provided when He divided the waters from the land—the broad, shallow, half-moon bay, protected from off-shore drafts by hills which rise behind the beach. No moles or docks reach out from shore. Ships drop anchor out in the bay and unload cargo into lighters.

The day we anchored in Joppa was remarkably warm for the season. The sun shone brilliantly, though we had had rains throughout the voyage. The water looked blue and inviting. I was sticky and verminous, and stale from many weeks' confinement in the worst ship on which I had ever traveled. I had only the meager comfort of knowing there was not a man aboard less verminous than I. I longed to leap into the bay and make the long swim to shore, but in spite of the sunshine's promise, spring had not yet come, and the water was much colder than it looked to be.

I needed bracing for the encounters ahead. My nights throughout the journey, with its tedious stops in every little harbor along the eastern end of the Great Sea, had been tortured by dreams of a cold and unforgiving Rhoda. My days had been haunted by the memory of Paul's reproaches.

I knew not how I was going to convince Rhoda that my follies were behind me, since I could scarcely convince myself. I wanted her desperately, till it seemed to me I would be of small use to God or the copper business until I had brought her to Salamis and made her mistress of my home.

How to convince Rhoda of the change in my feelings I did not know. There was nobody to tell me how willingly a young girl in love would listen to intelligence of that sort. Nor had I sense enough to realize that the insight which had revealed to her the emptiness of my heart would now reveal its fullness.

I went ashore in the third lighter. The sun was low and my shadow long as I stepped out onto the white, packed sand. I looked about, half hoping to see Nicodemus amongst the merchants. Failing that, I inquired of a Greek in one of the grain sheds where Nicodemus could be found.

He glanced toward the setting sun, then curiously at me. "The Christians keep the first day of the week as their holy day. You will find him with this sect at the house of Simon the Tanner." He stepped outside to point out the house, a wide, stone dwelling on an eminence south of the bay. It had no upper room, but a spread of tentcloth was visible above the parapet. On that roof Peter had seen the vision of the tentcloth filled with every creature which creeps or crawls or swims, the vision which prepared him for his mission to Cornelius in Caesarea.

In the multitude of my discomforts and anxieties on shipboard I had lost track of the days, even of the Sabbath, which was yesterday, since today was the First Day. I was ashamed to face the assembled ecclesia of Joppa unwashed. Yet I set out to climb the steep, narrow street which rose to the height above the bay.

I knew how often the fellowship of the ecclesias lasted from sunset far into the night's first watch. I had not the patience to search out the house of Nicodemus and go there to await the return of Mother and Rhoda. A doorkeeper would be posted on an evening when the ecclesia met. I would, I thought, give him a message for Mother and wait outside the gate till she came to me. Bearing the verminous bundle of my bed and clothing I followed the winding ascent of the narrow street.

As I approached the house the first hymn was heard, a hymn Silas had adapted, setting words from the Messianic prophecies of Isaiah to a lovely melody sung by the choir of Levites in our Temple for centuries. The sound of the familiar hymn in this strange city, after my miserable journey, brought a lump to my throat. Then the sound of Mother's clear voice soaring joyously in the hymn compounded my emotion. I judged from the singing that all the company, men and women together, was upon the roof.

Another voice struck upon my ears—the deep, powerful, true voice of Peter. No sound could have pleased me more. If I failed to explain myself to Rhoda, I could count on Peter's help.

I rushed round to the camel gate. It stood ajar, and my knock went unheard. I stepped into the court, set my bundle against the wall. The lad left as gatekeeper stood at the top of the stairway, singing joyously, his gaze bent upward.

Peter was in the podium, visible above the parapet, singing with all the power of his great lungs. I tried to get the lad's attention, failed, and went up to tap his shoulder. His jaw dropped when he saw me, and he sent a guilty glance toward the open gate.

Caught up in the music I began to sing. The boy grinned, reassured to find that I was of this fellowship, though a stranger.

Peter turned, hearing my voice added to the others, and strode across to embrace me, his welcome enveloping and compelling. The next thing I knew I was in the podium and Peter's great arm was around my shoulders. Mother's voice cracked, then soared happily. Her face glowed welcome. She was in the third row, very near, and Rhoda was beside her.

In the unguarded moment of surprise I saw the longing and the pain of Rhoda's love. Then she was singing again, nodding, smiling, her poise restored. I had to swallow before I could get my voice to working once more. I could not take my eyes from her. I longed to go to her, to whisper my love to her, but Peter's arm held me.

The song reached its close with the lines:

> He will feed his flock like a shepherd,
> He will gather the lambs in his arms,
> He will carry them in his bosom,
> And gently lead those that are with young.

The rustle of murmuring movement was quieted by Peter's strong, sure voice. "Friends and brothers in the Lord Jesus, this is Mark, son of Miriam of Bethany. In bonds of the spirit he is my son also, for we have shared journeys and labors, dangers, even prison. Come now. Welcome Mark into your fellowship."

They pressed forward to shake my hand, and give me the kiss of welcome. First came the men, Nicodemus among them, some two score people of various races in this backwater port. After the men, the women came, with Mother foremost among them and Rhoda lingering shyly in the shadows. Mother embraced me lovingly. "Mark, how well you look. What joy to see you. Peter told us . . ."

Peter's voice interrupted from the podium. "There will be time for greetings later, friends. Let us return to our places.

This young man has a witness you will want to hear. Simon, go ahead with lighting the lamps. We will proceed, for this promises to be a long evening."

Mother glanced with a wry smile at Peter but returned to her seat. Rhoda returned, shy and uncertain, to her place beside Mother. I had not even spoken to her. Now she sat with her eyes on her folded hands. I gazed at her steadily, but could not catch her eye. Well then, I had been prepared for this meeting, but my sudden arrival must have been a shock to the dear girl.

Peter drew me back to the podium. "Five months ago the Antioch elders commissioned Barnabas and Paul of Tarsus and this young man Mark to preach throughout Cyprus. Now let us hear Mark's report upon that mission."

This was typical of the fellowship of Believers, this welcome from strangers, this delighted assumption that whatever concerned one concerned all. These were the open, receptive faces of friends. I swallowed my emotions and plunged into the story of our Cyprus mission.

The tale took a while, for at every turn there were cries of pity or of thanksgiving, or demands for additional detail. In the telling I felt again all the drama of the experiences I had shared with Barnabas and Paul, the terror and triumph of the stoning, the scene in the governor's palace between Paul and Elymas, the baptism of the proconsul with his household. Rhoda was caught up in the story, as were Mother and Nicodemus and all the company.

Finally I spoke of Paul's illness, coming upon him while his body was still painfully bruised. I described him as I last saw him, sitting in the sun before the inn, while the distant mountains rose dark and threatening against the sky. "We talked of the dangers he and Barnabas would face in crossing those mountains. I urged Paul to rest for a while and recover his strength before undertaking that journey. He replied, 'When I have used the strength I have, God will give me more.' I have no doubt," I concluded, "that Paul and Barnabas are preaching even now, this very evening, somewhere in the vicinity of Antioch of Pisidia, to men and women who never heard the Good News until they came to tell it."

I concluded, "When the ship came, bound for Joppa, I bade them farewell, and came hither."

A sort of sigh went up, and the happy, attentive faces grew strange and bewildered. Peter voiced their question. "Why did you abandon Paul in his time of greatest need? Surely you longed to share that magnificent adventure! Surely you wanted to witness the marvels still in store. Why did you leave them?"

Nothing less than the truth would serve. Nor could I have imagined an alternative reason, for Rhoda was waiting for my answer as if suspended there beneath the canopy of black goat hair. I stepped toward her. I saw none but Rhoda as I replied, "I came to claim my bride."

Rhoda's lips parted, her eyes opened wide. She leaned toward me, half rising. A shout went up from the company, a chorus of delighted laughter. Rhoda ducked her head, clutching her hands together in embarrassment. Yet somehow I was beside her; my voice was for her ear alone. "You will marry me, won't you? Oh, Rhoda, I will cherish you. Truly."

She asked softly, "Did you really leave them, Paul and Barnabas and that wonderful journey—for me, Mark?"

"All for you, Rhoda. Only for you."

At that point Peter took charge once more. Evidently he thought I had had time enough to court the girl I had treated so coldly a year ago.

"Now, Rhoda, I must see you two married at once. The

hour grows late. Let's get on, for I must bless this marriage tonight, since I depart at dawn for Caesarea."

Simon the tanner moved in, an earthen lamp in his hand. He was a heavy, hearty man, and I'd have known him anywhere for a tanner by the cured-leather look of his hands and the unmistakable tannery odor. "Rhoda, my wife has been saving her wedding veil for our daughter. She wants you to wear it."

Mother said, "Mark, I have put aside for your marriage the ring your father gave me. Nicodemus will bring it while I help these good women prepare Rhoda." Then, joyfully, "Oh Mark, my dear, dear boy, this is a joyful night."

I protested, "But Rhoda has not consented. Give her a moment to say yes or no."

Rhoda's dark eyes searched my face. "Is this what you truly want, Mark?"

"With all my heart."

"Now? Tonight?"

"The sooner I can call you my own, the happier I will be."

"I will marry you. Tonight, or whenever you say."

Nicodemus cried exuberantly, "Now we have all we need— a bride, a bridegroom, a veil, a ring, and our beloved Peter to bless the union. As for the wedding feast, we will celebrate that tomorrow night. Meanwhile, you must all follow the bridegroom as he leads his bride home to his mother's house, and we will manage at least a little wine for everyone." With that he rushed away down the stairs. I saw him shoulder my bed and baggage as he went out the gate.

I put my lips to Rhoda's ear. "Tonight, my love, and for all my life."

My heart was overflowing with joy as I watched Rhoda go down to be decked for her wedding. Then I went over to Peter, who had somehow brought all this so swiftly to pass.

The whole place was in a clamor, with the women laughing and chattering downstairs and men bringing more and more lamps and torches to the roof, till it seemed as bright as noonday. Nicodemus returned, breathing quickly, carrying a magnificent scarlet robe over his arm.

"This was my bridal garment, my son," he said. "I could not let you stand up here in the presence of God and these dear friends wearing that travel-soiled coat. Now I have the ring secure in my scrip. I will give it to you when we get you ready."

Peter and Nicodemus tugged off my woolen coat and helped me into the rich, scarlet affair. They laid on me the scarlet headcloth and over it, securing it, a golden chaplet set with a single, large ruby. Then Nicodemus wound about me a splendid golden girdle and looped it so the fringed ends hung to the hem.

"Wear it with joy, my son," said Nicodemus, and embraced me. "God send you every good gift and many sons. You could not have found a better wife if you had searched the world for her."

Peter called down into the court, "Come, come. The hour grows late. How long does it take to lay a veil over a girl's head?"

"We are ready," said Mother.

The women began the bridal chant. Mother came hurrying, signaled to Nicodemus to come and lead the bride up from the court. Standing with Peter beside the podium I could see the procession form. Nicodemus and Rhoda led, the singing women by twos followed. They ascended to us, Rhoda with her hand tucked into Nicodemus' arm.

The bridal veil was a gleaming square of white linen, so large that, laid over the bride's head it hung down almost to the hem of her coat, covering her completely. A wreath of flowers had been bound to the silver chaplet and more flowers made a wreath over her shoulders. She approached proudly, very tall, very straight, leading the women in stately procession. Mother walked with the singing women. Her voice had never sounded lovelier. I am sure her face glowed with joy, though I could not take my eyes from the veiled figure of my bride long enough to look upon anyone else.

Nicodemus laid Rhoda's hand in mine. It trembled and was cold. I held it tenderly, the hand which had written many letters to me by firelight when the day's hard labors were done. Suddenly I was remembering, with a sweep of tenderness the dirty little gamin who had stared round-eyed at all the paraphernalia I had laid out for my bath after a day's work in the vineyard. I was remembering that this hand had been very grimy that day as it clutched the fig cake upon which she continually licked. Poor, hungry, neglected little waif. What she had been, and what she had become, had at last made for me all that had gone into that Bethany ecclesia worth while.

Peter spoke simply and beautifully of the views our Lord Jesus had expressed concerning marriage. As he spoke I felt Rhoda's hand grow warm. Its trembling ceased. And when Peter had spoken briefly, he blessed us, using a blessing I had read in the "Sayings."

"A man shall leave his father and mother and be one with his wife, for in the beginning God made them male and female, and the two shall become one flesh. What God has joined together, man must not separate."

Peter lifted Rhoda's veil and draped it back on her head so she could see and be seen. He kissed her. "May you bring to your husband as much joy as you have brought to our sister Miriam. God bless and keep you, dear Rhoda, and send you sons and daughters."

Before the people could again break into turmoil of re-joicing, Peter had organized the procession. Nicodemus lighted our way with a flaming torch. Rhoda and I followed, hand in hand. After us came Peter with Mother, then all the others, over the hill and down a street lined with blank-faced Jewish homes.

Late though it was, people emerged from these houses, brought from their rest by the lights and the singing. They called out good wishes as we passed.

And so I brought my bride to my mother's house. The act set the legal seal upon the marriage. Nicodemus led us to the roof, where a bridal chamber had been prepared. Damaris stood in the doorway, her face a moon of joy. She embraced Rhoda, then kissed me, weeping as always when I returned home, but this time with a flood of emotion. Mother led us into the room Damaris had prepared. The bridal bed was a wonder to behold. It had come from Egypt and stood upon wooden legs above the floor.

Nicodemus said proudly, "I bought it for Miriam. A marvel of comfort, with heavy strips of cotton cloth interwoven beneath the matting."

The singing women were all crowded into the room now, and divided their attentions between the bride and the Egyptian bed. I left my bride with them and returned to the court to drink wine and rejoice with the men, as was proper.

The joyful fellowship of these Joppa men continued into the night's second watch. The moon passed its zenith. The women had departed for their homes long before Peter rose to say farewell to us and return to Simon's house. Everyone left when Peter did.

I bade Nicodemus good night and went to the upper room, carrying a small copper lamp. I was dizzy with wine and good fellowship and other emotions natural to a bridegroom. The

Egyptian bed stood smooth as Damaris had left it. Where, then, was Rhoda?

In the dimness I heard a low sound, something between a hiccough and a sigh. Opposite the Egyptian bed a sleeping mat had been unrolled. Rhoda sat upon it, wrapped warmly in a white sleeping robe. She was weeping. I set the lamp in a niche and knelt beside her. "My beloved, why do you weep?"

She shuddered away from me. "Don't touch me. Mark, I'm so—ashamed."

"Ashamed? Rhoda, I am the one, not you, to feel . . ."

Her voice rose hysterically. "Don't touch me. I'm—dirty."

"Now how could that be?" It was not easy, after the long day and the longer night and all the good fellowship of the court to be reasonable with a hysterical bride.

"I don't know how it happened. I was sleeping, and I woke up feeling—oh, horrible—the way I used to feel, long ago, before Mother—before Mother scrubbed me clean and taught me to be as you are. I feel sticky and itchy and—and horrible. Things are crawling on me, and in my hair. I washed my hair only three days ago! I'm so ashamed!"

She threw herself down upon the bed, and I saw then what bed it was. I had brought it from the ship, and Nicodemus had brought it here.

I dared not laugh. The heart of my bride was breaking. I said, "You should have gone to sleep in that Egyptian bed, my darling."

She sat up quickly. "Oh, I couldn't! It's a bridal bed. I couldn't—alone."

I gathered her into my arms, smothering her protests with kisses. "No more tears," I said, when at last she was quiet. "Your husband brought you a wedding gift, direct from the dirtiest, most verminous ship on which I ever traveled. This bed is inhabited. So, by now, are you—and so am I."

She wailed, "I can't wash my hair in the middle of the night!"

I stripped off the scarlet coat and golden girdle. "Tomorrow we will scrub one another till we are fit to occupy that fine Egyptian affair over there. For tonight, my darling, we will remain where we are."

# VII .... *Rome*

# CHAPTER *24*

Peter had sent the letter by messenger to Antioch. Agabus brought it to me in Salamis. Agabus came often in his travels, now that he was bishop of Antioch. Our sons welcomed him as they would a grandsire.

Peter was not given to spontaneous letter writing. I did not have to be told the contents. Peter was summoning me to join him in Rome. He would never write to me for any less urgent reason. I held the scroll, the seal still unbroken. A summons to far-away Rome deeply concerned Rhoda as well as me. I would wait to read it until she returned from the errand which had occupied her all this morning.

I watched Phoebe and Agabus climb to the roof, followed happily by the youngest two of our four sons. Ah Peter, I thought sadly, could you not have waited six months longer? Four sons we have, and three were born while I was journeying with you. When Rhoda gives birth for the fifth time at the end of summer I will be gone again, and farther than ever before.

Peter had been the first bishop of Antioch. Five years ago, during Paul's long imprisonment in Caesarea and in Rome, Peter had resigned his office to make the difficult journey west

across the trans-Taurus region to bring comfort to the churches
Paul had founded, the churches to which he had returned
whenever he could in his successive missionary journeys. Our
youngest son was born while I made that journey with Peter
and his wife Perpetua, who had at last been liberated from
bondage in Caesarea by the death of her mother.

We had gone together, the three of us, to visit scores of
churches. When Peter and Perpetua settled down in Ephesus, I
took ship and returned to Salamis and to Rhoda and the sons
she had given me—James and Stephen, Levi and Aaron. Little
Aaron was born a month after I set out on that journey. He
was swarming all over the house before I returned, and had
twice fallen into the pool in the atrium before ever his father
set eyes upon him.

Peter and Perpetua remained in Ephesus for a time, then
crossed to Corinth. After three years in Greece they went to
Rome. These things I had learned from Agabus, who often
saw Christian travelers in Antioch, and passed along the news
they brought.

Paul also was in Rome. The princeps, Nero, had heard his
case, finally, and set him free. Now both Peter and Paul
preached in Rome, Peter in snyagogues and the Jewish ecclesia, and Paul to Gentiles. It would be well worth the voyage to
see them both again, and hear them preach. It would be fine to
see the capital of which Caesar Augustus had written, "I found
a city of mud and left a city of marble." But something more
was involved, this time. I went to the roof, moved by the wish to
discuss with Agabus the deeply stirring sense I had that what
lay before me was far more than a long sea voyage and a few
months or perhaps a year in Rome with Peter.

The years had been good to Agabus. They had given him
opportunity to use the wealth of talents with which he had
been endowed. When Peter left Antioch the elders elected

Agabus to the office of bishop. James was bishop in Jerusalem and Andrew bishop of Macedonia. John was bishop of Ephesus, Matthew of the churches in Ethiopia, and Thomas was bishop of Damascus. But Agabus was the first Greek bishop, and Antioch the largest bishopric of them all, and the most influential. After Agabus was made bishop of Antioch, Cyprus elected to join his diocese.

Phoebe sat on a rug, going through a heap of clothing Agabus had brought, sorting what needed mending from what could only be converted into scrubbing rags. Agabus was laying out scrolls he had brought along for distribution to the Cyprus ecclesias. Twenty-five years of ministry had whitened the curling fringes at his brow and chin, yet he had an ageless look. The eyes were living lights in the creases of the thin, brown face.

Agabus said, "What did Peter have to say to you, Marcus?"

I held up the scroll, seal unbroken. "I will read it with Rhoda when she returns."

Phoebe looked up anxiously. "Shall I send someone to fetch her?"

I shook my head. "This letter has been two months on the way. Another hour or two will do no harm."

Agabus said, "I have brought four copies of a letter Paul wrote to the church in Galatia. This is a strong letter, Marcus. A fine letter. Every church should have a copy."

"I read it," I said, "when I was in Lystra with Peter five years ago. It is an excellent letter. So is the letter he sent to Ephesus."

"Many copies should be made," Agabus said. "But who can find time for that?"

I patted Levi's curly head. "This boy can in a few more years. He has the scholarly bent his father lacked."

"I can copy things already," said Levi proudly. "Will you let me try, Agabus?"

"We will wait, lad. We will still need copies two years from now. We will always be in need of new books."

Phoebe observed, "Paul preached to more people while he was a prisoner than during all the years of his travels. And he will preach to uncounted thousands long after he is dead. Had he not suffered imprisonment he would never have found time to write the letters which now inspire the churches."

Agabus twinkled. "My wife seems to think I also might acquire a great name in the earth if I were held prisoner for a time."

Aaron was clasping Agabus' knees. "Tell me a story," he begged. He was a pretty little fellow, his face a small image of my mother's lovely face. He was not yet five years old, and could still crowd into Agabus' lap. But Levi had to be content to sit beside them and lean against Agabus' arm. Phoebe gathered up the mending and the rags and went out, as Agabus began a story someone had brought from Nazareth about Jesus' boyhood.

I was too restless to listen. I wandered down into the shop. James, our firstborn, was a man, though it was not easy to think of him so. In appearance he resembled me more than the others did. As a coppersmith he could fashion fine bronze wares with the best artisans. He was intent upon a miniature pitcher designed to hold precious perfume. I stood at his elbow watching, with the strange mixture of pride and envy a father must always feel, I think, when a son surpasses him at some particular skill. Beneath the miniature lip of the pitcher was a cluster of tiny lilies, so delicate they were a marvel to see.

"Such a vessel should be executed in gold," I said.

In his absorption James had not noticed me until I spoke.

He said irritably, "It is not finished! I wish you would not judge my work before I have invited you to do so!"

I sat down nearby. "I will not be here, James, to see it finished." I held up the unopened scroll. "From Peter. In Rome."

"You will not be here for my wedding." The long, skillful hands fell inert, palms up, as he said, "You will be gone a long time, this time."

"It seems likely that I will," I agreed.

James was betrothed to Rabbi Gershon's youngest grand-daughter. The date for the wedding had not been set. James was determined the girl should be baptized a Christian before they married. He was attending snyagogue for her sake, and she was attending the ecclesia for his. The problem was his, and he must work it out in his own way. I said, "You will be the head of this family in my absence."

"Oh, I wish things did not have to change," he said, but softly, not to be heard about the busy, noisy shop. Then, with a level look, "I will take care of Mother, and the children, and the little sister when she is born. But about the business—lay that responsibility upon Stephen."

"He's still a child!"

"He has a head for figures, and you know how apt he is in the marketplace. Let his duty lie where his talents lie. He will not take orders from me in any case."

I had laid responsibility upon this son. I dared not reject his first exercise of it. I went to the next room. Stephen's apprenticeship was in its second year. He was shoving a pan of metal deep into a furnace. His face was red with heat as he turned and saw me.

Rhoda had said of Stephen, "If any of our sons inherited the duplicity which cursed my father Ananias, Stephen is the one." Yet the lad had a merry way with him, utterly different from the Ananias I remembered. Stephen would rather dicker with copper merchants than master the skills of smelter and shop. He was not above driving a sharp trade with his brothers when he could. Well then, he would be dealing with men who were themselves sharp traders. Perhaps they could teach him what fifteen years of ecclesia sermons had not.

Stephen cried, "Take me with you," when I held up the letter from Peter.

"The House of Aaron can't spare you," I replied. "You will make the Paphos journey this year."

He had made the business trips with me for three years. He was not impressed, until it struck him that he would be in charge of them. "You mean—I am to write up the orders and everything? I am to make the deals?"

"You will be responsible," I agreed. "For getting the orders, for their execution, for their delivery."

"You'd better tell that to James." The merry face wore a triumphant twinkle. "I want to see Elder Brother's face when he knows I'm in charge."

"Elder Brother suggested it."

"He did?" The merry face sobered. "He's a smart fellow, you know it? I never expected that—not from good old Elder Brother." Suddenly he extended his hand. "I'll do it right, Father. I won't forget I represent you and the House of Aaron. Don't worry about me while you're away."

"I'll be gone a long time, Stephen. Rome is a far journey. And Peter is growing old. He may not release me again."

Suddenly the boy's arms were around me. His face was burrowing into my shoulder. "I don't want you to go. We need you. Mother needs you. So do I."

"Agabus arrived today. He brought the letter. Do you want to cross to Paphos in his company?"

The boy stood very straight. "If I can make ready in time. If

I do not set out with him, I will overtake him on the way. But these journeys take preparation. I don't have to tell you that, Father." How serious he looked.

"The House of Aaron will not suffer in my absence." I went back to the atrium. The House of Aaron would not suffer if I never returned. In the full tide of my mature years I was ready at last to give to the Lord Jesus what he had not demanded of me in my youth.

"I must first put my affairs in order," I had said to Paul at Perga. My affairs were in order. If God now laid it upon me to make the choice Peter and Paul and Barnabus and so many others had made in young manhood I would not refuse, even if my ministry took me so far from Salamis I never again walked through the pleasant rooms of this house.

God had given me these years. "If only I had your strength," Paul had said that day in Perga when I bade him and Barnabus good-bye. But God had another use for my strength. Out of it had come sons to minister to the second generation of our new era, for surely the Lord Jesus did not live, and minister, and die for one generation alone. Two sons for the House of Aaron; a third son, Levi, who might become another Agabus or another Peter. Besides these, other children whose destiny was not yet clear.

Lost in my vision I did not perceive that Rhoda had entered the atrium till she came up beside the pool and laid her hand upon me. "What is it, Mark? You look so strange."

I held up the letter, grown moist in my sweated palm. "From Peter. Agabus brought it."

I looked upon her, my beloved wife of more than a score of years, as if already I was taking farewell of her. She wore a blue coat and simple mantle of bleached wool, and sandals that had seen better days. No workingman's wife dressed more simply than did the mother of my sons. Whenever I brought her finery from my journeys to Antioch or Damascus she put away or gave away the garments.

"For some great occasion—James's wedding perhaps," she had said of the handsome saffron coat I had last brought. And when she gave away the one before that, "The good soul needs something better than the rags of charity. She needs a coat that will give her courage."

Rhoda took the scroll and broke the seal. "You have not even opened it," she said. The dark eyes met mine, and fear was in them. "From Rome! If he—calls you to Rome—" Then, straightening, "We have always known a time would come when you would be called to your real ministry. I do not think you will return while Peter lives. God was good to give us so many years."

I drew her down on the bench beside me. "A lifetime with you, my love, would be less than enough." I cleared my throat and began to read aloud.

"I, Peter, an apostle of our Lord Jesus, send greetings to my son Mark and to Rhoda his wife, and to the sons God has given, and to all who are of their household and fellowship. I send by the hand of Jude, a servant of our Lord who is bound for Antioch by ship. My wife Perpetua joins me in the prayer that grace and peace be yours in full measure, and also theirs who dwell under your roof, and all who meet with you in fellowship on the Lord's Day."

The writing was in an unfamiliar hand, but then Peter never wrote his own letters, and each handwriting was different from the last. As I read the opening passage Rhoda's eyes scanned what lay below. She now took the scroll, rolled it on, opening up a new section, scanning rapidly. She exclaimed, "He is losing the sight of his eyes. Oh my dear love, you must go to him at once, for he desperately needs you." She raised her voice. "Ken! Are you here, Ken?"

Ken's eldest son appeared from the kitchen. "Father went to spread the news that the bishop has come, my lady." The lad was the image of Ken at sixteen, a chunky, good-humored, friendly lad, useful so long as he was told exactly what to do and how to go about it.

Rhoda said,. "Run down to the harbor. Learn when the next ship will sail for Antioch or Ephesus! This is important, so make haste."

The boy's eyes held mine. "You are making a journey, sir?"

I had promised to take him instead of Ken when I made my next journey. "You and I are going to Rome," I said. "Peter needs us. Now scoot."

He scooted. His name was Epidopphilos. Since Ken refused to let anyone call his son by a shortened form of the unmanageable cognomen, we all called him simply lad.

Rhoda rose. Four sons had she borne me, and the fifth child was within her. My heart's love, my life's companion, I have had you for half my life and it is not enough, and now I must go to the mission to which Paul summoned me when I had lived a score of years, but to which God summons me only now. O God, do you call me now? With the voice of Peter, do you call me now?

Rhoda said, "I must go through your clothing. No need to buy anything new here, I think. It is better to travel light and buy what you need in Rome. You will find that Peter's needs can be supplied at the same time."

She moved quickly across the pavement toward my private apartment. As she reached the curtained doorway she turned back. "When I knew I was again with child I was sure Peter would send for you." Her eyes were spilling tears, and I crossed to join her in the privacy of our own shared room.

"How can I leave those I love? How can I go, from this place and from you?"

"You have no choice." Then, firmly, "If you stay away too long, Ken will bring me to you. Phoebe runs this house and always has, and Stephen and James no longer need their mother. I will bring the little ones—Aaron and Levi—and this daughter God will send me—and we will join you. So find a house for us in Rome, my darling. We will come before the autumn winds sweep the Great Sea."

She would not come this year. Travel takes time, and a message sent to her after I reached Rome would not come soon enough to get her safely to me this year. But the hope gave us strength for the parting.

That evening after the sunset meal Agabus spoke to our household about the letter Paul had written to the Galatians, showing by what logic Paul had set forth the danger that men would introduce into a new faith elements remembered from old beliefs and superstitions. After he had dismissed the company he gave me messages to carry to Paul and to Peter. Then he blessed me, for I would take ship early the next day.

I set out with Ken's chubby, eager, voluble young son for Antioch, traveling by the same ship on which Agabus had come. It was a small, ill-balanced vessel which made the passage back and forth between Salamis and Antioch regularly. From Antioch after three days we boarded a coasting vessel bound for Rhodes and Ephesus. From Rhodes we sailed direct to Syracuse and north through Messina Strait up the western coast of Italy.

At Pompeii we spent a day in harbor. The lad and I went ashore to walk through this handsome city of costly villas and impressive theaters, temples, and thermae. Pompeii was on the slope of Mount Vesuvius, with a fine view and a cool breeze from the sea. Many Romans of wealth had built summer villas there to escape the heat of Rome. The city had been severely shaken by earthquake a year or two ago, we were told. However, most of the damage had vanished in a program of rapid rebuilding. The slopes above the city were a lovely checker-work of verdant vineyards, yellow grainfields ripe for summer harvest, and silvery olive orchards. Yet in the midst of this beauty one saw the ruins of fine villas crumbled beyond repair in the earthquake, and even in the forum we found that the temples to Isis and Jupiter were still undergoing repair. I have always been glad for this brief visit to Pompeii, for it is the finest example I have ever seen of what Romans could achieve in architecture and decoration.

I never saw the city of marble in which Caesar Augustus had such pride. When we returned to the wharf after our sight-seeing tour of Pompeii we found crowds so dense we had to elbow our way through to the ship. The first refugees from a burning Rome had reached Pompeii. We were to see countless thousands of these refugees in the days and weeks which fol-lowed, but these were the first. We were to hear many versions of the catastrophe and the terror and the destruction, but none more terrible than the ultimate story in all its stark and fearful truth.

# CHAPTER 25

We crossed the bay by moonlight, carrying a score of Pompeians who were rushing to Rome to determine what had happened to property or relatives. We anchored in the fine roadstead of Puteoli soon after dawn. This was the end of the voyage. There were harbors nearer to Rome, but none half so commodious.

The grain, our principal cargo, would be unloaded into small craft here to be carried on to Rome. But the passengers would conclude their journey overland by way of the Via Appia.

This great highway was named for Appius Claudius Caecus, a censor who had, four centuries earlier, built the road from Rome south across the Alban Hills, through the difficult Pontine Marsh, and on to Capua. Other Romans had, with the centuries, improved and lengthened the road, extending it ever deeper into lower Italy until ultimately it reached the southeastern seaport at Brundisium.

The journey from Puteoli to Rome could be made in four days. But when I saw the refugees crowding the wharves of Puteoli and heard their shouts about the week-long fire, I would gladly have traveled night and day to reach Rome sooner and learn what had happened to our half-blind Peter in the burning city.

One of the Pompeiians shouldered his way in front of the lad as we were leaving the ship. Once on the wharf we moved against a tide of burdened refugees, their possessions on their backs or on donkeys. Suddenly the Pompeiian let out a great bellowing cry. "Police, Ho there, Police! Thief! Looter! Murderer!" He seized a wiry freedman who looked to be a Gaul, and who trundled a barrow laden with fine terra cotta art objects and vases wrapped in fine cloth which had once been draperies from some elegant dwelling.

I took the lad's arm and steered him around the melee, he looking back over his shoulder all the while. Behind us the Pompeiian was yelling that the barrow contained his daughter's wedding gifts, stolen from her husband's palazzo in Rome. I kept a firm grip on the lad, steering him toward the fine amphitheater on the hill north of the harbor. Peter had sent instructions for the final stage of my journey. "North of the amphitheater is the dwelling of Publius Quartus, a brother in the Lord Jesus. He will direct you to my house in the Regione Esquiline. He will give you a night's lodging before you start the journey, and perhaps even furnish you with a guide."

As we were passing the amphitheater, a barefoot porter burdened with two heavy wineskins overtook and passed us. I asked him the way to the house of Publius Quartus. He shot me a warm smile. "Follow me, Brother. I am going there myself."

Outside the kitchen portal of a modest dwelling a string of donkeys waited patiently while men milled about. Hampers and parcels of food and clothing were heaped beside the house. One of the men rushed nervously about, tall, lean, dark as a desert dweller from Africa. This was Publius Quartus, elder of the Puteoli ecclesia, host to Christians bound to and from Rome.

The lad cried, "Look, sir, they are taking gifts to the Christians of Rome. Why, it's just like being at home, sir, isn't it?"

"So it is." How familiar was the atmosphere, brotherly love at work in the hearts and minds of men.

Publius Quartus dashed over to me, his lean face contriving somehow to show both welcome and anxiety. "A friend of Peter! Thrice welcome, Marcus of Salamis. I fear for Peter—he is going blind, you know, the blessed man. He was in this house, with his good wife Perpetua, only two years ago. The only man ever to visit us who had seen the Lord Jesus and been with him during his ministry. Oh, a blessed experience. I know not whether he escaped the fire. Ah, the fire—a dreadful thing. God has surely sent you, Brother Marcus. We need more men to guard these gifts we must deliver to our brother Paul." Then with a shriek of anguish, "Brother Festus, look what you do! Never set wineskins on bread! Wife! Come and see to things, for I cannot manage it all. Felix! Grain is leaking from that sack! God help us, I don't know how we will get all this good food our excellent people have provided past the looters and the soldiers and safely into the burial caves where our homeless brethren have taken shelter!"

To make the journey to Rome at the slow pace of a donkey train was a depressing prospect. Yet the anxious author of all this liberality needed our help, and we needed his. For who could say what sorts of ruffians would be found upon the Via Appia in such times—whether looters from Rome, or robbers from the hills to prey alike on southbound refugees and on northbound travelers carrying succor to homeless friends and relatives. We needed one another, Publius Quartus and I. The lad and I fell to with a will to get the donkeys loaded. It was work we two at least had done before, though our experience had been with copper wares rather than foodstuffs. However, a donkey is a donkey, and the trick is to balance the load.

The sun was at its zenith when we set out, sweating in the heat of the day, for this was midsummer, the month the Romans had named for Julius, first and greatest of the Caesars. There were ten of us, and eight led donkeys. We reached the historic Via Appia at Capua at sunset, slept beside the road, posting a guard for each of the night's three watches. Each man carried a stick as a weapon, also food for himself for the journey to Rome and back, and a bed, rolled and bound upon him. The beds would be left with Christians who had not managed to save even that much from the fire.

We were on the way again at dawn, and now we walked upon the sturdy stone blocks with which the Via Appia is paved. There was less dust now, but walking on stone makes ankles and knees grow weary. We gladly paused for the noon-day rest in the days that followed. Traffic was as thick as on the Jericho road at Passover. At every stop we heard tales about the week-long holocaust.

The stories conflicted, but on one point most of them agreed. "The gods are punishing the princeps." Last year's earthquake at Pompeii had been a warning. Military disasters in outreaches of the empire had been a warning. "The princeps sins, and we suffer him. The gods are punishing us all for his sins."

How many murders had served to advance the interests of the young Nero? The murder of Claudius Caesar had brought him, at seventeen, to the throne. The murder of Nero's doting mother had ended her struggle to rule through him. The murder of Nero's wife Octavia, daughter to Claudius, had freed him to marry the ambitious Poppaea. There were other murders, and Nero had benefited, and nobody was ever charged with them or punished. Evil in high places had brought disaster to Rome.

The fire had started in the night, among the wooden benches of the Circus Maximus. It had spread rapidly east-ward over the Palatine and Velia and into the Esquiline. At the same time it spread west till it reached the Tiber and the Servian wall. Fire lanes were made by tearing out whole blocks of dwellings, but the fire sprang up in some new place whenever it was put out.

The lad said shrewdly, "Looters set fires to conceal their crimes. That is how new fires started after the old ones were put out." He had become quite a man of the world in our travels. He had struck up a great friendship with the barefoot porter Festus. Wherever traffic permitted, they led their donkeys side by side, singing together hymns which they had taught one another. The lad was improving his Latin every day. I was glad to see him taking advantage of his opportunities.

These new friends called him Philos, dropping the first three syllables of the name Ken had given him. The lad and Festus had the last two donkeys in our cavalcade, and I followed them as rear guard. Sometimes Publius Quartus dropped back from his place in the van of our procession to discuss with me the sweep of ecclesias throughout the world. He was overjoyed to learn that I had seen Jesus, however briefly, and had heard him speak. Nobody else he had ever known had seen the living Jesus, except Peter.

We spent our third night on the road at the Forum of Appius, where stands the forty-third milestone from Rome. Another day's journey should bring us to the hills south of Rome where Paul had taken refuge with a little colony of Christians. The Forum of Appius was thronged and the price of space in the inns there was outrageous, as was the price of food. Fortunately we had no need of this expensive hospitality. I had brought a purse of silver coins and, strapped against my body, a letter of credit drawn on a Jewish banker, Ezek ben Ezra. How I would find this banker in a disrupted Rome I could not know, nor could I be sure he had survived the fire. The reports were that of Rome's fourteen regiones only four had escaped the blaze. This was another of the nagging anxieties which disturbed my sleep during those hot midsummer nights beside the Via Appia.

The canal through the Pontine Marshes reached to this point. When we set out next morning we found the road fearfully congested by carts of grain, ox-drawn. Midsummer month is harvest month, and Rome regularly drew grain from every quarter of the Great Sea. So slow was our progress we began to despair of reaching Paul before nightfall.

We passed the Three Taverns at the end of the Pontine Marsh shortly after noon. As we wound through the Alban hills we had our first brush with bandits. As we were ten and our attackers four, we got off without serious injury—two sets of bleeding knuckles, a bruised head, the lad with a bloody nose, and I with a shinbone that ached from a savage kick. We were the better off, we thought, for we had acquired experience in the use of the heavy sticks with which we were armed. But in the end this experience proved of no benefit whatever.

We passed the viaduct and entered upon a roadway lined by tombs and funeral monuments to the great men of Rome's long history, mostly generals whose conquests had unified the whole world into the vastest empire ever known. Off to the right we occasionally saw encampments of the homeless. From hilltops we caught glimpses of the blackened waste of the city, with broken walls and lonely chimneys rising in a forest of desolation. The summer air was tainted with odors of burned wood and rotting flesh.

We moved in single file, the lad and I at the rear. We sang

as we marched, to lift our spirits and refresh our tired bodies. We had taken no noonday rest. The end of our journey was near. Soon we would learn at first hand what had happened to our brethren in Rome. Surely it would be better to know the worst than to imagine it!

I was watching the horizon and singing with the rest, when a blow caught me below and behind the left ear. I sank without a sound. When I regained consciousness a figure of filth and rags was tearing at my clothes, searching for hidden wealth. So avid was his search, so confident was he that I was done for, that I was able to send him over backward with a kick, and leap upon him and pinion him. I pressed one hand across his throat till his eyes rolled and he ceased his struggles. My purse was gone from my scrip, but I found it among his rags. My letter of credit was still bound against my ribs. I took my hand from his throat, saw him draw a ragged, aching breath, picked up my stick, threw his club into bushes far from the road, and rose.

The pain in my head was blinding, and my revulsion from violence joined with the pain to make me giddy. My companions had vanished around a turn in the road, unaware of the assault upon me. Now the road seemed strangely empty. Nobody had come around that turn ahead, southbound, since I roused after the attack upon me. What I had thought to be a buzzing in my ears was the sound of many voices up ahead, around that turn in the road.

I staggered toward the turn, then dizzily veered off into the bush, and fetched up against a wall of marble. This was one of the many tombs. It was set precisely within the bend the road made at this point. As I made my uncertain way around the building I saw engraved upon it the names of several of the Gracchi.

Now I was in the shubbery north of the tomb. Beyond was a

row of trees which bordered the Via Appia, and beyond the trees the road was filled with milling people. I had reached the trees when I heard a rough voice bellow in Latin, "Christian dogs, arsonists, thieves! Yield, or die here on the road!"

Our party, men and boys and donkeys, was surrounded by a squad of legionaries. Blood was again running from the lad's nose, and his face was filled with terror. Beside him on the stones Festus lay, dead, his head half severed from his body. Publius Quartus was shrilly protesting that he had come from Puteoli, bringing gifts to homeless friends, but a clout from the fist of a soldier silenced him. Soon all were bound and moving north. Soldiers now led the donkeys. Traffic began to move again. When I had gathered enough strength I went to the dead body of Festus, which someone had kicked off to the side of the road, took hold of the tough, bare feet, and dragged him into the trees, through the bushes, and over into the shadow of the tomb of the Gracchi. I wrapped his coat about him, laid a few branches over him, said a prayer, and left him there, for I could do no more. For a long time I knelt in the shade, my head pressed against the cool marble. When the sun had reached the tops of the trees I left the tomb and descended eastward, toward the hills where surely Paul was to be found.

For two days I searched the hills, wandering in and out of the catacombs, the quarries, the valleys. I had given my food and bed to a refugee family with whom I bedded down that first night, too weak to endure their burden. In return they pointed out a distant hill where there was a gravel quarry which opened into the catacombs. I don't remember much else about those days, except that my head throbbed, that any touch against the bump behind my left ear made me lose consciousness. Whenever I asked for information about Christians, people stared at me in hostile fashion and walked away.

On the third day—I think it was the third day—as I walked amongst wooded hills above a shallow sand quarry I heard in the distance a rich, passionate, unforgettable voice. The diction had grown lovelier with the years. Ah, the beauty of the sound! I stumbled toward it, among the trees, and came out into a glade on a gentle slope. A group of perhaps a score of people sat about on the grass, in the shade of oaks and cedars. Paul was preaching, and his listeners were so attentive they hardly noticed my entrance. I was behind Paul and over to the left. It proved to be the last sermon I ever heard Paul preach, and it echoes in my ears to this day, a measure of the cost to Paul when he gave over preaching to Jews to become the apostle to Gentiles.

"I speak the truth in Christ Jesus; I do not lie. I have great sorrow and unceasing anguish for my kinsmen by race. I could wish myself cut off from Christ for the sake of my brethren. To them belong the sonship, the glory, the covenants, the promises; to them, according to the flesh, is the Christ, our blessed Lord Jesus. Yet Gentiles who did not pursue righteousness have attained it, through faith. But Israel, who pursued righteousness through the law, failed to fulfill the law. For the law has become to the Jews a stone of stumbling."

I sank down in my weakness, and tears filled my eyes. Whether my emotion was because it was so wonderfully good to see and hear Paul again, or because my lonely search had ended, who can say?

The years had shrunk Paul's meager frame. He had endured many bouts with the fever; he had suffered shipwreck and imprisonment. Worst of all, perhaps, had been his struggles with Christians who dogged his journeys, seeking to force the Jewish law upon his converts, contriving instead to muddle and mislead them. Paul was my elder by only a decade, but the shriveled body and bent back might have belonged to a man well past his three score years. Only the youthful, vigorous, positive voice had not changed.

One of the women listeners presently noticed the state I was in and came toward me. Paul turned. "Mark!" he exclaimed, "oh Mark, most welcome! God bless you for coming to us at such a time." He knelt to embrace me, and I felt the sharp bones in his arms and shoulders as he pressed me against himself. When he sat back on his heels I saw that the eyes, deep-sunk in that shapely skull, held all their old fire. Paul was quite bald; but the beard, snow white, was as luxuriant and handsome as when I bade him farewell in Perga more than a score of years ago. All the deep lines which marked his face seemed but a frame for the warm, vital, intelligent eyes. The years had given Paul a warmth he had lacked in his young manhood.

"Paul, Barnabas was right when he said you were the greatest of us all. You are an ornament to our faith, an ornament to the Jewish people. You could stand with Jeremiah and Isaiah and feel no shame."

"I am the slave of the Lord Jesus. I do not aspire to be more. Where is Barnabas? Did he come here with you?"

"He is preaching in Spain. We had a letter from him at midwinter. He is well, and he is well-content with his mission there. He says that is where he will live out his life."

Delight spread over the lined, bony face. "Then I will see him. I will go to Spain when the sheep of this fold are sheltered once more. I would be gone before this, had not the holocaust prevented."

The Christians had moved in close while we talked. Paul introduced them, but I remember only two names, Naomi, the Jewess who had first noticed me, and her husband Titus, a

Greek. As I shook the hands of these good people, suddenly I was overcome with weakness. Then Paul saw the discolored lump behind my ear and bent to examine it. "Who did this? A thief? Or—a soldier?"

"Paul, I have sad news for you. I sailed from Salamis with my lad, Ken's son, and from Puteoli we made the journey with Publius Quartus and friends of his. They were bringing you eight donkeys laden with food and other gifts for the homeless Christians. I was walking at the rear of our procession and was knocked unconscious by a blow from a bandit, who then got so busy robbing me he did not notice when I awoke. I escaped after recovering my purse. The other nine men with the donkeys went round a bend in the road, where they were taken by legionaries who accused them of looting and arson. One was killed, the others bound and led away, while I still crawled about in the bushes, half-conscious and completely bewildered. I have always put my trust in Roman law. What has happened to Roman justice?"

"It is something new in the world, this seizure of Christians. People blame the princeps for the fire, and he needs a scapegoat. He found witnesses who swear they saw Chirstians start the fire and spread it. Now all Christians, by Nero's proclamation, are subject to arrest and imprisonment—possibly even crucifixion."

I turned my face to the ground. Paul concluded, "Christians are easy to identify. They sing, they pray. Many are slaves or freedmen, with no powerful friends, no influence. Mark, I am afraid you chose a poor time to come to Rome. Are you here on business?"

"Peter sent for me. Where is he? Is he with you? Is he—alive? Did he escape the fire?"

Paul sat beside me, his head in his hands. "Peter is safe. Rufus was with him, and got him out of the city. I believe

Perpetua suffered some injury but she also got away. There are catacombs west of the Tiber, under the hill of execution. Peter is there. Titus will take you to Peter, tomorrow."

"Thank God." A great burden had lifted from my heart. Then, remembering the wholesale seizure of Christians, I groaned, "What will become of him now, and of you, Paul—of all of you?"

"And of you, Mark? You are a Christian."

"But I was on the ship when Rome burned."

"You are a Christian. That is enough." Paul dropped his head onto his arms, which were crossed over his knees. "I sent for Publius Quartus. All those good men, our brothers, were in Puteoli when Rome burned. But I sent to them for help. Where are they now?"

Naomi brought us each a cup of cheap, sour wine. When I tasted it I remembered that I had not eaten in two days. Yet I knew not whether these friends had eaten, or whether they had food to give. I did not mention that some of the weakness and illness which afflicted me was due to hunger. The wine made me exceedingly giddy. No evening meal was served.

We stretched out on the grass. Paul was in the open, in the glade, and I nearby under the trees. We had much to tell one another. I gave Paul the messages Agabus had sent. I told him of the many copies Agabus had made of Paul's letters to the Galatians and the Ephesians for distribution to ecclesias. Paul was deeply moved to know his letters were being read in many places as a part of the worship at First Day services.

"I wish I had taken time to know Agabus better, when we ministered together in Antioch," he said. He continued to speak of Agabus but my mind wandered back to the present situation.

Why am I cast down, I wondered. I do not fear death,

whether for myself or those I love. The kingdom of heaven awaits us all.

Paul said, "I've had no news of Sergius Paulus and his daughter for many years. Do they still dwell in Paphos?"

"Malnor is in Paphos. She married a centurion, and is the mother of a son and three daughters. She is all she promised as a girl to become—a tower of strength amongst the Christians of Cyprus."

"And Sergius?"

"Nero sent for him to come to Rome five years ago. He was lost at sea."

Paul sighed deeply. "Malnor was a lovely young woman. Ah well, I have fought a good fight. I have kept the faith. Now it weighs upon me that I have finished my course. I wish it were not so, for I should have liked to go to Spain and minister there for a few years with Barnabas."

I knew then why I was cast down. I wanted my years of ministry—the years I had missed when I abandoned Paul in Perga.

I must have slept very deeply. When I wakened the sun was high amongst the branches. There was a strange quiet all about the glade. I sat up, and found that the throbbing of my head was less than it had been yesterday.

Naomi came through the trees, a loaf of bread in her hand. She gave it to me. She was weeping.

"Legionaries came at sunrise. They took Paul and Titus and four others with them. The rest of our people escaped. You slept so quietly here under the trees that they did not even notice you, Mark. When you are ready, I will take you to Peter."

"I have finished my course," Paul had said.

Twice, now, I had escaped when those with me were taken.

Was it chance? Or was it God's promise that my ministry would be granted, that my martyrdom would wait until God's time for it had come? When I rose it seemed that some of the mantle of Paul's great courage had settled over my own shoulders.

# CHAPTER 26

Where the Augustus aqueduct crosses the Servian wall we left
the green world behind and entered the blackened ruin left by
the fire. We crossed over two of Rome's seven hills. Here the
devastation was complete. We descended into the flat land
framed on three sides by a deep bend in the Tiber. Formerly a
cattle market, this open area, the Campus Martius, had been
set aside by the princeps as a shelter for the homeless. Here
free grain was distributed. Other foods were sold to whoever
could buy.

Here we separated, agreeing to meet at a bridge which
crossed the Tiber at the end of a street Naomi showed me. She
went to join the queue for free grain, and I went into the
bazaar to buy fruit and wine. I would not go to Peter empty
handed, as I had gone to Paul.

What would Roman merchants say to my Cyprus denarii, I
wondered, as I took out my purse. Then, for the first time, I
was struck by its weight. I opened it, and saw not only the
silver I had brought, but other coins of Roman coinage, some
of them gold. So my assailant had taken time to consolidate
his loot into one purse while I lay unconscious on the Via
Appia!

Seeing gold in my hand the merchant hastened to urge upon me a better wine in a larger bottle, but I replied in my best Latin, "Tomorrow! Tomorrow! I am in haste." I wasted only a moment's regret on the unfortunate victims who had been robbed for my enrichment. Should I have trouble finding Ezek ben Ezra I would surely need these extra coins. I passed on through the Campus Martius. The food displayed sent hunger and weakness over me in waves. I bought dates and crammed a handful into my mouth, and went on, spitting seeds onto the pavement.

The beautifully arched bridge led to the northbound road called the Triumphal Way. This road circled the hill of executions, marked by a row of crosses against the sky. Under the hill lay the catacombs to which Rufus had taken Peter and Perpetua when they fled the fire. We found the entrance in some bushes near the Tiber's western embankment.

Unlike the winding galleries of the catacombs south of the city, these fanned out from a large central crypt. The corridor we took to reach this crypt echoed with voices. I suppose at this time there were three or four score Christians amongst the refugees here. I never saw them all, however, for they found their own places in the many chambers. Peter was in the central crypt, where the gloom was lightened by a single torch. He moved about restlessly, peering before him in the dimness. I paused to look and to listen, for the sight of him, and the sound of his voice moved me deeply.

"When Rufus returns we will make a feast. I myself will make the funeral oration. No, my friends," he said, when protests rose from the shadows, "our beloved Perpetua is with the Lord Jesus, beyond pain, beyond sorrow, beyond the anguish our flesh is heir to—" He peered about as I moved forward. "Who is here? Rufus, speak up. We have been waiting your return."

"Peter," I said, "it is I, Mark."

He reached blindly and I rushed to embrace him. He clung to me with strong arms whose power had not been stolen away by the years.

Peter said, "I have repented summoning you to this troubled city, Mark. We need you, God knows, but these arrests continue, and we know not what is ahead. For now I remain, a coney in a burrow, but I cannot endure confinement long. Ah, my son, Perpetua would have joyed to see you before she died. We have opened a niche in one of the galleries, and will seal her in this day. If you are still in Rome when I am taken, reopen the same hospitable loculi and let these bones find their rest beside hers. No, no, my son, let us make no pretense. The princeps is in trouble, and finds in us a help in his distress. Now, no more. When Rufus returns with meats for the feast we will proceed with the business at hand."

"Peter, Naomi brought me here from the hills where Paul had taken refuge. Paul has been arrested, with Naomi's husband and some others."

"Paul!" He lifted his head as if looking at what was invisible to me. "Our brothers in the prison will be comforted by his presence among them. What matters, whether we are in the Mamertine or the catacombs? We are all in God's hands." He turned about, breathing deeply. "Friends, we will wait no longer for Rufus. Perhaps he is also a prisoner. We will dispense with the feast and proceed to the funeral."

"Peter, we brought food, Naomi and I. Let us not scant these observances. Now I have brought with me money to buy, and we will not lack for food."

My eyes were sufficiently adjusted to the dimness that I made out the bier upon which Perpetua lay. She was wrapped only in a coat of blue homespun. There were no spices, none of the usual linen wrappings. Naomi carried our food to the

women to prepare, and brought cups, and I poured wine for
Peter, and for myself, then gave the bottle to Naomi to take
charge of.

"The women will go to market hereafter," said Peter, and
sighed. "The Romans are not yet arresting women."

When we had eaten we carried the bier back into one of the
galleries, but not far. The loculi in the wall were bricked over
with a kind of terra cotta tile. One of these was open, empty,
with the tiles lying in a neat pile nearby. We laid Perpetua
there, then stood in the torchlight while Peter preached.

"Praise be to the God and Father of our Lord Jesus, who in
His mercy gave us a new birth into a living hope by the
resurrection of our Lord. The inheritance to which we are
born is one that nothing can destroy or spoil or wither. It is
kept for us in heaven, because we put our faith in God. We
are under his protection until salvation comes, as it has already come to our beloved sister, friend, wife. This is cause for
rejoicing, even though now we smart for a little while under
trials of many kinds. Even gold passes through the assayer's
fire, and more precious than perishable gold is faith that has
stood the test . . ."


I gave my purse into Naomi's keeping, lest in my errands in
the days that followed I be taken, and the money lost to those
who would need it. I could not remain underground, nor
could Peter much longer. For one thing, I needed to seek out
Ezek ben Ezra and present to him my letter of credit, for the
needs of our community were many and their resources few.

I made three journeys over the bridge and into the city,
wandering north and east and south from the Campus
Martius, but found no lead that could bring me to him.
Naomi and the other women made inquiries in the market
also, but heard only conflicting reports. Some said the banker

was lost in the fire; others that he had departed Rome to go to Alexandria, or to Athens, or to Jerusalem.

On Friday the women came white-faced from market. Christians were to be crucified on the hill above us Sunday morning. We had no reason to believe the Romans chose the day because it was our holy day. It was the first day of the week. This was reason enough to make it their day of executions.

"I am going to be on the hill when they come," said Naomi. "My man may be one of them. If he is not, perhaps I can get news of him."

One of the other women sobbed convulsively. "I cannot bear it. Don't ask me to go, Naomi. But try to get news of my husband."

"If our men can bear what will be done to them, I can bear to stand nearby for their sake," said Naomi.

As I lay awake that night I had it out with myself. When we wakened next day I brought Naomi over to where Peter was rising from his morning prayers.

"Peter," I said, "I must go with Naomi to comfort these men in their death."

"What folly is this?" he exclaimed. "Let the women go. They will comfort the men. If you go you will shame other men into going, and more of us will be taken. Soon none will be left. Be reasonable, Mark. You have never been a reckless man in the past. Moreover, you did not come all this way to die."

"Peter, the lad who came with me may be one of those crucified. He is far from home, and he came for my sake."

"They crucify men, not children. Mark, this is foolishness."

"Peter, you taught me your kind of foolishness. Do not ask me to deny what you yourself have taught. The angel who brought you alive from the Antonia in Jerusalem to give you twenty years more for your ministry will keep me safe, for my ministry is before me. Give me your blessing."

It was sheer recklessness, though it sounded like faith and courage. Yet I could not draw back. Something stronger than my own nature drove me. In the end Peter blessed us, Naomi and I, and we went out laden with messages, should the victims prove to be the husbands, or fathers, or brothers of our friends.

The hill was dotted with spectators as we came out into the early dawn. Five of the crosses had been laid flat upon the ground. This was the third month of summer, the month Romans had named for Caesar Augustus. Dawn was fresh and cool but the day would be a hot one before it ended.

We waited near the bridge. Soon the victims appeared, five of them. They had been scourged before they left the prison, and their coats were spattered with blood. They stumbled as they walked. When Naomi saw that Titus was not among them she drew a deep, shuddering sigh. None of the party from Puteoli was here. As the first man came abreast of us Naomi asked, "Do you know Titus of Corinth?" To each she put her question. "Have you seen Titus of Corinth?"

Their lips formed the word no, or heads were shaken as they passed us. The backs of their coats were drenched with blood but Naomi did not weaken.

As the fourth man came up she gave a little cry. "Rufus! You are Rufus!"

The man was large, powerful. I would never have recognized him as the son of Simon the Cyrenian who bore Jesus' cross to the Place of a Skull, the friend who had traveled with Peter or with Paul on so many of their journeys. His face was bruised out of shape, his head tied with a piece of cloth which came round under the chin. His eyes passed over Naomi and rested on my face with recognition and pleading.

The fifth man said, "He's Rufus. His jaw's broken. He can't talk."

An officer shouted, "Keep back from the prisoners."

I drew Naomi back a step. I said clearly, "Rufus, I will give your love and your farewell to Peter. I will be with him hereafter to the end."

His eyes spoke their gratitude. I walked beside him up the hill. Behind us the fifth man, Epaphras, was telling Naomi that Titus had been taken from the Mamertine Prison, that he could be seen among the men who were clearing and rebuilding the city. I asked him about Publius Quartus and Philos, but their names meant nothing to him.

We reached the hilltop. Our brothers here removed their bloody coats and lay down, as ordered, upon the crosses. All about us were men and women to whom this scene was a kind of circus. Bets were being made. I heard remarks such as, "The little ones last longest." "They die quicker when it's hot, like today will be."

I stood near Rufus, who in all the extremity of pain had made no sound. When his coat was removed and his back revealed I bit back a cry. I began, "Our Father, Who is in heaven, Holy be Thy Name . . ." whether for his comfort or my own I know not. He fixed his eyes upon my face. He was pushed backwards and fell upon the rough cross with a kind of grunt, as if the breath had all gone out of him. I raised my voice above the beat of the mallets upon the spikes, above the low, whimpering sounds which bubbled from the mouths of tortured men. From the man on the second cross came the anguished cry, "Lord Jesus! Lord Jesus! Lord Jesus!"

I have seen crucifixions where cords bound the arms to the cross pieces, where a lower crosspiece under the feet takes the weight off the hands and feet. The crucifixions I saw in Rome had none of these refinements. Since crucifixion is quite simply death from exhaustion, thirst, and pain, I am not sure how merciful are the minor mercies which serve to prolong life. Even the scourging, which greatly weakens the victim, serves to hasten death. The backs of all these men had been laid open, and clouds of gnats were soon all about them. Yet they prayed, and all our voices were soon blending as we repeated the Lord's Prayer over and over together.

A lad came up with a pitcher of sour wine. The first three drank deeply, but Rufus could not, and for his sake Epaphras refused. Then the crosses were lifted, and dropped into the earth. The sound of pain all the years of my life since that morning has been the thud of a heavy cross into its place, and the scream wrenched from the inmost being of a man affixed to it.

Now the crosses stood against the sky and the parade of the revilers began, for this too was part of the torture, the privilege of those who came to enjoy the day. Then Epaphras cried out in a loud voice, "My brothers, many men have been crucified, but we are the first to die thus for the sake of our Lord Jesus, sharing his agony for his sake. Let us remember his words from the cross to the repentant thief, 'Today you shall be with me in Paradise.' We share his death. We will share his glory. Let us praise our Lord Jesus, since those who kill the body can only release the spirit to dwell in the heavenly kingdom evermore."

He started a hymn. Naomi's voice joined his. Perhaps the tradition born that day would never have come into being had not Epaphras and Naomi each possessed a rich and beautiful singing voice. Yet I do not believe these things come by chance. They sang, and I joined them, and the men on the second and third crosses joined. Soon two women came out from the crowd of watchers to stand with us and sing, then came five more, Christians who had been more wise than courageous, until the singing overcame their fears. Before noon a score of men and women had come from the catacombs to join us. We sang, we witnessed, and the heat of the day increased, and the sun beat down, and one by one our brothers on the five crosses lost consciousness of their agony, escaping into the torpor which comes before death.

On the following Lord's Day the Romans crucified another five Christians, and this time the hill was black with watchers who had heard how strangely the Christians die, and how their friends stand about singing and praising God. Two score of us were there when the prisoners climbed the hill, and four score before the heat of mid-afternoon had stilled the last voice from the cross.

In the week which followed the women brought from the market daily more stories than before of the excitment aroused amongst all sorts of people by the way the Christians met agony and death. "They are not human. They do not feel pain as others do . . ." But on the following Lord's Day when the Romans came with seven men to be crucified, they carried whips to keep back the crowds as they passed through the streets and up the hill.

If there was a Christian left in Rome who did not appear upon the hill that day to join in the singing and the witnessing, he must have been either bedridden or in prison.

Peter preached to us that day, and to the men on the crosses. It was his last public sermon preached in the open air, and even the revilers listened as he spoke of the manner of man Jesus was, of his love, his power to heal the body and the soul. I will never cease to praise God that I was one of the listeners that day. I saw tears upon the face of the lad who had brought the pitcher of sour beer to the dying men. Today not a man on the cross had drunk the numbing draught. They chose the clear consciousness of pain. It was the price they paid to hear every word spoken by Peter to them, for them. It was their testament that Jesus had overcome death, not for himself alone but for them, for each of them.

At midday Peter's sermon ended. While the people sang hymns of the heavenly kingdom a squad of legionaries came marching briskly across the bridge and up the hill. We watched them come, knowing for what purpose they had been sent. The guards who served as executioners had never troubled us. Indeed, they had listened, some with interest, to our singing and our prayers. They had orders to crucify the prisoners, but they had no orders where we were concerned. This new squad came on briskly, however, and we waited quietly, for this had been the inevitable end which we had seen from the beginning. They bound Peter's hands first, and mine next, and thereafter they bound all the men, two score I suppose, who were in our company. Then they led us down the hill, across the bridge, through the Campus Martius, into the forum, and so to the Mamertine Prison.

# CHAPTER 27

The Mamertime Prison is under the Palatine Hill, facing on the forum. Originally a stone quarry, the one great room was originally entered by a trap door in the roof. Later it was sealed over and a portal opened onto the street. A second room was built above the great chamber, then a third room was excavated below it. When I knew the Mamertine it had still another room behind the large chamber, lighted and ventilated only by a grating in the door.

All this was hidden behind a splendid façade of concrete faced with marble, a façade worthy to stand beside the Temple of Concord, worthy of a place amongst the architectural splendors of the Roman forum.

The fire had melted the lead by which the marble veneer had been affixed to the rough concrete. The prison was not beautiful, even on the outside, when I entered it with Peter. I report only what I was told about that. The inside I know as I know the house I live in, yet even the dank, dim misery of the inside of that prison wears for me a veneer of beauty, for it is illumined for me by Peter's presence. From that prison I walked forth with Peter, more than a year later, to the unforgettable radiance of his death.

I do not know how many Christians were brought to the Mamertine in all. There were perhaps five score of us that night in the great chamber and the room beyond the grating. We were not chained. I moved about the room freely, seeking the lad and Paul, Publius Quartus and Titus. When I did not find them in the great chamber I went to the grating. I found that the door was not locked, and entered. These men had been longer in prison than those in the great room. Two had been there from the beginning of the seizure of Christians. I learned a good deal from them, but not all.

The sick were in the upper chamber of the prison. Paul had been taken there after a bout with the fever. The lad Philos and Publius Quartus had been taken to work gangs, who were housed elsewhere. The strongest and soundest prisoners were taken for labor gangs and the sick were above us, and these who remained were destined for crucifixion.

"The Romans are great organizers," I said.

They asked about the crucifixions. Was it true, all they had heard about the courage of the Christians? They wanted to hear the details, over and over.

We had no comforts of any kind. Each of us had been stripped and searched when we entered. My letter of credit had been taken. My purse, thank God, was with Naomi, and would provide food for the women for a while yet. I myself was now as poor as the poorest. Still, my confidence remained that my years of ministry would not be taken from me.

That first night Peter moved along the wall of the big room, his hand following the pattern of stone worn by many hands, over many, many years.

"We shared our first prison, Mark," he said softly, for many of our fellow prisoners were sleeping. "This one, I think, will be my last—my vestibule into the heavenly kingdom, where I shall be evermore with the Lord Jesus."

When morning came I was taken with perhaps a score of other prisoners out into the sunlight and the heat to be delivered to guards set over the prisoners who labored at the restoration of Rome. I was taken to the top of the Palatine Hill, over the crest to the southern shoulder. Here various Caesars had built their palaces. Here also were palaces built by men famous in Rome's history, our former governor Cicero among them. The destruction among the palaces was not complete. Men with barrows were hauling away rubble. Men with ropes were dragging broken pillars and slabs of usable stone to assorted dumps. I was set to separating marble and terra cotta bricks from refuse. This was not easy, since everything was blackened. But the penalty of failure was clear. I was too much occupied that first day with my work to seek familiar faces amongst those black, unrecognizable faces all around me.

In the end it was the lad who recognized me. He was one of five men dragging a broken column. As they passed near me Philos dropped the line with a glad shout, "Marcus! Sir!" He flung himself upon me, embracing me, kissing both my cheeks, while tears of joy streaked his sooty face.

I got my feet under me and held him off to look him over. He had no wounds and he looked healthy. "This is a great adventure you have had with me, lad," I said, and wiped the back of my hand across my cheek. "But you *would* come!"

"Better me than my father, sir. Did you find Peter?"

"I found Paul and Peter. Both are in the Mamertine. Do you have news of Publius Quartus?"

"He was claimed as a runaway slave." The lad's face sobered.

"How could that be? He was no slave!"

"Tigellinus claimed him. He has a farm near Brundisium where he breeds race horses. He said Publius Quartus had run away from his farm. Who can argue with Tigellinus?"

Tigellinus was captain of the princeps' own Praetorian Guard. "Don't grieve for Publius Quartus, Philos. God has many ways of sending His messengers to spread the good news. Perhaps soon there will be an ecclesia at Brundisium."

The lad's face brightened. "For all of us, while we live, in whatever condition we find ourselves, there is opportunity to witness. As do the men who are crucified. Have you heard how they die, sir?"

"I have heard. I have seen. They are magnificent."

"Sir, I have learned a wonderful thing. I do not fear death. At home in Salamis it was only a theory. Here it is truth. I love living, even this life we lead here, but I do not fear death."

The men had dragged the column away. Now they were returning. A guard strode past them and over to where we stood. He shouted, "Get to work, lazy Greek! We'll string you up next!" The knotted rope he carried crashed onto a concrete slab from which I had been trying to pry away a marble facing. It missed the lad by a finger's breadth.

Philos looked up with a bright smile. "Truly, Alex, I will work twice as hard now, for I have found my master, Marcus of Salamis, who brought me to Rome." To me he said, "This is Alex, sir. A Greek, a very kind man."

The lad rushed away, joyously telling his news to one and all, and faces all over the hill grew bright at the sound of his voice. Alex stayed to poke amongst my heaps of marble and terra cotta, and to show me a better way to loosen the marble from the concrete.

"Is it true that uppity Greek was on a ship when the fire burned this city," he inquired.

"It is true. We heard of the fire from refugees in Pompeii and Puteoli. The lad was arrested before ever he reached Rome."

I did not speak to Philos again that day, but I heard him

singing. He was teaching the Roman Christians songs Agabus had made, in which words from Jesus' sayings were fitted to familiar Greek tunes. Once I saw Alex singing with them, though he sang the old Greek words.

We bedded down at night in an underground passageway Nero had constructed between the palaces of Caesar Augustus and Claudius Caesar.

On the third day as I was examining a fine terra cotta vase I had found, Alex came toward me followed by a handsome, heavy Jew in a scarlet robe embroidered in gold thread. The Jew had a remarkably luxuriant growth of side curls.

The guard bawled, "This banker has business with a Cypriot Jew, Marcus of Salamis. Come, prisoner, are you the man?" He knew I was, for Philos had said so.

I stepped toward them. "I am Marcus of Salamis."

"Can you identify yourself, prisoner?"

"I cannot. I was stripped of everything I brought to Rome."

The Jew said, "I am Ezek ben Ezra. I have a letter which concerns Marcus of Salamis. Can you tell me the contents of the letter?"

I laughed. "I had lost faith in Roman law and order. Well, then—it is a letter of credit drawn upon you by the House of Aaron. We are copper makers."

"In what amount was the letter drawn?" The Jew was looking me over with a mixture of compassion and amusement.

"The amount was unspecified. The letter says unlimited credit, sir."

The banker said, "Thank you, Officer. I will take this man with me." Their hands touched briefly. How much, I wondered, is a proper tip for such a service?

Ezek ben Ezra extended his hand. I looked at my black and blistered one, then at my filthy tunic. "Let me shake your hand after I have washed, sir."

He glanced about at the workers who swarmed the hill. "So these are the arsonists who destroyed our city." He spoke loudly.

Work stopped. Eyes turned to him. A few protests were heard, but most of these men simply stared at this vistor from another world.

He looked upon them kindly. "Rome has been a firetrap for three centuries, with miles of hovels lining narrow streets. I tell you, friends, the Jews were the first choice of our princeps as scapegoat for this inevitable calamity. But the gracious lady Poppaea interceded on our behalf. She pointed out to the noble Nero that only those Jews who worship the crucified Galilean had a hand in the arson, since they sought revenge against Rome for his crucifixion."

A wave of protests swept the hill. He raised his hands. "The people must blame someone. Better to blame an obscure sect than our worthy princeps. You make excellent targets for abuse. You have turned the crucifixions into a circus with all that singing and praying. If you would consent to die ignobly, the spectacle would lose its value. Still, I thank you for taking my place, and the places of my two-score relatives upon those crosses and upon this hill."

He turned. "Come, Mark. We must find a bath for you."

I saluted my brothers. I had come to know them and love them in the dungeon under the palace of Caesar Augustus.

At the foot of the street a chariot was waiting. We mounted it. The driver shouted and flicked his whip, and the horses set out toward the hills west of the city. The hills were green with shade. Ezek ben Ezra said, "I have the good fortune to live in one of the four regions to which the fire did not spread. You will find us overrun with friends and relatives less fortunate than ourselves, but we can find a place for you to bathe, and we can find clothing fit for a copper merchant to wear. What brought you to Rome?"

"I was summoned here by a dear friend who was one of the disciples of the Lord Jesus during his lifetime."

The urbane expression of the banker cracked just a little. "Do fishermen and carpenters summon the head of the House of Aaron?"

"Spoken like a Roman, not a Jew," I replied quietly. "I have had the great happiness of being this man's disciple whenever he calls me, over the past twenty years."

"Is his name Paul of Tarsus?"

"No. Why? Have you news of Paul?" A sharp pain was lodged in my breast. The unaccustomed motion of the chariot seemed to make it sharper. What was I doing here with this man when those I loved were helpless?

"Paul was beheaded two days ago. As a Roman he could not be crucified."

When I did not speak, he said, "It was inevitable—twice he came before the princeps as a hatcher of disturbances."

I said, "The world is poorer with Paul gone from it. But heaven is richer."

"Perhaps. Now come, how can I help you if you don't give me weapons to use on your behalf?"

"Why should you help me? I am a stranger to you."

"You came to Rome to do business with me. A man cannot do business with a martyr. Whom did you come here to see? Which of the Christians?"

"The apostle Peter. He is an old man, almost blind. He is in the Mamertine Prison. You seem to know a great deal about what is going on. Can you help me get him away to safety? He lost his wife because of that fire."

"I will do what I can. The lady Poppaea does business with our firm upon occasion. But if this man is a ringleader of the Christians—well, we will see. Can you prove you did not engage in arson?"

"I was on shipboard when Rome burned."

"What ship?"

"The Twins."

"Her captain was in Rome last week. Perhaps he can be found."

"I must insist that my servant, a young lad, be released also."

"Your servant, certainly. If this Peter is not released, we can get you free access to him, I hope."

We had left the burned over sections behind and were in a shady region of fine homes, of beautiful pavements, of handsome cedar trees.

"Here we are," said Ezek ben Ezra. "Come along. You will need a lot of hot water."

We entered a spacious dwelling, typically Jewish in architecture. Off the main court was a small court with a sunken pool. Here I soaked the soreness from my body and scrubbed the filth from my hair and from every part of my person.

White linen was waiting for me, and a richly textured blue robe embroidered about the neck and sleeves with silver. When I came out into the court, which was filled with well-dressed, important-looking Jews, Ezek ben Ezra crossed toward me, looking me up and down.

"Yes," he said. "Yes indeed. A bath makes quite a difference. That is my son's coat. Well now, I shall take you to Nero. You can plead your case for yourself."

# CHAPTER 28

We set out for the palace of the princeps as the day's heat was beginning to pass. "It is the hour of prayer, for any proper Jew," said Ezek ben Ezra.

"My first excursion with Peter came at this hour. I was a lad of fourteen. This was the summer after our Lord Jesus was crucified and arose and came forth from the tomb." And I went on to tell the story of the healing of Korah, and the arrest which followed, and our hearing before the Sanhedrin.

"Do not tell that story to Nero, Mark. He is at least halfway convinced that Christians employ demons to do their bidding."

We circled half the city to reach the palace Nero had preempted when his palace in the Palatine filled with smoke and drifting ash. Nero was in the garden, dressed in a loincloth, practicing weight lifting. Behind him was a long paved pool, with a fountain plashing noisily at the far end. He had the heavy body of a wrestler or a weight lifter, and the strangely innocent face of an habitual self-deceiver. He was actually twenty-eight years old at the time, but he looked younger, perhaps because one surprised bewilderment so often in the large, blue eyes. A beard would have become him by hiding the heavy folds of flesh about his big jaws. His hair lay in sweated ringlets over the broad forehead. He glanced toward us then bent to a great stone at his feet, fitted his big hands carefully over the ends. I had been handling stones recently. I would have said one man could not lift this one, but the princeps did. Muscles bulged, eyes fairly popped as he slowly straightened. Little by little the stone rose higher till it was level with his shoulders. The princeps' face grew redder. Sweat poured, and the stone was level with his eyes. It was above his head. He leaned forward, and dropped it into the pool with a tremendous splash.

Nero fell to the earth, panting, while sweat poured from the great body. A sound of clapping came from under a nearby tree. A young Greek wearing a loincloth, beautifully muscled and bronzed, came running forward. "Bravo, sire. A great feat. A very great feat." To us he said, "I had this stone cut to the size of the great stone of Olympus, the heaviest ever cast by the greatest champion of them all."

"Cast!" exclaimed the sweating Nero. "You said nothing about casting it!"

"That is for the next time, sire. These things take practice. A splendid feat, sire!"

The heavy lips pouted. "I break my back to lift it and you said nothing of casting it!"

"Sire, you will sweep the games. No Greek has ever won more than four events. You will show the world greatness it has never seen in five thousand years of competition."

Still pouting, though less markedly, the princeps turned upon Ezek ben Ezra. "You saw it, Ezek. What do you think?"

"I would have wagered my house and my farm that such a stone could not be lifted, sire. Yet if any man could do it," he shrugged, "it would have to be the greatest athlete in the world." He presented me to the princeps.

I stepped forward and made the proper obeisance to the man who ruled the world.

"Well," said Nero, "what did you think of it?"

"I did not believe it could be done, sire."

"Have you ever handled stones?"

I glanced at my blistered hands. "Yes, sire."

"Then you know. You have to handle stones to know their weight." He eyed me speculatively. "You are not young but, for a Jew, you move as an athlete. Do you wrestle?"

"No, sire. In my youth I was a swimmer. I still prefer walking to riding."

"Do you run?"

"Sometimes." I added, forcing myself to the courtesy, "These things are for young men, like yourself, sire. I am beyond the age for sports."

"I am not young. Oh, to be sure I command my body and it obeys. But the man who rules the world carries an ageless burden. I have carried the world upon my shoulders for eleven years. That stone seems light, by comparison."

He rose, and from somewhere a young slave came running with a coat, which he wrapped about his glistening body. He turned to Ezek. "Now I know you did not come to watch me sweat, nor to hear me read my poetry. Nobody calls upon the princeps for pleasure. Why are you here? Did Poppaea summon you? If you lend her more money this year I cannot be responsible. All Rome is eating from the trough I must fill."

"Sire, I found this Cypriot copper merchant, head of an international firm, grandson and great grandson of merchants to whom Rome awarded the boon of citizenship in return for their contribution to the wealth of the empire—I found this man amongst the prisoners who are sorting stones on the Palatine."

"You—what?"

"He was imprisoned in the Mamertine. His letter of credit to me was found upon him, and fortunately the duty officer brought it to me. So here we have the unfortunate spectacle of an important business man from the provinces seized without recourse and set at hard labor, though he did not reach Rome until after the fires had been extinguished. I knew this was something you would want to know about directly, sire. I brought him to you as soon as he had bathed and dressed."

The princeps' face was redder now than when he lifted the stone. "You—you are of that devil breed who cast spells and cannot feel the pangs of death!"

"I am only a man. One night when I was a lad I saw a man pray in our orchard—my father's orchard—at Jerusalem. 'Let this cup pass from me,' he prayed. But when the soldiers came and arrested him he submitted. When he was tried for conspiracy he made no defense. He was hanged on a tree, and before he died he prayed, 'Father, forgive them.' That was many years ago, but I have loved that man and have longed to be like him."

His anger did not abate. "You are a Christian. Admit it."

How long ago had the question been put to me by Sergius Paulus. Joy filled me that this time, and to this man, I could make a straightforward reply. "Sire, I am a Christian."

"You say that to me, knowing what I can do to you?"

"You can kill the body. The soul is immortal."

The princeps threw back his coat to ventilate his sweating flesh. "The Christians are a cutthroat gang of runaway slaves! What can a substantial business man have in common with such rubbage?"

"Sire, the Nazarene accepted his destiny, which was to die.

'Love one another as I have loved you,' he said, and I heard him say it. Then we went to his death for love of all mankind."

"And because his death came on a Roman cross, my city was burned by his fanatic followers. What kind of love was that?"

"Sire, the Romans did not arrest him. The Romans did not accuse him. We hold no grudge against the Romans. Sire, let me explain this mystery. Men are mortal. Men do evil. Each man carries in his conscience the memory of deeds he has done which he knows were evil, and which he would like to forget."

A terrible longing crossed that strangely childlike face. He looked like a fat, unattractive child who knows he is disliked by others because he dislikes himself.

I continued, "The Lord Jesus, a sinless man, accepted death with anguish and shame, having been tried under the just laws of a just government and found guilty. He was found guilty because he made no defense. He made no defense, sire, because he took upon himself the guilt of every man. He bore our sins, our guilt, our wrongdoing to the cross, and was punished.

"Now, sire, every man who humbly accepts Jesus' punishment as his own punishment can in Jesus' name accept God's forgiveness, the cleansing of the slate, the washing away of sin, of even the memory of sin, if he will have it so. Every man by faith in the Lord Jesus can feel himself a clean and righteous man, henceforth to live a life of love with the help of the Breath of God, which has come to dwell within him. This is what it is, Sire, to be a Christian."

A spasm crossed the heavy face and left it cold and empty. "We have such stories, Marcus. Virgil wrote something like it, in the Aenead. But men of intelligence are able to separate imaginative works of fiction from the truth of life and death. I suppose if a man were gullible enough, such a belief would help him to live well."

"It would, sire. And to die well."

Nero laughed. "Indeed, the Christians die too well for their own good. Ordinary crucifixions attract only ghouls. But the death of Christians has become a very successful public spectacle. You Christians tempt a Caesar, for where could he find cheaper entertainment for his people than by the continuing crucifixion of more and more Christians?"

He rose, bland as butter. "You have given me excellent entertainment, Marcus of Salamis. I give you a gift in return. Your life. You may come and go, while you are in Rome, without fear. I will see that a document is prepared which you can get from Ezek."

"If you will, sire—there is my servant."

"Who is your servant?"

"A lad, a Greek lad who grew up in my house in Salamis. We traveled together to Rome on the ship called The Twins. We reached Puteoli after the fire had been extinguished. We were greeted at the wharf by scores—hundreds—of refugees, also looters who brought valuables they had stolen from Roman houses. I have no doubt at all, sire, that these looters set fire to houses they robbed. They were the arsonists."

"Where is this servant of yours now?"

"He is hauling stones on the Palatine Hill."

A smile of pure evil marked the fat face. "I do not deprive a man of the lad who gives him pleasure. You shall have the comfort of your—companion."

I stood my ground. He had twisted my concern for Philos into something common enough among Romans, but which he surely knew was anathema to Jews.

"Sire, one thing more. Among the prisoners in the Mamertine is a very great man, one who followed the Lord Jesus throughout his ministry. He is now old, blind, but with such a store of memories to share with other men! Give Peter the protection you would give to Virgil, were he living, that he may tell—"

Nero waved his big hands in a shooing motion. "Enough! You have had your audience. Go!"

Ezek ben Ezra plucked at my sleeve. "Come, Mark. The princeps has been very kind—more than generous—"

I said, "Sire, there are hundreds of Christians who would go to the cross willingly to give Peter a few more years—"

"Must Caesar speak twice to a Christian? I have given you your life, and your servant. Go, before I repent my clemency."

# CHAPTER *29*

I was at the portal of the Mamertine Prison early the next morning, armed with a pass from Nero, and bringing fruit and a new coat for Peter. The pass and my freedom made poor telling when I learned that a score of Christians had gone to their crucifixion at dawn by special order from the princeps. A score! And it was not even Sunday! To make it all worse, I had to bring to Peter the news of Paul's death. Yet all these good men rejoiced in my freedom as if it had been their own. Some, it is true, gloomily predicted that Nero would as readily revoke a pass as give one; that a protector in the position of Ezek ben Ezra could become a liability, in case the princeps should choose to liquidate Poppaea's debts by liquidating her banker.

"Let us not fret about tomorrow," Peter said. "While we live, let us draw each breath with thanksgiving to the author of life, that when we die we may return to our Maker knowing that death is also God's gift, and is not to be feared or dreaded."

The prison was less crowded than when I left to work on the Palatine Hill. In addition to the crucifixions, the labor quotas had claimed another score of men. Others than Tigellinus had claimed Christians as slaves escaped during the turmoil of the conflagration.

One event that morning gave me unalloyed satisfaction. I went up to the Palatine Hill, found Alex, showed him my document for claiming Philos. Then I took the lad to Naomi with instructions for getting him cleaned up and clothed. Thereafter he would be her companion and assistant on all her shopping trips.

Before the summer ended he had helped her find the district where Titus was working and reassure herself that he was in health.

Peter spoke often of Paul in the days that followed. "You and I, my son, launched him upon that first missionary journey. So great a power was he that I can scarcely imagine a world in which Paul is not somewhere preaching or writing letters. Now that he has gone before me into the kingdom of heaven I can confess how often I envied him his trained and excellent mind, his fluent Greek and passable Latin, his power as a winner of converts. I preached to Jews in cities where Paul preached to Gentiles, but never were the Jewish ecclesias as large or as enduring as those Paul established.

" 'Feed my sheep,' the Lord Jesus said to me. 'Feed my lambs.' That has been my true labor, nourishing converts others had won. A pastor rather than a missionary or evangelist. I shared with our Lord all the blessed years of his ministry, yet I realize that our movement would scarcely have been established in this generation had it not been for Paul."

I wanted to give Paul his due, but not at Peter's expense. "Perhaps more Jews would be Christians had not Paul made an issue of flouting the law."

"My son, the Lord Jesus did not minister and die to create another sect among the Jews, for the Jews, of the Jews. His mission was for the world, including the Jews but excluding nobody. It took Paul to see we could not share our Lord with all peoples yet remain securely within the warm and comforting cloak of Judaism. Our Lord came into the world a Jew, but he brought love and redemption to all men. I could wish we had had another Paul, however, whose mission was to preach to the Jews. That was my mission, and I failed. There are scores of Christian Greeks for every Christian Jew. This is tragic, and I have lived to see it, and to acknowledge myself a failure."

"Now that is going too far." I was ready to weep with love and pity. "You were never a man to whom confinement comes easily. You were confined in the catacombs for weeks before they brought you here, and something must be done. Come, we will walk about this large room and be thankful it is not such a dungeon as we shared below the Temple."

Peter took my arm, and we circled the big room, and by ones and twos and fours others fell in behind us until Peter found to his great delight that he was leading a parade of prisoners round and round the cavern which had once been a quarry. Soon all had formed the wholesome habit of walking briskly morning and evening. And Peter learned to know every part of the prison flooring so well he could lead a parade of his fellows over the rough stones without stumbling. And after the walk all would sit down together, and Peter would talk to them.

Concerned for the prisoners in the upper chamber, now that Paul was no longer with them, Peter sent me up to visit them and report on their condition. Here, among the sick, I found Silas. He had been in prison when Paul was brought in, had gone to the upper chamber with Paul to take care of him when he was stricken with fever, and here he had been left when Paul was taken away. Here he had remained all the weeks of the hot summer among the sick and the dying, ministering to them with nothing but cold water and a gentle touch and voice. Silas, formerly steward to our neighbor Simon the Leper of Bethany, had gone with Paul on his second missionary journey and on other journeys afterward. The same gentle spirit which had distinguished him in his youth marked him still. We embraced one another with warm affection, and I promised to bring him medicines for his patients, also paper and pens.

"I must write to the churches about Paul's last days," he said. Then, with longing, "If only I could see Peter again, and hear him speak, I would be content."

Thereafter I took paper and pen myself, and wrote down as much as I could of what Peter said to his fellow prisoners, and when I went up to visit Silas I took these daily messages of comfort and reassurance to him. He read them to his fellow prisoners, and made copies of them, rolling each copy into a scroll. "These are the letters I will send to the churches," he said. "Help me, Mark. Find someone who can carry the letters for me."

"You shall take them," said Peter, when I told him of these scrolls Silas had prepared. "You shall travel to each church, to Corinth, to Thessalonica, to Ephesus, and on across Galatia and comfort them and take them each one their copy of Peter's first letter to the churches."

"I will never leave you, Peter."

"I must send someone. Who else can go?" Then, "We will find the way. God will show us the way." He began speaking to the prisoners, and to the guards who also moved up whenever Peter sat down to deliver his daily exhortations.

"Who is going to wrong you if you are devoted to what is good? Yet if you suffer for your virtues, count yourselves happy. It is better to suffer for well-doing if need be than for doing wrong. For the Lord Jesus also died for our sins. In the body he was put to death; in the spirit he was brought to life.

"Lead an ordered and sober life, given to prayer. Keep your love for one another at full strength. In all things so act that the glory may be God's through the Lord Jesus; to him belong glory and power forever and ever, Amen.

"My dear friends, do not be bewildered by the fiery ordeal that is upon you. It gives you a share in Jesus' sufferings, and that is cause for joy; when his glory is revealed, your joy will be triumphant."

To me now he spoke directly. "The letter must close in this fashion: 'I write you this brief appeal through Silvanus, our trusty brother and fellow prisoner. Greetings to you also from my son Mark. Greet one another with the kiss of love. Peace be to you all who belong to our Lord Jesus.' "

As I finished writing and rose to go for my daily visit to Silas I looked directly into the face of the guard who daily admitted me to the chamber above us. He often stood at the grating listening while I read to those men and to Silas the messages from Peter. Now, as he climbed the stairs ahead of me, I asked, "When a prisoner dies, what is done with the body?"

"We carry him out to the pit. We throw a little dirt over him."

"What if you make a mistake, and the prisoner awakens in the fresh air?"

"A sword thrust would take care of that. If his recovery is noticed."

I returned to Ezek ben Ezra for a large sum of money, for travel expenses for two. Silas would need clothing, sandals, a bed, and so would Philos. A bribe for the guard—ten denarii was enough. He liked the assignment. They were to follow the Via Appia to Brundisium and there take ship for Corinth by way of the Corinth Sea. It was a short route—a week's journey should get them near to Brundisium—three weeks should see them in Corinth. There they would separate, Silas to take the long northern journey to Thessalonica, Philippi, then by boat to Pergamum and Ephesus, and afterward inland across Asia to Tarsus and Antioch. The lad, however, would take ship from Corinth to Salamis by the quickest route, for he carried my first letter to Rhoda. She must have heard rumors enough by now to be sadly in need of reassurance. This Philos better than anyone alive could surely give.

Still, it would be a winter journey. There were hazards, if one chose to dwell upon them.

With the coming of spring Peter's restlessness increased. "When I go from this place I want to find a city where nobody has ever yet preached the good news. Alexandria is much in my mind—if only because it is the one city where Paul never went. Would you consent, my son, to come with me to Alexandria?"

My heart leaped. In Alexandria Rhoda could come and be with us, and the youngest of the children, Aaron and Levi and the little one who by now was half a year old, whom I had never seen. Ah, what a beautiful dream. Freedom for Peter, a new ministry in that sundrenched city in which we would share. We talked of it for days.

"We must build a separate house for worship," Peter said. "We must not continue to meet in the homes of our members. With a separate house where we worship the Lord Jesus, where we remember the Lord's Supper with wine and some token food which offends neither Jew nor Greek, all Christians would be able to meet without the schism which bars our people from one another. For all are equally precious in the sight of the Lord Jesus."

Peter would pace about the prison, afire with the dream.

"To heal the breach—that would be my greatest work. I could then go into the presence of the Lord Jesus and stand beside Paul without feeling myself dwarfed."

He reached to touch me. Here in the dimness his sight was quite gone from him, and he had to touch me to be sure he knew where I was.

"There is much vanity in me, my son. Yet our Lord Jesus does not censure me for so human a desire. He visits me, Mark. In the night, when sleep does not come, he sits beside my bed, and these dim eyes see him clearly, and we talk together as in former times."

Nero had gone to Greece to enter the Olympic competitions, and Tigellinus had gone with him. With their absence from Rome there were fewer crucifixions, though there had been no letup in the work of rebuilding the city. Spring green had covered the waste and the blackness. Rome was taking shape, with wider streets, a new design less subject to the devastation of uncontrollable fire. Spring had brought hope to us all, hope that Peter might indeed survive the long confinement, that he might yet reach Alexandria and the new ministry of which he dreamed.

On a spring morning Peter was pacing about the great stone chamber when I entered. He had long since memorized the four sides of the room, the walls rough from quarrying tools, the floor worn smoother than the walls because it had known the traffic of so many feet. And when I fell into step beside him he put his hand upon my arm, put his hand to his lips for silence, and so we circled the room once and took a diagonal course across it, followed by the score of men who shared the big chamber. And Peter went to his place and sat upon the floor, and beckoned the men who shared the chamber to gather near. Not all were Christians, and some were thieves who had been in and out of the Mamertine two or three times before. Yet all came to hear Peter, for how better can you pass the time in such a place?

"It troubles me, Mark, that we who remember our Lord Jesus and all that he did in his ministry are growing old. The Sayings are written down as Agabus heard them that first summer, when all was so fresh and clear in our memories. Surely the hand of God was upon him in that. Yet this is not enough. My son, have you paper and pens here at hand?"

"Some. I will bring more tomorrow."

"Good. Now I shall begin at the beginning, and tell of Jesus' ministry, of the places where our Lord preached, of how he was received, of the events which occurred before and after the sermons Agabus recorded, and of situations and questions which evoked the many parables."

"Paul spoke of the need for such a book," I said. "Yet I wish some better scholar than I could write it all down for you, Peter."

"You are a better scholar than I am, my son, and if we each do our best, God will use our efforts. Never doubt this. You will find all your life that you will do better than your best, if you put your trust in God and lean upon Him."

So Peter began the narrative at the beginning, that is, at the point where he and his brother Andrew first encountered Jesus at the Jordan River. Day by day the story continued. Sometimes Peter spoke in Aramaic, sometimes in his halting Greek, and I made my notes in whichever language he used. It was soon clear that Peter no longer recalled events in the order of their occurrence, but one event would remind him of another, and so it would go. Some mornings he would begin with some event which had been with him in the night. Some of the things he told us seemed to me likely to have occurred after the resurrection, as when he told how Jesus came to him, walking upon the sea. The stories were filled with little homely, daily events, and often when he lapsed into Aramaic his listeners would begin whispering, "What did he say? What was that?" Then Peter would pause, if he was not too deeply involved with his memories, while I repeated in Greek the story they had missed.

Summer had come before the narrative reached an end. Nero had returned from Greece, triumphant because the Greeks had wisely awarded him the laurel crown for every event in their competitions.

With the return of Nero and Tigellinus the rate of crucifixions was stepped up and the arrests began again. On a rainy day in the beginning of winter I found Peter lying flat on his back, his great hands behind his head, his unseeing eyes wide open.

"My work is done, Mark," was his greeting. "I will never preach in Africa. You will preach there, my son. You will write the book there. And you will build churches where the ecclesias you organize will meet together. And when you write the book, be sure to tell how often we who were closest to our Lord failed to understand his meaning, for that is part of the story. Give me your promise, my son, for after today you will see me no more."

"I promise, Peter." I knelt and laid my head against his great chest.

He must have felt my tears, but he made no sign. He might have been looking straight into the kingdom of heaven, judging from his expression. "This day I will be with our Lord Jesus in Paradise. The years have been so long. I marvel, my son, remembering what we were, and what we became. Today marks the end of the long separation. When the sun sets for you in Rome, think how the eternal sun of God's presence will have risen, for me."

In the entry men were already being prepared for crucifixion. How many times had I sat in this prison with Peter while men who had shared its darkness and its fellowship were in the entry undergoing the scourging which preceded and hastened death upon the cross. When they came for Peter he dropped his robe, and I saw upon his broad back the ancient scars of other scourgings. And he went out, and I walked ahead, blinded by my tears, ashamed that I could not stand beside him while he endured in his feebled flesh an anguish I had never known.

I followed slowly the well-known path the prisoners took, over the bridge and up the hill, and after a while I saw Peter coming, stumbling a little on the unfamiliar terrain. But the soldier who held the cord by which he was led did not offer any abuse, but let the blind old man make his way as best he could. Then I walked back to move beside him, and he knew before I spoke that I was there. "God bless you, Mark. God bless you, my son." But I did not speak, for I could not inflict upon him the weakness of my grief and my tears.

We came to the place of the crosses. Three men hung there, two seemingly drunk on the wine and barely conscious of the rain upon their naked flesh. But the third man, a Greek and a Christian, called out, "Peter, brother Peter, I shall die in better company than I deserve."

"We share our Lord's death, my brother," Peter said strongly. "We do not deserve to be so honored. And when the pain ends we will be with him. Be of good courage."

The man on the cross said to the Roman soldiers who were busy stretching Peter upon his own cross, "What can you do against men who do not fear death? Doesn't your princeps realize that for every Christian who dies, a hundred men who see his joyous death are converted?"

The watching crowd drowned the soldier's reply with their reviling. I took up Peter's bloodied coat and rolled it together. Peter turned his face toward me, the serene face of a man who has conquered all earthly agonies. "Mark, my son, do you remember how we laid my beloved Perpetua in her tomb?"

"I remember, Peter. I remember the promise I made you, that day. I will fullfill the promise, Peter."

While two Romans held his arms upon the cross piece, a third raised the heavy mallet and brought it down. And when the spikes were driven through, Peter said, "My hands are pierced, as his hands were. The death I shall die is the death he died."

Yet when all was done, and the cross was to be raised, Peter cried out, "I am not worthy to die as my Lord died. Set the cross head down, friend."

The guard grunted, as he went round from the head of the cross to lift up the other end, "It's your death, friend. Take it any way you like."

# VIII ... *Alexandria*

# CHAPTER 30

The pen dropped from my cramped fingers. I could write no more. Those scrambled notes I had brought from the Mamertine Prison, written partly in Aramaic, partly in Greek, had lain in this desk, a reproach and a reminder for five years.

My eyes rested upon the heap of papyrus sheets. Dear Peter, I thought, I have written the story as you told it to me. The ending is strange, yet in some odd way it pleases me. The work does not have the warmth of your living voice. Can it ever set fires blazing in men's hearts as you did when you spoke of all these things? But it is written, and it is the best I can do. It had to be written down against the time when none remained alive who still could say, "I remember . . ."

I rose from the low desk at which I had spent so many hours and walked about the room, stretching my legs. I could hear Rhoda moving about the room below. She was ordering our household—the household of the bishop of Alexandria, with all that involved of charity for the needy, counsel for the confused, comfort for the troubled. She would hear me moving up here and know the book was finished, for I had promised myself I would not stop until the final events were recorded. I walked back to look down at the last page, which lay on top of all the others. A strange ending. Yet somehow it suited me.

I went out onto the balcony which overlooked the spreading city. We dwelt in the district beside the western harbor, from which the grain of Egypt is shipped to Rome. Separating the eastern and western harbors was the ancient mole, built by Alexander's engineers when they founded the city four centuries ago, a mole which connected the mainland with Pharos Island, whose monstrous lighthouse dominated the skyline. Theaters, temples, palaces, and the two tall obelisks of rose-red granite called Cleopatra's Needles rose against the sky, but all were dwarfed by the lighthouse. Buildings concealed our view of the blue, blue sea I had known all the years of my life, and upon which so many journeys had been made by those who carried the good news.

My thoughts were not on the vast city, with its quarters divided by two intersecting, colonnaded avenues in the fashion copied by the builders of Syrian Antioch. My eyes went to a low, unpretentious building nearby, made of white sandstone which glittered in the African sunshine. It had been built by Christian hands, mine with the others. I have made good use of of the years, Peter, I thought. Had you been here, you would have preached to the people and built the church before writing the book, as I have done.

Ah Peter, you would have joyed to preach in our church, I thought. You would have joyed to worship in a house built for worship, where Jews and Gentiles can pray together, sing together, and together drink the wine and break the bread of our simple, symbolic Eucharist.

Below the balcony Rhoda appeared in the open doorway with her guests, three women of our ecclesia. Our fifth son, little Peter, was grasping a handful of her blue coat, listening in his serious, intent way to all they said. I called down a greeting to the women as they departed. Rhoda left little Peter in the care of young Aaron and came up to join me.

"How goes the book?" Then, with a glance at the writing on the top page, "Oh, I was hoping it was finished."

"It is finished. That is how it ends."

"Oh?" She frowned down upon the page, then turned to join me on the balcony, tucking her arm into mine. "I wonder if Peter knows—about the book, about the church, and the village churches you have organized all around this area. I wonder."

Rhoda frequently speculated about the unknowable. I did not reply. I could not even speculate as to the thinness of the veil which separates the heavenly kingdom from the earthly.

She went back to pick up the top sheet. She read the ending aloud. " 'They went out and fled, beside themselves with terror, and they said nothing to anyone, for they were afraid.' Why do you end there? All the glorious things they did later . . ."

"I have written the story to which Peter bore witness. I have added only one scene of my own—the scene in the orchard— the betrayal by Judas and the arrest. Peter said I must include that. If I went on past this point it would be my witness. This is as Peter told it to me."

"Will you call it the Book of Peter?"

"Its virtues are Peter's. Its flaws—and there are flaws—are mine. I will call it 'The Good News according to Mark.' "

Rhoda's eyes lingered on the page. "It seems so strange to end it with the crucifixion, and the despair of the disciples. Did Jesus know, when they fled in terror, what they would become?" It was another of her unanswerable questions. Presently she answered it herself.

"I hope he knew. Oh, I hope he knew that those who fled would one day turn and stand. I hope he knew that when his voice was silent a hundred—a thousand voices would rise to teach what he had taught. That those who were driven from one city would stand and preach in another. I hope he knew that those imprisoned would preach to their guards, that those who died as martyrs would die blessing the name of the Lord Jesus."

My memory of a night in our orchard revealed the answer, clear and sure. "He knew the soldiers were coming. He knew the death he must die. He surely knew what his disciples would become, after he was parted from them. He surely knew how many men and women would spend the rest of their lives saying to all men and all nations, 'I remember . . .' "

Rhoda said thoughtfully, "You are right to end the book as you do. We were not heroic people, but we have lived heroic lives. The men who fled in terror lived to become heroes and evangelists and martyrs. The boy who fled in an orchard, leaving his coat in a soldier's hands, stood courageously beside the cross on which Peter was delivered from this earth into the heavenly kingdom. But that is a different story, and you are right to end this book as you do."

I kissed her, my beloved, my wife, of whom James had said on the last day of his life, "Her price is above rubies."